I0822163

WAR OF THE NAMELESS

Other Fiction by A.J. Calvin

THE RELICS OF WAR
The Moon's Eye
The Talisman of Delucha
War of the Nameless

The Ballad of Alchemy and Steel

Serpentus

THE CAEIN LEGACY
Exile
Guardian
Harbinger
Legend

HUNTED

WRAITH AND THE REVOLUTION

WAR OF THE NAMELESS

A.J. CALVIN

THE RELICS OF WAR
Book Three

This is a work of fiction. All of the characters and events portrayed within this book are fictitious, and any resemblance to living people or real events is purely coincidental.

WAR OF THE NAMELESS
Second Edition

ISBN 979-89883193-2-0

Absolutely no portion of this book, including its artwork, was generated using artificial intelligence.
Human authored registration # 9891569,
https://authorsguild.org/human

Cover illustration and design by Jamie Noble
(www.thenobleartist.com)

Map illustration by Dewi Hargreaves (www.dewihargreaves.com)

Chapter tile illustrations by A.J. Calvin

HUMAN AUTHORED

For Eric

You've been a fan of my writing for so many years, and I'm incredibly lucky to have your support. Thanks, cousin.

AUTHOR'S NOTE

The Relics of War series is a project that has been on-going for more than twenty years. In its first iteration, the series was not marketed. It was published only for the enjoyment of a few close friends and family members.

Fast-forward two decades. I've decided the stories are worth sharing with a wider audience. All three books have undergone a complete rewrite, significant editing, and many updates. This is the version of the series that I have always envisioned, and this is the version I am sharing with the world.

The Relics of War is meant as a series of novels for adult readers. I want to stress the importance of this statement, as there are passages that depict violence, abuse, and torture within. There is also some language that may be offensive to some. Please be advised that I do not recommend these books for a younger and/or sensitive audience.

For those who don't mind reading about some of the uglier facets of humanity, I truly hope you enjoy the series that launched my aspirations to publish.

On a side note, there are several references contained in War of the Nameless that stemmed from a novella I wrote. That work features the story of Jal'den and Sal'zar prior to the events of this trilogy. If you would like to read The Ballad of Alchemy and Steel, it's available free to subscribers of my newsletter, or it can be purchased from the usual ebook retailers.

I hope you enjoy this final installment in The Relics of War.

Thank you,
A.J. Calvin

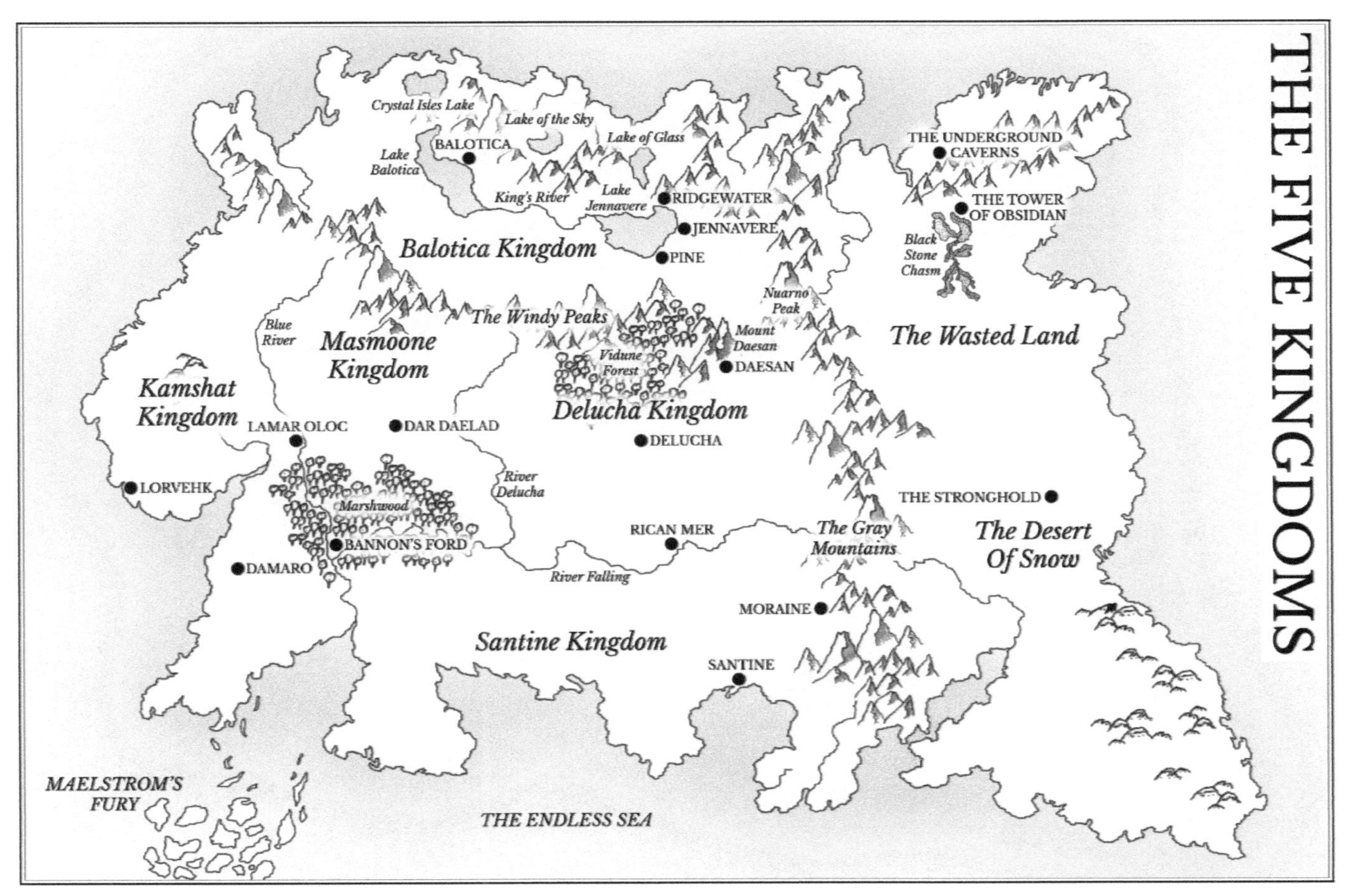
THE FIVE KINGDOMS
Crystal Isles Lake
Lake of the Sky
Lake of Glass
BALOTICA
Lake Balotica
King's River
Lake Jennavere
RIDGEWATER
JENNAVERE
PINE
Balotica Kingdom
THE UNDERGROUND CAVERNS
THE TOWER OF OBSIDIAN
Black Stone Chasm
Nuarno Peak
The Windy Peaks
Mount Daesan
DAESAN
Vidune Forest
Blue River
Masmoone Kingdom
The Wasted Land
Kamshat Kingdom
Delucha Kingdom
LAMAR OLOC
DAR DAELAD
DELUCHA
LORVEHK
River Delucha
THE STRONGHOLD
Marshwood
RICAN MER
The Gray Mountains
The Desert Of Snow
BANNON'S FORD
DAMARO
River Falling
MORAINE
Santine Kingdom
SANTINE
MAELSTROM'S FURY
THE ENDLESS SEA

CHAPTER ONE

THE QUEEN'S FINAL INSULT

Ravin leaned against the window sill, his gaze fixed on the crowded street below. Trumpeters marched along the thoroughfare, blaring a brassy fanfare ahead of the first of many attractions that wended their way through the city of Delucha. The queen had spared no expense when it came to ensuring the celebratory parade would garner the public's attention. A team of horses bedecked in silks with feathers in their manes followed the first wave of musicians, their riders in gold-plated ceremonial armor for the occasion. They carried blunted lances adorned with colorful ribbons that rippled in the light breeze.

Ravin sighed and shook his head. The parade was a waste of time and resources the queen could scarcely afford in the wake of the recent battle. The young monarch had insisted on the festivities, eager to flaunt her wealth to the masses while many of the townspeople still mourned their losses. It was nauseating.

Beside him, Adalin peered wistfully at the celebration. By rights, they should both have taken part in it, though Ravin was silently pleased he wasn't forced to. The thought of mingling with the crowds below made his skin crawl. He'd never liked large gatherings. The duchess, however, thrived in such settings. They made an odd pair, but their unexpected friendship was steadfast.

"I hope the others are enjoying themselves," she remarked as a troupe of acrobats began performing below.

Ravin chuckled. "Emra didn't want to partake, so naturally, Patak was reluctant to go as well. Vardak thought it was a waste of time—he has a thousand items requiring his attention as it is. Taven was reticent, but he warmed up to the idea once he learned his two friends were excited for the parade."

"It's Taven now, is it?" Adalin flashed a knowing smile. "You've taken to him during the past two weeks more than you've let on."

Ravin shrugged. "He needs a mentor, and—"

"—You're best suited for the job," she finished for him. "I wasn't trying to argue with you, Ravin. I think this role of guardian suits you. It's a far cry from the dour man with little patience I first met in the palace."

"Hmm." He frowned at the street below, though his eyes didn't focus on the festivities currently taking place. "When we met, I believed you were nothing more than a court floozy."

She tipped her head back and laughed merrily. "Then my farce to keep my place in the palace worked better than I'd believed."

"Yes, I suppose it did." He sighed and pushed away from the window. "I'll miss your company when the army departs, Adalin. There have been too few people in my life to call friends, but you are one of them."

She placed her hands on her hips and fixed him with a knowing gaze. "And as I've told you countless times, I'll be waiting for you once this business with the Soulless is over. I'll be of little use to the army, although a part of me believes I'd be safer in the field than here in Delucha."

"The queen can't risk making a spectacle of you," he replied swiftly. "Jasom's note indicated she wanted to have both our heads, but it would be poor publicity for our dear monarch. And she certainly can't pursue Emra or those with her unless she wants to be seen as an ally of the Soulless." He smirked. "There were too many important witnesses to that vision, Adalin. You are safe."

"About Jasom's message… Are you planning to accept his invitation?"

Ravin scowled and looked away. The queen's consort had managed to secure Ravin a place at the feast that was to follow the current parade as a show of gratitude for Ravin's service during the battle. Ravin doubted the queen was aware he'd sent the missive, and was certain she'd be livid if Ravin appeared in the palace. Additionally, he simply didn't wish to go. The royal feasts he'd attended during his time as the queen's advisor had been tiresome and crowded affairs.

"I'd rather stay here," he growled.

"Oh, Ravin," she replied, exasperated. "As you've just stated, the queen can't risk harming you. There must be a reason Jasom asked you to the palace. It may prove useful if you go."

Her point was valid, but it didn't change the fact he wanted nothing more to do with the queen. The woman was a murderer without remorse. He groaned and raked one hand through his dark hair.

Adalin touched the side of his face, forcing him to meet her gaze. "Ravin, he may have information for you that he doesn't wish to share with the queen. Have you considered that?"

"I…No." He sighed. "He also may have sent the invitation out of pity. Of all those who stood on the walls or charged through the gates to defend this city, I was the only one she refused to invite."

"I think you should go, Ravin. What can it hurt?"

An hour later, Ravin found himself in the palace's outer courtyard, waiting for his invitation to be verified by the chamberlain's staff. He crossed his arms in displeasure as a pair of palace guards leered at him from the entrance. He wasn't certain what rumors the queen had spread in the wake of his resignation, but given the reception he'd received upon his arrival, it was clear he was no longer welcome in Her Majesty's grand abode.

He resisted the urge to abandon his folly and return to The Three Roses Inn—and Adalin. They'd grown closer since fleeing the palace, and she'd dropped the last of her courtier's façade. He enjoyed her company and the lengthy discussions they often engaged in; she possessed a keen intellect and a sharp memory. Despite the many insinuations from outsiders, they were not romantically involved. He suspected Adalin desired more from him than he was willing to give at present, but he wasn't prepared to take that step with her—or anyone else, for that matter. His focus was needed elsewhere.

After several minutes spent frowning at the palace guards, the chamberlain himself appeared and waved Ravin inside. "It's good to see you're doing well, Ravin. Lord Jasom indicated he invited you, but it seems word did not filter down to my staff."

Ravin shrugged as he was led down the familiar, tapestry-lined corridor toward the great hall. "I wasn't planning to accept it."

The chamberlain frowned with concern. "Her Majesty will not speak of the reasons you gave for resigning, and Jasom has been equally close-mouthed."

"We had a difference of opinion that could not be reconciled," Ravin replied evasively. "It's better if you don't learn the details."

The chamberlain grunted. "I suppose that business is between you and the queen."

He said more, but his words were lost in the sudden onrush of sound as they entered the bustling great hall. Ravin noted most of the other pivotal figures from the recent battle were present and seated at a long table near the front of the room. More tables formed rows across the vast space, crammed with nobility eager to be seen in the company of heroes, wealthy merchants who had likely bought their position at the night's feast, and many officers from the royal guard and the city watch.

Ravin was led to an empty seat at the end of the main table next to a Santinian he recognized as one of Emra's officers. He couldn't recall the man's name, though he knew he was involved with the army's cavalry.

"I'm sorry, Ravin," the chamberlain said in a low tone. "This is the best seat I could wrangle at the last moment. You deserve better after all you've done for this city."

Ravin shrugged indifferently and took his seat. "Don't fret over my placement—the queen is angry with me. This is better than I'd expected."

Ravin peered along the tabletop as the chamberlain excused himself to attend other matters. Emra sat in a place of honor at the center, flanked on either side by the Scorpion Men brothers; her general and the captain of her personal guard. The Green Sect Master from the Council of Auras was seated at the far end of the table with several other wizards, including the young trio that had accompanied them, one of whom was still considered an apprentice. Nearer to his location was the small Felene guardsman that Emra employed—Ravin wasn't entirely certain what his role in her army was, but since he was here, it was something of importance. Danness, one of the two Airess, chatted with the Felene amicably, and on his other side was the Santinian Ravin sat next to.

He noted with some amusement that Aziarah and the other Drakkon were absent; he was certain she'd refused the invitation, and likely in her characteristic blunt manner. Also absent was the other Airess, though hers came as little surprise. She was a skilled healer and had spent countless hours tending the wounded since the battle. She was either busy with her trade or exhausted and in need of rest.

"You must be Ravin," the man at his side said, offering his hand in greeting. "I'm Danian. I've taken charge of Emra's cavalry now that…" He shrugged uncomfortably.

"I understand," Ravin replied. "I didn't know Lucas, but you have my condolences."

"From what Emra tells me, many of us owe you our lives. Without your preparations before the battle, it could easily have gone in the Soulless' favor."

Ravin nodded tersely. At least Emra's people understood the enormity of what he'd accomplished for Delucha even if the queen did not. No one in history had managed to secure one of the five peace talismans—not only had he done so, but he'd wielded it as a weapon and effectively turned the tide of battle in their favor. Emra and many others had played key roles in the city's defense as well, but the talisman he kept hidden in his pocket had been instrumental.

They fell silent as trumpeters began to play across the room, heralding the queen's arrival with her consort. Ravin considered remaining fixed in his seat as a show of irreverence and defiance but thought better of it. He rose and followed her progress across the room as she smiled and nodded to her audience. When her eyes met his, her expression soured and she whispered angrily into Jasom's ear. He replied in kind and shrugged. If the queen's gaze had grown any more heated, he would have combusted in an instant.

Clearly, she was furious with his presence. Ravin grinned insolently and resumed his seat. He'd have a tale to tell Adalin once he returned to the inn.

He sat through several courses of the extravagant meal the queen had ordered for the occasion. With each pass, the servants brought his plates last and cleared them away first. He was certain the queen had demanded they make the festivities uncomfortable for her former advisor, but he refused to allow her silent barbs to affect him. He'd come to learn why Jasom had invited him—but he was forced to admit he relished the notion that his mere presence antagonized the young monarch. It was no less than she deserved.

As the final course was being served, the queen signaled for the attention of her subjects. She rose elegantly from her seat at the head table, Jasom on her arm. The pair were bedecked in dark velvet and ivory lace. Ravin noted the slight swell in Her Majesty's midsection that indicated her growing pregnancy; she'd attempted to hide it for some time, but could no longer.

"I must thank all of you for joining us tonight." Her voice carried easily over the room. "It has been my great honor to host the wielder of Fireblade in my halls, as well as her officers and associates. Without Emra's assistance, I'm certain our fair city would have fallen to the Murkor army. I must also thank the Council of Auras for their support and their continued work to aid the wounded."

Her gaze swept across her guests as applause rang through the hall. Ravin leaned back in his chair, unable to hide his smirk. He'd expected her to ignore his own contribution to the city's defense, had anticipated she'd refuse to acknowledge him. It was meant as an insult, but he found it amusing. It was a typical display of her petty nature.

"Please enjoy the final course. There will be dancing and music to follow."

As she finished speaking and seated herself once more, Jasom disentangled himself from her arm and made his way toward Ravin. If he was aware of the furious scowl she sent in his direction, her consort ignored it.

Jasom leaned down to speak without being overheard. "She won't tell me why you left, Ravin, but I felt obligated to extend the invitation to you. You've done so much for Delucha, and for us. It wasn't right to exclude you."

Ravin shrugged. "She is fickle, Jasom, and I've earned her disfavor. You may wish to remind your wife that once I leave Delucha, the protections I put in place go with me. Perhaps she'll realize the error she's made."

"You're leaving, Ravin? But where will you go?" Jasom was genuinely shocked by the news.

"As you are aware, I aim to defeat the Soulless. I'll be leaving with Emra's army."

Ravin rose from his seat and offered his hand to the young man. They shook, and Jasom said, "I can't believe you'll be leaving."

Ravin shrugged and glanced toward the queen, who continued to fume. "I've worn out my welcome, it seems. If you have need of me before we depart, I'm staying at The Three Roses—though I suggest you keep any dealings with me a secret if you know what's best for your marriage."

He flashed another insolent grin in the queen's direction before striding across the hall toward the exit. Adalin would no doubt reprimand him for antagonizing her, but after the long hours of petty nonsense he'd been forced to endure during his tenure as the queen's advisor, he felt his behavior was justified. After all, he'd kept the truth of her ascension mostly to himself—if she wanted to start a war with him, he held the trump card that would result in her downfall.

CHAPTER TWO

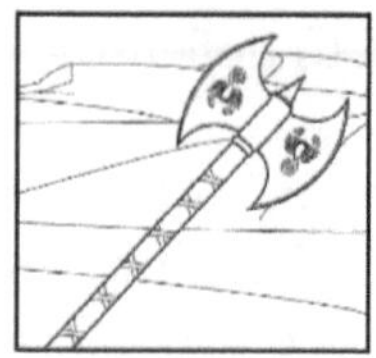

AN UNLIKELY SUMMONS

The parade had been a waste of his time, the feast a show of extravagance the queen could have forgone, and the tedium that ensued left Vardak irritated. There were a thousand items and more that required his attention, and each moment spent acting out this farce was a lost opportunity. He itched to leave, to follow in Ravin's wake—though without the obvious display of antagonism the mage had shown to the young monarch.

Instead, he picked at the final course of the lavish meal and listened half-heartedly as his brother regaled Emra with tales from their desert homeland. The final dish was comprised of a fruit filling ensconced between layers of flaky dough and drizzled with copious amounts of honey. It was far too sweet for his taste, and he had little interest in consuming more than the first bite he'd taken.

He sighed and pushed the plate aside, glancing briefly at Emra as he did so. Her attention was upon Patak alone; he'd be forced to endure the festivities until she determined it was time to leave, or he could convince her to allow him to depart. He'd attempted to avoid coming in the first place, but she'd explained his absence would be seen as an affront to the queen. They required solidarity, the unity of their cause with Delucha's. Now, he was grudgingly here in support of Emra and the hope she represented. And time was wasting.

Beside him, Maryn leaned back in his seat, his feline ears twitching as he studied the crowded room. His plate remained untouched, but Vardak was unsurprised. Felenes were strict carnivores; their final course was inedible for him. Maryn's green eyes shifted to meet his, a sly smile crossing his furry, orange-striped countenance.

"I think the mage had the right idea."

Vardak nodded. "As do I."

"Do you think she'll force us to sit through the dancing?"

Vardak looked at Emra again. She was turned away from him, her gaze fixed on Patak's. He couldn't hear what she said, but Patak's return smile was warm and filled with longing. Vardak turned away with a sigh.

"Yes. I've no doubt Patak will ask her to dance at least once—and make a fool of himself in the process." Vardak sat back and crossed his arms with a smirk. "Our people are capable of great speed, but intricate footwork can be problematic."

Maryn snickered, his eyes flicking briefly to Vardak's lower half as he took in his scorpion legs and tail. "How much coin are you willing to bet that Patak's legs become tangled and he finds himself sprawled across the floor?"

Vardak shook his head, amused. "I'm not about to take that bet. My brother owes you enough as it is."

"I'll wager he doesn't fall at all," Danian interjected from Maryn's other side. The dark-skinned Santinian flashed a grin. "She's too enamored with him to allow him to make a spectacle of himself. She'll dance—but slowly. For his sake."

Vardak rolled his eyes; Maryn had found his next gambling victim. "It's your coin, Danian."

Maryn tipped his head back and laughed. "Vardak knows it's unwise to bet against me, but I'll be happy to take *your* money. I'm in need of another dagger or three."

Their banter continued for some time. As the palace staff began to clear away the last of their plates, Vardak was approached by the palace chamberlain, who spoke in low tones to avoid being overheard.

"I'm sorry to interrupt you, sir, but a messenger has come for you from the temple of Armistral in the city."

Vardak's eyebrows rose in surprise. His dealings with the gods had never included Armistral, and a summons from the peace god's temple to one of Blademon's chosen was as unlikely as a tarantula sprouting wings.

"Did the messenger say why they've come?"

The chamberlain shrugged helplessly. "I'm afraid not. She stated she would speak only with you, Emra, Patak, Tavesin, or Ravin—and Ravin has gone. She awaits you in the foyer."

"I'll speak with the others," Vardak replied as he stood.

He watched the chamberlain scurry away, then moved to stand behind Emra and Patak. The pair didn't seem to have overheard his exchange with the chamberlain, nor did they acknowledge his presence immediately. He crossed his arms and cleared his throat to garner their attention.

Patak flashed a grin. "What brings you here, little brother?"

Vardak frowned at him, nonplussed, then relayed the message. Emra's smile faded to a look of concern as he spoke, while Patak merely appeared confused.

"Armistral?" his brother asked.

Vardak shrugged, while Emra said, "The summons may not have come from Armistral himself, but merely his temple. It is the nearest to the palace. Regardless, the involvement of any god is troublesome." She glanced toward the queen briefly before continuing. "I'll speak with Her Majesty and inform her of our early departure. I doubt she'll be pleased, but we cannot ignore the gods. Take Tavesin with you to the temple. I'll liberate Fyrmane from the stables and seek Ravin. No doubt he's returned to the inn."

"I'll not leave you alone, Em," Patak protested.

"We don't have time to argue, Patak. Go with your brother. I'll meet you at the temple." She rose swiftly from her seat and made her way toward the dais and the queen's table.

Patak glowered after her. "Gods-damn it, she is stubborn."

"She can take care of herself, Patak."

"I know, but I don't have to like it."

Vardak suppressed a sigh and made his way toward the trio of human boys at the end of the table. Of the three, Tavesin was the most subdued, his blue eyes flicking between his friends as they engaged in animated conversation. Rostin straightened at Vardak's approach, dark eyes alight with anticipation.

"Taven, you've been summoned to the temple," Vardak said quietly. "Patak and I must accompany you."

Rostin was unable to hide his disappointment. "Only Taven?"

Vardak nodded. "I'm afraid so. We can practice your swordsmanship tomorrow if you'd like. I will make time for you in the afternoon."

Placated, Rostin grinned and turned his attention to the third boy, while Tavesin climbed to his feet. Tavesin glanced nervously between Vardak and his brother but did not speak until they were some distance across the room.

"What is this about, sir?"

"I don't know." Vardak glanced over his shoulder to note Emra was still in conversation with the queen. "There is a messenger in the foyer. Perhaps she can tell us why we've been called away."

"A fine time to interrupt us, too," Patak groused. "I was planning to ask Em for a dance."

Vardak snorted. "It looks like it's finally Maryn's turn to pay out on one of his bets."

"What? Who did that little scamp lose to?"

Vardak chuckled and shook his head, but didn't answer as they entered the palace's foyer. A diminutive woman garbed entirely in white stood near the door, and as her gaze met his, he understood she was the messenger from the temple. Her dark hair was bound into an elaborate braid and piled atop her head, adding several inches to her height. She stared up at him as they neared; even Tavesin was taller than she was.

"I've come from the temple of Armistral," she said by way of greeting. "My name is Evalin. I am training to become a priestess there."

Vardak introduced himself and the others, and she nodded sagely.

"The priest, Corvin, said I must bring you to the temple without delay. Armistral came—with his twin." She glanced between Vardak and Patak nervously. "I assume Blademon arrived to speak with the pair of you."

They followed her into the torchlit courtyard beyond the palace doors and into the cobblestone street beyond.

"It's likely Blademon is paying a visit to my brother," Patak replied with a grin in Vardak's direction.

Evalin shrugged and drew her snowy cloak more tightly around her shoulders. "I cannot say, but the war god's presence in Armistral's sacred space is unnerving. They arrived together, so I can only assume they are working as one."

Vardak exchanged a glance with his brother. First Blademon, then Flariel and Solsticia, now Armistral… It was unheard of for the gods to interfere with one person's life so readily, and even rarer for more than one to do so. Yet Vardak was plagued by not one, but four of the gods, and he could see no means of wrenching himself free of their grasp.

"That's strange," Tavesin said quietly. "Blademon and Armistral never cooperate."

"It's certainly unexpected," Evalin replied stiffly. "Corvin doesn't like the implications. Nor do I."

"Why was I sent for?" Tavesin asked. "Vardak I understand, and Emra. Even Ravin…"

"I didn't ask questions and was only given names." Evalin's expression softened as she seemed to take in Tavesin's youth for the first time. "I've been taught it's unwise to demand answers from our fickle deities, for it serves little purpose. They will do as they wish. I didn't know your identities until you arrived in the foyer, though I recognized *your* name from the recent battle," she said to Vardak. "And Emra's, of course. Where is she?"

"She went to fetch Ravin," Patak growled, unable to keep his displeasure with her decision to himself. "She'll meet us at the temple."

They fell silent as they followed Evalin through the city's darkened streets toward the temple. Vardak stewed over his current predicament with the gods, his frustration mounting the further they traveled. He'd completed his duty to Flariel when the Moon's Eye was handed to Tavesin and her strange message delivered to Ravin. Blademon was a different matter, however. Vardak was obligated to follow the war god's commands, no matter how inconvenient they proved to be. It was the price he paid for his advanced training at arms and the unusual knowledge he'd been granted.

They rounded a corner, and the temple loomed suddenly before them, an elegant domed structure ringed with filigreed columns. Attached to each column were a pair of torches that flickered and danced in the night. Vardak made out Emra's silhouette alongside that of her tall warhorse. Another figure paced not far from her; as it turned to make another circuit, the firelight illuminated Ravin's dark features and set his golden eyes aglow.

"I didn't think she'd arrive before us," Patak muttered.

"Ravin probably transported them here," Tavesin replied. "It's faster than walking."

Patak chuckled and smiled down at the boy. "Yes, magic. It's not a thing our people typically consider when it comes to traveling."

Evalin quickened her pace as they neared the columns, and as a group, she led them inside. The interior of the dome was an open space lit by hundreds of white candles placed in small niches along the rounded walls. At the center of the room, a circular obsidian mirror was inset into the tiled floor. Upon it stood Armistral and Blademon. The two gods towered above the dozen priests and priestesses that flitted about the room in their pristine white garb.

Standing side by side, it was clear the gods were brothers, though they'd taken different forms. Both were fair-haired and light-skinned, with the strangely incandescent eyes that marked them as gods. Their facial features and torsos were nearly identical, but the similarities ceased there.

As the patron god of the Airess people, Armistral sported a pair of golden, moth-like wings on his back but was otherwise humanoid in appearance. He was dressed in a flowing robe of white. Blademon's form was that of a scorpion from the waist down, the patron of Vardak's people. He was clad in black plate mail, and a pair of sword hilts were visible behind each of his broad shoulders. While Armistral's expression was welcoming, Blademon's was stern. Both deities observed their approach with unconcealed interest.

"Leave us," Blademon ordered the white-robed priests as Vardak and the others came to stand before them.

"Our words are for them alone," Armistral agreed in a gentler tone.

Vardak was accustomed to Blademon's gruff demeanor, but the others appeared decidedly uncomfortable. Tavesin began to fidget; Patak shifted his weight and skittered slightly from side to side while Emra stared at the floor. Ravin crossed his arms and frowned up at the pair, the only one other than Vardak who was unfazed by their presence.

Once they were alone, Armistral spoke while Blademon continued to study them each with an impassive gaze.

"We've come to warn you that the Nameless god stirs in his prison," Armistral said, his voice earnest. "He has not moved in this manner since we caged him, long ago."

Emra's head snapped up at his words, and she met his gaze with a fierce one of her own. "What can we hope to do? Four of the Soulless still live, and they've fled—"

"They've returned to their tower, yes," Blademon replied. "They gather their strength while you gather yours."

"It has been decided that should the Nameless break free and join his servants in battle, then we must join your cause to oppose him," Armistral added. "Even I must stand against him if he breaks free, though it goes against the very fabric of my nature."

Vardak's gaze met Blademon's. "We must move our forces nearer to the mountains."

The war god's mouth twitched into a semblance of a smile, a sign of his unspoken approval. "Yes. But there is more."

"Your relics must be kept safe," Armistral said, addressing Ravin and Tavesin. "The time will soon come when they must be used—*in the manner they were designed for.*"

Tavesin's eyes widened and he gaped openly at the gods. "You mean…?"

"There is but one way to make certain the Nameless cannot achieve his goals," Armistral replied. "The tower where much of his power is stored must be destroyed."

"Acquiring the relics cannot be enough," Ravin said dryly. "As with all powerful magics, there must be a process, a method for unraveling what he's put in place."

"There is," Blademon confirmed, "but it is not our place to speak of it."

Ravin snorted. "I'm not inclined to contact my mother."

"Even your mother does not know the ritual," Armistral replied.

"There is a wealth of knowledge trapped within the palace's library," Blademon said. "As you well know, Ravin. We believe something lies within that may be of help."

Ravin groaned. "I'm not welcome in the palace any longer."

Blademon shrugged. "That's not our concern. Your mother claims you're resourceful. Prove it."

A brilliant flash of light shone from the mirror's center, and both gods were gone, leaving the others to blink away the after-images.

"Gods-damn it all," Ravin swore. "It's so damned typical. Vague responses and impossible demands!"

"We *can* prepare the army to move," Emra said quietly.

"We'll need a suitable location," Vardak replied, his mind sifting through and rejecting a dozen possibilities. "I'll look over the maps once I return to the inn. I'll come up with a plan."

"And the palace library?" Ravin demanded. "Even if I transported myself there, one of the servants will likely come across me. I can't sort through books and scrolls from within the Aethereum."

"Radosan was granted access to the library," Tavesin said. "The queen told him all *wizards* are welcome there. I can look, Ravin."

Some of the mage's frustration dissipated, and he nodded his agreement. "Gods, I'd forgotten about that. Speak with Adalin before you go, Taven. She may have an idea of where you can begin the search."

CHAPTER THREE

THE MASTER'S TEMPLE

Dranamir, your skills are required.

She bolted upright as the Nameless god's words rang through her skull, awakening in an instant from a deep and dreamless sleep. The summons included a brief snatch of image. The large room at the top of the tower with its long glass cases filled with relics swam before her eyes, and at its end, the dark, oblong mirror in its twisted crimson frame. Within the smoky depths of the glass were a pair of narrowed, yellow eyes.

The eyes of the Nameless god. Her master, the proprietor of her soul.

She rose without hesitation and dressed hurriedly. Garin usually sent such summons; this was the first time since her revival the Nameless had deigned to call her directly. Her pulse accelerated with both anticipation and dread. Her existence was tied to the god's whims; she was both his devoted servant and cowering subject. His favor would grant her power and glory, but his displeasure would result in an eternity of suffering as he meted out his punishment.

She could recall nothing in her recent past that would earn his disfavor, and she began to wonder why she'd been summoned in the darkest hours of the night. Had he called the others, or her alone?

She ran a comb through her long tresses, then opened a portal into the Aethereum. It was the fastest means of traveling to the topmost floor of the tower, though her stomach twisted with momentary dread as she stepped through the opening. The Aethereum was Ravin's domain, and he'd recently acquired several powerful allies. Her time within the magical realm must remain brief, lest she risk discovery by her greatest adversary. Ravin may have thwarted her plans in Delucha, but she'd make certain he paid dearly for his decision to ally with Fireblade's wielder. It was simply a matter of time.

She transported herself instantly to the tower's top floor and promptly exited the Aethereum. She would not keep the Nameless god waiting.

To her dismay, the others were emerging from their own portals as well. Garin was the first to arrive, and he went directly to the mirror where it hung overlooking the room. Its glass was dark in the half-light that emanated from the tower's walls. He glanced over one narrow shoulder at her, crimson eyes narrowed in suspicion or concern.

"I must establish a connection," he told her. "I'm surprised he's called you."

With his words, another portal opened to reveal Alyra. She stumbled through and corrected her balance by grasping the edge of the nearest relic case. Dranamir studied the other woman dispassionately; the last vestiges of her former beauty were gone, replaced by puckered scar tissue from her recent injury. She was still recovering from the blow Ravin had wrought against her during the battle two weeks past, her strength all but depleted with the effort to stand upright. The right side of her face was red and raw as the burns continued to heal, and her right eye was a milky, sightless orb.

Garin possessed some healing abilities, and he'd done what he could for Alyra once they'd returned to the tower. It was enough to spare her life, but she'd remain scarred for the remainder of her days. For a woman who once used her flawless good looks to gain power and prestige, her current state must seem an enduring nightmare. Dranamir smirked at the thought; Alyra deserved her current misfortune, and more.

Garin frowned thoughtfully as Kama emerged moments later. "We've all been summoned?"

"It seems so," Alrya replied, her voice strained.

Dranamir watched as Garin placed his palms against the mirror's glass. She sensed the workings of his magic as he made contact with the Nameless god, but his manipulations were clouded and indistinct. She frowned; it seemed his unique bond with their master prevented her from uncovering the secrets behind his ability to contact their god directly.

After a few moments, Garin stepped back. The same malevolent, yellow eyes she'd glimpsed in her summons appeared within the glass, but she could see nothing more of the Nameless god's form. The eyes locked upon hers, and his words thundered through her skull with such force she nearly collapsed.

The time has come, Dranamir, my first and most cherished. The others have received their own orders, but yours are paramount to my plans. Remove the seals you placed over my temple and ensure the treasures within are in order.

Ecstasy flooded her veins with his statement. The Nameless god, her master, the deity she'd devoted her life to, wished for his temple to be restored. It could mean only one thing. He'd grown strong enough to break free of his prison and would soon join her in the world. Long ago, he'd promised her power and glory, a place at his side, so long as she fulfilled her obligation to see him released from his cage.

Heat suffused her core as she gazed longingly at his fierce, yellow eyes. "I will see it done, master."

Soon, our time will come.

The eyes faded from the mirror, and she felt his departure keenly, as though a part of herself had vanished with him.

She drew a breath and shook her head, her gaze scanning the others within the room. Garin and Kama glared fiercely at one another while Alyra had fallen prostrate upon the tiled floor, weeping joyously. He'd spoken to them each privately, it seemed.

Kama crossed his arms and glowered at Garin's pale countenance. "I don't like the idea of leaving the army unattended for this business," he said. "I hope you have a plan."

Garin nodded. "I do, but it's not without risk. The Aethereum is no longer safe."

Kama snorted. "I'm aware."

"What has he tasked you to do?" Alyra gasped as she struggled to her feet. "I believe I received different instructions."

Garin flicked his gaze toward her, then to Dranamir. "Yes. He chose each of us for a specific purpose, and it seems the time has finally come to fulfill them. Kama and I are to seek the Twilight Stone."

"Why does he seek the talismans?" Dranamir demanded. "We've attempted this before, and Ravin has proven problematic."

"It is essential for the ritual that will set him free," Garin replied. "The power of the talismans is unrivaled."

"And what of you?" Kama asked as his eyes raked across her form.

"Our master wishes his temple be restored," she replied. "I alone can unravel the wards placed over his most sacred abode, and I alone can access the treasures sealed within."

Alyra gasped. "He's asked me to gather the necessary materials to create the elixir that will restore him. I believe several of the items I require are within his temple."

Dranamir scowled. "I will provide you with a list of what I find. You will not accompany me and sully our master's sanctum with such blatant evidence of your ineptitude."

Alyra's expression was stricken as she gingerly touched the side of her marred face. "That was cruel even for you, Dranamir."

"Then perhaps the next time your lover betrays us, you shouldn't run blindly from the scene, screaming at the 'injustice' of his execution." Dranamir folded her arms and sneered. "Ravin has always been a man of opportunity, and you left yourself vulnerable to his attack. I've no sympathy for your weakness. Your scars are warranted."

"Enough." Garin's tone was unyielding. "She has suffered for her mistakes, Dranamir. Your energy is better spent carrying out your duty to our master rather than antagonizing her."

She leveled an icy glare in his direction. "You won't remain untouchable forever, Garin. Remember that."

As dawn broke over the sky above, painting the thin, wispy clouds in shades of pale orange and gold, Dranamir exited a portal at the bottom of Blackstone Chasm. She peered at the tiny sliver of sky visible above the vast crevice, the Wasted Land above seemingly leagues away. The chasm's sides were uneven and comprised of obsidian. Jagged shards and razor-sharp edges glittered dangerously in the faint illumination that filtered into the depths. Scattered haphazardly across her path were shattered fragments of bone, the remains of the unfortunate souls cast into the natural void over the course of centuries.

Idly, she wondered if Shan'tar's body had reached the bottom and if it had begun to decay. His was the most recent addition to the chasm's lengthy list of victims, though he'd been dead when his body was cast over the ledge.

Few had ventured into this place. Many believed the chasm to be bottomless, a rumor she'd always found amusing. From the land above, the bottom was invisible, lost to the shadows. To her knowledge, only the Soulless were aware of the temple hidden in the abyss—and only she was capable of unlocking it. Alyra lacked the power to dismantle the wards, and Dranamir had designed them to be fatal should a *man* attempt to unravel them. She'd added that final touch in the unlikely event Ravin learned of the temple's location, but he'd fallen into a trap of a different making and been eliminated. Or so she'd believed.

Thoughts of Ravin soured her mood. She shoved them aside and strode across the chasm's rocky bottom toward an arched opening near its southern end. The opening was a deeper black than the glittering obsidian surrounding it, a void within the darkness.

Just beyond the feeble reach of the sun's light and nestled within the arch was the ancient ward she'd woven centuries ago. She reached toward it with her power, probed its structure tentatively, and was pleased to find it had not been tampered with nor diminished over time. A pair of brittle skeletons lay beneath the arch, a testament to the only fools in history who'd attempted to break into the Nameless god's sanctuary. Her magic had protected his temple from those deemed unworthy, and they'd paid for their folly with their lives.

She smiled maliciously at the skeletons as she began to undo the intricate tapestry of magical threads comprising the ward. It took her little time, but required a significant expenditure of energy to complete the task. She leaned against the arch's smooth interior for several minutes once she was finished, gathering her remaining strength for the journey within.

Though drained, she pushed away from the arch and ventured inside. She created a magical light to guide her steps, though she'd traversed the path numerous times and knew each twist and turn it would take. Unlike the walls of the chasm outside, the walls of the tunnel leading to the temple were smooth and polished into a reflective sheen.

She smirked at her reflection, pleased with the figure she beheld in the obsidian. Her long, dark hair remained lustrous and thick, despite the changes her bond with the Nameless had wrought. Though her skin no longer possessed the ivory tone it once had, the grayish flesh she sported was not off-putting. Her eyes blazed crimson, the same shade as the gown she presently wore. She'd retained much of her natural beauty after bonding to the Nameless god, whereas Alyra's had been corrupted prior to her recent deformation at Ravin's hands. Alyra's allure had once been legendary, a source of contempt for Dranamir, but now the tables had dramatically turned.

The corridor opened into a rectangular chamber. Several rows of intricately carved columns ran the length of the room, each carved into a life-like rendition of various fanciful creatures. Carefully chiseled obsidian eyes followed her progress toward the dais at the far end. Each corner of the dais was supported by a column sculpted into the likeness of the ancient race known as the builders. Leathery wings tipped with finger-like talons spread wide from each column, while their lupine faces gazed at a point near the center of the dais where a silvered mirror was set into the floor.

Dranamir admired the artistry of the temple as she walked. The builders had been the greatest craftsmen and artists in history, and their skill was present in every carved facet of the temple's interior. It was a pity they'd betrayed their patron god when he'd set out on his first conquest; he'd cursed them and denied them their eternal rest in retaliation for their crime. Little remained of their legacy beyond the Nameless god's temple and Stonewall Hall.

She ignored the mirror and continued toward an alcove in the wall beyond. The mirror served little purpose at present but would become useful once her master was freed. The alcove contained several shelves lined with colored glass bottles and ceramic urns. A label was painted upon each item in a precise script. Many of the bottles contained rare and valuable ingredients, the like of which would cause any Murkor alchemist to salivate with longing. The urns held various other items of importance to the Nameless god; the ashes of the last loyal builder priest, poison glands from the giant scorpions that once roamed the desert to the south, fangs from the giant serpents of the Marshwood, and a collection of small glass spheres swirled with color.

Dranamir wasn't certain what purpose the collection served, but she'd preserved it when the Nameless requested it of her. Everything was in place.

She could have provided Alyra with the list of items before departing the tower, but she'd chosen to postpone the conversation and minimize her time spent with the other woman. She would give Alyra access only to the items she required to create her elixir. The remainder would be stored, untouched, for their master's use alone.

CHAPTER FOUR

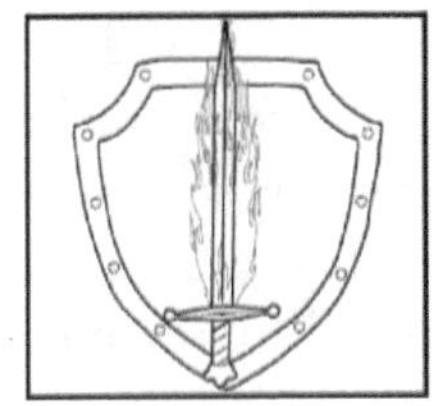

A GROWING ARMY

"I'd planned to ask you for a dance last night before the gods decided to interrupt us."

Emra looked up from the stack of correspondence she'd been skimming over, eyebrows lifted in surprise. "I didn't think your people danced, Patak."

He flushed slightly and ran a hand through his short blond hair. "Normally, we don't, but…" He shrugged and grinned sheepishly.

Her heart fluttered in response; since the battle, he'd dropped his remaining pretenses and made his intentions unabashedly clear. She'd expected the opposite reaction after he'd witnessed Fireblade's power first-hand, but Patak continued to surprise her. She loved him for it.

"From what I know of your people, perhaps Blademon did you a favor when he called us away."

He chuckled while she rose from her seat and walked around the table to where he stood near the door to the inn's corridor. She took his hands in her own and gazed up at him, a coy grin on her face. She'd waited long enough; the more she learned about the towering captain of her guard, the harder it became to deny what she felt for him.

"Em?" he asked uncertainly.

"Perhaps it's time," she replied softly. "If Aeon upholds his promise, I cannot continue to wallow in my own indecision."

His smile faltered, replaced by a look of unease. "Em, I—"

She rose up on her toes to interrupt his words with a kiss. If this life was to be her last, she would not squander it—or ignore the passion she felt for the man before her. Startled, he nearly pulled away before he recovered himself and returned her sentiment with a passionate one of his own. His arms encircled her waist and drew her in, lifting her slightly away from the polished wooden floor.

When their lips parted, she lifted one hand to touch the side of his face while he grinned. His skin was warm and rough with blond stubble that her eyes could not detect. Gods, he was handsome. She'd fallen for him long before she realized the extent of her attraction; it did not matter that he wasn't human.

"I've been trying to work out how to make this moment happen for weeks," he said quietly. "Nothing seemed right."

"Sometimes you must ignore the how and simply do."

His grin widened. "I like the way you think." He bent toward her for another kiss as the door burst open.

She sighed, disappointed, as they disentangled their limbs and he set her on the floor. Maryn's orange-striped feline countenance smirked at them from the corridor, his green eyes flitting between them mischievously.

"Well, I suppose it's fortunate Vardak asked me to deliver this message and didn't come himself." Maryn waved a folded sheet in one hand.

"Vardak and I have come to an understanding," Patak replied with a laugh. "Tell him all you'd like."

Maryn snickered. "And if I embellish my tale?"

Emra shook her head in mock exasperation. "You won't, and we both know it, Maryn. What is the message?"

Maryn shrugged and handed it to her. The message was folded carefully, a wax seal impressed upon the overlapping edges. She studied the seal for a moment; it was familiar, yet unexpected. She traced the ridges of wax with her forefinger as they formed a fox standing atop a smoldering volcano.

"This comes from Kamshat," she said quietly. "The noble house of Corbetehk bears this insignia."

"It was brought to us from the city walls," Maryn replied. "I happened to be with Vardak when it arrived and offered to bring it to you. He has a hundred other things demanding his attention. But to your point, I'm not certain who sent it."

"A friend," she replied. "Or rather, one of his descendants."

Janasu Corbetehk had been a brilliant strategist and a decisive leader. She'd named him general during her life as Arianna and believed without his assistance in the war against Kama, the outcome may have been vastly different for the world. Seeing his family's crest again was a welcome sign. Whoever the sender truly was, she was certain they were an ally.

She broke the wax seal with her thumbnail and unfolded the message. It was brief, written in a scrawling hand that was almost unintelligible at times, but she understood the contents well enough. Five hundred Kamshati soldiers were stationed on the eastern outskirts of the city, and their leader, a woman by the name of Alori, was requesting an audience. No mention of the Corbetehk family or its ties to Fireblade's wielder were present in the missive, though the seal was indication enough that she ought to meet the newcomers.

She looked up from the message to meet Patak's questioning gaze.

"Gather the rest of the guard," she told him. "We've a meeting to attend."

Patak nodded and ducked past Maryn into the hall while the Felene eyed her meaningfully. "You're taking *all* of your guards, Emra?"

She nodded. "I'd like to believe this message comes from a potential ally, but her motive is yet to be seen. I will not walk into her camp unescorted, and Patak's blade may not be sufficient if we're walking into a trap. Inform Vardak of my plans, but tell him not to send anyone unless we don't return by sundown."

"What of Ravin and the wizards?"

"I'll leave the telling of my plans to Vardak's discretion."

"He won't be pleased." Maryn turned away, then glanced over his shoulder with an impish grin. "You'd best return—your paramour still owes me ten gold pieces, and I intend to collect."

It took more than an hour before Patak had located and assembled her full contingent of personal guards, and another quarter-hour before all were armed and armored. When all was readied, Patak returned to her makeshift command quarters inside The Three Roses and escorted her outside. Thirty-two men and women stood in formation in the stable yard next to the inn, their trappings a mismatched conglomeration of styles from their various homelands.

She knew them each by name, though she didn't know all of their backgrounds. Patak had hand-picked them either for their skill or for their unwavering devotion to her cause. He knew them well, and he'd built a strong rapport amongst the group with his easy manner and ready smile—not to mention his fierce loyalty and determination. No matter what awaited them in the Kamshati camp, she would be protected.

Only steps away from the inn, their group began to draw the attention of the townspeople. Since most did not own horses, they marched on foot, with Emra and Patak in the center of the formation. People paused in their business to watch them pass. She wasn't certain how many of the onlookers recognized her, but it was clear they knew someone of importance moved in the heart of the throng. She could have done without making a spectacle of their journey through the city, yet she knew it could not be helped.

Several of the city watch saluted as the group passed beneath Delucha's western wall. She waved in acknowledgment while Patak chuckled uneasily at the exchange.

"They ought to be watching the road beyond the walls," he growled, casting a disapproving look toward the guards.

"You're beginning to sound like your brother," she replied with a laugh. "Relax, Patak, and save your energy for the Kamshatis. If I'm wrong about their motives, we'll be in for a fight."

With a shrug, Patak relented. "I suppose it's possible the watchmen don't know a Kamshati army is on their doorstep. How they'll keep a force of five hundred concealed from the city's defenders, I can't say." He shook his head, then raked one hand through his short blond hair. "Vardak will have my head if anything goes wrong, Em—brother or no."

In that moment, she understood the source of his agitation. Patak wasn't concerned about his or the others' ability to defend her. He was worried he'd anger his brother by unquestioningly following her lead.

"Patak, let me deal with your brother when we return. He's more reasonable than you give him credit for."

Patak snickered. "Perhaps he is with *you*, Em. I'm his brother. Reason has no place in our discussions."

She laughed in spite of herself. "Promise me you'll never lose your sense of humor."

It wasn't long before the Kamshati's sprawling encampment became visible along the length of open road that trailed west from Delucha toward the kingdom's border with Masmoone. There were few trees to provide shade or shelter in the grasslands, and though it appeared the Kamshatis had made an attempt to conceal their tents from prying eyes, it was easy to discern them. Armored sentries patrolled the camp's perimeter, and most wore thick cloaks with the same fox insignia the message had borne.

Emra withdrew the letter from within her blue cloak, while her right hand strayed to Fireblade's hilt. She prayed for a peaceable outcome but was prepared for the worst. Beside her, Patak loosened his broadsword in its leather scabbard across his back, though he did not withdraw the weapon. He nodded to her, then began to issue wordless commands to the guards, gesturing to several who seemed to understand his hand signals. Their formation tightened around her in preparation of the encounter and many reached for hilts or arrows.

Several of the sentries ceased their patrol as they took notice of her approach. One broke into a jog as she disappeared between the tents, while three others clustered together and began to stride forward toward Emra's position. Their weapons remained sheathed, and the woman in the center of the trio held up her hands to demonstrate her peaceful intentions.

Emra breathed a soft sigh of relief, hopeful the Kamshatis would remain friendly. As the two groups met, she pushed forward to stand between her guards and introduced herself.

The woman, who seemed to be the leader of the group, flashed a crooked grin. "Alori will be pleased you've come. She wasn't certain you'd recognize the seal on her message."

"I know that mark well. What ties does she have to the Corbetehk family?"

Laughter met her question. Emra looked up to find a tall woman striding toward her, her dark hair pulled up into an elaborate braid that accentuated her angular features and sharp nose. Dark eyes regarded her knowingly, while a faint smile played upon her lips. The woman was dressed in tooled leather armor, the same fox insignia worked into each piece though her features alone marked her as one of Janasu's descendants. Not for the first time, Emra wondered what sort of life her former commander had led after the conclusion of Kama's War.

"I am the youngest daughter of the Rais, Draevo Corbetehk. Call me Alori." She offered her hand in greeting, and the two shook. "My father was livid when he learned of my plans to lead this contingent across the Five Kingdoms to meet you, but the king himself granted my leave. It's a pity we arrived too late to partake in the battle."

Alori motioned for Emra to follow her. "Come. We shall speak in a more private setting."

"My captain will accompany us," Emra replied as she fell in beside Alori and Patak brought up the rear. "If you know my history as well as you let on, you'll understand my need for caution."

Alori grinned and paused to sweep an appraising eye over Patak. "I do. I suppose I shouldn't be surprised the Scorpion Men have joined you. They've always had a thirst for war."

"When your patron is Blademon, it's to be expected," he replied with a laugh.

"Tell me," Alori said to him, "is it true your poison can kill a human in under five minutes?"

"No, but my venom can." He returned her grin with a feral one of his own.

"You shouldn't encourage him," Emra replied, amused.

Alori laughed as she led them to the large pavilion erected at the center of the camp. "We may speak freely inside."

A teenage boy sat within the pavilion, huddled inside his cloak, shivering. Alori smiled apologetically at Emra as they entered. "It seems my son has refused to allow me to meet with you alone."

The boy scowled up at his mother. "It's not fair—" he began, then cut himself short as Patak ducked through the narrow opening. He gaped openly, unable to tear his eyes away from Patak's.

Patak chuckled as he came to stand between the two women. "I take it you've never encountered one of my people before. What is your name?"

"Jundo, sir."

"If you'd like to learn more about the Scorpion Men, I'll be happy to tell you a few tales while your mother speaks with Emra."

Emra smiled up at him, grateful for the intervention. "Thank you," she whispered.

Patak motioned to Jundo, and the pair exited. She could hear Patak's voice, muffled through the pavilion's canvas sides, moments later.

"I wished for him to remain home, where he would be safe," Alori said quietly after a time. "I left him in the care of my father, but he ran away and found his way to our camp the first night of our journey. He refused to be left behind when I was embarking on such a grand adventure."

"What of his father?"

Alori shook her head. "He is with Aeon."

Emra looked away. "I'm sorry."

"I only pray my son lives to see the conclusion of this war and does not join him prematurely."

An uneasy silence settled over the pavilion while Emra considered her next words. She had a dozen questions and more to ask Alori; it was simply a matter of deciding where to begin. Outside, she heard Jundo laugh at something Patak said.

"Why have you come, Alori?"

Alori's dark eyebrows lifted in genuine surprise. "Janasu Corbetehk was one of my forebears, a man of great renown, spoken of highly in the legends. He was your commander. When word reached us from Dar Daelad of your reappearance, there was no question of what I must do."

"You mentioned the king gave his blessing. There is no doubt in my mind that you are a Corbetehk—you have the look about you—but why did he choose you specifically?"

"I've trained at arms since I was seven years old. As the Rais' youngest child, I was granted the rare opportunity to forge my own path," Alori replied. "I chose to become a soldier and have served the king's army faithfully for years. I begged the king to allow me the honor of following in the footsteps of my ancestor. He gave me charge of the others outside and promised to send more troops once they could be gathered."

"Janasu was a brilliant strategist and is held in high esteem by my current general." Emra studied Alori's reaction and was pleased when she detected no disappointment in the other woman's expression. "We are preparing to depart Delucha for a location nearer the mountains. I'll make certain Vardak speaks with you before that time."

"Thank you. Will we have time to resupply in the city before the departure?"

Emra nodded. "It will be another few days at least before we're prepared to march. If there is anything you cannot find in the marketplace, make your way to The Three Roses Inn. I've made it my temporary headquarters. If I'm not available, ask for Danness, my quartermaster."

Vardak was awaiting her when they returned to The Three Roses. He paced across the ground floor room she used as her meeting room, arms crossed, a glower upon his face. He paused to scowl in her direction as she entered with Patak.

"Maryn told me where you've been."

Patak snickered. "Don't tell me you finally chose to take a break this afternoon, only to spend your time wearing a path in the floorboards, little brother."

"No, I arrived here only minutes ago." Vardak frowned at his brother. "I planned to wait until nightfall, and if you didn't return, send half the army to liberate you."

"There was no need," Emra replied before Patak could interject with another quip. She apprised him of the situation and the additional aid the Kamshatis promised. His expression softened with the news, and his tension visibly decreased.

"We'll need every willing soul for this fight," Vardak said once she'd finished.

"Yes. It doesn't explain why you've come seeking me, however." Emra eyed him knowingly.

"The Deluchan soldiers that were trailing the Murkor arrived," he replied. "The queen's military advisor has promised they will follow your banner when we march. The city has its own defenders, and he believes they'll benefit our cause more than the queen's." He shook his head. "He seems to be of the same mind as Ravin, though less…*overt* in his reaction."

Patak snorted. "We all know what transpired between them, and I can't say I blame Ravin for leaving her employ."

"The queen's business is less important than our own," Emra cut in. "I'll not become mired in court intrigues, no matter their source, and I won't have either of you tangle yourselves in them, either. Focus on our planned departure and the battles that await us in the future. The queen will pay for her crimes one day, but it is not for us to dictate when."

CHAPTER FIVE

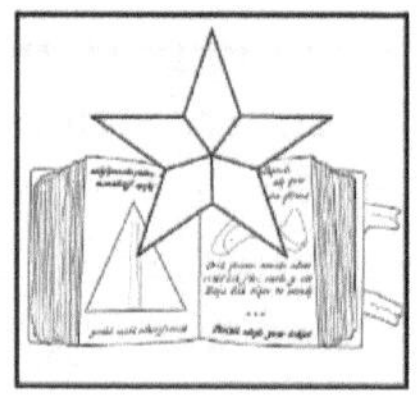

LETTERS FROM ABOVE

Tavesin's heart raced as he stared at the open page before him, his eyes fixed on the detailed drawings on the aged parchment as though they were a source of horror. Perhaps, he reflected, they were.

He'd scoured the palace library for hours, following Adalin's instructions. Most of the tomes he'd wrested from the crammed bookshelves had failed to provide him with any new information and detailed nothing of the black tower. The book spread open on the table in front of him was different, however.

He moved a candle nearer to the page to better read the tiny script as the daylight began to fade from the window. An artist's rendering of the black tower filled one page, while depictions of several of the tower's floors filled the next. Beneath both drawings were copious notes explaining the magic involved in its assembly and creation.

Though he didn't fully understand the passages, he was certain this was the book Blademon and Armistral had urged them to locate. He glanced surreptitiously toward the door to the corridor as he hefted the tome in his arms. There was no one outside, and he'd been alone with his studies for some time. He drew a breath and created a portal into the Aethereum, clutching the book to his chest. He must take it to Ravin, and theft seemed to be the only way.

He cast a final glance around the empty library and darted through the shimmering blue oval that would take him into the magical realm. It wasn't his first time pilfering an item of significance, but his previous act had been the taking of a relic from the black tower. The Soulless were the enemy, and he'd been able to justify his actions. This time was different. The queen wasn't the enemy, and if she learned of his theft, it was likely he'd find himself thrown in a cell.

It was a risk he must take. The gods had led him down the path to finding the book after all. Unlike Ravin, he feared incurring their displeasure and would act accordingly. He'd believed the Scorpion Men were fearsome, but after meeting Blademon, he realized they were people not so different than himself. It was the gods who traversed an echelon of their own.

He transported himself to the room he'd been given at The Three Roses, formed a second portal, and exited the Aethereum. He shared the space with Rostin and Badolo, but neither were present to witness his arrival. He suspected Rostin was in the stable yard below, training at arms with one of the Grays, and Badolo was likely with the Drakkon. It was just as well; he didn't relish the notion of explaining why he'd returned clutching an ancient text when both of his friends knew he'd been in the palace library. The fewer who knew of his theft, the better.

His room was on the topmost floor, several doors down from Adalin's. There was a good chance he'd find Ravin with her, and he hoped she was within. He scurried down the hall, his feet thudding loudly on the floorboards. In his haste, he drew the attention of a maid bearing a basket of fresh linens to one of the other rooms. She shot him a frown of disapproval as he passed, but in his excitement to bring his find to Ravin, he ignored her and continued on his way.

He rapped loudly on Adalin's door and prayed the duchess was within. Even if Ravin was not with her, she would know his whereabouts.

When Adalin opened the door, she frowned at him curiously while her gaze flicked to the book clutched in his hands. "Taven? Have you found something?"

He nodded emphatically, eager to impress the duchess. "Is Ravin here?"

She glanced over her shoulder and released a sigh. "Yes, but he's in a foul temper."

"With good reason," Ravin growled from within. "It's no matter. Let the boy inside, Adalin. I'd like to know what he's discovered in the palace."

She rolled her eyes and gave Tavesin a long-suffering look before ushering him inside. "I'll pray whatever you've found puts him in a better mood," she whispered.

Tavesin shrugged uncomfortably, unused to acting the role of mediator between adults at least thrice his age. He spied Ravin near the room's window, his gaze fixed on something beyond the darkened panes of glass. The mage held his hands clasped behind him and did not turn to greet Tavesin as he entered. His scowl was fierce.

"Ravin," Tavesin said hesitantly, "I've found the book."

Ravin spun away from the window, eyebrows raised. "*The* book? The one the gods mentioned?"

"I believe so."

Tavesin offered him a sheepish smile as he opened the book to the pages he'd discovered while in the library. Adalin peered over his shoulder while he pointed to the incomprehensible text beneath the diagrams.

Ravin chuckled darkly. "I'm not certain which makes me happier—that you've found what we were seeking, or that you stole this from the palace."

Tavesin blanched and looked away. "I didn't know what else to do."

Ravin clapped him on the shoulder amicably. "You've done nothing wrong, Taven, and Adalin spoke true. I've been difficult this evening."

"A greater understatement has never been uttered," the duchess replied dryly. She reached around Tavesin to tap a fingernail against one of the passages on the open pages. "While this doesn't state how you must use the relics, it does indicate where. This room must exist beneath the tower's ground floor, but I see no stairs leading to such a level."

Ravin smirked. "That's where the Aethereum comes into play. I wasn't aware of this chamber. Now that I am, I should be able to reach it easily enough—so long as Dranamir hasn't left any nasty surprises."

"Do you mean wards?" Tavesin asked.

"Among other things." Ravin nodded thoughtfully. "It's a start, and I'm certain there will be more information within this book. We'll need to make time to read through it."

"The ebb and flow of time works against you, son of Solsticia."

Tavesin froze at the words and glanced around the duchess' room. The voice had seemed to come from nowhere, yet filled the space with its cloying presence. It was a feminine voice with an ethereal quality, unlike anything he'd previously heard.

Ravin stepped in front of Tavesin and Adalin in a protective manner, his dark features twisted by fury. "Show yourself."

Amused laughter accompanied his demand. "You do not wield the power to command the gods, Ravin. I will not."

Tavesin glanced at Adalin, eyes wide with fear. "A goddess?" he whispered.

Adalin shrugged, but the voice laughed again. "The boy understands his place."

"Why are you here?" Ravin growled. "I'm not interested in your games."

"Ah, but you should be. You've been mired in them since your birth." The voice paused, and a light breeze whirled through the room, ruffling the pages of the book Tavesin still held in his hands. The candles on the room's only table flickered and danced. "Your mother and I have a very long history, Ravin De'vor."

Ravin stood rigid, his hands clenched into fists at his sides. Tavesin knew enough of the mage's past to understand the goddess' words had angered him deeply. Fearful that Ravin would lash out and enrage the invisible deity, Tavesin swallowed and spoke up.

"Which goddess are you?"

"One matter at a time, child," the voice replied. "Ravin's question shall be addressed first. I bring you this."

A pair of envelopes fluttered lazily from the ceiling. One landed on the floor in front of Ravin, while the second found its way atop the book in Tavesin's hands. The envelopes were constructed of fine, ivory-hued paper and sealed with a shimmering green wax. The image impressed into the wax depicted an hourglass ringed by stars.

"Minora…" Adalin breathed to the accompaniment of receding laughter. A moment later, the goddess' presence was gone.

Tavesin met Adalin's eyes and shifted uneasily. "Why would Minora visit us?"

"The timing is no coincidence," Ravin growled as he stooped to pick up the envelope at his feet. "I've no doubt this has to do with your finding that book, and she's simply been waiting for this moment to reveal her hand. Whatever it proves to be."

"I don't like this business with the gods, Ravin." Adalin folded her arms and cast a glance through the room, as though worried Minora remained lurking in the shadows.

"Nor do I. It was one matter to be summoned by the twins—I chalked that up to our proximity to Vardak. But this is different. Minora and my mother…" He scowled and raked one hand through his hair. "I've no doubt Solsticia is involved if the Time Guardian is."

"What aren't you telling me, Ravin?" Adalin demanded. "I know that look. It's the same as you wore countless times in the catacombs when I attempted to learn of your past."

"I learned something of my mother's plans for me while we sought the talisman." Ravin sighed and seemed to deflate, much of his anger evaporating with his words. In its place, Tavesin saw helplessness and despair war across the mage's features.

Adalin went to him and took his hands in hers. "Ravin, I am here to help you—as a friend. Whatever you've learned, we will work through it. Together."

Ravin's golden eyes clouded with emotion and reluctantly, he nodded. "The day the queen summoned you, and I ventured into the catacombs alone, I encountered an area that could not be crossed from the physical plane. I was forced to enter the Aethereum in order to proceed."

"What does that have to do with anything?" Tavesin asked, confused, as Adalin drew a sharp intake of breath.

Ravin glanced at him, his expression troubled. "It means the Aethereum was built before my birth—or mother put that piece of the puzzle in place with Minora's help afterwards. She told me that realm was constructed for *me*, and as you are aware, my strength while there is unparalleled. Regardless of the timing, I alone was meant to acquire the talisman." He sighed. "What I'm trying to say is this: I believe my path was preordained by my mother and likely by Minora, as well. I've striven so gods-damned hard to correct my mistakes, but the more I learn, the more I can't shake the sense that my free will is nothing but a fallacy. I'm nothing more than a damned pawn in my mother's games."

"I'm sure that's not true," Adalin replied gently. "Perhaps this message will provide you with more insight—and some peace of mind."

Ravin snorted. "I doubt that." He peered over the duchess' head at Tavesin. "Why don't we see what yours says first? I'm not yet ready to face my mother's schemes."

Tavesin looked down at his letter, unable to hide his trepidation. His hands shook as he placed the book on the floor, and he fumbled with the wax seal. He chewed his lower lip and glanced at Ravin before he opened the envelope, seeking reassurance. When the mage nodded his encouragement, Tavesin withdrew a carefully creased sheet of parchment and unfolded it. A beautiful, flowing script graced the page. He scanned the message twice before raising his gaze to gape at the others.

"Minora left a book in my room. She claims it was the journal written by Morganus the White."

Adalin's eyes lit up with his statement, and she flashed an excited grin at Ravin. "Surely even you know the name," she said to Ravin. "Morganus is the wizard who stopped the first Soulless. There have always been rumors surrounding his death, and speculation about why no one ever located his personal possessions after the battle. They'd vanished, or so the legends say."

Tavesin shook his head. "He gave them to Minora, and now she's given his journal to me."

CHAPTER SIX

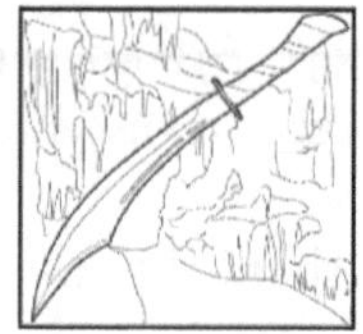

DIRE MACHINATIONS

The night sky spread like a curtain of velvet overhead, dotted with myriad pinpricks of light. The sky was clear, marred only by a few wisps of clouds far to the south, and illuminated by the starlight alone. The moon would not rise for several hours.

Aran'daj gazed upward as his feet carried him along the perimeter of the Murkor camp, situated between the edge of Blackstone Chasm and the black tower, looming ominously like a beacon of strife yet to come. As commander of the army, he was not required to partake in patrol duties, but on this night, he'd come to the perimeter to clear his head. The preceding weeks had been trying, a weight upon his conscience.

He considered his precarious position and the waning time he had left to walk the earth. He was certain once Jal'den's injury had sufficiently healed, Sal'zar would make his move, and Aran'daj's fate would be sealed. He'd come to peace with the inevitability of their scheme and understood it was the only way to see their people freed from the oppressive yoke the Soulless had placed over them. If Sal'zar succeeded—and he prayed the alchemist would—someone must pay the price for the Murkors betrayal. Aran'daj knew with cold certainty it would be his blood demanded by the Soulless, his life forfeit to grant his people hope of survival.

He'd kept his distance from both Sal'zar and Jal'den since their last meeting in the alchemist's tent when the Kal's plan had been laid bare. He was uncertain if either of the young men understood the enormity of what the scheme demanded of him, but it was of little consequence whether they did or not. He would not burden them with his innermost thoughts. It was better Jal'den remained ignorant, in any case; the Arms Master would undoubtedly protest, or perhaps throw himself foolishly into the fire in a misguided attempt to spare his commander. It was a possibility Aran'daj could not allow to happen. Jal'den was young and must live to see the end of the war—if not for himself, then for his partner.

Aran'daj's track began to curve toward the dark mouth of the chasm with its glittering sides of obsidian. He wondered if, when his time came to face his Soulless executioners, he'd be thrown over the jagged edge to tumble through space for an interminable time before crashing to his death at its bottom, leagues below. His wouldn't be the first such body to find its end in the shadowed depths.

He tore his gaze away from the chasm to scan the cracked and barren landscape beyond, then whispered a prayer to the gods to grant him the mercy of a swift death. If he must give his life to secure the future of his people, he did not wish to endure a prolonged and agonizing end.

He paused in his patrol and lifted his eyes to the moonless sky, taking solace in the tranquility of the stars above. He missed the days of peace that had preceded Shan'tar's arrival in his people's lands. Since the wizard's coming, the quiet life of the Murkor had been turned on its head. He prayed he would find solace when he entered Aeon's realm.

After a time, he became aware of the sound of footsteps behind him, coupled with quiet conversation. Reluctantly, he turned around to face his visitors. The tall, black-clad form of Jal'den, his right arm cradled in a sling, strode toward him alongside the tall, yet slighter, green-clad figure of Sal'zar. Aran'daj was at once pleased to see the pair, yet dreaded their pending conversation.

"Commander," Jal'den said by way of greeting, ducking his hooded head slightly in deference.

"Arms Master. I'm glad to see you're mending."

Jal'den tilted his head toward Sal'zar with a chuckle. "He wouldn't have it any other way, sir."

"Contrary to what he might tell you, he still requires some time to heal." Sal'zar crossed his arms. "Jal'den's health is not why we've come, sir."

"I thought not." Aran'daj motioned for the pair to walk with him as he continued his circuit of the camp. "I assume you've come about the Kal's plan."

"In part." Sal'zar paused to gather his thoughts. "I was within the tower prior to coming here, Commander. The Soulless are maneuvering forces beyond this army, forces that ought not be tampered with."

Aran'daj suppressed a shudder at the alchemist's insinuation. He suspected he understood the meaning behind Sal'zar's words, but dreaded hearing his worst fears confirmed. "What do they plan, Sal'zar?"

Sal'zar glanced at Jal'den as though seeking reassurance. When the Arms Master nodded, Sal'zar said, "They're seeking to release the Nameless god from his prison, sir. It's as the Kal feared."

Aran'daj focused his gaze on the empty landscape before them as he grappled with the enormity of the news. He knew Sal'zar must act soon to carry out the Kal's desperate scheme to shield some of their people from the inevitable hardships yet to come. And with the alchemist's move, his own fate was sealed.

"You cannot delay much longer, Sal'zar." His voice was strained, but he forced himself to continue. "The Kal's plan must be enacted."

"I know, sir." Sal'zar's tone was despondent. "My greatest fear is that this plan will fail, and we'll all suffer for it."

Aran'daj nodded, and the trio moved in silence for several minutes, each lost in his own thoughts. The Kal's plan hinged on the volatile temperament of the Soulless, the questionable protection of the very gods who seemed to have forsaken the Murkor, Sal'zar's guile, his own ability to deceive their dangerous overlords, and a thousand unanswered prayers. Yet the Kal believed it was their only hope to regain their freedom, and despite his misgivings, Aran'daj agreed.

"There is no other way," Aran'daj said finally. "You must carry out the Kal's orders, Sal'zar."

Sal'zar drew an audible breath and nodded. "The soldiers the Kal has chosen to accompany me have all received their orders. They know to look for my signal when the time comes."

"I'm pleased to hear it."

"Gods, I wish you'd let me help you," Jal'den muttered sullenly.

"We both know that would end poorly for you, *ama*," Sal'zar replied. "The Kal wishes to see us both survive this war. For that to occur, you must allow me to act alone."

They'd discussed the same topic on his previous visit, but it seemed the passage of two weeks had not alleviated Jal'den's displeasure with the situation nor weakened Sal'zar's resolve. Aran'daj prayed Sal'zar would not waver in his conviction to see the Kal's will done. So much of their plan rested on the young alchemist's shoulders, and if Sal'zar's plot was uncovered prematurely, he would pay the price meant for Aran'daj. Losing Sal'zar would break Jal'den.

"Trust your partner in this," Aran'daj advised. "It is the only way our plans will bear fruit."

"I will, Commander," Jal'den growled, "but I don't have to like it. He risks too much."

"I'll ensure you both know when I plan to depart with the others," Sal'zar replied wearily. "There are still some preparations we must make. It will take time, but I will urge everyone to be ready before the month is out." He turned toward Jal'den. "There is one more thing I must ask of you, *ama*."

Jal'den shrugged. "You plan to leave with my heart. What more do you require?" he asked, his tone heavy with despair.

Sal'zar sighed, exasperated. "The vial I gave you before I was sent to the tower. If you haven't yet used it, I wish to have it back. We may need it..."

"The stealth potion?" Jal'den asked. "Yes, I still have it, and you may take it."

Aran'daj listened to their exchange silently, recalling the night when Jal'den had mentioned Sal'zar's parting gift to him. The Arms Master had offered to use it, to attack one of the Soulless directly if Aran'daj commanded him to do so. He'd managed to convince Jal'den to keep it for a better time, then had promptly forgotten their conversation. He was pleased that Sal'zar would have it at his disposal, should the need arise.

"Thank you, Jal'den," Sal'zar replied, relieved. "I feared you would argue with me on that point, as well."

Jal'den snorted. "I will not argue with you any longer since I can see there is no other path for us to follow. But know this: if you don't survive, I will tear the world asunder to avenge you, and even the gods will rue the day they set our people on this damned course."

Sal'zar fell silent at his words and looked away.

Aran'daj studied the pair for a time. He empathized with Jal'den; the two had been kept apart for most of the time they'd been named *ujar'havel* due to circumstances beyond either's control. Both were frustrated by the situation, yet both understood the necessity of what must be done. Neither were happy with the proposed outcome.

Aran'daj suspected Jal'den still had not made the connection between their plan and Aran'daj's own bleak fate. Once the Arms Master learned his commander's life would be forfeit, Jal'den would burn with rage, a rage he must suppress in order to fulfill the Kal's orders. As his second, Jal'den would be named Commander, then would be forced to stand in battle against Sal'zar's battalion when the war resumed in the spring. It was a heart wrenching-position that could not be avoided unless they abandoned the Kal's scheme altogether.

As he watched the alchemist and the Arms Master, Aran'daj believed neither would waver from the roles their people's leader demanded they play. The knowledge was comforting as he contemplated his last days.

"I will pray for your success, Sal'zar," Aran'daj said quietly, breaking their long silence.

"Thank you, sir. I should return to the tower before my absence is noted."

Jal'den sighed. "I will walk with you to the far side of the camp."

After the two were gone, Aran'daj turned to make his way toward his tent. He would compose one final letter to the Kal, his grandfather, and another to Rej'amin, the love he'd been denied in his youth. He prayed his parting words to them would provide them with a measure of peace once they learned of his death.

CHAPTER SEVEN

A PREDESTINED FATE

Ravin wanted nothing to do with the unopened letter clenched in his fist. Minora may have been its bearer, but he was certain it came from his mother. Since he'd uncovered Solsticia's involvement in the defenses of Delucha's talisman, he'd planned to confront her but had continually put it off. There were dozens of other tasks to occupy his time, and what would become a contentious discussion with the celestial goddess was not something he looked forward to. He'd procrastinated, and now, he was being summoned. He would be forced to face his mother on *her* terms rather than his own.

He scowled at the thought as he trailed behind Tavesin and Adalin toward the boy's room. He realized he was delaying the inevitable once more by allowing Tavesin to uncover the book Minora had left for him. He didn't care. His last conversation with Solsticia had ended in a heated argument, and he'd refused to speak with her for years. He resented her meddling in his affairs and detested his own inability to prevent it. She was a goddess, after all—there was nothing to be done.

Tavesin darted ahead, narrowly avoiding a collision with one of the inn's maids, who shot him a glare. Unfazed, he careened through the corridor to his room and flung the door open without regard for anyone who may have been within. Ravin was aware he shared the room with the two other young wizards that had traveled to Delucha, but it seemed Tavesin's focus was solely upon Minora's "gift."

Ravin followed the boy inside once it was clear they were alone. Tavesin edged toward a cluttered table shoved in one corner of the crowded room, where several books were stacked amongst an untidy heap of someone's soiled garments. Two of the three narrow bunks were unmade, clothing was strewn across the floor, and a pile of rubbish was pushed against the wall nearest the door. Ravin grimaced as he took in the disarray within the room, but he supposed it was to be expected from three young teenagers. The room reeked of unwashed bodies and stale rations.

Beside him, Adalin frowned and held one hand over her nose. "Gods, this reminds me of my late husband's son," she whispered, disapproval thick in her tone. "Do all boys strive to live in utter squalor when there is no need for it?"

Ravin chuckled. "It's a phase that will pass, Adalin."

"I suppose it must. Otherwise, how would any man win a woman's heart?"

Across the room, Tavesin placed his pilfered book from the queen's library carefully atop the table and retrieved a slimmer, leather-bound tome that appeared newly-made. Tavesin turned the book over in his hands with a confused frown, then looked up to meet Ravin's eyes.

"She said this book belonged to Morganus," Tavesin stated helplessly. "I don't understand how it's possible. He died a thousand years ago."

"Taven," Adalin said gently, "this was gifted to you by *Minora*, Time's Guardian. Think on that."

He continued to frown at the book as he picked his way across the disheveled room. "Oh, I think I understand," he whispered, and his expression suddenly brightened.

He stood before Ravin and Adalin as he opened the pristine cover to reveal the first page of text within. Ravin peered down at the compact handwriting and shook his head. Morganus' book began with a rendition of the Legend of Creation, a tale most children learned by the age of five. What purpose did its inclusion in his journal serve?

"It seems you'll have some reading to do, Taven," Adalin said, as though intuiting Ravin's thoughts. "I believe we'll leave you to it. Ravin has the matter of his own message to deal with."

Ravin suppressed a groan and clenched his fist, crumpling the envelope further. She pierced him with an unyielding gaze while Tavesin closed the journal and stared uncertainly at the two adults.

Ravin drew a breath and reluctantly tore open the envelope to reveal its contents. It was a message, as he'd anticipated, though it was not his mother's handwriting that greeted his eyes.

Ravin De'vor is hereby summoned to the Windmaker's temple north of Delucha city. Delays will not be tolerated.

The script was precise yet flowing, and he wondered if Cirrus himself had penned the brief missive. Or perhaps it had been Minora. He supposed it didn't matter which deity had decided to plague his evening further with their demands; he welcomed none of them. He growled wordlessly and handed the letter to Adalin.

"I suppose this means you're leaving, Ravin?" she asked.

"It's not my mother's hand," he replied. "She may tolerate my defiance to a degree, but the others will not. Yes, I'll be going." He looked between the duchess and Tavesin, then said, "If anyone should come seeking me, tell them what you will."

"Ravin," Adalin replied firmly, "whatever comes of this summons, we can discuss it afterwards. You do not need to bear this burden alone."

He nodded, grateful for her support. "I'll seek you out once I'm finished," he promised.

She nodded, satisfied. "Good. Now, go, Ravin, before you offend the gods further."

He chuckled and created a portal in the corridor without regard for the inn's staff or other patrons who might happen to see him. After the recent battle, there was little reason to hide his abilities as he'd done in the past. He cast his senses throughout the Aethereum as he stepped inside, but located no threats within. He transported himself to the temple dedicated to Cirrus, the wind god, and exited to the physical realm without hesitation.

The temple was a cylindrical tower topped by a twisted spire, set against the backdrop of the low, rounded mountains known as the Windy Peaks. Its outer walls were comprised of a pale gray stone, shot through with veins of silvery blue. It was leagues north of Delucha city, and only a deity aware of his access to the Aethereum would have demanded he arrive without delay. The trip would have taken days on horseback, perhaps more than a week on foot.

A luminous blue-white crystal hung suspended above the temple's closed double doors, providing light enough to guide his path. He recognized the crystal as being of Murkor craftsmanship, an unusual feature for a location so distant from their homeland.

He shivered as he neared the doors, momentarily frustrated with himself for departing the inn without his heavy cloak. A stiff breeze cut through his clothing and threatened to chill him to his core. He glanced at the sky apprehensively but was relieved to note it was cloudless; there would be no snow this night.

He pushed through the heavy doors and entered the temple foyer. The space was similarly lit with Murkor crystals, revealing a triangular room constructed of the same pale gray stone. Several large tapestries adorned the walls, each depicting the winged, reptilian countenance of Cirrus, the patron god of the Drakkon people. A single open door exited the room opposite his position at the entrance. There were no priests present in the foyer to note Ravin's arrival.

He shrugged and crossed the room toward the open door. Peering beyond the threshold, he was met with another empty space, this one smaller than the foyer; it housed the base of a wide, spiral staircase that led upward toward the tower's apex. More tapestries furnished the walls, decorating the path of the faithful as they ascended the steps.

Ravin glowered as he began the trek. While he'd known the approximate location of the temple and could use that as his guide in the Aethereum, he'd never before entered Cirrus' sacred space. He didn't know the structural features of the temple; it would prove too risky to transport himself without the ability to visualize the precise details of the interior destination. He hoped he'd meet someone to guide his path on one of the lower levels, rather than be forced to traverse the entirety of the staircase to the tower's top.

The first two landings he encountered were empty, the rooms beyond dark and silent. Muttering a curse under his breath, he continued to the top floor, where he was greeted by a pair of Drakkon. Both were male, marked by their large stature and the sharp, bony protrusions along their brows. They wore flowing robes of sky blue with swirls of silver embroidery, the color contrasting with their crimson scales. The shorter of the two ruffled his leathery wings in agitation at Ravin's appearance while the other studied him with dark gray eyes.

"The gods have been expecting you," he informed Ravin. "Come."

Ravin frowned; the priest's use of the plural confirmed his suspicions. His mother was behind the summons, though she'd attempted to disguise her machinations through Minora and Cirrus. It was typical.

He allowed himself to be led into the circular room beneath the temple's spire. More crystals lit the space, and on the wall opposite the door he spied the largest mirror he'd ever seen. Its surface was polished and free of blemishes, reflecting the room and enhancing the crystals' light. His eyes were drawn to the room's center, however, where the towering forms of Cirrus and Solsticia stood.

He understood Cirrus' presence; they were within his temple, after all. As patron of the Drakkon people, he sported their winged, reptilian form, but unlike the priests, he stood well over ten feet tall. Cirrus' arms were folded across his broad chest, and a look of disdain painted his features. His sky blue eyes tracked Ravin's progress as he moved across the room.

Ravin's gaze met Solsticia's last. She was the patron of the human species, though far more beautiful than most women Ravin had ever met. Her dark hair curled toward her waist, and her golden eyes—identical to his own—studied him. A faint smile played upon her full lips, as though she were pleased to see him. Her expression unsettled him. He'd expected disappointment, perhaps anger. Their last encounter, before he'd created his soul-stone, had ended when she'd ordered him from her sight.

He stopped several paces from the two gods and knelt to indicate his deference, while his priestly escort did the same. He studied the smooth, stone floor while a lengthy silence enveloped the room. Finally, Cirrus broke the stillness with a leathery rustle of his enormous wings.

"Leave us," he ordered the priest.

Ravin remained kneeling while the priest exited the room. After he heard the soft click of the door closing behind him, Solsticia said,

"Stand up, Ravin. We've much to discuss." Her tone was gentle, welcoming. In spite of himself, he smiled.

"My part is finished in this business," Cirrus stated, casting a pointed look in Solsticia's direction. "He has come, as you intended."

She nodded graciously. "I thank you, brother."

Cirrus paused to frown at Ravin while his words were directed at Solsticia. "I'd be less lenient with my blood than you've proven to be. The irreverence he showed the twins is infuriating."

"It will be addressed," Solsticia assured him.

Cirrus grunted, unconvinced, before abruptly winking out of sight.

"You've summoned me here for a scolding, mother?" Ravin demanded, unable to mask his irritation. He crossed his arms and stared a challenge at her while she continued to smile.

"No, Ravin. You've suffered enough in your life. I will not add to it."

Ravin sighed and looked away, uncertain what he ought to say. Compassion was not the response he'd expected after Cirrus' remarks. He was further startled when she abruptly knelt down to look him in the eye.

"Ravin, I'd never intended for you to endure the hardships life has presented you with. I know I've been absent much of your life, and I will always regret my decision to remain distant."

He studied her silently, noted the earnest expression in her eyes and the sincerity in her voice. His previous anger began to subside, and he wondered at the change in her demeanor. Perhaps his millennia-long imprisonment had afforded her the time required to accept his choices—if indeed they'd been choices at all.

"What has changed?" he asked.

She sighed. "You've been in contact with Vardak for some time. Surely you've heard his story and how he came to possess the Moon's Eye."

Understanding flooded him then. The relic had come into Vardak's possession only after a young woman who'd become one of his friends had sacrificed her life to break its ages-long curse. The woman had been the daughter of Flariel.

"I will not lose you as my sister lost her child," Solsticia said quietly. "I will aid you as I can during the remainder of this war."

He frowned. "Isn't directly influencing mortal conflicts forbidden, mother?"

She shook her head. "This time is different, Ravin. The Nameless has grown strong once more, and we must defeat him. He cannot be allowed to break free." She eyed him critically, some of her former disapproval seeping into her expression. "You'd understand this if you'd paid better attention to the twins' words rather than pouring your energy into provoking them. Armistral was understanding enough of your behavior, but Blademon was not. If you were not my son, he'd have taken your head to decorate his compound."

Ravin lifted his eyebrows in surprise. "I don't recall saying anything to warrant my execution."

"And you've no previous experience with the god of war," she countered. "Blademon is fierce and unyielding. He is unused to disobedience from mortals, and you've garnered a reputation amongst my siblings for being exceedingly difficult."

Ravin snorted. "I simply don't trust their motives—or yours. My life has been toyed with enough."

"Ravin…"

"No, I need to say this, mother." He clenched his fists at his sides, overwhelmed by frustration. "While I was in the catacombs beneath the palace, I realized one of two things. Either you and Minora warped time significantly in order to protect the talisman, or you set me on this path long before I first drew breath."

Solsticia released a pained sigh. "You have every right to be angry, Ravin. We vowed never to interfere in mortal conflicts and to minimize our roles in your affairs. But with your power, I couldn't simply leave you to your own devices. Your path *needed* to be guided, Ravin. Without a predestined fate, you would have proven too dangerous. My siblings would have seen you killed."

He turned away from her with a snarl. "And the only alternative was to see me fall into Dranamir's gods-damned trap, tortured, and killed, only to have my soul bound for over *one thousand fucking years?* All so I could retrieve this damned talisman and fight in your senseless war? Why not take the fight directly to the Nameless and leave the rest of us out of your blasted schemes?"

His shoulders heaved as he continued to seethe. He stared at the floor, refusing to meet her gaze while his temper raged. He should not have said half of what he'd just done, but he felt better for having expressed his anger. Her admission that his life was not of his own design would continue to sting for years to come.

"Ravin, look at me."

Although her voice was pained, he briefly entertained the notion of ignoring her. He knew if she truly wanted to force him to obey, she could do so easily. She was a goddess, and he was merely her mortal pawn. Grudgingly, he peered at her from the corners of his eyes.

"When I became aware of the magic you harbored, I was forced to tell the others. My choice was simple, Ravin, albeit selfish. I refused to lose you, so I allowed Minora to weave your fate into the tapestry of time. I was unaware of all she'd set upon you—she refused to speak of it, stating that I would learn as each event came to pass." She looked down, genuinely anguished. "Since your resurrection, I've argued with her continually. She was against me coming here until tonight, though I've desperately wished to tell you how deeply sorry I am. You have every right to be angry, Ravin, and I will not fault you if you choose never to speak with me again."

Her words diffused his rage, but he didn't believe he could fully trust her again. "Is it truly my choice, or is it hers?" When she opened her mouth to speak, he shrugged and shook his head. "It doesn't matter. I won't refuse to see you, mother, but I require time to think over this evening."

Her smile was strained. "I suppose that is the best outcome I can hope for. I have always loved you, Ravin. You are my son, my only child."

He nodded wearily, feeling suddenly drained. "I'd like to return to Delucha."

"Of course. Allow me to take you. It's the least I can do."

She returned him to the corridor outside Adalin's room but did not make an appearance herself. She'd understood his need to speak with the duchess, or perhaps she was simply aware of the promise he'd made to her before departing for Cirrus' temple. Either way, he was grateful despite the depression that had settled over him like a dark mist.

Adalin opened the door moments after his knock, as though she'd been awaiting his return. She took one look at his haunted expression and ushered him inside.

"Ravin, what happened?"

He went to the window and peered down at the darkened streets below. His voice was hollow as he related what had transpired between him and his mother, and by the end of his tale, he found himself on the verge of tears.

Wordlessly, Adalin drew him into a warm embrace, offering what comfort she could.

"Was this moment written for me a thousand years ago as well?" he asked.

His voice cracked and the last of his defenses fell away. Tears fell unbidden from his eyes while Adalin held him. He'd allowed no one to see him give way to his emotions since his childhood, but he knew the duchess would not judge him for his lapse. It was in that moment he realized the true depth of his feelings for her.

Even if every event of his life had been carefully orchestrated to fulfill Minora's agenda, he was grateful she'd seen fit to allow him to know true friendship at long last.

CHAPTER EIGHT

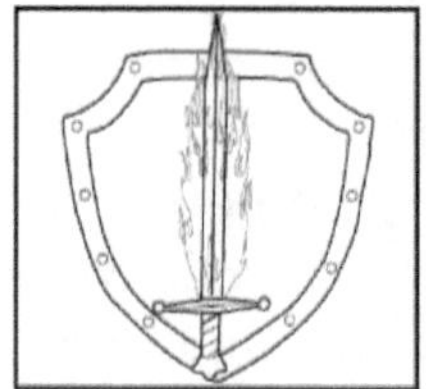

A PLAN FOR DEPARTURE

As midday approached, the private dining room Emra used as her primary meeting room and temporary command center began to fill rapidly. She'd summoned each of the prominent figures associated with the various aspects of the army, as well as the leader of the wizards and Ravin. Vardak had made a determination regarding their destination for the winter, and while most gathered were aware she planned to depart Delucha soon, there was still much to do.

Patak loomed on her right side, unable to stand still. His legs tapped a steady rhythm against the wooden floor while he observed the others within. Vardak stood on her left, bent over the table in front of them as he continued to study maps and sift through correspondence. She knew he would not stop his work until she began to speak. He was tireless in his determination to see every aspect of their military was running smoothly.

Across the room, Maryn spoke quietly with Danness, his feline ears twitching and tilting as he eavesdropped on the conversations of others nearby. She smiled in amusement; it was typical of the Felene watch commander. Danness held several long sheets of parchment in his hands—a list of needed supplies and recent acquisitions, no doubt. Like Vardak, her quartermaster's work was never finished.

Jadosin, the queen's military advisor, lounged against one wall as he spoke with Alori, while the wizards' leader in Delucha, Radosan, listened intently. Ravin stood apart from the others, his arms crossed. Dark rings encircled his golden eyes, which were bloodshot and weary. Emra was aware of his summons to Cirrus' temple the previous evening but was not privy to the details. He'd said only that he'd spoken with his mother, though the encounter had clearly taken its toll.

"Where's Danian?" she asked of the two Scorpion Men who flanked her.

"He was meeting with several smiths this morning," Vardak replied without looking up from his work. "Many of the horses need reshoeing before we depart, but he said he'd be here."

"Relax, Em," Patak added with a grin. "Everything will come together, you'll see."

"I certainly hope so," she said, unable to mask the concern in her voice.

Vardak's chosen destination would take them nearly two weeks to reach with the size of their current group, the weather had grown cold, and she was still uncertain what would await them when they arrived. The Murkor army attacked Daesan some time before reaching Delucha city, and while Ravin and the Drakkon had confirmed the army was in the Wasted Land once more, the path might still be dangerous.

Her gaze flitted across those gathered once more as she realized Aziarah was missing, as well. "And Aziarah? Where is she?"

Vardak shrugged. "Likely with Tavesin or Badolo."

"We both know she wouldn't miss this without good reason," Patak replied. "The Drakkon are nothing if not dependable."

Moments later, the leader of the Drakkon mages entered, pausing to nod at Emra before she joined Maryn and Danness. As she began to speak, Danness scribbled notes in response.

"It seems the Drakkon are in need of supplies as well." Patak flashed another grin. "I told you she'd be here, Em."

She smiled. "Yes, I should know by now that between the two of you, I don't need to be concerned. You are both very efficient in your respective roles."

Patak snorted. "I rarely forget, and Vardak…" he shrugged and gestured toward his brother, who continued to pore over documents. "I'm not sure he knows how to relax."

Vardak pushed his work aside and smirked at Patak. "Better?"

"For now, yes."

Vardak pointed toward the door. "Danian has arrived. I'd have to break regardless."

Emra laughed as Patak rolled his eyes dramatically. "Only you, little brother. Only you…"

Emra waited until Danian closed the door to the hall before she called the group to attention. "I understand that each of you is busy, so I'll try to keep this discussion brief. There are many logistics to consider as we plan to move the army."

"Have you determined when we'll leave Delucha?" Aziarah asked. "My people are prepared for a lengthy journey, if that's what is required of us. The Drakkon can depart on a moment's notice."

Emra nodded. "I plan to march in five days' time. That should provide us with the opportunity to acquire any final supplies. As we all know, the gods have begun to involve themselves more thoroughly than even I have experienced. We cannot delay any further."

Murmurs and nods greeted her words, though Ravin muttered darkly under his breath. His latest encounter with Solsticia must have gone more poorly than he'd admitted.

"Where do you plan to lead us?" Radosan asked.

Emra shifted her gaze to meet Vardak's. "General, I believe this question is yours to answer."

Vardak appeared nonplussed, but it was his duty to inform the others of his plans. She understood he disliked being thrust into the center of attention, but she also believed he was the right person for the role. He needed to learn to accept the aspects he found distasteful just as he had everything else. His battle prowess and mind for strategy would only gain him the respect of some, but if he rose to the challenge and proved himself a true leader, he would earn the respect of all.

After a moment, Vardak nodded. "We'll march along the track the Murkor followed until we reach Daesan."

"Why Daesan?" Radosan asked.

Ravin frowned at the wizard. "Isn't it obvious?"

Vardak drew a breath and said, "For those who do not know the geography of eastern Delucha, there are two reasons why I've chosen Daesan." He leveled a glare at Ravin. "First, Daesan is near a merchant track that can be used to traverse the mountains in the spring. It is the fastest route through the mountains. Second, Daesan lies at the foot of a volcanic mountain. I believe we can utilize it to work the forges, even if the town has been razed."

"It has," Ravin snapped. "I've told you this previously."

Vardak's expression was unyielding. "Not everyone present is privy to your reports. I speak so they will understand. I don't care what transpired between you and your mother last night, but I do not appreciate your gods-damned temper when we're simply trying to explain the situation."

Ravin closed his eyes with a pained expression and looked away. "You're right, of course."

Emra looked between the pair with surprise. Vardak had handled the mage's foul mood better than she'd anticipated, but she was genuinely shocked by Ravin's admission. While it wasn't an apology, she suspected it was the closest they'd come to receiving one.

As a heavy silence began to descend upon the room, Emra said, "We will march for Daesan in five days' time. Make certain you and your people are ready."

Dismissed, the others quickly began to depart. Emra crossed the room before Ravin reached the door, intent on uncovering the events of the previous evening. She knew he'd likely confided in Adalin—though the nature of their relationship was still a mystery to her, they seemed to provide one another with an essential support system. After learning of his past, she understood why he was often skeptical or suspicious of others, and she realized the conversation they must have would be difficult.

"Of everyone here, I believe I understand your frustration with the gods best," she told him quietly. "I think we ought to speak."

He groaned, then nodded reluctantly. "Adalin suggested the same. She knows your story better than I, and seems to believe you might be of help." He shook his head in frustration. "Prior to last night, I hadn't spoken with mother in years. I was twenty-six. I'd say it was two decades ago, but we both know that isn't true."

He paused, scanning the room as the others exited. His golden eyes fell on Patak, and he said, "I'd prefer we spoke in confidence—away from your partner."

Emra felt her face flush. "I believed we'd been discreet."

"When your watch commander has a few drinks in him, he's rather talkative."

She looked down, her face heating further. "Maryn. Of course." She drew a breath, then forced herself to meet his gaze. "There is no one else I trust as implicitly as Patak, but I agree to your request. He won't be pleased. They still don't fully trust you."

Ravin snorted. "The mistrust of others seems to be my life's theme."

She ignored his final comment and went to Patak, where he continued to stand near the table with his brother. "Ravin has agreed to talk, but without your supervision."

Patak's smile faltered and he scowled across the room. "Is this wise, Em?"

"He's proven himself so far," she replied. "Besides, we cannot accomplish what the gods demand without him. We'll talk later."

He cracked a sly grin. "I hope you plan to do more than just talk, Em."

Beside them, Vardak groaned. "I think it's time *I* depart, as well. I don't need to hear this."

Patak snickered and accompanied his brother outside. "You're merely jealous, little brother."

She smiled to herself as she listened to the pair's banter. She prayed the war wouldn't change Patak's demeanor; it was the first thing that had drawn her to him. Reality often failed to mimic dreams, however, and she'd seen it happen enough times to prepare her heart for what the stress and brutality of battle might do to him. That he was one of Blademon's people gave her some comfort in the midst of her dark thoughts. They were made familiar with combat and its aftermath from a young age. Perhaps his personality would emerge unscathed.

She forced herself to focus on the matter at hand and turned to face Ravin. The mage wore a contemplative expression as he met her gaze.

"Tell me what happened last night, Ravin."

He began with Minora's unexpected visit, his certainty the message she left him had come from his mother, and his reticence to open it. It was only after Adalin's urging that he'd done so. He described his trip to Cirrus' temple in the north, the wind god's disparaging remarks, and the conversation that had unfolded between himself and Solsticia.

"My life has never been my own," he said bitterly. "It's a realization I have been unable to come to terms with. Perhaps I never will."

Emra empathized with his plight. Since Fireblade's forging, her own destiny had been dictated by the gods, though she believed she'd been afforded a measure of free will that it seemed Ravin had been denied.

"Adalin was right, you know," she told him quietly. "I *do* understand. My fate has been dictated by Aeon time and again. He's refused to grant my soul rest until the Soulless are vanquished and the Nameless is brought to heel."

It was something even Patak was unaware of, and as she spoke, she wondered why she believed Ravin would keep her confidence where the man she loved would not. Perhaps, in spite of his prickly exterior, she sensed a kindred spirit in Ravin. Or perhaps it was merely Patak's unabashedly open nature that gave her pause.

Ravin's gaze was locked on the floor between them. When he spoke again, his tone was weary. "If what Adalin told me of your history is correct, you at least had a say in your current predicament, once. Mine was determined before my birth." He raked one hand through his dark hair in his agitation. "I've always believed my choices were my own. Learning that I've been wrong on every count is...gods-damned devastating." His final words were growled through clenched teeth.

"If ever you need to talk, I am available, Ravin."

He forced a smile and looked up to meet her eyes. "Thank you. I will make an effort to be less surly. It does none of us any good, as the duchess is fond of reminding me."

"Will she be joining us when we depart?" Emra asked, still uncertain what his ties to Adalin truly were.

He chuckled. "Gods, no. She'll remain here, where she'll be safe—so long as we're successful, that is." He smiled to himself. "I've promised her I'll return when I'm able, though I seem to need her more than she does me. When we were first introduced, I wanted nothing to do with her. It's amusing to realize how quickly that changed."

"Yes. Matters of the heart often develop unexpectedly." She smiled, her thoughts once more on Patak. "I'm glad we've spoken, Ravin. I think it's done us both some good."

CHAPTER NINE

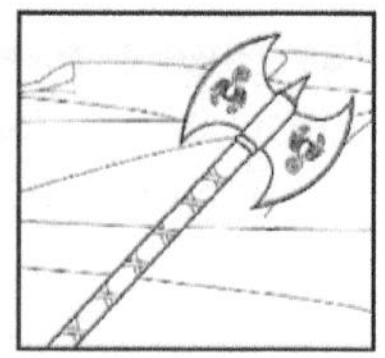

BALOTICAN SUPPORT

"If we had another strong wizard or two, we wouldn't be required to travel on foot. We'd be able to transport the whole army directly to Daesan."

Vardak nodded in acknowledgment of Ravin's words, though he felt speculating on the issue served little purpose. The fact was, they lacked the aforementioned wizards and must travel in the traditional sense. Only the Santinian cavalry and a handful of others possessed horses, while the majority of Emra's army was forced to march on foot. Vardak had tasked the cavalry with acting as scouts, simply due to their ability to travel more swiftly than the others.

"Perhaps the Shining Tower will send more wizards once they learn the full scope of Emra's plans," he replied without looking at the golden-eyed mage.

Ravin snorted. "It's doubtful. Radosan has spoken with the Radiant often enough, and it seems the wizards currently with us are all he is willing to spare. It's ludicrous. Does he not understand the magnitude of the threat we face? If we fail, it will only be a matter of time before the Soulless make their way to Dar Daelad."

"While I agree with your assessment, what more can we do?" Vardak countered. "We cannot force them to join the fight. Radosan and the others here came of their own volition."

Ravin scowled and looked away. "The Radiant is a gods-damned fool."

Vardak made no reply. He agreed with Ravin's sentiments and understood his frustration to a degree, but there was nothing he could do to improve the situation. Emra had pleaded their case to the Radiant on more than one occasion, but they'd received nothing more than the handful of wizards that had traveled with them to Delucha.

His gaze swept the column of soldiers ahead. Most chatted amicably with their peers, while others joked and laughed amongst themselves. Spirits were high, though they were only three days east of Delucha. The army still had at least a week of marching ahead of it, provided the weather remained calm and clear. The air was cool, but the sky showed no indications of Maelstrom's wrath on the horizon. He prayed it would remain that way. A storm would not only cause a delay, but it would dampen morale.

Vardak noted a disturbance in the ranks ahead as he studied the soldiers. A man on horseback was galloping along the side of the road against the flow of the march, a plume of dust trailing in his wake. As he drew nearer, Vardak recognized the green and white Santinian crest on the man's shield, depicting a winged serpent with bared fangs. He was likely one of the advance scouts.

Vardak glanced at Ravin as he began to make his way toward the road's edge. "I think he has news."

"I'll accompany you," the mage replied swiftly. "There's little else to do, and I may be of help."

Vardak shot a skeptical glance over his shoulder but said nothing. Since their departure from Delucha, Ravin had striven to make amends for his previous foul temper and was often found in discussion with Emra when he wasn't busy acting as mentor to Tavesin. He'd made an impression on Patak, and Vardak grudgingly acknowledged his initial assessment of the man may have been premature. Ravin was as much a victim of the gods' games as he—perhaps even more so.

The two made their way toward the scout as he reined in his mount. "Sir, there's movement ahead. Judging by the amount of dust, there are a large number of people on the move."

Vardak narrowed his eyes as he considered his options. "Did you ride near enough to determine who they might be?"

He did not need to elaborate on his concerns; the scout intuited the implication that the group may prove hostile. Though the Murkor had fled across the mountains, a human army might prove to be equally dangerous. The Soulless had recruited human soldiers in the past.

"No, sir." The scout looked away with a grimace. "We're not far from Delucha, and I believed—"

"What's done is in the past," Vardak replied, silencing the man's excuses. "To leave without further assessing the situation was a mistake, but we'll deal with the matter."

"Vardak," Ravin said slowly, "allow me to investigate."

Vardak studied the mage silently for a moment, then nodded. "As I understand it, you are critical to the Immortals' plans. Don't get yourself killed."

Ravin smirked. "It's the newcomers that ought to be worried."

Vardak returned his attention to the scout as Ravin created a shimmering blue portal and disappeared within. He tried to ignore the crawling sensation that ran across his skin at Ravin's display of power. His people didn't possess magical talents, and the strange abilities Ravin and the wizards employed unnerved him, though he'd never admit it openly. Since the battle in Delucha, he'd been more wary of the magical folk that accompanied the army. He focused on masking his discomfort in order to perform his job and succeed in his role without drawing the ire or suspicion of the mages.

"Report what you've seen to Emra. She ought to be a quarter-mile back with Danian and Patak."

The man saluted before urging his mount into a canter. Vardak watched him ride away and remained in place as he awaited Ravin's return. He'd learned the mage often reappeared in the same space he departed from, though he didn't understand the workings of the magic involved in his rapid transport between locations.

It was only a matter of minutes before a second shimmering oval appeared and Ravin stepped from within. The mage wore a rare grin, and Vardak knew he bore good news. He fell in step beside Vardak as the pair began to march forward again.

"There is indeed a large group ahead—a hundred or so Baloticans." Ravin glanced behind them, seeking someone within the ranks of soldiers. "Their leader stated his name is Jonathan *Castledowns*. He claims he's a cousin of our leader."

"Do you believe he spoke true?" Vardak asked.

Ravin nodded. "There's no denying they're kin. Same hair and eye color, similar features…"

"I see. Emra didn't mention any family in the Balotican military." Vardak frowned; there was something about the situation that continued to trouble him, though he couldn't pin down what it was.

"They're not soldiers, unless I'm terribly mistaken," Ravin replied. "A few had piecemeal armor, but I wouldn't call the tools they carried weapons. I'm not certain *why* they've journeyed so far to lend their support, or if she'll even welcome their arrival. What I can say is this—they aren't hostile."

"How far away were they?" Vardak pressed.

Ravin shrugged. "It's difficult to determine distance from within the Aethereum. Perhaps your scout will know."

Vardak suppressed a disappointed sigh and nodded his thanks to the mage. He paused to peer down the long line of soldiers traipsing along the road but could not locate Emra amidst the throng.

"I'll inform her of our visitors," Ravin stated. "Or would you rather I bring her to your location, so that you might discuss our options?"

Vardak hesitated while he considered the request. He needed Emra present when their group met up with the Baloticans in order to verify her cousin's identity, but he was reluctant to allow Ravin's further involvement. This was a military matter, not one of magic.

Finally, he said, "I need to speak with her before the Baloticans arrive, if you don't mind."

Ravin smiled knowingly. "It's not so difficult to trust me, is it, General?"

Before Vardak could form a response, Ravin disappeared inside another portal. Vardak sighed and shook his head before resuming his march, frustrated by the interaction and Ravin's apparent ease at reading his unspoken sentiments. He briefly wondered if the mage had conjured a means to magically eavesdrop on his thoughts, but discarded the notion as absurd. Perhaps, he reflected, Patak wasn't merely teasing him when he claimed Vardak's expressions were a clear indicator of his emotional state, and Ravin had merely learned to read him.

Moments after Ravin's departure, he returned with Emra. She sat astride Fyrmane, whose eyes rolled with fright as she exited the latest portal. She took a few moments to calm the terrified steed, who snorted in agitation at her murmured words.

"I don't think we ought to try leading him through your realm again," she informed Ravin as she coaxed Fyrmane forward with her knees. "He doesn't care for it. I can't say I do, either. The light gives me a headache."

Ravin appeared thoughtful. "Adalin has mentioned the same. Yet you're a mage—I didn't believe it would affect you adversely."

Emra arched one eyebrow in his direction. "Perhaps it has nothing to do with one's Ability or lack thereof, and simply affects those not blessed by your mother with Aethereal magic."

At the mention of Solsticia, Ravin scowled. "Perhaps you're right."

Vardak looked between the pair while he waited for Emra to address him. The exchange was markedly more friendly than those they'd shared while within Delucha, a sign that Emra had accepted Ravin as an ally—and perhaps a friend. He knew he must do the same, though he struggled to forgive the mage for withholding critical information on the eve of battle. His trust was not as easily regained as Emra's seemed to be.

Emra shifted her gaze from Ravin to meet Vardak's. "Ravin mentioned there are Baloticans on the road ahead."

Vardak eyed the mage curiously. "Ravin scouted ahead and spoke to their leader. I'm surprised he didn't tell you more."

Ravin's expression was unreadable. "I didn't feel it was my place to do so. I came to offer my services to the army, not to interfere in its workings."

With a sigh, Vardak told Emra what they'd learned of the Baloticans. At the mention of Jonathan, she brightened.

"Jonathan's a blacksmith," she said with a grin. "He may not be a soldier, but I'm certain we can utilize his skills." She twisted in her saddle to look at Ravin once more. "Were all of the Baloticans craftsmen?"

"Perhaps. They certainly weren't soldiers."

"Jonathan's influence amongst the various trade guilds is strong," she replied. "It's possible he's convinced others—armorers, fletchers, and the like—to join him." Her smile faltered, and she sighed. "It's likely he also left our homeland without the blessing of the king. He isn't known for his patience."

"Will that be a problem?" Vardak inquired.

"It's difficult to know for certain. I'd like to speak with him first."

It was another hour before the Baloticans became visible along the road ahead. Vardak issued a halt while he accompanied Emra forward to meet with her cousin. Patak and two of her personal guards trailed behind them. His elder brother refused to allow her to go unescorted, even though she was meeting with her kin.

One of the Baloticans drew away from the others as they neared, and within moments Vardak knew the man must be Jonathan. Many of his facial features strongly resembled Emra's, though he was several inches taller than she and was nearly twice as wide. His muscular build reminded him poignantly of Travin, who was also a smith. Idly, he wondered how his middle brother fared, and if he'd be able to return to the Stronghold prior to the birth of Travin's first child. It was Vardak's wish to be present in the life of his future niece or nephew.

He refocused his attention on the blond human that approached them alone, unconcerned by the presence of Emra's escorts. He grinned broadly when she dismounted Fyrmane and rushed forward for a brief embrace.

"Jon, we weren't expecting to see anyone from home," she said as she stepped back to examine him further.

He shrugged. "Rumors came to us some time ago that you were in Dar Daelad. That was my original destination, you know. We were going to follow this merchant's road west until we met you. I wasn't expecting to find you in Delucha."

She grinned. "We're on our way to Daesan. I'm pleased we've met up with you." She paused to introduce Vardak and the others, then told him of the recent battle.

Jonathan whistled. "Gods-damn, Em. The Soulless? And…what did you call them?"

"Murkor," she replied. "Hooded Ones, as our stories call them."

"Well," he said, scratching the back of his neck in apparent discomfort, "we'd heard of the Fireblade's return, but this is…unexpected."

"The army can use your talents," she replied, "and Daesan is renowned for its forges. I recall you once told me you'd give your left arm to travel there."

He chuckled uneasily. "I did, at that."

Jonathan's gaze flickered to the rest of his group, and Vardak was certain he was concerned for their safety. He understood he must say something to ease the man's fears.

"Craftsmen are valuable," he said. "I'll ensure those who cannot or don't wish to fight will be protected if they plan to accompany us."

Jonathan blinked in surprise, then managed a smile. "I wasn't expecting such understanding. Forgive me, but I've always been told your people frown upon those who refuse to wield a blade."

Behind him Patak snorted. Vardak motioned for his brother to remain silent and shook his head. "Many of our people become warriors, but not all. It's true that most are trained for battle from a young age, but our society still requires those like you to function. Not everyone is suited for a life of combat."

Jonathan grinned. "I'll speak with the others. I can't guarantee everyone will wish to remain with the army, knowing now what we face, but I, for one, will join you."

As he began to turn away, Emra said, "Jon, were you granted permission for this expedition?"

He laughed over his shoulder. "When have I ever bothered with such things, Em?"

CHAPTER TEN

THE NAMELESS GOD'S WILL

Garin smirked knowingly as Dranamir entered the tower's topmost room, his expression a mixture of malice and gloating. Alyra paced not far from his position near the mirror, seemingly unconcerned by his present attitude. Dranamir glared in his direction, which caused his smirk to widen into a cold smile. Uncertain of his motives, she hastily shielded herself from any potential magic he might deign to throw her way. Something had occurred that left the deceptively frail man in a haughty mood, and she knew she wouldn't like whatever he planned to say.

Garin glanced between the two women, his crimson eyes alight with sudden anticipation. "Where is Kama?"

Dranamir snorted. "I'm not his keeper, and as I recall, the two of you have been working rather closely of late. Shouldn't *we* be asking that question of *you*, Garin?"

Garin flashed an icy grin, revealing a row of yellowed teeth. "With what I plan to do today, you ought to thank me, Dranamir. I'm eager to begin—and Kama is late."

"He's likely with the army," Alrya cut in. "Shall I—?"

"No," Garin cut her off, his tone unyielding. "You will remain here. Kama will arrive soon, or he'll face our master's wrath."

Dranamir lifted her eyebrows in question at Garin's tone. He was eager, yet edgy, a dangerous combination.

A portal opened next to Alyra, and moments later, Kama emerged. He scowled across the room as his gaze met Garin's. "Fucking gods! I thought I'd be granted more than an hours' rest after our return. This had better be important, or I'll—"

Garin interrupted him with a bitter laugh. "You'll do nothing, and we both know it, Kama. Your threats against me are hollow. I summoned you here for a very *momentous* occasion."

Garin's words failed to impress Kama, who continued to glower. "Fine. Let's get this over and done with."

Dranamir observed the pair warily, maintaining tight control over her invisible defensive barrier. Garin was scheming and she did not trust his motives. Of the four Soulless, he was perhaps the most dangerous, given his unique bond with the Nameless. Garin took a moment to look at each of them individually, an icy smile twisting his lips. She'd rarely seen him show any emotion beyond anger and his expression made her wary.

Finally, he reached into the pocket of his dark tunic and withdrew a polished onyx stone carved into the shape of a howling wolf. It was small enough to fit in the palm of his pale hand as he held it up for all to see. A satisfied smirk crossed his lips as Alyra gasped.

Dranamir kept her emotions in check while she studied the object from across the room. Prior to its withdrawal from Garin's pocket, she'd failed to sense its presence. Now that it was on display, she understood why he continued to gloat; it was the most powerful relic she'd encountered, with the exception of the one Ravin had wielded during the recent battle. A tingle of anticipation ran along her spine as she suddenly understood the relic's significance and the reason behind Garin's summons.

"With Kama's assistance, I have acquired the talisman from Kamshat. The Twilight Stone." Garin closed his hand around the relic as he spoke. "I informed our master immediately, of course, but he demanded a second meeting—with everyone."

Alyra fell to her knees as tears began to leak from her crimson eyes. "I have waited years to hear his voice again. I have longed for it."

"Your former beauty and your charm do not impress him," Dranamir sneered.

She knew when the Nameless returned to his former glory, it would be her, not Alyra, standing at his side. The arrangement had been made long before Alyra joined their cause, and Dranamir believed their master would keep the promise he'd made to her all those years ago. He'd never failed her previously, and her devotion to him was steadfast. The same could not be said for the sniveling bitch kneeling on the floor.

Alyra opened her mouth to argue, but Garin interjected. "*Enough.* I will summon him now."

Garin stashed the talisman inside his pocket and turned to face the oval mirror that had served as a backdrop for most of their gatherings. Its glass was dark and smoky, its frame carved to resemble the gnarled branches of a bramble, complete with thorns. The mirror had been a fixture in the tower since they'd overtaken the Council of Enlightened millennia ago, but rarely had Dranamir witnessed it put to use. It was now the second time in as many weeks.

Garin placed his hands upon the glass, his palms pressed firmly against it. Dranamir once again sensed the intricate workings of magic in the air, but the exact mechanism of Garin's summoning remained clouded from her sight. She frowned, envious of the apparent power the small man wielded over them.

Dranamir sensed a shift in the atmosphere before Garin stepped away from the mirror. The air grew thick around her, almost tangible, as she became aware of his essence; rage, desire, danger, cunning—a hundred dark emotions coalesced to form the Nameless god's presence. Within the shadowy depths of the mirror, a pair of incandescent yellow eyes with vertically slit pupils stared into the room. The eyes darted between Garin and Kama, flitted to Alyra, then landed upon her. They lingered for several moments, drinking in her presence while she was consumed with a yearning she'd long suppressed.

Her master was *here*. The Nameless god. The ancient Harbinger of Death.

His voice rumbled through the confines of the room, rolling like a dark tide to wash over her with his blessed words. They were felt more than heard.

You have done well.

The words reverberated through her skull, but unlike his previous communication, she sensed his approval. He did not intend to command her as he'd done before. She smiled at the eyes glowing balefully in the mirror, reveling in the Nameless' attention.

The others will receive their own instruction. We speak privately, Dranamir. I sensed the protections you placed over my sacred domain were removed as instructed. Was anything amiss within?

"No," she whispered. "All was as it should be."

She sensed pleasure in his nebulous essence, acceptance, and passion. The force of his emotions threatened to take her voice, to leave her a quivering mass of unmet desire huddled on the polished tile floor. She suppressed her yearning and continued to meet his gaze.

Amused laughter echoed through her skull. **I am pleased your strength has not diminished with time.**

"It will not fail me, nor will it fail you," she promised.

I have instructed Alyra to create an elixir. She will require some of the ingredients stored within my temple. Has she spoken of this to you?

She briefly considered telling him Alyra had not, but he was adept at detecting falsehoods. "Yes. I will assist her, if that is your wish."

It is. She must create the elixir on the darkest of nights for it to be most effective. The winter solstice approaches, and with it, a new moon.

"Then we have a fortnight to collect what she requires."

Yes.

The time had come, and soon the Nameless god would be freed. She drew a breath, savoring his presence, and knew what she must say next.

"I wish to create a gift to celebrate your return."

A chuckle coupled with an intense wave of desire washed over her. **I assumed you would ask this of me. You have my blessing, Dranamir. Pray that this gift is more successful than your last.**

His tone shifted from one of yearning, to dire threat laced with unadulterated rage in an instant. His final words struck with such force her knees gave way, and she found herself sprawling across the floor. As quickly as his essence had appeared, it vanished, leaving her hollow and shaken. She stood up and straightened her clothing with trembling hands.

She understood the meaning behind his words well enough. Her first gift to him, though useful while she lived, had turned against his army and followers with her death. They'd built a magically protected and heavily fortified home for themselves at the conclusion of the war, and their descendants continued to thrive. She did not see her gift as a failure, but clearly the Nameless was displeased with their betrayal. There was but one way to rectify her perceived mistake—her next gift would not be bound to her existence, but *his*. He was a god, eternal and unyielding. Her offering would be the same.

As she scanned the room, she noted the others were rising from the floor, similarly shaken. Even Garin's pallor appeared more profound than usual.

Kama muttered a string of curses under his breath as he regained his feet and cast a furtive glance in her direction. His gaze no longer held its former lascivious undercurrent, nor did it hold disgust. Instead, she noted barely concealed terror and wary apprehension. He continued to stare at her even as she looked elsewhere.

Garin shook his head as if trying to clear it and staggered toward the glass case nearest his position. He leaned against it for support, his energy depleted. He did not look up.

Alyra was the last to rise and took several moments to smooth perceived wrinkles from her long skirt. Dranamir's eyes were drawn to the woman's ashen neck, which appeared swollen and bruised. Alyra glanced at Kama, then turned to face Dranamir. When she spoke, her voice was hoarse.

"He demands the elixir. I'll need your help."

Dranamir smirked, reveling in the other woman's discomfort. "I know."

"Then I'd like to—"

"As I stated once before," Dranamir replied acidly, cutting her off, "provide me with a list of the items you require. I will deliver them to you. You will not set foot within the temple until our master deems it necessary."

Alyra swallowed painfully and grimaced. "Fine. You will have your list. Tomorrow."

Dranamir focused on Kama once more. His gaze remained haunted, fearful. She wondered what had transpired between the tall Kamshati and the Nameless god that would instill such terror in his heart. A cold smile touched her lips; she preferred his terror to his misplaced lust.

"I'll have need of the human prisoners kept by the Murkor," she informed him.

"How many do you require?" His voice was somber, cool.

"All of them." Her smile became cruel as she anticipated their screams, their horror when learning what she had planned. They would be made to serve her master, once they'd been remade in his honor. They would become her gift to him.

"Dranamir…" Alrya rasped, her eyes wide with understanding.

"If our master is to return, I will ensure his army is unparalleled. Surely you would welcome more than Murkor support," she said to Kama.

He stared at her impassively. "I don't know what you plan, Dranamir."

She laughed. "Then you will soon learn why our master has chosen me, why I was named Soulless before any other." She crossed her arms and sneered at them. "You'll have your army, Kama, and you'll thank me afterwards."

CHAPTER ELEVEN

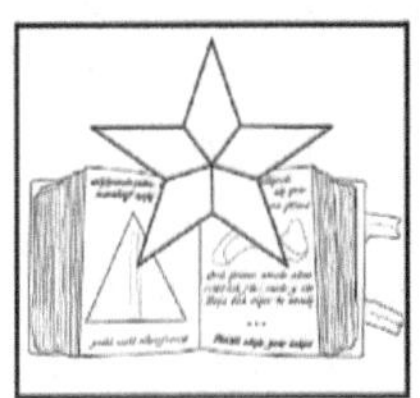

HOPE

Tavesin collapsed ungracefully near the fire, weary from the long days of travel. He wished there was a way to move the army through the Aethereum directly to Daesan, but Ravin insisted it was impossible. A stray thought would transport even those without the talent for Aethereal magic anywhere within the realm, where they might become hopelessly lost. It was a risk Ravin was unwilling to take. Tavesin understood, albeit grudgingly; he was convinced there must be a faster way to travel that involved far less marching.

Badolo sat down carefully beside him, a smooth disc of stone in his hands. He flashed Tavesin a grin. "It seems we're both busy with studies tonight." He pointed at the unopened book Tavesin held in his hands. "I haven't seen that volume previously. What is it?"

Tavesin looked at the carefully bound leather book with its unadorned cover. It was Morganus' journal, though Tavesin wasn't certain if he should tell his friend its contents. Minora hadn't sworn him to secrecy, yet something gave him pause.

"It's something I'm investigating for Ravin."

Badolo nodded, unconcerned, and held up the stone disc. "If I complete this tonight, Radosan says he'll contact Lilyna tomorrow to schedule my challenge." He grinned. "I'll have it done before nightfall."

Tavesin brightened at the prospect. If Badolo was summoned for his challenge, he'd need someone to facilitate his travel to the Shining Tower, which meant either Tavesin, Ravin, or one of the Drakkon must escort him through the Aethereum. Before they'd departed Dar

Daelad, the Radiant had indicated he expected the duty to be fulfilled by Tavesin. A change of pace from the long days spent trudging along the rutted merchant's road was something he sorely needed.

"I hope they send you soon," he replied. "I'd like to spend a day in the tower."

Laughter behind them caused them to turn. "You're just tired of marching, Taven," Rostin stated as he sat down carefully between his friends. He twisted his sword belt slightly, seeking a more comfortable position for the blade he was scarcely seen without. "Admit it."

Tavesin shrugged. "Yes. My feet are sore, and I think I'll need new boots before we reach Daesan." He studied the older boy pensively. "I thought you had sparring practice tonight."

Rostin sighed and his face fell. "I did, too. But with the Baloticans' arrival, Vardak's busy, and Jerizyen's been sent on a scouting mission."

"What about Patak? Or one of the other guards?" Badolo asked.

"I see what the two of you are doing. You want me to leave," he teased.

"No, Rostin," Tavesin began as Badolo said, "You can stay, so long as you're quiet. I need to finish this."

Rostin snorted. "And Taven wants to read. That's the book you found in Delucha, isn't it?"

Tavesin looked between the two boys; they sought answers about Morganus' journal that he was uncertain he ought to provide. He'd skimmed the first portion before they'd departed with the army. It was a lengthy passage that retold the story of the gods, their individual roles in the world's creation, and their continued influence into the present time, with one marked exception—it spoke of the Nameless god as *Necronus*.

Each time he spoke with Ravin, it was to learn more of the Aethereum or how to better deploy his powerful defensive shields. At times they worked on offensive magics. Tavesin had been so consumed with bettering his role for the good of Emra's army that he'd neglected to read Morganus' journal any further, nor had he inquired of Ravin or Emra about the reference to Necronus. He was certain that only they might understand why the god's name had been included in the journal when it had been stricken from the histories everywhere else.

Reluctantly, Tavesin nodded in response to Rostin's question. "I've been tasked with reading through it by Min—by myself. I haven't gotten far, but Ravin's expecting me to learn something from it soon."

Rostin ignored his near lapse and accepted his answer with a grin. "And I thought we'd be done with books and lessons once we were named wizards."

Tavesin managed a laugh as Badolo said, "When one ceases to learn anew, they are lost. My father says that often," he added when Rostin gaped at him.

"There is much wisdom in that line," a voice said to them from behind, causing the trio to turn. It was Radosan.

"Good evening, sir," Tavesin said. The others echoed his sentiment.

"Several of the Grays are available for sparring this evening," the Green Sect Master told Rostin. "I understand you prefer to train with Vardak, but you shouldn't bypass an opportunity when one presents itself."

Rostin rose swiftly to his feet. "You're right, sir. I'll be on my way."

As he departed, Radosan settled himself in the space Rostin had vacated and turned his attention to Tavesin. "Ravin informed me of your book."

Tavesin glanced at Badolo warily, but the younger boy was hunched over his stone, diligently working his confounding brand of magic, and paid them no heed. Sensing his discomfort, Radosan offered to walk with him so they might achieve some privacy. Grateful, Tavesin accepted.

They left Badolo alone to complete his latest relic, then made their way toward the camp's perimeter. The sun was beginning to sink beneath the horizon in the west and the air was becoming cold. Tavesin hoped their conversation would not take long; his feet continued to ache, and he missed the heat from the campfire.

"What did Ravin tell you, sir?" Tavesin asked cautiously.

"That your book came from Minora and seemed to be the missing writings of Morganus the White." As Radosan smiled, the thin, white scar that marred the left side of his face stretched and puckered.

"That's true, though I haven't found much time to read since she gave it to me." He looked at the tome in his hands longingly.

"When you are finished reading it, what do you plan to do?" Radosan asked.

"I don't know, sir. I haven't considered it."

"Morganus' writings have been sought for centuries, Tavesin. If Minora allows it, I request that you donate it to the tower's library. The knowledge it contains is invaluable." Radosan paused to study him, his green eyes wary. "I continue to find it strange the goddess deemed you alone worthy of its possession."

"I didn't question her, sir," Tavesin admitted sheepishly. "Even if I had, she left before I knew what she'd given me."

"Hmm. While I should report your gift to the Radiant, I hesitate to do so. Things in the tower are…strained, at present."

Tavesin whipped his head around to peer at Radosan directly. "What do you mean, sir?"

"Forget I said anything, Tavesin. I'm certain you'll learn what goes on in the tower soon enough." He sighed and glanced at the camp. "We should return before it grows any darker."

Tavesin nodded silently and followed the Sect Master back to the fire where they'd left Badolo. He considered Radosan's words while they walked, certain something was amiss in Dar Daelad. He wondered if Radosan kept the truth from him because of his age, or if he'd been sworn to secrecy by the Radiant. Determined to learn more, Tavesin made up his mind to speak with Ravin and Aziarah. Though neither was a member of the Council of Auras, both were adept at gleaning information from the wizards.

Radosan left him wordlessly at Badolo's side. The younger boy continued to focus his attention on the stone disc until Radosan was out of earshot, then abruptly leaned forward with an expectant gleam in his dark eyes.

"What did he want, Taven?"

Tavesin shifted uneasily and looked away. "He made a suggestion about my book, but that's not what troubles me." He divulged the latter part of their conversation to Badolo. "Something's happening, and he wouldn't tell me what it is."

Badolo flashed a mischievous grin. "I have a plan. I'm to meet with Aziarah after I inform Radosan my relic is complete. I'll try to learn more, then I'll tell her. The Drakkon will wish to know if there is trouble in the tower."

Tavesin nodded eagerly, pleased to have an accomplice. "And I'll speak to Ravin."

Ravin proved busy that evening, and Tavesin found himself alone beside the fire. He spent his time poring over the carefully written text contained within Morganus' journal. Though much of the writings were illuminating, Tavesin had yet to uncover why Minora had been asked to safeguard the book, nor what its connection to the Soulless or the black tower might be.

Tavesin had known for some time that Morganus belonged to the White Sect, and it was apparent in his journal. He chronicled the history of his era diligently, explaining first the rumors of war in the east, then his mounting frustration with the council for failing to send aid. As Tavesin continued to read, he realized the hierarchy amongst the wizards had changed little over the centuries; in Morganus' time, just as now, the Radiant and Sect Masters were hesitant to commit the forces required to face the Soulless' army.

Tavesin turned another page and froze as he read the name scrawled across the top. Dranamir. He'd overheard Ravin and Emra discussing her on several occasions, and he understood her name was synonymous with terrible acts. Ravin had been tortured by her, and she'd become the first of the Soulless. Tavesin shuddered in spite of the heat radiating from the fire and forced himself to continue.

We have finally learned the name of the enemy's monstrous leader: Dranamir. I was tasked to learn all I could about her past. Though I've uncovered little, none of it is good.

As her name suggests, she is Deluchan, though I cannot find records of her surname. Hers is an unusual name, which allowed me to find the few documents I did. She was born approximately thirty-five years ago to an unmarried woman who did not survive the labor. Dranamir was taken to the nearest temple and given to the priests for adoption. Her record vanishes for nearly twenty years.

She resurfaces in Santine after several noblemen were found murdered in their beds. Numerous witnesses described her fleeing the scene of each crime, often spattered with blood. There was no doubt of her guilt. She was arrested and sentenced to death. While awaiting her execution, the jailors returned to her cell one morning to find it empty. Again, her records disappear.

Now, she leads an army of Murkor and half-human abominations of her own creation. It is said she is no longer human herself. Rumors abound that she gave up her soul in exchange for power granted by the Nameless god, the one formerly called Necronus. Without meeting her in person, I cannot verify these claims, but I know with a certainty she brings war across the Five Kingdoms and wields a magical power equal to my own.

"I was told you were seeking me."

Tavesin gasped and closed the book, twisting in his seat to find Ravin standing over him. He exhaled, relieved it was the golden-eyed mage who had been peering over his shoulder rather than someone else.

Ravin chuckled and seated himself nearby. "It seems you've found some interesting reading?"

Tavesin nodded then reopened the book to show him the page regarding Dranamir. Ravin's expression became grim.

"I can fill in the gap between her scheduled execution and her reemergence as the first Soulless," he growled. "One of the more influential members of the Council of Enlightened, a man named Godazi, was in Santine seeking new recruits. He could sense her power, though she was unaware she possessed it. He freed her from the prison and took her to the black tower for training. Most of the council leaders were appalled. She was a murderer—and unrepentant."

"Why did they allow her to stay?" Tavesin asked, fascinated.

"Godazi spoke for her and claimed she could be redeemed, that she merely needed guidance and purpose in her life. He truly believed she could be saved." Ravin shook his head, his gaze locked on the dancing flames of the campfire. "I learned years later that Godazi was not the altruistic soul he pretended to be."

Tavesin wanted to ask another question, but he knew Ravin didn't like to speak of that time. Instead, he remained silent while Ravin gathered his thoughts.

"She was a follower of the Nameless god for many years prior to the murders in Santine, and Godazi held similar beliefs." Ravin closed his eyes with a grimace. "One of the council's leaders discovered their loyalties a few days before I left for my final tenure amongst the Drakkon, but by then, it was too late. They'd recruited dozens of others."

"What did they do?" Tavesin asked, unable to suppress his curiosity any longer.

Ravin raised his eyebrows and glanced at Tavesin. "You were present when I spilled my tale in Delucha. They staged an insurrection and killed the council's leaders."

"And she became Soulless." Tavesin shuddered.

"Eventually, yes." Ravin sighed and tilted his gaze skyward. "I've often wondered what led up to the events in Santine. I knew only what Godazi presented to the council, and it mirrors the account in your book. It seems even Morganus was unable to uncover the truth of Dranamir's past."

"Do you believe it may be important, Ravin?" Tavesin asked.

"I...I don't know, Taven. Minora held that journal in her possession for centuries, but has given its care to you. Dranamir's past may be the key to the puzzle we've been ordered to solve, or it may be nothing more than a diversion, irrelevant." As he looked down, his shoulders slumped. "I can't shake the notion that we've been set an impossible task."

Tavesin chewed his lower lip as despair washed over him. If even Ravin believed the gods' commands could not be fulfilled, what hope did he have of success? He was merely a teenage boy, one of the few wizards traveling in support of Emra's army. Overwhelmed by the enormity of the situation, he closed his eyes.

Images flooded his mind. Scores of dead soldiers, both human and Murkor, laying bloody and broken in the brittle grasslands surrounding Delucha gave way to a magical barrage of deadly energy streaking across the dawn sky toward him. The pale, distorted features of the Soulless named Garin appeared, taunting him as he kicked Tavesin savagely in the ribs. Garin's face disappeared, giving way to a curtain of flame that sliced its way through countless hooded figures who screamed in sudden agony. Finally, he was greeted by the battered features of Arra as he'd last glimpsed her in the Aethereum, her body broken and spirit shattered.

White-hot rage enveloped his being as the memory of Arra overtook him. He could not give in to the black depression that threatened to overtake him. He would not allow her capture to go unavenged. The Soulless must be stopped, and Arra must be saved. He would wallow in despair no longer.

When his eyes snapped open, he found Ravin eyed him warily. Tavesin's fists were clenched so tightly his hands ached, but he did not relax them for fear he would lose control of his temper and lash out.

"Taven?" Ravin's voice held a note of concern.

"There are no impossibilities," he stated through clenched teeth. "I will not believe everything has been in vain. I will not give up, Ravin. I won't lose her."

Ravin's expression softened, and he nodded in understanding. "I've allowed my fears to stand in our way, it seems. I'm sorry, Taven. I'm a poor example to follow."

Tavesin crossed his arms, his anger making him brazen. "I will not let you give up, either. I can't do this alone." When Ravin did not respond, he added, "If not for Arra, then do this for the duchess. She's counting on your return."

Ravin startled, then leveled a glare toward the fire. "What did she tell you?" he growled.

Tavesin hesitated, his previous ire dissipating in an instant. He knew he'd prodded the mage too far, but he would not apologize. He needed Ravin's guidance. "She told me nothing, Ravin," he replied quietly. "I may be young, but I've seen how you look at one another."

Ravin shook his head, his scowl replaced by a mystified expression. "I can't believe I'm having this conversation with *you*. A boy. Gods-damn it, I'm a fool, aren't I?" He paused briefly, then said, "Don't answer that."

"Do you love her, Ravin?"

Rather than answer, Ravin rose to his feet and chuckled to himself. "You've given me reason for hope, Taven, and much to think upon. We'll speak again in the morning."

"Ravin?" He asked again, though he knew his attempt at prolonging the conversation was futile.

Ravin smiled as he walked away, leaving Tavesin alone with his book once more. He couldn't fathom why Ravin refused to answer his final question, though he was pleased to see his outburst had lifted the mage's spirits. Whether Ravin would admit to it or not, Tavesin was certain he was in love with the duchess—and she with him. He would use his newfound knowledge to ensure Ravin did not falter. He felt empowered and emboldened.

What he'd admitted to Ravin was true. He could not undertake the gods' mission alone and succeed, but now he grasped a thread of hope that previously had eluded him—and so, too, did Ravin.

CHAPTER TWELVE

THE ALCHEMIST'S GOODBYE

Sal'zar held his breath and waited for the footsteps in the stairwell beyond his door to fade. It was well after midnight, a time when the majority of the tower's denizens should be in the depths of sleep. Even the Soulless were rarely active during this period of time. The echo of the footfalls as they continued to ascend the tower unnerved him.

He drew a silent breath and shook his head. After what he'd learned that afternoon, he could delay no longer. He must return to the Murkor camp and spread word to those selected that his signal would come soon, and they needed to be prepared for departure on a moment's notice. The Soulless had announced their plans to those they called the Enlightened; the human prisoners were being escorted to the tower as part of a grand "gift" Dranamir was creating to celebrate the Nameless god's imminent return.

Sal'zar had never been so thankful for the anonymity his hooded attire provided. Though he didn't know the details of the Soulless' plans, he understood enough of the implications to be appalled. One of the humans had begun to retch at the news and was swiftly killed for his apparent weakness. Sal'zar had been unable to sleep after the meeting, the image of the man's broken corpse haunting him each time he closed his eyes.

The announcement, coupled with the murder, spurred him into action. He leaned against the heavy door and strained to hear the footfalls that had forced his present delay. They were high above, faint, nearly indiscernible. He breathed a sigh of relief and eased the door open to peer along the stairwell. It was empty as far as he could see.

He wished he'd taken the stealth potion from Jal'den on his previous visit to the camp, but he believed it was safer with his partner than inside the tower where one of the Soulless might discover it. He would collect it tonight. He wasn't certain if he would see Jal'den again, and this may be his only opportunity for a proper goodbye. He hoped he'd find his partner alone rather than in discussions with the commander.

At the thought of Jal'den, his hand strayed to the wide pouch on his belt. He felt the outline of the thin tome he'd secreted within, the book that detailed their story. He'd completed his portion earlier in the night and planned to present it to Jal'den. He wasn't certain if his partner would add anything more or if he'd simply pass it on to the Kal during his next journey to the caverns, where it would be included in the collection of Murkor histories housed within the Matriarch's complex.

Sal'zar smiled faintly beneath his green hood, pleased the book was finished. Thinking of Jal'den and their combined story gave him a measure of strength as he pressed on.

He slipped across the threshold and began to descend toward the ground floor. His room was near the base of the tower, its location meant as yet another slight against his race, or perhaps the fact that he was resistant to the Nameless' brand, but he was grateful for the placement now. It lessened his chance of discovery on the nights he disobeyed the Soulless' orders and found his way to the Murkor encampment.

He channeled a thread of magic to silence his footsteps and increased his pace, fearful the person he'd heard earlier would decide to return. He could not risk an encounter with one of the Soulless, nor any of the others, for that matter. Though he suspected some of the humans were in the tower under duress much like himself, he didn't believe any of them could be trusted. If they weren't loyal to the Soulless, they would report him out of fear for their merciless overlords. No, it was best he kept his nightly visits to the camp and his dealings with the Kal to himself while simultaneously avoiding detection. It was the only way to accomplish the ambitious task the Kal had set before him.

The long, winding stairwell was lit dimly by the polished obsidian walls themselves. He sensed it was an ancient magic, but one that he could replicate if he desired to. It was a bit of knowledge he would reserve for later. At present, the light was more than sufficient for his Murkor eyes to see by.

He hurried down the remainder of the steps, then paused as he reached the threshold of the tower's foyer. He glanced across the vast space, relieved when he saw no one within. He sprinted the distance between the stairs and the exit and did not slow his pace until he was halfway to the camp.

He paused to catch his breath and glance over his shoulder toward the tower. There was no movement; he had not been followed. He forced himself to take several deep breaths, imparting calm throughout his being. Each time he'd ventured away from the tower, his reaction had been the same. The Soulless would kill him if they learned of his disobedience. They'd made it clear he was expendable, a lesser being unworthy of second chances.

If Jal'den knew the truth of his predicament, he'd be livid, but Sal'zar vowed he would not tell him. They'd argued enough during the past weeks, and Sal'zar refused to leave his partner with a final memory distorted by anger. Jal'den deserved better—they both did.

No longer winded, he continued his journey through the night-darkened landscape toward the Murkor camp. A handful of fires twinkled amongst the tents, most clustered in the small area reserved for the craftsmen and cooks. Several dozen sentries patrolled the perimeter at intervals, and as he approached, one of them called out to him in the common tongue. He chose to respond in their own language; he greeted the sentry and made his intention to visit Jal'den known.

"The Arm's Master is on patrol," the black-clad sentry informed him. "Shall I send for him?"

Sal'zar nodded. "I will meet him at his tent."

It would take the sentry some time to reach Jal'den. Sal'zar made his way into the camp, scanning the hands of the soldiers he passed for the silvery, identifying marks that would yield their name. He'd memorized the long list of soldiers the Kal had provided him with and knew if he spoke to only a few, word would reach the others. He prayed it would not spread beyond those selected. If the Soulless learned of their plot, their people would be massacred, whether they'd been involved in its planning or not.

He pushed the thought aside. He must remain strong and maintain his composure for the sake of the others. For Jal'den.

He was not far from Jal'den's tent when he spied the first Murkor from the Kal's extensive list. Dav'rim, based on the markings he could see on the backs of his hands. Sal'zar motioned to him, making certain his own tattoos were clearly visible. Dav'rim glanced warily at their surroundings, then strode toward him.

"The time will be soon," Sal'zar informed him in a low whisper. "Not tonight, but very soon. Make certain the others know."

Dav'rim bobbed his head. "Of course. The Kal's bidding shall be done."

He encountered a handful of others as he loitered outside Jal'den's tent, awaiting the Arms Master's return. He told each soldier the same, and each promised to fulfill his duty to their people and the Kal. At the conclusion of each interaction, Sal'zar prayed the Soulless would not uncover their plan.

He was on edge. When Jal'den finally appeared, it was a relief to be finished with his covert business, a comfort to know he could spend some time—however brief—with the Murkor he loved. Jal'den beckoned him into the tent wordlessly while Sal'zar finished speaking with the latest of the Kal's chosen.

As soon as he entered the tent, Sal'zar was swept into a fierce one-armed embrace. Jal'den's hood was pulled back, revealing his striking features, the swirl of silvery familial tattoos that marked his cheeks and forehead—and his mischievous grin. He shook his own hood free and smiled, their desperate situation temporarily forgotten. Their lips met, and Sal'zar sensed the urgency, the *need*, in his partner. He was certain Jal'den sensed the same emotions from him.

"How long do I have you, *ama*?" Jal'den asked as they parted.

Sal'zar looked away, unable to hide his pained expression. "Not long."

With a sigh, Jal'den dropped his arm to his side. "I am weary of these momentary glimpses of you, Sal'zar. After all we've been through simply to be acknowledged, it's not fucking fair."

"I know, and I agree with you." Sal'zar's tone was hollow. He shared Jal'den's sentiments, but there was nothing to be done at present to remedy their situation. "I came tonight so that I might see you one final time, *ama.* I…We must act soon."

"I've been dreading this conversation."

Sal'zar swallowed; he feared it, as well. "I'll do everything in my power to live through this war. Gods, I don't want to leave, but we both know there is no other way."

Jal'den moved to the corner of the tent and knelt beside a battered satchel. "You'll need this," he said quietly as he fished out the vial of stealth salve Sal'zar had concocted for him not long after he'd been forced to leave for the tower.

As he took the vial from Jal'den, he said, "I have something for you, as well." He withdrew the book and placed it in Jal'den's calloused hands.

"Sal'zar…" Jal'den looked up from the slim tome, pain and frustration warring across his midnight blue features.

"I've finished my part," he replied quietly. "I wasn't certain if you'd wish to add more, or simply give it to the Kal—"

"I have nothing more to add, *ama,* but I'm not relinquishing this to *anyone* until we're together again." Jal'den drew him into another fierce one-armed embrace. "We will give this to the Kal after we've been reunited. Until then, I will keep it with me as a reminder of you."

"Then you'd best survive this war," Sal'zar replied, blinking away tears.

The book contained their combined story, a Murkor tradition between those paired as *ujar'havel.* It included the details of how they'd met, the struggles they'd endured to be accepted—Jal'den's more so than his own—and a few passages describing their time together once the ceremony had been performed. Traditionally, such books were kept in the Matriarch's library and made available to any young Murkor who wished to learn about their predecessors' unity ceremonies. The Kal had impressed upon them during their own that their story was more important than most, and Sal'zar agreed.

"You as well," Jal'den replied. "I will pray to the gods with every dawn that you remain safe and that we'll see one another again."

Sal'zar nodded, overcome with emotion. He'd never liked goodbyes, but this one was proving the hardest of his life. "How is your shoulder?" he asked instead.

"Thanks to you, it's stronger every day." Jal'den managed a strained smile. "I will continue to follow the instructions of the other alchemists, but I was told only yesterday that I should be able to forgo this damned sling by the end of the week."

"I'm glad to hear it."

"Sal'zar," Jal'den said slowly, "promise me that I'll see you again."

He longed to acquiesce, to speak the words Jal'den desperately wanted to hear, but he feared they would be nothing more than a hollow vow, one he could not keep. He would not lie to the Murkor he'd given his heart to.

"I wish I could." His voice was little more than a strangled whisper. "I love you, Jal'den."

Jal'den tightened his arm around Sal'zar's shoulders and rested his forehead against his partner's. "What I told you before was true, *ama*. Even the gods will rue your death if they deign to take you from me prematurely."

He met Jal'den's pale eyes through a veil of unshed tears. "I will pray for our success. It is all I can do."

Jal'den kissed the top of his head before releasing his arm. "I've kept you long enough, *ama*. You should return to the tower."

Sal'zar nodded sullenly. "I hope my fears are unjustified. I cannot imagine life without you."

"Nor I, without you. Be safe, *ama*. Be strong. Have faith we'll see one another again."

CHAPTER THIRTEEN

PREPARING THE GIFT

In the moments after awakening, Dranamir experienced a clarity of purpose, a certainty of her plan that could only be explained as a vision from the Nameless god himself. For the first time, she knew what the future of the human prisoners would be, down to each finite detail. They would be molded into an exact replica of her vision, the greatest gift she could conceive for her god's return.

A malicious smile crossed her lips as she rose and prepared herself for the day, certain even Garin would be impressed with her results. She garbed herself for exploration and hunting; a light-weight blouse, leather trousers, and matching vest. She pulled her long, dark tresses into a thick braid and paused to examine her appearance in the mirror beside her wardrobe. The others might remark upon her unusual attire if she encountered them, but she would pay them no heed. Where she planned to travel was no place for finery or skirts.

She created a portal and stepped into the Aethereum, then transported herself to the large meeting hall on the ground floor of the tower. She exited swiftly and paused to survey the room. It formed a large square with a high ceiling. Rows of wooden chairs filled two-thirds of the space. A raised dais faced the many chairs, adorned by large banners depicting the symbol of the Council of Enlightened at either end; a downward triangle in red drawn within an upward triangle in white. In the center of the red was a single yellow eye. She smiled faintly, pleased the design she'd created had withstood the passage of centuries.

She turned away from the dais to inspect the chairs. They were solidly built with slat backs and sturdy arms. She estimated there were chairs enough for nearly one thousand. The number might be sufficient, but she needed to learn the true number of human prisoners the Murkor held. Kama would have the information she sought. With a grimace, she reentered the Aethereum and made her way to the heart of the Murkor encampment where she suspected he would be.

She stepped out of the magical realm and into the glaring sunlight of midmorning in the Wasted Land. The army's camp was quieting as most of its denizens turned in for the day, but as she'd anticipated, Kama was in conversation with the Murkor commander outside of his spacious tent. The commander stiffened as he noted her approach, no doubt considering himself fortunate that Kama had stayed her hand weeks ago. Without the Kamshati's intervention, she would have made a painful and bloody example of him for his failure to conquer the Baloticans at Pine.

She ignored him and focused her attention upon Kama. His expression soured, though his eyes remained wary. She wondered what the Nameless god had said to him during their latest summons two days past. His demeanor had changed markedly since that date, much to her satisfaction. His fear of her was titillating.

"Dranamir," Kama said uneasily as the commander saluted and disappeared within his tent.

She smiled icily. "Kama."

"Clearly, you have some plot afoot, based on your attire. Why are you here?"

"I merely have a question, one that I'm certain you have the answer to." She crossed her arms and eyed him, deliberately pausing for effect.

He clenched his jaw, a flash of anger passing through his crimson eyes. "Yes?" He growled through clenched teeth.

She laughed, pleased her needling had yielded results. "How many prisoners are held by the Murkor?"

"This again? You've already requested all of them brought here, Dranamir, and I've issued the orders. They'll—"

"You fail to understand my intent, Kama," she cut in. "I know very well *all* of them will soon be marching their way here. I need to know an exact number to complete my preparations."

Kama's graying flesh paled at her words. "I don't know what you have planned, Dranamir, and I'm not certain I want to."

"I wasn't aware *you* had a weak stomach. It's no matter—you'll benefit from my work, just as our master will. When I'm finished, you'll thank me."

He shrugged noncommittally. "That remains to be seen."

"And see it, you shall. Now answer my question before I grow impatient."

"At last count, there were just over nine hundred prisoners."

She grinned coldly. "Perfect. When they draw near, be certain to inform me. They will be taken to the tower's meeting room and held there until I can begin my work. I intend to be ready for them."

"You plan to repeat what you did to the Scorpion Men," he said, stunned at his realization.

"The Nameless has given his approval, and I will not disappoint him."

Kama eyed her, horror and admiration warring across the angular planes of his face. "Do you plan for the prisoners to…bolster our army?"

"Of course, but only after they have been broken, remade, and brought under our heel. I will improve the command link, as well. They will be compelled to obey even if I fall in battle. I will tie the command collars directly to the Nameless god—so long as his power remains, so too will their obedience."

"Infallible," he replied, impressed.

"Unlike certain others of our number, I learn from my past mistakes."

"Perhaps you would do me the honor of allowing me to observe your work?" The familiar lust had returned to his gaze; the man couldn't seem to divert his desires for long.

She shrugged, unfazed by his advances. "If you wish, Kama. Based on your previous statements, I'm not certain you possess the fortitude. Perhaps you will prove me wrong."

She returned to the tower after speaking with Kama, then made her way to Alyra's door. Alyra had yet to provide her with a list of ingredients to obtain from the Nameless god's temple, but that was not the reason for her errand. Alyra was adept at crafting magical devices, and she required nearly one thousand control collars. She'd created a vast quantity of them once before—and without assistance.

She rapped on the door loudly and paced along the landing while she waited. It was several moments before Alyra appeared, her thin hair disheveled and a thin robe clutched around her bosom. Dranamir smirked, certain the other woman had not been alone in her quarters—despite the addition of the disfiguring scars that marred the right side of her face.

"Dranamir? What's this about?"

"I require control collars for the prisoners. Perhaps you and your current paramour will oblige?"

Alyra cast an uncertain glance over her shoulder, then shook her head. "He lacks the talent for crafting relics, Dranamir. How many do you need? I assume this has to do with your 'gift' to our master."

"It does. One thousand should suffice."

Alyra blinked in surprise. "That will take some time, and I—"

"You have five days. Recruit help or not—I leave that to you." She smiled maliciously. "I'm certain you're capable of meeting this deadline. It's for the Nameless, after all."

Alyra's hand strayed toward her throat and she rubbed at the area where her own collar had recently hung. "Of course. I'll not disappoint him." She paused to study Dranamir warily. "Once the collars are in your possession, I want no further part in your abhorrent schemes."

Dranamir had anticipated the response. Alyra had complained tirelessly about her role in the Scorpion Mens' creation, claiming it was a weight on her soul she could not bear. Dranamir did not tolerate the weak nor the tenderhearted, and it continued to puzzle her that Alyra had been chosen as Soulless after her previous fall. She had her uses, but she was no proper leader for the Nameless god's conquering army.

"It's best you avoid the meeting room at the tower's base, then," Dranamir replied. "I'd hate to be reprimanded if you inadvertently found yourself caught amongst the prisoners and molded into a design of *my* choosing."

Alyra gaped, outraged. "You wouldn't dare."

"Try me."

"Our master wouldn't allow it."

Dranamir chuckled mirthlessly. "I have his approval, Alyra. Make the collars and deliver them to the meeting room. And provide me with your list of ingredients. The new moon is swiftly approaching."

Alyra's gray-green features blanched as she nodded. "I have the list prepared. I'll just be a moment…"

Dranamir rolled her eyes as the other woman darted inside her room. It was typical for Alyra to avoid her until she could no longer drum up excuses—even when it came to a matter as critical as the elixir. Perhaps if her own gift to the Nameless pleased the volatile deity sufficiently, he would reward her with the taking of Alyra's head. The prurient bitch deserved it and more.

Alyra returned moments later to thrust a scrap of parchment toward Dranamir. "Here. Everything should be in the temple."

Dranamir scanned the list and nodded once. "Yes. When I'm finished gathering my own supplies, I'll collect yours."

"You're unusually gracious this morning, Dranamir."

Dranamir grinned wickedly. "Not even your paltry excuse for existence can dampen my mood today. My plans for the prisoners are *exquisite*."

Alyra flinched, disgust clear in her eyes. "Then I'll not delay you any further. You'll have the control collars, as the master demands."

"Good."

Dranamir created another portal and stepped through as Alyra disappeared behind her door once more, no doubt to return to her latest conquest's arms. Dranamir couldn't fathom how men continued to throw themselves at Alyra after the ravages of becoming Soulless had distorted her once beautiful face. She'd retained her figure; perhaps that was enough to satisfy her endless line of partners. Alyra's behavior was appalling, a disgrace to her position and to women everywhere.

With a shake of her head, she transported herself out of the tower and into an area of southern Masmoone kingdom she'd discovered only weeks ago when she'd expended her rage with Garin on an unassuming village. Garin's red-haired pet, the girl he'd stolen from beneath the wizards' noses, had come from there. After she'd razed the village and left nothing but burned corpses and charred stone in her wake, she'd calmed enough to take in the further surroundings.

Now, as she stepped out of the Aethereum and into the ruins of the village, she studied the dense forest that would soon swallow the space as if it had never existed. The trees were tall, with thick trunks covered in smooth, gray bark. Even in winter, the trees retained their broad, silvery leaves and the air remained warm and cloying. The scent of mud and decay wafted through the air on a whisper of breeze. Vines twined around the broad trunks and between branches, while reeds and thorny bushes filled the spaces between. Sunlight filtered between the leaves, creating a dappled pattern on the soggy ground. The locals referred to the area as the Marshwood.

Her eyes drifted to the vine-laden branches. Her quarry should be there, camouflaged against the greens and grays of the forest, but visible to those who knew what to search for. The faint sheen of sunlight glimmering off scales, the rapid flick of a forked tongue, the faint rasp of reptilian skin against bark. She sought the marsh constrictors, snakes twice as long as a man was tall with thick, powerful bodies capable of crushing large prey. The snakes would be relatively docile during the daylight hours, where they would be found sunning themselves on tree branches.

She'd considered using the constrictors during her first attempt at forging a hand-crafted army for the Nameless god, but had discarded the idea in favor of the giant scorpions that had once roamed the Desert of Snow. The notion of soldiers equipped with deadly venom had been too tantalizing to pass up. Now, the scorpions were extinct and she required another, equally intimidating predator to meld with the hapless prisoners. The snakes would serve her purpose splendidly.

So near to the ruined village, she doubted she would find the great serpents. A rutted road led from one end of the decimated site to the other, disappearing into the dense foliage on either side. She followed the road south, her passage marked by the squelching of her boots in the mud. The sounds of the forest quieted as she walked, as though the creatures within understood a predator more deadly than the rest was on the prowl. She smiled grimly and continued to scan the branches overhead for signs of the prey she sought.

She walked nearly a mile before she spied the first glint of sunlight reflecting off reptilian scales above. She paused and peered up at the creature where it wrapped itself around a thick branch, apparently drowsing in the morning's warmth. A pattern of interlinked diamonds of slate gray broke up the snake's otherwise emerald green exterior, while its underbelly was a lighter, pearlescent shade of gray-green. It blended well with the foliage. She found the coloration strangely beautiful, at odds with the creature's deadly nature.

It was a shame such a majestic animal must be sacrificed to mold the human prisoners into a vision worthy of the Nameless god, but concessions must be made in order to further his goals. The serpents she collected today would be transported to the tower, where they would be kept alive until her planned ritual took place. The serpents would give their lives for the betterment of the wretches that would soon bolster their army in service of the Nameless god.

She smirked at the snake as it shifted its broad head to fix its green eyes on her. It did not know it faced the greatest predator in the forest.

She seized her power and struck the serpent before it realized the threat she represented. She held it firmly in place, then unwound its thick body from the branch it clung to. She lifted it through the air and brought it to her position in order to inspect it more thoroughly. It showed no signs of illness or injury, though it was clearly terrified of its current predicament. It was a pristine specimen and would serve her purpose sufficiently.

She leered at the snake as she guided it through a portal, into the Aethereum, and to the meeting room in the tower she'd designated for her ritual. It was but the first of many she would collect. Her gift to the Nameless god would be flawless, a testament to her devotion to him.

CHAPTER FOURTEEN

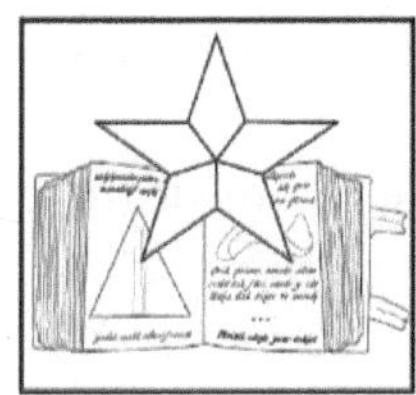

AN UNWELCOME RIFT

"I have a favor to ask of you, Tavesin."

Tavesin glanced up from his reading expectantly at the Sect Master's words. He believed he knew what Radosan was about to ask; Badolo had finished crafting his latest relic and was due to begin his challenge any day. Tavesin was expected to escort his friend through the Aethereum to the Shining Tower.

"Of course, sir." He closed the book he held carefully, marking his place with a scrap of paper.

"Well, perhaps I have *two* favors." Radosan smiled kindly, which caused the scar on the left side of his face to pucker. "First, Badolo is to begin his challenge tomorrow morning. I'd like you to escort him to the tower."

Tavesin nodded. "He told me it would be soon."

Radosan chuckled. "I've no doubt he did. He's eager to finish his apprenticeship."

"What is the second favor, sir?"

Radosan's smile faltered; he fell silent for a time as he contemplated his answer. Tavesin resisted the urge to fidget impatiently as curiosity assailed his mind.

"The wizards—all of us—have been summoned to the tower. I know you cannot transport all of us alone, Tavesin, but Ravin's gone to pay his lady a visit. I was hoping you might seek him out and ask for his assistance."

"What about Aziarah?" he blurted, confused why Radosan hadn't mentioned the Drakkon.

The Sect Master shrugged uneasily. "I broached the subject with her earlier, but she refuses to become entangled in what she deems 'tower politics.' I suppose I cannot blame her. This business is… It comes at an inopportune time."

Tavesin frowned, unable to mask his confusion. "What business, sir? Why have we all been summoned?"

"I don't have sufficient details myself, I'm afraid. Something has occurred in the tower that has the other Sect Masters on edge, and the Radiant has been detained. I know nothing more." He sighed. "As I said, the timing is deplorable. Can I count on you to seek Ravin's help?"

Tavesin snickered, recalling his last conversation with the mage. "Yes. If he's gone to visit the duchess, he won't be difficult to find."

"Thank you. Badolo was gathering his things when I came to speak with you. He should be ready soon."

As Radosan walked away, Tavesin looked down at Morganus' journal. He would need someone to keep it safe for him while he was away, and after his previous conversation with Radosan, he wasn't certain it would be prudent to keep it on his person while he was within the tower. He knew he ought to be able to trust the other wizards, but a nagging suspicion of their motives held him back. With Ravin involved in his task, he couldn't leave it with the mage, which left him with few options. Aziarah and the other Drakkon had not been informed of Minora's gift to him, and he thought it wise to involve as few people as necessary. This left him with Emra or one of the Scorpion Men.

He suppressed a sigh and rose from his seat, reluctant to leave the warmth of the campfire. The day had been cold with a sharp, biting wind, and though the stew he'd eaten for supper had helped warm him, the nearby flames were a comfort he was loath to part from. He studied the tents that surrounded him; most were occupied by wizards, and several emitted the soft glow of magical light from within. The wizards were camped on the southern outskirts of the army; it would take him some time to reach the command tent at its heart.

He trudged to the tent he shared with Rostin and Badolo, Morganus' book clutched tightly to his chest. He peered inside to find

Badolo fastening his cloak in preparation for the journey. He grinned at Tavesin, a bright gleam in his dark eyes.

"Has Radosan spoken to you, Taven?"

"Yes." He explained his desire to speak with Emra before their departure, and Badolo nodded his agreement.

Together, they made their way through the bustling camp. Many of the soldiers were outside of their tents despite the cold, some busy mending garments or sharpening blades, while others gambled at dice games or regaled their fellows with tales of battle and glory. Tavesin was no longer overwhelmed by the presence of so many armed men and women, though he didn't believe he'd ever grow accustomed to their typically crude language.

As they neared the command tent, the camp quieted around them. Several of Emra's personal guards patrolled the area, their eyes sharp and their hands upon weapon hilts. Badolo trailed behind him silently, his cloak drawn tightly around his shoulders while he shivered. Tavesin tugged at his own cloak, though it did little to dispel the cold. He did not see Emra or either of the Scorpion Men outside, but he fearlessly approached the guards stationed outside her tent. He'd visited them frequently enough since leaving Dar Daelad that the guards instantly recognized him.

"Tavesin, isn't it?" the woman lounging near the tent's entrance asked. When he nodded, she said, "Emra's inside, but I'd best announce you. The, ah, captain's *with* her, if you take my meaning."

Tavesin frowned in confusion before realization dawned on him. He gaped, feeling his face flush several shades of crimson while she chuckled in amusement. Behind him, Badolo muttered, "I wasn't certain that was even possible."

"Believe me, it is, though I can't imagine myself in her position." The guard snickered, then smacked the palm of her hand roughly against the tent flap several times in a staccato pattern. "She'll likely appear in a few minutes. Might as well make yourselves comfortable."

Tavesin glanced at Badolo and the two shared an uncertain look. After a moment, they settled themselves on the opposite side of the entrance from the guard.

"Did she mean they were…?" Tavesin grimaced at his friend as he struggled to find the words to finish his question.

"Intimate? Yes," Badolo replied quietly, a faint flush rising into his cheeks. "At least they are somewhat discreet. You'd be surprised how some of the nobles at home behaved when they'd had one too many drinks."

Tavesin's eyebrows rose of their own accord. "What?"

"When I was seven years old, I stumbled across a Rais with one of the palace staff right outside the kitchen. Neither was more than half-dressed. I turned around and ran back to my room before they knew I was there, but I'd seen enough to wonder why they were in the corridor rather than somewhere else." Badolo shook his head, baffled. "I told my father the next day. He laughed and told me I'd see much worse during my time in the palace. The nobility of Kamshat aren't known for their discretion, it seems. He was right."

Tavesin stared at the book clutched in his hands, stunned. For the first time since he'd learned Badolo was a prince, he truly understood how different his upbringing had been. The worst scandal Tavesin could recall from his hometown was when the baker caught his wife sneaking into the wagon of a traveling merchant one night. They'd at least had the decency to remain indoors, away from the watchful eyes of the rest of Rican Mer's residents. He couldn't imagine walking down a corridor to find a pair of adults in the midst of an intimate act, yet Badolo acted as though his experience was nothing unusual.

"Sometimes I forget you're from a small village, Taven."

Tavesin shrugged uncomfortably. "As Rostin likes to remind me, my life has been rather sheltered."

He was spared any further discussion as Patak and Emra emerged from within the tent. Emra turned to speak with the woman at the entrance while Patak scanned the area, a mischievous glint in his blue eyes. As he spied the two teenagers huddled in their cloaks, he grinned.

"Em, it seems we have visitors."

The boys stood up as Emra turned her attention to them. "I see. Come inside and out of the cold."

Tavesin hesitated a moment before following her inside, but his discomfort with her previous activities was overshadowed by his desire to escape the frosty air. Patak reentered the tent as well, but he remained near the exit, near enough to overhear their conversation but distant enough to provide the illusion of privacy. The tent was neat and orderly as it always was when he'd come to speak with her, though he spied a tangled mound of blankets shoved in one corner. He averted his gaze quickly and focused his attention on Emra.

"What brings you here tonight?" Emra asked kindly.

"I need to return to the tower. We all do," he explained, his words tumbling over one another in his nervous state. "The wizards, I mean."

Emra's gray eyes narrowed thoughtfully. "Radosan mentioned this but wouldn't elaborate. It still does not explain your presence in my tent."

Tavesin looked down at the book clutched in his hands. "I don't want to take this with me," he said. "And Ravin's away. I was hoping you might…?" He trailed off and looked up at her hopefully.

Her concerned frown deepened. "Do you not trust the other wizards, Tavesin?"

He sighed as helplessness overcame him. "I don't know if I can," he admitted. "Badolo and Rostin, yes. But the others…Radosan has already asked that I donate this to the tower's library. Minora entrusted me with its care for a reason and I…I don't know if it's safe in the tower."

Beside him, Badolo's eyes widened. "Minora? Taven, you never told us—"

"I thought it best not to," he muttered, angry with himself for his lapse.

"He was under instructions to keep the origin of this book a secret," Emra cut in, fixing her gaze on Badolo, "and now, so are you. Yes, Tavesin, I will safeguard it until you return."

Relief flooded his veins and he managed a tremulous smile. "Thank you. I would have asked Ravin, if he were here."

Emra chuckled. "I understand. He's gone to Delucha for a few hours, but he'll return by morning."

They said their goodbyes and made their way outside. Tavesin glanced at Badolo as they exited; the younger boy was somber and said nothing until they were some distance away from the command tent.

"Tavesin, what was that book? And what is going on with the wizards?"

Tavesin studied his friend uncertainly, but rather than answer immediately, he waved his hand to create a portal into the Aethereum.

"I'll explain inside." He offered his hand. "Don't let go. If you become lost, I'm not certain I can find you on my own."

Badolo nodded and gripped his hand tightly as the pair entered the magical realm. Badolo winced as the unnaturally stark, blue-white light hit his eyes. "This place makes my head ache."

"Ravin said it sometimes affects people that way." He shrugged helplessly. "It doesn't seem to bother anyone gifted with Aethereal magic, only those who aren't. I'm sorry."

"I'd appreciate if you explain what's going on quickly, then." Badolo grimaced and held his free hand over his eyes in an attempt to shield them from the glare.

"Minora gave me the book and said it will help us in the fight with the Soulless. It belonged to Morganus the White."

Badolo's eyebrows rose in surprise. "That's…incredible."

"As for the wizards, I don't know," he added. "Radosan said we're all to return to the tower. After I bring you there, I need to find Ravin. I can't transport everyone alone, and Radosan said the Drakkon want no part in whatever is going on. That's all I know."

Badolo nodded and squeezed his eyes shut. "Perhaps I can learn more tonight. Let's go, before my head implodes from this infernal pressure."

Tavesin nodded and transported them to the garden at the foot of the Shining Tower. In the Aethereum, the tower's brilliance was muted, outshone by the realm's strange illumination. He created a portal and pulled Badolo through as the younger boy continued to grimace. Once outside, Badolo breathed a heavy sigh of relief.

"Gods, I don't care to repeat that journey, Taven."

"I'm sorry," he said again and offered his friend a sympathetic smile. "We're here, though. Good luck tomorrow."

Badolo brightened. "Thank you. I'm prepared for this challenge. When next we speak, I'll be named wizard, too."

They bade one another goodbye, and as Badolo entered the tower, Tavesin returned to the Aethereum. Now that he was alone, he considered traveling to Rican Mer in search of Arra, though he doubted she would be there. His final encounter with her was etched into his memories, a painful scar that only he knew existed. He prayed she still lived, prayed she would endure long enough for him to fulfill his promise of a rescue. She was the reason he'd traveled with the army—not the Soulless' threat to the world he knew nor the meddling of the gods. The path he trod was for Arra alone.

He shook his head. If he ventured to Rican Mer alone and Ravin learned of it, the mage would be livid. Tavesin believed he could defend himself against the Soulless if he encountered one of their number, but Ravin had cautioned him time and again to avoid placing himself at risk. He knew Ravin had his best interests at heart, and he should follow the mage's advice. It tore at his conscience to know that he must ignore his desire to seek her and wait for the proper time. Tonight wasn't it, no matter how strongly he wished it to be otherwise.

With a despairing sigh, he transported himself to the stable yard adjacent to The Three Roses inn, where he knew Ravin would be. He was struck by a blast of icy wind as he stepped into the yard. He clutched his cloak tighter and scurried toward the open door of the inn and the promise of warmth it foretold. He shivered as he stepped through the door and scanned the common room. It was busy, though not filled to bursting as it had been while Emra's army was in the city. To his surprise, Ravin was seated at a table near the corner hearth, and Adalin across from him. He'd expected to find them in her room.

Ravin glanced up as he threaded his way through the room. His golden eyes narrowed with concern while a frown creased his dark features. He said something to Adalin that caused the duchess to twist in her seat to look at him. She smiled warmly and beckoned Tavesin toward them.

He quickened his steps and grinned, eager to feel the warmth of the nearby fire. He took the open seat next to Ravin, who continued to eye him with a troubled expression.

"Taven, why have you come here?" he asked.

"Oh, Ravin, let the boy have a moment to warm himself before you begin the interrogation." Adalin smiled, and Tavesin was reminded once more of his mother. Both women were of the same age with dark hair, blue eyes, and striking features. Tavesin believed Adalin was more beautiful than his mother, but their demeanor was much the same. He immediately felt at ease in her presence and was grateful for her patience.

Tavesin removed his cloak and draped it across the back of his chair before he made his reply. "Radosan sent me. He needs your help."

Ravin listened silently as he relayed his conversation with the Green Sect Master, his expression growing darker as he considered Tavesin's words.

"And he told you nothing more about these events? What crime could be so dire that they've detained the Radiant?" Ravin asked in a low tone. He glanced surreptitiously at the nearby tables, but no one seemed to be paying them any heed.

"No, he told me nothing else. He said he didn't know the details, but…I'm not certain I trust him," Tavesin admitted. "Something doesn't feel right."

"I agree with you on that point." Ravin leaned back in his chair and gazed toward the ceiling as though seeking answers in the rafters above. "And I agree with Radosan that the timing of this business—whatever it may be—is terrible. We've other, more important items to concern ourselves with. Your council's infighting and politics should wait."

"I know." Tavesin stared at the polished tabletop miserably. "I was tasked with transporting our people to the tower as needed. I have to help, Ravin."

Ravin chuckled, causing him to look up. Amusement danced in the mage's eyes. "I didn't say I wouldn't assist you, Taven. The gods know, I don't like the idea of you traipsing about my realm alone, and powerful as you are, you can't manage several dozen others on your own. You'll have my help, though I'd like something from you in return."

"Ravin," Adalin hissed in disapproval.

He flashed a grin, causing the duchess to blush. "I only seek information, Adalin. You know I would never put his welfare at risk." To Tavesin, he said, "Whether your wizards wish me to learn the details of this trouble or not, I ask that you report all that happens within your council to me. Like you, I'm not certain we can trust Radosan's motives, and Emra certainly has a right to know if we're suddenly without the wizards' support."

Tavesin blinked, stunned at the insinuation. "Do you believe they'll order us to return for good? I won't do it, Ravin. I can't."

He would not abandon Arra to the Soulless, no matter what the council decided, and amongst the wizards, he was the only one gifted with Aethereal magic. They could not force him to remain in the tower. He would escape, return to the camp, and see his final promise to Arra through. If it meant his excommunication from the Council of Auras, so be it.

"I was merely speculating, Taven," Ravin replied evenly. "Without knowing the nature of this summons, there are a number of possibilities—but you ought to be prepared for the worst. Will you tell me what transpires?"

Unnerved by his words, Tavesin managed a nod. "Yes. Emra should know everything, and so should you."

"Thank you." He smiled wistfully at Adalin and said, "I suppose this means I must return earlier than I'd hoped. I'm—"

She held up one hand, and he stopped abruptly. "Don't apologize, Ravin. I understand. We can carry on our conversation later."

Ravin grinned. "I look forward to it." He rose from his seat and motioned for Tavesin to do the same. "We should go."

Once they were outside, Tavesin peered up at the mage, his curiosity gnawing at him. "What were you and the duchess talking about?"

Ravin smiled and shook his head in amusement. "It doesn't matter."

"But—"

"I'm not yet ready to discuss it, Taven," he replied firmly. "Let's return to camp and see about the wizards."

CHAPTER FIFTEEN

THE SERPENTUS

Dranamir surveyed the mass of writhing, serpentine bodies that filled the meeting room. She was weary, yet thrilled that her task was complete. She'd acquired enough marsh constrictors to pair one with each of the prisoners the Murkor were presently leading to the tower. The snakes' sinuous movements as they slithered about the space were hypnotic, a continuous transition between green scale and gray. The snakes seemed unperturbed by the change in their location and paid her no heed as she strode through the room toward the door.

The smile that graced her lips was frigid, yet subtly pleased. Everything was in place, save the prisoners.

She secured the door behind her with a magical ward while pointedly ignoring Kama's presence in the tower's foyer behind her. She suspected he'd returned to the tower to provide her with an update on the prisoners' status, but his news could wait. The snakes were her priority. Without the creatures, her gift for the Nameless' return would be meaningless.

Kama began to pace restlessly while she worked, making his impatience known. When she finished and turned to face him, his grayish features were twisted into a scowl. "Were you planning to make me wait all fucking afternoon?" He snarled.

"It would be a shame if any of the serpents were to escape," she replied coldly. "I've tricked them into ignoring me, but anyone else would be in grave danger. They're capable of consuming prey as large as yourself."

Kama's eyes glittered ominously. "Do you consider me prey, Dranamir?"

She snorted. "Don't mistake my words for a threat, Kama. You're beneath my notice."

He ground his teeth together and clenched his fists. "I am no gods-damned insect. One day, you'll regret your treatment of me."

"I may not know exactly what our master said to you upon our last meeting, Kama, but I believe I understand enough of what he commanded based on your recent behavior." She sneered. "There is little you can do to me that he will not punish."

Kama's eyes narrowed dangerously, his expression akin to a cornered and desperate wolf. "Perhaps not, but a man can dream." He crossed his arms and scowled at the floor. "I didn't come here to start an argument, Dranamir."

"Then stop provoking one." Her patience had worn thin, and she longed to strike him down for prodding her temper. The Nameless would be furious if Kama found himself dead, but inflicting pain on him might satisfy her sudden craving for blood.

"The human prisoners should arrive by dawn," he stated, his eyes fixed on the floor. "I assume you'll want them escorted directly here?"

"Yes. I'll be waiting for them. If you'd still like to observe my work, you may, but I'd advise you remain well away from any of the prisoners—or the snakes." She smiled cruelly. "As I've told Alyra, I cannot be held responsible if you become entangled in the magical web I must weave."

Kama's eyes flicked up to meet hers, a dangerous light in their crimson depths. "Perhaps you don't know me as well as you believe, Dranamir. I won't tolerate your gods-damned threats."

"It's not a threat, Kama. I simply state the facts. Stand in the wrong location, and you will become part of my gift to the Nameless god." She tossed her head with a smirk. "If you plan to observe, you'll need to remain on the dais, near me. Otherwise, stay clear of this room while I work."

His expression became wary. "You aren't lying. Shit."

She laughed mirthlessly. "Why would I lie? This is not the first time I've prepared for such a ritual, after all."

"Yes, I've heard the tale." Kama cleared his throat uncomfortably and glanced at the warded door. "I'll send word to you once the prisoners arrive."

After the bothersome conversation with Kama, she traveled to the temple in the depths of the nearby chasm to retrieve the items Alyra required for the elixir. The ashes of the temple's final priest, an assortment of natural toxins and plant-based compounds, the like of which she'd never encountered in the Five Kingdoms or the Wasted Land, bone fragments from a variety of species… The list went on, but each item had been stored in the temple ages ago. The Nameless god had not been idle during his long imprisonment, and now he was on the brink of breaking free.

A thrill of elation coursed through her at the notion. She'd devoted her life, then her soul, to the death god. It was his unexpected kindness during her darkest hours that had earned him her undying devotion. He'd spared her from a fate worse than death in the months prior to her first journey to the black tower. All he'd required from her was the blood of her tormentors and the promise that she would become his champion.

In retrospect, she believed the Nameless god had noticed something different in her nature, a dark, twisted facet that many others lacked. He'd nurtured it until it blossomed into a terrible force, then unleashed her upon the world. She smiled fondly at the memory and gave silent thanks to the only god who had deigned to answer her long-ago prayers.

She placed Alyra's ingredients carefully inside the satchel she'd brought with her, then returned to the tower to deliver them. It was after sundown by the time she rapped on Alyra's door. When it opened, she was unsurprised to find the other woman disheveled and once again in a state of semi-undress.

She dangled the satchel carelessly in one hand. "I have the components you asked for."

Alyra's eyes lit up and she reached toward the satchel eagerly. Dranamir drew it beyond her reach with a shake of her head. "First, the collars."

"Fine," Alyra replied with a scowl. "I've nearly finished. There are only another fifty to enchant, but I can have them to you in the morning."

"No. The prisoners will be here before dawn. I must have them tonight."

The control collars were an essential piece of her planned ritual; without them, her creations would retain their free will and may pose a greater danger to their conquest than even she could foresee. She would not have her finest gift to the Nameless be ruined by Alyra's ineptitude.

Alyra's shoulders slumped and she nodded in resignation. "Fine. I'll have them completed by midnight, but don't mistake me Dranamir—I do this for the god we serve. I am *not* doing this for you."

Dranamir smirked. "As it should be. When you deliver the collars, you may have this." She held up the satchel once more before turning on her heel to march up a short flight of stairs to her own quarters. She heard Alyra splutter indignantly behind her, but ignored the other woman's half-formed protests. Alyra would have her ingredients only once she'd fulfilled her part of the bargain.

Once in her chambers, she settled down to sleep for several hours. She was awakened just before midnight by a light tap on her door. She knew immediately it was Alyra, eager to be rid of the control collars and acquire her precious ingredients in exchange. It was the first time in several encounters that Dranamir opened the door to find Alyra fully clothed, with her hair brushed and styled. Perhaps she'd sent her latest conquest to his own quarters while she worked, though Dranamir suspected he was eagerly awaiting Alyra's return—wherever he might currently reside.

Behind Alyra was a large wooden crate filled with the slim leather collars she'd enchanted. Dranamir peered inside greedily, unable to hide her malevolent delight. A rough count told her the crate contained the full thousand she'd requested.

"They're finished." Alyra eyed her warily, discomfort apparent in her every gesture. "I recall how the prisoners reacted when you performed this ritual the first time, Dranamir. I do not envy their fate."

"Nor should you. Their lives belong to the Nameless god—whether they wish it or not." Dranamir smirked. "I think he will be quite pleased with the new addition to our army once I've finished with them."

Alyra visibly shuddered. "I will pray he is, for all our sakes. Might I have those ingredients now? I've fulfilled my obligation to you." It was clear she was eager to be rid of Dranamir.

Dranamir retrieved the satchel from the small table near her door and passed it to Alyra. "Everything you requested is inside. Perhaps if our master is pleased with you after your task is complete, he'll allow you entrance into his domain." She grinned wickedly. "I wouldn't count on it, though. Even Garin has never been inside the temple."

Alyra's expression soured further. "Good night, Dranamir. I'll pray I won't be forced to speak with you again any time soon."

Dranamir continued to smirk as Alyra turned away. She'd struck a nerve.

She waited until Alyra's footsteps faded from the winding staircase, then opened a portal into the Aethereum. Wrapping the crate in strands of magic, she pulled it through after her and made her way to the meeting room at the base of the tower. Upon exiting, she noted her ward remained in place, untampered with by curious Enlightened or the other Soulless. She left the crate beside the magically-guarded entrance, then returned to the Aethereum to travel to the tower's topmost floor.

The room was empty, as she'd anticipated. Even Garin was forced to succumb to sleep on occasion, no matter how closely his being was tied to the Nameless' whims. A thrill of anticipation ran along her spine as she approached the center of the long glass case housed along the room's eastern wall. A trio of softly glowing orbs were housed within, each a different color—one gray, one green, one yellow. The light emitted from each was oily and swirled upon itself, while their surfaces roiled in constant motion as waves of magic undulated within.

If the histories were correct, it had been more than a thousand years since she'd last used them, a millennium since her previous gift to the Nameless had been wrought. The orbs had endured the passage of centuries, and not one of the others—or the Enlightened who followed them—had possessed the ability to utilize them properly. Perhaps, she reflected, it was her innate aptitude for both creation and destruction that had drawn the Nameless god's eye. The orbs were her means of carrying out the ritual, facilitators of her creative nature.

As she withdrew them from the case, the power they contained crackled against her grayish skin, sending a ripple of exhilaration through her core. Each orb was the size of her palm; she cradled one in the crook of her elbow while holding the others during her return journey to the tower's meeting room. She would link to each at the onset of the ritual, her magic and theirs intertwined while she manipulated the prisoners and the serpents. The thrill that coursed through her at the prospect was incomparable.

She released the ward protecting the meeting room and entered, once more moving the crateful of collars behind her with magic. She secured the door behind her, cognizant of the restless serpents' desire to be freed after several days spent confined to the tower.

The serpents largely ignored her presence, though a few made a show of slithering away from her as she traversed the length of the room. She placed the crate carefully at the base of the dais at the far end of the room, then stepped carefully upon the dais to arrange the orbs in a triangle surrounding the single, comfortable chair that sat overlooking the rest of the space. The green and grey orbs she placed on either side, within arms' reach of the chair, while the yellow was positioned in front, near where her feet would be.

All was in order. The only piece remaining for the ritual was the prisoners.

She settled into the chair and allowed her eyes to roam across the room. The serpents slithered across the tiled floor and over one another, their green and gray scales glinting faintly in the magical light emanating from the walls. They were restless and on the prowl in spite of their present surroundings, but she knew they'd settle and become lethargic as the hours ticked toward dawn. She was pleased they were nocturnal creatures; if that facet of their biology transferred into the prisoners, it would prove beneficial to their work alongside the Murkor.

Her gaze drifted to the yellow orb near her feet. Perhaps with three of the orbs to aid her in the ritual, she would have more control over the outcome than her first attempt had allowed. Then, she'd only possessed the gray and the green. She'd been satisfied enough with the results, and the Scorpion Men had proven fierce adversaries, but perhaps she could have molded them more efficiently with the third orb to aid her. A wistful expression crossed her features as she considered what might have been.

She was drawn from her musings as a heavy knock sounded on the door. She smiled grimly. It was time.

She crossed the room and opened the door to reveal Kama's tall and angular frame. He glanced beyond her and grimaced as he took in the large serpents that filled the space. "The prisoners are outside."

She nodded. "Bring them in. I will link with the Oldaran Orbs and pacify the reptiles in preparation for their arrival. Ensure each is secured *firmly* to their seat, Kama. I cannot have even one of them break free while I work."

His gaze raked her head to toe appraisingly. "Of course. I will stand by on the dais to observe."

She smirked. "Perhaps you'll even learn something, Kama."

"Perhaps." His smile was tight. "I'll see to the prisoners."

She strode toward the dais and linked with each of the orbs as she did so. She could feel their power enhance her own, could feel the pulsation of energy flooding her being with each beat of her heart. The orbs had been created for a benevolent purpose, yet she had warped them to fulfill her own desires, twisting their magics toward a dark practice that only she and the Nameless god fully understood. Kama could observe all he wished, but he'd never learn the mechanisms in play. He lacked the proper aptitudes.

She wove a net of magic across the room to entrance the snakes. They became still as they awaited her unspoken command. She compelled each to coil beneath the chairs reserved for the prisoners, where they would remain until she was prepared to initiate the next step of the ritual.

She watched impassively as the human prisoners were led inside and secured to the chairs one by one. Kama strode toward her and came to stand adjacent to the green orb at her left, while dozens of hooded Murkor shackled the humans to their fate. Most appeared in good health and uninjured, though their clothing was torn and soiled. The Murkor had treated them well enough, it seemed. The prisoners' expressions ranged from dejected to defiant; some had accepted their inevitable fate, while others refused to acknowledge it.

There were a handful of sickly prisoners who would never survive the ritual. She glanced at Kama, who stood with his hands behind his back and a steely expression upon his face. "There are several who will not serve my purpose. Either they leave with the Murkor, or they die."

His dark eyebrows rose in surprise. "You would allow them to leave, Dranamir?"

"The army is your purview, as you've so often reminded me," she replied acidly. "I am granting you the opportunity to spare their wretched lives, if that is your wish."

"Very well. Which are unfit?"

She pointed them out, and to her astonishment, he seized his power and struck at them mercilessly. An invisible shockwave careened into each with such force they were thrown against the far wall of the chamber, their bodies broken and crushed from the impact.

"Impressive," she said to the sound of horrified cries in the room below.

He grunted. "I cannot allow you to steal all of the fun, Dranamir."

She suspected it was yet another misguided attempt on his part to win her favor and perhaps satisfy his lust. He would receive neither, but she was in no mood for debate. "This will take some time, and I cannot be interrupted. Do not leave the dais, Kama. I won't remind you of the consequences."

He shook his head while his eyes darted warily across the room. "I understand."

She scanned the room a final time. Each prisoner appeared secure, each serpent was under her thrall, and the Murkor had closed the doors to the chamber when they departed. She drew as much power from the orbs as she could safely wield and felt the crackle of energy as it coursed through her and into the room beyond. She closed her eyes and began to unravel the creatures before her, unmaking them only to rebuild them in the fashion of her choosing.

She ignored the chorus of screams, the shouts of horror, the sobs and broken moans that erupted from the human prisoners. The serpents hissed, adding their own displeasure to the cacophony before their voices were abruptly silenced. She sensed Kama beside her, rigid with tension, though he spoke not a word.

With the third orb's power, she was granted a clarity that had been hazy during her previous attempt. She sensed every bone, every muscle and tendon, each organ and vein in both the humans and the serpents. She severed some parts while knitting others together, molding her creations into a vision worthy of the Nameless god's praise. The process was bloody and painful for its victims.

She poured more energy into the task, drawing deeply from the reservoirs of magic contained in the trio of orbs. She bound them each with a control collar, then tied the collar's effectiveness to the essence of the Nameless god himself. The new segment of their army would be compelled to obey him, so long as his power remained. He was a god—their servitude was now eternal.

The process took several hours; by the time she'd finished, her magic was depleted and she knew she'd be unable to stand due to her exhaustion. She severed the link she'd established between the orbs and sagged backward into the chair.

"Dranamir?" Kama's voice was a bare whisper, laced with concern.

"It's finished. I am spent."

There was a pause, then he said, "I know. They're remarkable."

She forced her heavy lids open in order to inspect her handiwork. Most of the prisoners had survived the grueling process. They'd retained their human forms from the waist up, but below, their bodies had melded completely with those of the serpents. Like the Scorpion Men before them, they were now only half human.

Some wept silently at their plight, while others stared maliciously at the dais, hatred burning in their eyes. They remained shackled to the chairs, but she lacked the energy to free them. With the collars secured about their necks, the restraints were no longer necessary.

A faint smile crossed her lips. "They are the Serpentus," she said, giving name to her creation. "They will obey our commands without question. Perfect soldiers."

Kama chuckled darkly. "A fitting name. I'll see to it they are integrated into the Murkor ranks. The Nameless will be pleased."

She smiled once more and closed her eyes, content for the first time in many months. The Nameless god would reward her once he was free.

CHAPTER SIXTEEN

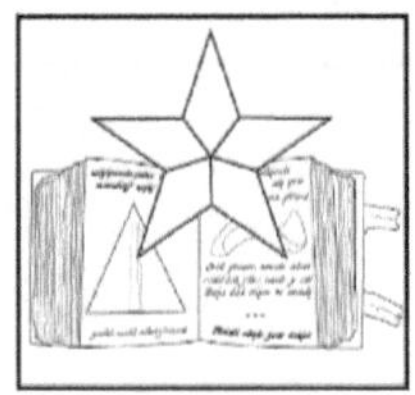

A NEW LEADER

It was uncomfortably noisy in the vast meeting hall housed on the Shining Tower's second floor. More wizards than Tavesin had ever witnessed gathered in one place were crammed into the space, and it seemed each had an opinion to share or gossip to spread. There were at least a dozen conversations carrying on in his immediate vicinity and too many voices to keep track of. He resisted the urge to sink lower into his chair and hold his hands over his ears. He'd never believed he would miss the controlled chaos that was the army's camp, nor favor it over the relative sanctuary he considered the tower to be.

Rostin and Badolo sat on either side of him, Badolo sporting his new yellow cloak marking his acceptance into the Sect. Rostin's eyes were squeezed shut, and he wore a determined expression on his face, as though he could will away the din that surrounded them. Badolo appeared alert and interested; he was clearly eavesdropping on several conversations at once. Unable to relax, Tavesin released a heavy sigh that was immediately lost amongst the unceasing susurration of voices.

He wished Ravin were present. At least then he'd feel secure, knowing the mage would uphold his promise of protection. It was a foolish notion; Ravin would never set foot within the Shining Tower.

"Look!" Badolo hissed. He nudged Tavesin painfully with his elbow and pointed toward the dais at the room's center.

Tavesin directed his attention there and was astonished to find Ukase had appeared. The god towered above the humans surrounding him while his pale, faintly luminescent eyes scanned the room. Ukase was garbed in dark robes that only revealed his midnight blue hands and hairless face. Indecipherable patterns of silver marked every inch of his exposed skin. Tavesin had seen likenesses of Ukase in the temples, but had never encountered him in person. That the Judge of Mortal Affairs had deigned to appear at the latest council meeting sent a ripple of fear along his spine.

Beside him, Rostin gaped. "That's Ukase, isn't it? Why would he be *here*?"

Tavesin shrugged, but it was Badolo who answered. "Radosan told us the Radiant had been detained. This can't be a coincidence."

A hush fell over the room as others began to take note of the god's unexpected appearance. The shuffle of feet as the wizards took their seats filled the space for a time, then the vast room fell into an eerie silence. Tavesin clasped his hands together as anxiety gripped him. He wished again that Ravin were present; he'd understand the scope of the situation and offer insight.

"Be at ease," Ukase's voice rumbled through the room. "The proceedings shall begin soon."

"What happened while we were away?" Rostin whispered across Tavesin to Badolo. "Did you learn anything since your challenge?"

Badolo shook his head helplessly. "Only that the Sect Masters were at odds with something the Radiant has done, and he's been detained. Radosan told us as much at the camp."

Rostin grimaced and sat back in his chair. "Whatever has happened, I don't like it."

Tavesin nodded his agreement and continued to watch Ukase. His arms were crossed, but his expression was unreadable as he studied the gathered wizards. Tavesin wasn't certain what to make of the god's demeanor.

The room fell silent once more as the rear doors were pushed open. The five Sect Masters began to descend toward the dais, the Radiant in their midst. Stripped of his ceremonial, multi-hued cloak, his hands shackled behind him, the Radiant was far less intimidating than he'd once seemed. A look of weary resignation etched his features, and he kept his gaze downcast. Whatever he'd done to deserve a trial was dire indeed.

The Radiant was made to kneel before the dais while the Sect Masters fanned out on either side of him. Each bowed low to Ukase, who studied them impassively for a time. Tension filled the room as each wizard sat forward to better observe the proceedings. The silence stretched for several moments before Ukase spoke, his low voice like thunder.

"Berasin Jarens, Radiant of the Council of Auras, I have been informed of the charges laid against you."

The Radiant hung his head but said nothing in response.

"The first charge brought against you is one of negligence. You knowingly allowed Varasen Jarens, your brother, to raise an army in the Wasted Land under the name Shan'tar. You were aware of his activities and failed to both inform your council and act to stop the threat he posed." Ukase glowered at the Radiant, who visibly trembled. "Shan'tar acquired a relic known as the Shalin Stone, which he then used to resurrect the Soulless."

Gasps erupted throughout the room, Tavesin's among them. He stared wide-eyed at the news and glanced between Rostin and Badolo. His friends appeared equally shocked. They'd known for some time that Varasen Jarens and Shan'tar were one in the same, but that he was responsible for the Soulless' return was unforgivable. Tavesin's mind raced as scenes of his beating at the hands of Garin and the knowledge of what he'd done to Arra spun through his head. Between those flashes of memory, he was forced to recall the horrors he'd witnessed from the wall in Delucha as the Soulless sought to take the city. The Radiant could have prevented it all.

He gazed with newfound fury at the kneeling man in the center of the room, his hands clenched painfully into fists. If not for the Radiant, Arra would be in Dar Daeland, safe and secure. He would not have been forced to fight against the Murkor and their Soulless overlords, and his nights would not be plagued by horrific dreams that not even Aziarah or Ravin could cure him of. Rage and hatred for the man at Ukase's feet threatened to overwhelm him.

A gentle hand on his arm startled him from his thoughts. Badolo peered at him, concern clear in his dark eyes. "Taven?" he whispered.

Tavesin swallowed and forced himself to relax his hands. "None of this had to happen."

Badolo nodded in understanding. "I know. Will you be alright?"

"Yes." He released a shaky breath and returned his attention to Ukase.

The god stared impassively at the Radiant. "Do you have anything to say in your defense?"

The Radiant drew a breath, seemed to gather himself, then tilted his chin up to face Ukase. "As you stated, Varasen was my brother. I wasn't aware of his madness until it was too late. By then, he'd already gathered the Murkor into an army." He looked away and sighed. "I believed I could stop him alone, that I could help him—cure him. I didn't want to involve the council in what I believed was a family affair."

"Your intentions were admirable, but foolish." Ukase crossed his arms with a frown. "Many deaths and many more hardships would have been prevented if you'd reacted to the news differently."

"I am keenly aware of that," the Radiant replied, defeated.

Tavesin was only moderately consoled by the remorse the man showed. It was difficult to set aside the pain he'd endured, the abuse Arra continued to suffer, and the atrocities he'd witnessed in Delucha. His heart ached as he blinked away unwanted tears. The Radiant was a man of influence and power. He should have stopped his brother before matters escalated. He'd failed—and Tavesin was reluctant to forgive him.

"The second charge is far more serious. It is partially the reason behind your colleagues' desire to have me oversee today's proceedings." Ukase eyed the man kneeling before him with a measure of distaste. "There are a number of apprentices who have gone missing during your time as Radiant, apprentices whose whereabouts have remained a secret to the majority of your council."

Ukase gestured toward the White Sect Master, an aged woman with the dark complexion that marked her as Santinian. Like the others of her rank, she was garbed in the ceremonial colored robes of her chosen Sect, her garments as snowy as her sweep of thick hair. She unfurled a roll of parchment and began to read a list of names.

"Carmyla Val'sen. Jasom Riversend. Kiria Nonsehk. Lorra Misthaven. Arra Shannin…"

Tavesin's heart wrenched within his chest as Arra's name was spoken. There were other names listed, but he could not focus on the

Sect Master's recitation as his ears began to ring with panic. He grasped the arms of his chair so tightly his knuckles ached and the skin of his hands grew pale. Was the Radiant somehow responsible for Arra's fate? He stared unblinking at the shackled man at Ukase's feet, torn between striking him down and collapsing into sobs.

Ukase's next words forced his attention back to the god. "I have been informed each of these apprentices were, in fact, abducted from within your ranks. Several have been traced to the black tower, while others remain missing."

"It's true," the Radiant rasped.

Gasps and angry shouts erupted across the room. Ukase held up his hands for silence. After a time, the incensed wizards quieted again.

"While this fact is not without precedent," Ukase stated evenly, "your reaction to the news was. Rather than admit to your council and the families of the missing apprentices that you were aware the Soulless were involved in their disappearances, you chose to send word that they'd run away from the tower."

His ears continued to ring, and without realizing it, Tavesin rose to his feet, unable to contain his anger any longer. "Arra was *taken*!" he shouted. "She's been tortured and might die! And you had the gall to tell her family *she ran away?*"

He felt hands on his shoulders, whether they belonged to Badolo or Rostin, he wasn't certain. He pulled free of their grasp and stormed down the row of chairs toward the aisle as tears began to stream from his eyes. He could endure no more of the trial.

Once free of the chairs, he turned toward the exit and fled as sobs escaped his throat unbidden. He heard Ukase's voice as he reached the doors.

"Do you see how callous your actions appear, Berasin? There are far more people affected by your apathy than you realize."

Tavesin yanked the door open and sprinted into the corridor beyond. He continued to run once he reached the stairs, even as his vision was blurred by tears. He crossed the tower's foyer, heedless of its splendor for the first time since his arrival. Its beauty and wonder was inconsequential in the face of the Radiant's corruption. He raced outside and into the garden where Ravin had promised to await their return.

True to his word, Ravin was perched on a sculpted bench beneath magically altered trees, their broad leaves still lustrous and green despite the winter air. Ravin held the book Tavesin had stolen from the Deluchan queen's library in his hands, but looked up with concern as he heard Tavesin's approach. He closed the book and set it aside, swiftly rising to his feet.

"Taven?"

He came to a halt paces away from the mage. "He lied to everyone about Arra," he blurted before bursting into a fresh wave of tears.

He felt Ravin's arm encircle his shoulders while he was led to the bench. Ravin helped him to sit, then settled down beside him. "Take your time, Taven. When you're ready, tell me what occurred."

Tavesin told him everything through a haze of tears. His faith in the Council of Auras was shaken, his trust in the wizards, shattered. Ravin listened quietly, only breaking his silence to pose questions when Tavesin paused. He felt marginally better afterwards, though his heart continued to ache with sorrow and despair.

"I want to go back to camp," he said sullenly as he finished his narrative. "I don't want to be here any longer."

Ravin's expression was understanding, yet filled with concern. "I know. But I'll need your help once the others return."

Tavesin released a shaky sigh. "What if they don't?"

"I doubt that's a possibility. Ukase will see to it that Berasin is punished for his crimes, and your council will—"

"I want no part of the council. Not any longer." The vehemence he heard in his own words stunned him, but he shrugged it away. "They've left Arra to *die*, Ravin."

Ravin studied him for several moments, and Tavesin began to wonder if he'd made a mistake in allowing his anger to consume him. Finally, Ravin nodded.

"I understand. *The* council will elect a new leader once Ukase is finished with him," Ravin amended. "It's part of the process, is it not?"

Tavesin nodded glumly. "It is."

"Then perhaps the new Radiant will prove a more competent leader." Ravin sat back and crossed his arms, his eyes trained on the tower's entrance. "I don't wish to see you walk away from them, Tavesin. You should not aspire to become like me."

Tavesin glowered at the ground between his boots, frustrated by Ravin's words. "Why shouldn't I? You have the freedom to do as you please. I want the freedom to save Arra, and they won't give it to me!"

Ravin rose to his feet and turned to face Tavesin in one swift movement. His hands gripped Tavesin's shoulders fiercely, almost painfully. Anger flared in his golden eyes.

"Did you not listen when I gave my story in Delucha?" Ravin growled. "You do not want to follow my path. It will lead you only to despair. You will become friendless, feared, and hated. You will be *alone*. I would not see you live a life such as mine."

Tavesin peered up at him sullenly. "You aren't alone. You have the duchess."

Ravin's expression softened, and he nodded. "Yes, but I suffered greatly before meeting her. She is far better than I deserve." He released his grip on Tavesin's shoulders and stepped back with a sigh. "Will you trust me on this matter, Taven? Do not give up on the wizards yet."

Tavesin wanted nothing more than to disagree, but a small part of him understood the wisdom of Ravin's words. Perhaps with a change in leadership, the Council of Auras could redeem itself. Reluctantly, he nodded.

"Good. You ought to return to the meeting."

"No." Tavesin sighed and looked away. "Rostin and Badolo will tell me what I've missed. I'd rather stay here."

"Very well." Ravin returned to his seat and picked up the book once more. "Perhaps this will give us an opportunity to discuss what we've learned about the black tower and the gods' plans for us."

Grateful for the change of topic, Tavesin managed a smile as Ravin began explaining what he'd uncovered from the stolen book. Their discussion carried on throughout the afternoon, and by the time wizards began to emerge from the tower, he'd set much of his previous anger with the council aside. He would give the wizards a second chance, but no more.

Badolo and Rostin were among the first to reach him. Rostin was uncharacteristically subdued and allowed the younger boy to recount all that Tavesin had missed.

"After you left, Ukase explained the last of the charges against the R—Berasin," he said quietly. "The Sect Masters acted immediately once they learned what he'd done. There were several wizards he excommunicated on the grounds that they were spies for the Soulless. He used a relic, Taven..." Badolo hung his head and lapsed into silence.

"Lilyna called it a sensation blocker," Rostin told him in a low tone. "It places a barrier between the person and all of their senses."

Ravin was on his feet in an instant, eyes ablaze. "Such relics should be destroyed," he hissed before storming toward Radosan, who had only just exited the tower.

Tavesin watched him go, unsettled by his unmitigated rage. "What do you mean?"

Badolo drew a breath and steeled himself. "Imagine a world in which you cannot see, cannot hear, or feel the wind against your skin. The relic also blocks the sensation of magic."

Tavesin stared at his friend, horrified. "Why would the wizards keep something like that?"

Badolo shrugged helplessly, but Rostin said, "When the Sect Masters explained what it was that he'd used, Ukase was enraged. He summoned Solsticia, who collected the relic and disappeared."

Tavesin grimaced and glanced toward Ravin, who was speaking animatedly to Radosan. "Perhaps it's fortunate Ravin wasn't inside. He's angry enough without a confrontation with his mother."

Rostin glanced over his shoulder and nodded warily. "It doesn't matter. I doubt Solsticia would have noticed he was there. The relic is gone, and the Rad—*Berasin*," he corrected himself, "was sentenced to a life of servitude in Ukase's temple."

"Ukase *bound* him, Taven," Badolo added, his dark eyes wide. "He can do nothing unless Ukase wills it. He's become little more than the god's slave."

"Ukase even controls his use of magic," Rostin said uneasily. "My mother always warned me never to infuriate the gods. Now I understand why."

"Who leads the council now?" Tavesin asked.

"Virano—the Gray Sect Master," Rostin replied. "He's ordered all of the Grays and Greens to join Emra's cause, and as many of the Blues as can be spared. The others may join if they wish, though most of the Whites and Yellows will remain here, it seems. The tower is going to war, Taven."

Tavesin blinked, stunned, yet relieved at the news. The council's inaction had put too many lives at risk for too long, but at least something was now being done.

He glanced toward Ravin, but failed to catch the mage's eye. He was thankful Ravin had calmed him and forced him to see reason when his anger would have otherwise blinded him to reality. The Council of Auras might redeem itself, after all.

CHAPTER SEVENTEEN

ROGUE SOLDIERS

The summons went through the tower at mid-day. Sal'zar was awakened by insistent pounding on his door, and not for the first time, he cursed the humans and their diurnal schedules. He hadn't managed enough sleep in weeks; there was always someone that required his presence or his particular skillset, or who simply wished to goad him. It wasn't enough that he was a curiosity amongst them, but he was an alchemist. Someone with the ability to concoct potions and salves, flares, light crystals, and countless other rare and useful items.

He kicked off his blankets and tugged his hood in place while stifling a growl. The months of abrupt awakenings had taken their toll on his temper, but he did his best to keep it under control. His position was precarious enough without a surge of anger to land him in the Soulless' sights. He swallowed his urge to shout at his unwanted visitor and instead stumbled to the door without a word.

It was one of the Enlightened, a human woman with a crooked nose and cruel, dark eyes. He recognized her from his months spent in the tower, but he did not know her name.

"The Soulless have called a meeting of the council," she informed him with a sneer. "See that you're downstairs quickly, blue-skin."

Sal'zar nodded once before he closed the door. Her insult rankled, but it was the least of the slights he'd endured within the tower. He retrieved his boots from the corner of the small room and tugged them on, determined to ignore the festering wound to his pride. Amongst his own people, his skills were celebrated and his position admired. The humans of the black tower were malicious and entitled, and seemed to reserve a special brand of vitriol for the lone Murkor within their ranks.

If Jal'den knew half of what he'd been forced to withstand, his partner would have torn through the ranks of Enlightened in a rampage—and forfeit his life in the process. It wasn't worth the risk to Jal'den's welfare to share the details of his tenure. Perhaps one day he would tell him, but Sal'zar was certain that time remained distant.

He exited his room and joined the stream of bodies descending the tower's spiral stairs. Since his room was near its base, the journey to the meeting room took little time. He took a chair in the back corner of the room with the knowledge that if he attempted to sit anywhere else, it would cause an unwanted stir amongst the humans. Attention was the last thing he desired.

A faint, metallic scent filled the room, coupled with an equally slight odor that he could not describe. The first he attributed to blood; it was no secret the Soulless had led scores of human prisoners into the room in the early morning hours the day before. What transpired after the doors closed, he did not know, but he assumed it could not have been anything pleasant for the unfortunates the Soulless had gathered.

Upon the dais in the front of the room, he spied three of the four Soulless. Dranamir stood in the center, arms crossed as she eyed the room with a sneer. Kama and Garin flanked her, but Alyra was nowhere to be seen.

Sal'zar grimaced beneath his hood. Without Alyra's presence to temper the trio on the dais, events could rapidly devolve into bloodshed.

The room filled rapidly, and within minutes nearly half of the seats were taken. The council lacked the numbers to properly fill the space, but Sal'zar considered it a blessing. The fewer resources the Soulless had at their disposal, the better. Once the trio at the front of the room seemed satisfied that everyone summoned was present, Sal'zar sensed a wave of magic permeate the air, and the heavy doors at the back of the room closed with a loud thud.

Moments later, Alyra emerged from a shimmering blue portal to join the others on the dais, a pair of armored humans in her wake. From Sal'zar's vantage point at the rear of the room, he could see little of the pair, though gasps issued from the lips of those seated nearer the dais. Though he wished to gain a better view, he knew it was too late to switch seats and standing would only draw the Soulless' attention.

He leaned forward in his chair but could see nothing beyond the pair's head and shoulders. Both sported light complexions and brown hair, and both were garbed in boiled-leather armor. One had dark eyes and a scar on his forehead, while the other had blue eyes and more refined features. Both men wore slim, leather bands around their necks fastened with iron buckles, and neither appeared pleased to be there. Hatred and fury burned within the depths of their eyes.

"We have gathered you here today for two very important matters," Garin intoned in a voice that seemed too deep for his small frame. His words silenced the whispers that had erupted with Alyra's appearance.

"First," Dranamir stated, a terrible glint in her eyes, "I present to you the Serpentus." She gestured toward the men with Alyra, who moved to stand atop the dais with the Soulless.

Sal'zar gaped beneath his hood, horror sending a chill through his core. The men were not human any longer. Both retained much of their human form above the waist, but below, they had the form of large serpents, replete with reptilian scales. They managed to stand as tall as their human counterparts in the audience, though Sal'zar wasn't certain how they managed to move and remain upright without great difficulty. Their upright stature seemed at odds with their serpentine lower bodies.

He had no doubt they'd been amongst the prisoners brought into the tower on the previous day, and he now understood the scope of the atrocities the Soulless were capable of. He knew the stories of the Scorpion Men and their origins, but had long believed it a fable, a tale of warning for others to never anger powerful wielders of magic. His hands shook as he gazed at the pair on the dais; they were helpless victims of circumstance, transformed into unnatural creatures by the twisted whims of the Soulless. It was little wonder both men appeared enraged.

"My newest creations have been integrated into the army's camp," Dranamir continued with an icy smile. "They will bolster our soldiers' numbers and are completely loyal to our cause." She stepped forward to finger the leather band on the neck of the nearest man. "The control collars compel them to do our bidding. They have been instructed to take commands only from the Soulless and the army's commander. Should any of you find compassion in your hearts and attempt to remove the collars, I will personally make certain you suffer immeasurably before your death."

Sal'zar swallowed a wave of bile and clenched his fists to his sides. He could tolerate no more of the Soulless' abuse. With the "creation" of the Serpentus, they'd gone too far. He understood the concept of the control collars; those under their influence were compelled to obey, no matter how strongly they wished to do otherwise. Their plight was more dire than his own, but with the threat of death, he could do nothing to assist them. They were under the Soulless' thrall, enslaved to the most merciless and brutal of taskmasters.

Sal'zar's conscience would not allow him to sit idly by to witness their suffering. Signaling the other Murkor selected by the Kal was his only hope of salvation—and his only hope of sparing the former humans from further humiliation and abuse. He resolved to leave the tower for the final time that night. By morning, a third of the Murkor soldiers would be gone, never to return. He'd put off the Kal's plan too long already in a misguided attempt to prolong Aran'daj's life and spare Jal'den the pain of another separation.

He could wait no longer.

Garin spoke again, and Sal'zar's attention was forced to return to the Soulless on the far end of the room. "As I stated previously, there were two matters we wished to discuss. The Serpentus were but the first. The second is far more important." He paused to scan the room with his baleful, crimson eyes while his words sank in. A twitch of smile quirked his lips as he continued. "We are on the brink of releasing our god, the Nameless god, from his prison. I suggest you all prepare yourselves accordingly."

Sal'zar resisted the urge to leap to his feet and flee as the statement reverberated through the chamber. Many of the humans cheered and applauded while his gut twisted and roiled at the news. It was as he'd long suspected and as the Kal had feared. He'd run out of time to further their scheme and must make his move tonight. He prayed the

Murkor chosen to accompany him were prepared and would understand his desperate signal. It was the only hope his people might have to survive the coming conflict.

The Soulless said more, but he could not make out their words over the ringing in his ears as he struggled to maintain his outward composure. When the others began to rise and depart, he joined them, his thoughts a tangled whirlwind on the brink of panic. He wished to send word to the Kal, but there was no time, and he had yet to master the art of long-distance communication with anyone other than Jal'den. He would deal with a message later; at present, he needed to gather his essentials and await nightfall.

He returned to his room and began packing his necessities into his battered satchel. When he picked up the vial he'd retrieved from Jal'den, he placed it on his small table rather than into the satchel. Though he'd prefer to save its contents for a later time, he could not shake the nagging feeling that he'd need it to safely flee the tower's premises.

Once finished, he sat down on the edge of his narrow bed and gazed through the room's small window. Beyond the warped pane, a distorted vision of the barren plains of the Wasted Land spread toward the western horizon. The sun was a handspan above the earth, its light blessedly muted through the dark glass. He could not risk leaving for several hours.

He sighed and wondered if Jal'den was awake. His partner had never been a sound sleeper, often rousing hours before nightfall to dwell on unspoken concerns. Sal'zar knew it was a risk to contact him on the very night he planned to steal away, but he needed to hear Jal'den's voice to calm his own anxiety.

He closed his eyes, sought his strange, magical power, and formed the now-familiar link with Jal'den's mind. To his relief, Jal'den was alert, and though he seemed startled by Sal'zar's unexpected contact, he was also pleased.

Sal'zar? Jal'den's voice echoed in his skull.

Sal'zar smiled. *I'm here. I don't have much time.*

A flash of frustration coupled with despair rushed through their connection. *You're leaving tonight, aren't you? I know what was done to the humans.*

Sal'zar sighed. *Yes, I must leave. I've delayed too long already, and the humans… I cannot abide what was done to them. It is unnatural. Wrong.*

I know. A wave of sadness enveloped him before Jal'den continued. *Be safe,* ama. *Your forced departure tears at my gods-damned heart.*

Mine as well. I love you.

Sal'zar severed their connection before Jal'den could reply, a lump in his throat and an ache in his chest. He wasn't certain he'd be able to speak with Jal'den in that manner again—once he fled the tower, it would be unsafe to attempt further contact. He would not place Jal'den's life at risk unnecessarily. He hoped Jal'den would understand.

There was activity on the staircase outside of his door for many hours after the sun had set. Finally, as it neared midnight, the unceasing tread of footsteps began to fade into silence. He knew he could not linger, but the risk of discovery remained forefront in his mind. The safest course was to use the salve he'd once given to Jal'den and pray it allowed him to blend with the shadows as he'd designed it to.

He uncorked the vial to reveal a pale, oily liquid. He poured a small amount into his hands and marveled as they seemed to fade into shadow before his eyes. The substance worked, but he had only enough to coat himself and his satchel. Fearful the Soulless would investigate his chamber once they discovered his disappearance, he stashed the empty vial in a pocket and scurried from his room, little more than an animated shadow amongst the tower's dark walls.

He moved as quickly as he dared down the staircase toward the foyer. He was nearly invisible, but his footfalls could still be heard if he trod too forcefully. Uncertain how long his shadowy guise would hold, he was forced into more haste than was comfortable.

He reached the foyer without incident, but was halfway toward the exit door when he heard heavy footsteps on the stairs behind him. He sprinted toward the nearest wall and froze, his breath caught painfully in his throat as he slowly glanced over his indistinct shoulder. Seconds later, the form of a burly human male appeared. Sal'zar recognized him as an initiate, though he knew little else about him. The newcomer's dark eyes swept the foyer before he turned to lumber toward the Initiation Chamber, seemingly unconcerned.

As the man reached the door, a shimmering portal appeared in the foyer's center and Alyra emerged. Sal'zar pressed his shadowy form further against the wall and prayed his concoction would last until he reached the safety of the darkness outside. Alyra paid him no heed and strode toward the man gracefully. They spoke briefly as Alyra explained the Initiation process and what would be expected of him.

Sal'zar glanced at his hands and was relieved to find they remained concealed. He prayed the pair would enter the chamber soon, but they continued to talk while his nerves continued to fray. His time as a wraith was limited.

Seconds that seemed to last an eternity passed. When Alyra finally opened the chamber door and escorted the man inside, Sal'zar released a breath he didn't realize he'd been holding. He glanced at his hands once more, noted the shadow seemed to be coalescing into flesh, and darted toward the exit, all pretense of silence abandoned. He ran across the darkened landscape until his legs ached and the fires within the army's camp came into view.

He altered his course and veered south toward the chasm's edge. Only when he was due south of the camp did he pause to catch his breath. He glanced toward the tower, silhouetted against the night sky, but could see no sign that he'd been followed. His hands trembled as he gulped air; he was visible once more. Alyra's unexpected arrival had nearly cost him his escape.

When he'd calmed enough to proceed, he knelt down and fumbled through his satchel, seeking the dark-violet flare he'd stashed within. He'd chosen to use the color knowing it would be difficult to detect against the night sky, but the Kal's chosen knew to look for it. He prayed the handful of soldiers he'd spoken with on his last trip into the camp had been able to inform the others.

The flare was housed in an unassuming brown tube marked with Murkor symbols to indicate its color and alchemical maker. A thin cord extended from one end. He tugged the cord, then set the tube on the ground and stepped back. Moments later, it shot skyward in a wide arc, deep purple sparks trailing in its wake.

Within an hour, scores of Murkor had followed his signal and joined him at the chasm's edge. Most wore the black of soldiers, though there were a handful of brown-clad craftsmen and several other alchemists as well. Following the Kal's instructions, he began to lead them west, toward the Gray Mountains and a little-used entrance to the Moraine Mines. They would remain there until they received further instructions.

Sal'zar risked a final, longing glance over his shoulder when they were some distance from the camp. He prayed Jal'den would remain safe and they would be reunited one day, against the odds the world had leveled against them.

CHAPTER EIGHTEEN

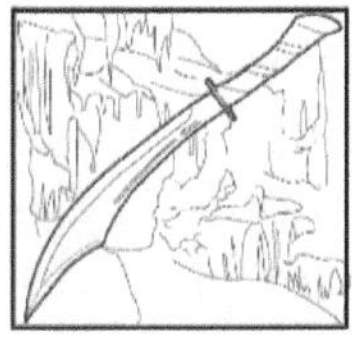

A FINAL SACRIFICE

Aran'daj was speaking with Jal'den outside of his tent when the violet flare arced through the southern sky. Sal'zar had chosen the color wisely; if his focus had been anywhere else, he would not have noticed the signal. Jal'den's back was to the flare, a blessing in Aran'daj's eyes. The Arms Master had oscillated between sullen and enraged for days, and witnessing Sal'zar's silent summons would have pressed him beyond the brink.

Aran'daj forced his eyes away from the signal and focused on Jal'den's plans for large-scale drills. Jal'den would require the work to serve as a distraction once he learned Sal'zar and the others were gone. Aran'daj gave his approval for the plans, then extricated himself from the conversation. On what he was certain would be his final night alive, he simply wished to be left alone.

He returned to his tent, knelt at its center beside the brazier, and began to pray. He sought Ukase's protection for Jal'den and Sal'zar, and begged his patron deity to ensure the Soulless would be served proper justice one day. He implored Blademon to lend his strength to Jal'den, so the Arms Master might survive to see the conclusion of the war. He asked Armistral to mend the rift that would inevitably form between the ranks of Murkor with the departure of Sal'zar and the others. Finally, he sought Aeon's guidance during his final hours. He prayed the Soulless would deem him worthy of a swift death and forgo a prolonged and torturous one.

He received no immediate answers, but such was the way of the gods.

As dawn began to lighten the sky, Aran'daj sought his blankets, though he knew sleep would prove elusive. On the narrow chance the Soulless did not demand his head in exchange for the army's losses, he must keep up an appearance that nothing was amiss. He would feign slumber during the daylight hours and await the events fate had in store, for good or ill. The Kal's plan was finally in motion and there was nothing he could do to change the outcome. He accepted his role, and with it, the inevitability of the Soulless' wrath.

He gazed at the canvas stretched taut overhead and watched as the light outside shifted from muted gray to orange, and finally to brilliant white. He was aware of the passage of hours only by the warmth the daylight brought with it.

His mind was strangely blank. He felt peace in spite of the threat that loomed in the nearby tower; he'd done all he could to secure a future for his people. The rest was in the hands of the gods, the Kal, and the two young Murkor now pitted against one another. His part in the long scheme was finished. His only regret was he'd been unable to see Rej'amin a final time—but perhaps one day they would be reunited in Aeon's dark realm.

It was nearing midday when the shimmering blue portal opened at the center of his tent. Aran'daj shifted in his blankets to gain a better view of which Soulless intruded upon his personal space, but he did not rise. He knew what was about to unfold, knew its outcome, and knew he'd made peace with it some time ago. He'd been awaiting this moment. He was calm, serene, prepared to give his life in sacrifice if it meant even some of the Murkor people would be spared.

Kama emerged from the portal, a murderous glint in his eyes. Aran'daj felt an invisible wall strike him, and the breath was expelled forcefully from his lungs with the impact. He gasped for air, then found himself bound within a tangle of the air itself. He attempted to break free, but could do little more than quiver in place.

Kama strode toward him, his expression a storm cloud of rage. "You have much to explain, Commander."

Aran'daj felt his body pulled through the air toward the shimmering oval at the tent's heart, but he said nothing to contradict Kama's words. He wasn't certain the magic that bound him would allow for speech, in any case.

Frozen in place by the Soulless' magic, he was guided through the portal into a world that mirrored his own. There was no sun, yet there was light, permeating everything and searing his eyes. The air was warm and unmoving, as though wind did not exist on the unnatural plane. Aran'daj was unable to turn his head to take in the strange realm he found himself in, but his curiosity was tempered by Kama's looming presence at his side.

Kama grasped his shoulder roughly, his chipped fingernails digging into Aran'daj's flesh. "The others have gathered at the chasm's edge. You will be judged for your part in last night's betrayal. Pray that your wretched fate rests in my hands, Commander, for if it lies with Dranamir, you'll wish for death a thousand times before she finally grants your gods-damned wish."

"What…happened?" Aran'daj croaked, feigning ignorance. It seemed he was capable of speech while suspended, though it proved a struggle.

Kama sneered at him, his lip curling with disgust. "Either you're fucking incompetent, or you're playing at innocence to save your blue hide. And I know you're not incompetent."

Before Aran'daj could form a reply, the world around them blurred and shifted. Suddenly they were on the lip of the chasm, due south of the army's encampment. It was the same area Sal'zar's flare had issued from. A pang of worry shot through him—had the alchemist and the others managed to escape as planned? Or were they now detained, prisoners of the Soulless? After their recent maltreatment of the humans, he feared what they would do to Murkor captives.

Kama waved one grayish hand, and a second portal appeared. "My beliefs are irrelevant, Commander. It is Garin—the Nameless god's thrall—who will oversee your interrogation."

As he was drawn through the portal and into the glaring sunlight of the Wasted Land, he realized Kama's words did not instill fear; rather, he felt only acceptance. Since the day Sal'zar finally divulged the details of the Kal's plan, he'd known this confrontation would come.

He tried to close his eyes to shield them from the sun's glare, but his lids were immobile. He grimaced; the light from the other plane had pained him, but it was a minor discomfort when compared with the harsh rays that now beamed down upon his uncovered head. Kama maneuvered him toward the chasm's dark ledge, where the others of his kind awaited. Several Murkor were gathered as well. He recognized the markings on the hands as belonging to the army's officers, and Jal'den's tall form was unmistakable with the curved, black saber of Arm's Master on his hip and the large steel broadsword, his gift from Blademon, sheathed across his back. The Soulless planned to make a spectacle of him, a warning to the others what the price of failure—or betrayal—would be.

He was made to stand before the other Soulless while Kama took his place alongside Dranamir. The cruel-eyed woman sneered at him, openly hostile. Garin stood on her other side, his expression unreadable and arms crossed. Alyra was the only one of their number who appeared uncomfortable, pity and compassion warring across her damaged features. Garin stepped forward to assess the commander with a critical eye.

"Do you know what has transpired during the night?" Garin demanded. His unusually deep voice carried through the air and echoed along the chasm's jagged sides.

Aran'daj met his gaze but remained silent. They'd already determined his guilt; he had nothing to say.

"Over a third of the Murkor soldiers vanished into the darkness." Garin crossed his arms again and scowled. "Under your watch, Aran'daj."

Aran'daj bristled at the use of his name by the corrupted man. It was clear his title was rescinded, his rank inconsequential, but for one of these abominations to speak his name while he remained unhooded was the greatest insult he'd endured. He ground his teeth together and again refused to speak.

"I suspect you were aware of their departure," Garin continued, his tone becoming dangerous. "I believe you were complicit."

Aran'daj looked beyond the Soulless, toward the gaping maw of the chasm beyond. A flash of movement caught his eye, and he spied the dark, feline form of Aeon in the distance. Aeon raised one furred mitt in salute and bowed his head before vanishing from sight. In that moment, Aran'daj knew Aeon had heard his anguished prayers. The last vestiges of his fear drained away and he faced the Soulless with a renewed sense of purpose.

"I knew of their plan."

With a snarl, Garin pivoted. His fist connected with Aran'daj's torso with enough force he felt ribs crack. "You dare betray us?"

Garin swung again, this time knocking the air from his lungs. Aran'daj was helpless, trapped as he was in the bonds of Kama's foul magic. He grimaced, gasped for breath, then said, "You've created...abominations."

A cold laugh escaped Dranamir's lips. "The Serpentus are my finest creation."

"What you've done...is wrong."

"No, Aran'daj," Garin countered. "The Nameless god has deemed the Serpentus a worthy addition to our army. You are a disgrace." The small man turned to face the others. "Since military matters are your affair, Kama, I shall let you mete out the punishment. Aran'daj must die for his betrayal."

Aran'daj gave silent thanks to Aeon for his intervention. To die by Kama's hand was a mercy; Dranamir would see him tortured endlessly before she was finished, and Garin was little better. At least with Kama, he knew his end would be swift.

Kama strode forward to sneer at him. "Karmada smiles upon your soul this day," he hissed in a low tone meant for Aran'daj alone. "Dranamir begged for the chance to take your gods-damned head."

Aran'daj met Kama's heated gaze without expression, while Kama continued to study him. Finally, the tall Soulless released a snarl and spun around to face the gathered Murkor.

"The rest of you have been gathered here to witness your former commander's demise. Let this be a warning to you. We will not abide failure, and we will not tolerate betrayal. Your loyalty is to us and the Nameless god we serve, or your life is forfeit." Kama gestured to Jal'den. "Give me your sword."

Jal'den nodded and began to unsheathe the curved saber at his hip.

Kama shook his head with a growl. "Not the fucking saber. I want your *sword*."

Aran'daj understood Jal'den's reluctance to part with the weapon, and it was clear Kama did as well. This was to be the first of many tests for Jal'den as the Soulless assessed his allegiance. Aran'daj watched Jal'den silently, praying he would comply. The Kal's plan would falter if Jal'den refused Kama's demand, and Jal'den would land himself in the same position as Aran'daj.

Jal'den nodded. "Apologies, sir." He withdrew the broadsword and offered it, hilt-first to Kama.

Kama studied the blade for several moments. "I doubt Blademon imagined this weapon would be used to execute one of your own."

Jal'den merely nodded to Aran'daj's immense relief.

Kama whirled to face Aran'daj once more. "Kneel."

Bound by Kama's magic, Aran'daj could not comply with the command, but he felt himself repositioned as Kama strode toward him. His knees hit the parched earth with force enough to leave bruises, but the minor injuries were no longer relevant. There would be no escaping from this mire—his only path forward was death.

His chin was forced upwards, his eyes made to gaze at the corrupted Kamshati looming over him.

"Do you have any final words?" Kama demanded.

"Justice will be served one day. You will not succeed in your conquest."

Kama snarled, incensed. He moved faster than Aran'daj believed possible, Jal'den's blade a deadly silver arc in his hands. Aran'daj experienced a moment of excruciating pain before his world grew dark and his soul was pulled forcefully toward the netherworld. His time upon the earth was done, but he hoped his death would serve to protect at least some of his people.

Insubstantial, yet somehow maintaining his corporeal visage, Aran'daj took several moments to orient himself. He stood before a pair of towering golden gates inlaid with a myriad of gemstones in every hue imaginable. The gems glittered in a diffuse, rosy light, soft enough that it did not pain his sensitive eyes. He gazed upward to find a sky split at its zenith; one half was the brilliant blue of daylight, though lacking the harsh rays of the sun, while the other was the deep indigo shade of midnight, replete with thousands of twinkling stars.

The legends of Aeon's realm fell short when describing the wonders it beheld. Aran'daj looked down after several moments spent gaping, awe-struck by the sight. Standing in front of the gates was the dark, furred form of Aeon, his body seemingly as ethereal as Aran'daj now was. Aeon's blue-white eyes fixed upon his own, and the Underworld's guardian smiled.

"I cannot speak for my siblings, but I have heard your prayers. Come. You are welcome here."

CHAPTER NINETEEN

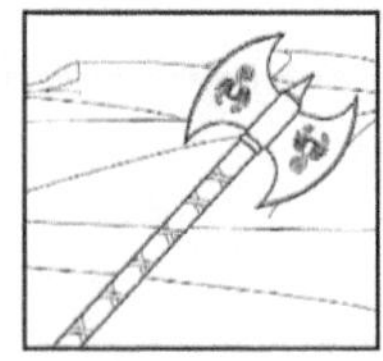

THE WARLEADER'S PLEDGE

Though it was early afternoon, the air temperature was frigid. Vardak drew his cloak about his shoulders and silently cursed the weather. The cold made his leg joints ache, his reactions sluggish, and he wanted nothing more than to seek a roaring campfire in which to thaw his hands. It would be some time before a fire could be managed, however; Daesan had been sighted by the scouts, and Emra was eager to press on in order to reach the ruined city before nightfall. His people were not built to endure the harshness of winter.

From his position near the center of the army's ranks, he could see nothing of the city, but Mount Daesan loomed ominously over the landscape, its lopsided crown a potent reminder that it was no ordinary peak. Tendrils of dark smoke rose into the clouded sky from the mountain's apex and he prayed Flariel would mind her temper. Flariel detested him; he almost expected her to send the mountain into an eruption simply to antagonize him, the remainder of the army be damned.

A sudden glimmer of blue drew his attention. He watched as Ravin emerged from a portal, visibly shuddered, and drew his thick, woolen cloak around himself. Vardak was continually amazed at the mage's ability to pinpoint his location as accurately as he did from within the other realm.

Ravin jogged toward him, breath steaming in the air. "Gods-damn it, it's cold," he said by way of greeting.

Vardak nodded. "I'll be glad to reach a fire."

"As will I." Ravin shivered again. "As you are aware, I was visiting Delucha this morning."

"Yes." Vardak knew something was troubling Ravin; it was unlike him to stall.

"There are reports from dozens of villages throughout the Five Kingdoms. They've been razed, often during the night, and there have been few survivors." Ravin's gaze shifted to a point in the distance. "I suspect I know who is responsible. When Adalin told me what she'd heard, I was determined to put a stop to it, but she persuaded me to follow the path of reason rather than revenge."

"It's one of the Soulless?" Vardak asked, though he knew what Ravin's answer would be.

"Yes. Most likely it's Dranamir." A flash of anger passed through Ravin's golden eyes as he spoke the name. "It's her style. I want nothing more than to confront her, end her, and be done with this business, but Adalin reminded me why I've joined forces with you. Tavesin needs guidance, and from what we've uncovered about the gods' task for us, he cannot complete the work without me." He sighed and ran a hand through his dark hair. "Dranamir will kill hundreds if left unchecked, but if we fail to stop the Nameless' plans, millions will suffer."

"The duchess was right," Vardak replied with emphasis. "Your skills are needed here, but perhaps there is still something that can be done about Dranamir?"

Ravin frowned and shook his head. "None of the wizards are a match for her power. Even Emra would be hard-pressed to deal with her. Besides, I want to see the look on her gods-damned face when I finally destroy her."

Vardak eyed the mage warily and wondered if his desire for revenge would prove problematic in the future. Ravin had indicated he'd suffered for weeks as Dranamir tortured him relentlessly. He couldn't fault the man for seeking retribution, but on the same token, there were many other factors to consider as they prepared to make war upon the Soulless' army. He couldn't allow Ravin to become reckless or succumb to tunnel-vision when so much was at stake.

"I hope you don't plan to do anything rash," Vardak replied.

Ravin snorted. "Perhaps I would have a few months ago, but your worries are misplaced. I will heed Adalin's advice—and yours."

Vardak made a mental note to thank the duchess if he was afforded an opportunity to see her again. He wasn't certain anyone else was capable of forcing Ravin to see reason when he was blinded by his thirst for revenge.

"Have you spoken to Emra regarding these attacks?" he asked.

Ravin nodded. "I spoke with her first. She is easier to locate from the Aethereum than you are. You have no magic about you." He shrugged. "She asked that I tell you my news, and suggested you might have some ideas on how to counteract Dranamir's attacks using non-magical means."

Vardak's eyebrows rose in disbelief. He knew little of magic, and even Blademon's imparted knowledge provided him with little information. Emra's assumption that he knew anything of the sort was ludicrous.

Ravin chuckled. "I gather from your expression that you do not."

"No."

Ravin fell silent for a time, his expression drawn and thoughtful. Finally, he said, "Once we reach Daesan, I can seek my mother's guidance, much as I'd prefer not to. There is a shrine to Flariel on the mountainside."

Vardak brightened, an idea forming in his mind. "Perhaps that isn't a bad idea. We could use the forges in Daesan to craft weapons and armor with the help of Jonathan and the others who came with him. But we'll need Flariel's blessing."

Ravin smirked. "You'd rather I take the brunt of the Fire Maiden's wrath, Vardak? How very noble of you."

Vardak groaned. "That was not—"

Ravin cut him off with a laugh. "I jest. I'd rather speak with Flariel than my mother, in any case. Consider it done."

It was another hour before they reached the outskirts of Daesan. By that time, almost half the army had arrived. Some were pitching tents, while others repurposed the abandoned buildings that were still structurally sound. Campfires roared to life in the streets, and hearths were stoked. Eager to be away from the cold, Vardak paused to speak with the first group of soldiers they came across, a half dozen from the Santinian cavalry.

He was greeted with salutes while he sidled toward their fire with the hope he could bring some life back into his frozen hands. "Have you seen Emra?"

"Word has it she's gone to the forges at the center of town," one replied. "The damage is less there."

Relieved by the news, he nodded and glanced toward Ravin, who stood holding his hands over the flames. "We'll seek her out once we've warmed ourselves."

"You're always welcome, General," another stated with a grin. "It's damned cold."

"I haven't experienced a winter this harsh in ages," a third chimed in. "Bloody fucking Maelstrom and his blasted fucking temper."

"We've at least arrived without a storm to delay us further," Ravin replied without looking away from the flames. "Maelstrom's temper can be far worse than this."

"I've no doubt," the soldier conceded, "but I don't have to fucking like it."

"There is shelter here, and with the mountain nearby, plenty of flame," Vardak replied evenly. "It's not a bad place to overwinter, provided Flariel keeps her temper."

One of the soldiers snickered. "I wouldn't count on that, sir. We've all heard tales of your run-ins with the fire goddess."

Vardak glowered at the campfire and fell silent. He prayed Flariel wouldn't react adversely to his presence so near one of her shrines, but the soldier's point was valid—his proximity alone might be enough to incur her wrath.

They lingered only a few minutes longer before departing in search of Emra. As the soldiers had indicated, the damage to the buildings grew less noticeable as they traveled toward the city's heart. Where some of the structures were reduced to rubble on the city's outskirts and its walls were sundered in several locations, the interior had survived nearly unscathed.

They located the forges easily enough. Vardak was impressed by the scale of the smithing facilities; he gauged more than a hundred craftsmen could easily set up shop within. The forges themselves were cold, but if Ravin was successful in his promised meeting with Flariel, they would soon be burning fiercely. The army would be resupplied, the horses reshoed, and all necessary repairs could be made before they marched again in the spring. The knowledge eased some of his ever-present concerns.

Emra was not at the forges, though they spied several of her guards nearby. When he approached, one hiked a thumb over his shoulder and grinned. "She's in the smith's guild building, just there."

Vardak nodded his thanks and led Ravin in the direction indicated. The mage had been silent for some time, his expression contemplative as his strange eyes studied their surroundings. It was just as well; Vardak remained wary of Ravin's motives, particularly after their earlier conversation concerning Dranamir, and he had little else to say.

The building that once housed the smith's guild was a two-story, brick affair decorated with intricate iron scrollwork around the windows and main entrance door. Another pair of Emra's guards kept watch outside, bundled against the cold. They waved Vardak and Ravin through silently.

The interior of the building was marginally warmer than the outside. A brazier had been lit in the foyer, and the crackle of a nearby fire could be heard from the adjacent room. The door to the room was open, and peering within, Vardak found Emra, several of her guards, Patak, Maryn, and Danian. Patak noted their arrival first and waved them forward with a broad grin. Grateful for the warmth pouring out of the hearth, Vardak made his way toward his brother while Ravin moved to speak with Emra.

"We were beginning to wonder when you'd turn up." Patak glanced toward another door at the far end of the room, and his smile faltered. "Blademon's here."

Vardak suppressed a groan. "I suppose he's here for me."

Patak nodded uneasily. "Makta's with him."

Vardak was unable to hide his amusement at the statement and smirked. Makta was the Warleader's niece, a blade smith well acquainted with their brother, Travin, and one of Patak's former love interests. He assumed Sevic had sent his niece to deliver a message, and perhaps to aid the army's weapons needs. He didn't know the details of her split with his eldest brother, but Patak's discomfort explained more than his words ever would.

Patak shifted uneasily and looked away. "It's not funny, Vardak. It's my worst nightmare come true. Makta and Emra in the same room…" He sighed and raked a hand through his hair. "You shouldn't keep Blademon waiting."

"No, I shouldn't," he agreed, "but I can't wait to see what *she* says when she learns about your latest conquest."

Patak groaned and crossed his arms while Vardak made his way toward the other door. It led into a smaller room furnished with a small desk and several chairs. Blademon loomed in one corner, his gaze impassive as Vardak entered. Makta, significantly shorter than the god and Vardak both, had settled herself on the ground nearby. She was of an age with Patak and muscular from years working the hammers in her forge. Clad in leathers, her chestnut-colored hair bound in a long braid, she rose to her feet as he entered.

Blademon spoke before Vardak had the opportunity to greet Makta. "I've been in contact with your Warleader. Your people will send soldiers to bolster your numbers once you cross the mountains in spring."

Vardak nodded as relief coursed through his veins. Sevic was reliable and a man of his word.

"There is more," Blademon continued. "A contingent of Murkor will join you as well. Ukase will handle communications between this army and theirs."

Vardak frowned in confusion. "Murkor? They would never turn against their own people without the Kal's involvement—"

"The Kal orchestrated their desertion," Blademon replied. "The Murkor understand what is at stake, as do we. You will have their aid, even if it means they fight their own."

"Thank you, sir."

Blademon chuckled mirthlessly. "Do not thank me yet, Vardak. I will ask much of you before this war is over." He disappeared in a flash, leaving Vardak alone with Makta.

"I suppose this means you're to stay here?" he asked her.

"Yes. My uncle wanted to be certain your army had a proper blade smith, and when Blademon told him you were overwintering here, he was eager to see what I might accomplish in the famed forges." She turned to retrieve a bundle from the floor behind her and hefted it over one shoulder. "I've brought my own hammers, of course."

"Of course." He paused to consider Blademon's words. "Did Sevic have any messages for me?"

"He said only to tell you he will defer to your command once the armies are united." She eyed him knowingly. "My uncle does not defer to *anyone*, Vardak. I do not know what Blademon told him, but he is mightily impressed by whatever you've done."

Vardak looked down, speechless. Sevic was proud, unyielding as steel, and nearly undefeated in combat. That he would defer to Vardak's command was unthinkable.

She patted him roughly on the shoulder as she passed. "You've gained his respect. Now, I have one other message to deliver, one I've been waiting three years to dispense with. Your brother can't avoid me any longer."

Vardak trailed her as they exited the room. She skittered across the floor toward the hearth—and his brother—without hesitation. "Patak!"

Patak turned around just in time for Makta to land a solid right hook to the left side of his jaw. He gaped at her, stunned into silence.

"You've had that coming for a good long while," she stated before turning toward the foyer with her chin held high.

Patak rubbed the side of his face and stared after her in shock. His face was already beginning to bruise from the impact of her fist. Given his brother's history with women, her reaction to his presence was unsurprising. He made a note to ask Patak if her proximity would become problematic—the last thing any of them needed was fighting within the ranks.

Maryn broke the silence with a snicker. "Fucking gods, Patak, what did you *do*?"

Patak muttered under his breath and turned away, a clear indication he wanted nothing more to do with the conversation.

Vardak wasn't privy to the details of his brother's love life, but he guessed Makta was justified in her actions. Patak's history with women was no secret within the Stronghold, and this wasn't the first time one of them had cornered him to make her displeasure known. He hoped for his brother's sake the burgeoning relationship with Emra would last. If it fractured, he'd likely find himself in exile alone.

CHAPTER TWENTY

RESTORING THE FORGES

Ravin observed the forges from his window seat across the plaza, loath to part from the warmth of the abandoned warehouse he and several of the wizards had secured as their headquarters. Fine tendrils of frost patterned the outer pane of glass, the sky was overcast, and he was certain snow would begin to fall by the end of the day. Several dozen smiths and other craftsmen were at work tidying the forges; sweeping away debris, inspecting anvils, arranging tools. Many sported cheeks reddened from cold.

They required fire from the nearby volcanic peak to operate the forges and he was in a position to secure it. He'd given Vardak his word, despite his misgivings. After his previous meeting with Solsticia, he wasn't eager to speak with her again. It was one of the few things he'd rather avoid—but he would not break his promise.

Reluctantly, he rose from the crate he'd been perched on and crossed the room to gather his cloak. To delay any further would risk darkness and icier temperatures as he made his descent from Flariel's shrine. It was past midday; he'd procrastinated enough.

As he donned his cloak and paused near the door to savor the last vestiges of warmth he'd encounter for some time, Tavesin and his ever-present pair of friends appeared. Tavesin was aware of his errand, and Ravin was certain the others knew of it, as well.

"Ravin, sir," Tavesin began, "we have something for you."

The smallest of the trio, a young Kamshati with inquisitive dark eyes, withdrew a disc from his pocket and placed it in Ravin's palm. Upon contact with the smooth stone, Ravin was immediately aware it was a magical device, though he could not discern its purpose without linking with it. He arched an eyebrow at the boy in question.

"It's meant to protect you from the cold, sir," he said shyly. "All you need to do is keep it with you. It works without magic."

"I've never encountered a relic such as this," Ravin replied with a smile. He recalled the boy had been working with the Drakkon to learn the process of creating such items. "Did you make this?"

"Yes, sir. I've made several, but Radosan gave the others to Emra for the scouts." The trio glanced surreptitiously around the room, and the boy lowered his voice. "Radosan doesn't know I made this one."

Ravin grinned. "You have my thanks. This will be our secret—your wizard friends don't need to know everything that goes on, now do they?"

"I told you he'd say that," Tavesin replied as he nudged the boy with his elbow.

As the trio laughed and began to chatter amongst themselves, Ravin pulled his cloak around his shoulders and exited the warehouse. The air was frigid, but as the boy had indicated, he did not feel its effects. It was as though he were enveloped in a bubble of summer, absconded with by magic months ago. With a pleased grin, he set off.

He'd never traveled to Flariel's shrine or Mount Daesan, but Emra had indicated a trail led northeast from the city and up the rocky slopes to his destination. Without a memory to guide him, he could not safely appear in the shrine while in the Aethereum. Before the boy's gift of the relic, he'd contemplated entering the Aethereum to make the journey on foot, if only to avoid prolonged exposure to the biting winter air. His concerns regarding the weather now moot, he decided to make the trek in the physical realm.

He made his way past the forges toward the northeastern quadrant of the city, which remained largely vacant, despite the army's presence in the city. Signs of the recent battle were more prevalent there—few buildings remained intact, and large scorch marks punctuated the streets where wooden structures had been set alight. Rubble from toppled stonework was strewn across his path, refuse and rubbish littered the road; the whole sector of the city had the sense of ruin and abandonment. It would take significant resources to rebuild portions of Daesan, and the northeastern sector seemed to have taken the brunt of the Soulless' initial assault.

The wind began to gust as he neared the city's wall and the gate that hung open like a gaping maw, revealing a broad dirt track beyond. He was aware of the wind's force as it sought to sink its icy fangs into his exposed flesh, but thanks to the relic he carried, it only managed to swirl his cloak and ruffle his hair. The creation of such devices was not a talent he possessed, but he understood what the boy had done was remarkable. Relics that could be activated without the use of magic were exceedingly rare.

He followed the road through the gate as it began to wind its way along the mountain's flank. The path became steeper and rocky as he continued. Gouts of foul-smelling vapor issued from jagged vents rent in the earth, and as he continued, the sensation of heat beneath his boots became discernable, though not uncomfortable. The mountain was as volatile as the goddess whose shrine he sought.

After an hour of climbing, Ravin paused in his ascent to catch his breath and study the landscape from his new, higher vantage point. The city of Daesan was nestled at the mountain's base; beyond it, vast plains stretched toward the horizon in three directions. Far to the south, he spied what appeared to be another city. He committed the observation to memory. They'd need to trade for supplies before long, and a nearby settlement would prove useful.

Rested, he trudged on. The path wound through a series of steep switchbacks before it reached a slight decline. The shrine came into view near the mountain's apex, wedged between a pair of large boulders. Beyond the shrine, the cone of the peak was visible, alight from within by its molten core. Acrid smoke billowed from the cone, dense and black against the backdrop of the gray sky.

The shrine itself was little more than a marble statue depicting Flariel with a small slab in which to place one's offerings near its base. The Fire Maiden's sculpted hands held a small, oval mirror of smoked glass.

Ravin drew a pensive breath as he stood before the statue; to call his mother from Flariel's shrine might be considered an affront to Flariel, but he wasn't prepared to face the Fire Maiden directly without

Solsticia's presence. Vardak's tales of his interactions with Flariel gave him reason for concern.

With a shake of his head, he pocketed the relic and was immediately assaulted by the biting wind. He pressed his palms to the glass of the mirror and silently evoked his mother's name, then stepped back and grasped the relic once more. Sudden warmth blossomed around him as he shivered violently. The weather was growing fouler as the afternoon wore on.

Solsticia appeared moments later. She towered above him and the marble statuary beside her. Immune to the wind's effects, her midnight blue skirts remained motionless even as Ravin continued to be buffeted by the gusts. Her golden eyes met his with a frown.

"My sister will be furious that you've used her shrine to summon me, Ravin."

He shrugged. "It couldn't be helped. I need to speak with you, and there doesn't happen to be a proper temple in this area."

Solsticia sighed. "She may prove lenient since you are my son, but don't count on it. Why have you called me?"

In truth, he'd called her only as a means of support for his discussion with Flariel, but he felt obligated to give her something more. She would not remain behind when he summoned the Fire Maiden without further reason for doing so. Only one thing came to mind, and as much as he detested what he must say, he pressed on.

"I came to apologize. I've had time enough to consider Minora's involvement in the events of my life, and I can't continue to blame you for what she's done to me."

"Oh, Ravin…" She was on her knees in a flash. Her arms encircled him as she drew him into a fierce embrace. "If there had been any other way to spare your life, I would never have agreed to her meddling."

"I know."

She rocked back on her heels, and he was stunned to see tears in her eyes. "If there is ever anything I can do for you, all you need is to ask. I owe you that much, Ravin."

He suppressed a smile; his plan had worked better than he'd anticipated. "I've also come to speak with Flariel on Vardak's behalf. The forges—"

"I will call her," Solsticia replied swiftly as she stood. "It will spare you her anger for misappropriating her shrine."

Before he was able to form a response, Flariel appeared beside her sister, her molten countenance swathed in flame. Her incandescent gaze flicked between Solsticia and her mortal son, eyes narrowed in suspicion.

"What is the meaning of this?" she demanded.

"I borrowed your shrine in order to speak with my son," Solsticia replied. "Surely, you understand?"

Flariel crossed her arms, but relented. "Of course. Why have you called me, sister?"

Solsticia gestured toward Ravin, an indication she wished for him to speak. "I came on Emra's behalf," he began, careful to omit Vardak's name to the goddess who loathed him. "Her army is in need of fire for the forges."

Flariel's features twisted into a frown. "I understand the army's need, and I'm aware there are a number of smiths amongst your ranks, but I will not provide what you seek without conditions."

Ravin steeled himself and bit back several choice curses. It would serve no one's interests if he provoked Flariel's temper. "What are your demands?"

"I will provide fire so long as Vardak—your *general*—does not sully my forges with his presence."

Solsticia groaned, exasperated. "Will you never set aside your petty feud for the betterment of this cause? We both know what is at stake, Flariel."

Flariel shrugged indifferently. "Vardak must agree to my demand, or your smiths will be without my flames. Those are my terms."

"I'll speak with him," Ravin promised.

"And I'll be watching you, mage," Flariel replied coldly. "I will know when he agrees—and if he breaks his word." Without waiting for a reply, Flariel vanished in a shower of sparks.

Solsticia shook her head in frustration. "Flariel will never change. I will speak with my other siblings about her 'conditions.' I doubt they'll be pleased." She sighed. "Take care of yourself, Ravin."

He made the return trip to Daesan within the Aethereum, able to transport himself directly to the smith's guild hall. He found Vardak within the innermost room of the ground floor, where he was speaking with several scouts. As he took note of Ravin's presence in the doorway, he dismissed the others.

Ravin waited until they'd gone before he crossed the room. "I've spoken to Flariel."

Vardak's expression was wary. "I fear to learn what she's said."

Ravin chuckled. "She is fickle. Even Solsticia was displeased by her words—but I have secured fire for the smiths. There is only one condition."

Vardak glowered at the floor. "That's no gods-damned surprise. What did she want?"

"The agreement you will not set foot within the forges."

Vardak nodded tersely, unable to mask his anger. "Fucking gods, I should have known! Fine. If that's what is required, I'll agree to her terms. We need those forges."

"I'll inform the smiths, if you'd like," Ravin offered. He understood Vardak's frustration keenly and would do all in his power to assist. The gods' meddling was tiresome and petty.

"Yes. Thank you. And if you see Flariel again, tell her I won't act her willing pawn forever."

Ravin made his way into the wintery city once more. The forges, only a short walk across the plaza from the smiths' guild hall, were bustling even though it would soon grow dark. More people crowded the space than was necessary for the smiths and their assistants, but it wasn't until Ravin pushed his way past some of the onlookers that he understood the reason for the unexpected throng.

True to her word, streams of molten fire now flowed through channels toward the forges, but it was not Flariel's generous act that had drawn the people's attention. At the center of the space were Blademon and Aeon. The two gods performed a blessing ritual at each smithing station; their words, though quiet, carried across the bitter air.

Ravin was stunned. He'd heard of Blademon favoring a smith on occasion, or Aeon offering his protection to a mortal in peril, but he'd never encountered a tale of the pair working together in such a manner.

He wondered if his mother were behind their unusual benevolence, or if there was more at play than the gods had let on.

"The products of this forge shall be blessed in battle. May their bearers rejoice in the sharpest blades and stoutest armor," Blademon intoned.

"And the items crafted here shall be doubly blessed," Aeon replied. "Armor created here shall protect the wearer from the darkest of death magics."

Aeon's feline eyes met Blademon's. The two studied one another for a time, nodded, then abruptly vanished.

"Well," said the burly man standing beside Ravin, "that was certainly unexpected."

Ravin scanned the space for Emra or one of her guards, and found her not far away. He wasn't certain what the gods had said before his arrival, but he needed to know. With each new instance of the gods' involvement in the war, his unease grew. He elbowed his way through the dispersing crowd until he reached her.

"It seems we have you to thank for Flariel's cooperation," Emra said as he drew near. "Vardak told us you planned to pay her a visit."

He nodded. "I did, but I wasn't expecting the others' help."

"I don't like it," she replied. "I've faced the Soulless in battles four times, and never have the Immortals deigned to take an active role in my army's defense."

"For what it's worth, I don't like it, either."

CHAPTER TWENTY-ONE

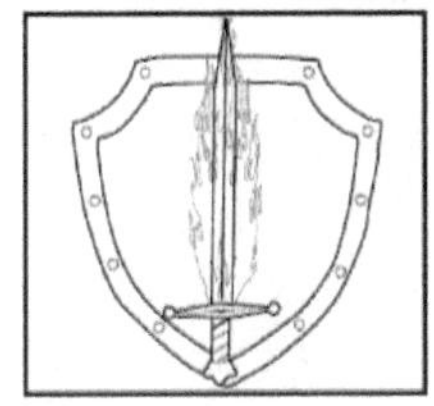

AEON'S VOW

Weak daylight filtered through the gaps between the blanket used to cover the room's single window and the wall. Emra sat up blearily, the vestiges of an unpleasant dream replaying in her mind. Beside her, Patak was sprawled facedown, his head supported by a wad of blankets and one of his forearms. He continued to snore, undisturbed by her movement. She smiled, thankful he'd come into her life despite the odds they faced. His fierce optimism often overshadowed her doubts—it was exactly what she needed.

She rose carefully so as not to wake him. She'd slept fully dressed in the hopes of warding off the winter chill, but as soon as she left the warmth of their blankets, the cold struck her viciously. She shivered as she pulled on her boots and made her way toward the window.

Pulling the makeshift curtain aside, she noted the pane was frosted both inside and out. Near its center, she was afforded a warped view of the plaza and the forges beyond, with the smiths' guild hall looming in the background. The building they'd taken as their personal quarters had once been a storage facility of some kind, but the walls were solid, the roof intact, and it was at the heart of Daesan. A number of craftsmen were at work near the forges, while their assistants scurried about on various errands. She wove her long blond hair into a braid as she watched the folk in the plaza begin their daily tasks.

Patak stirred behind her and muttered unintelligibly. Suppressing a laugh, she let the blanket fall across the window once more and turned to find him stretching. With both his upper and lower body aligned, he nearly spanned the length of the small room. After a moment, he pushed himself upright to resume his usual position. The dark bruise on the left side of his face appeared painful, but he seemed unbothered by it this morning.

As the blankets fell away, he grimaced. "Gods, it's cold! How do your people stand it?"

"During winter, we typically remain indoors next to a roaring hearth." She grinned. "You're not in the desert any longer, Patak."

His eyebrows rose as he stared at her, nonplussed. "I'm keenly aware of that. Where might we find a decent fire? And where did I leave my damned cloak?"

"I'm expected at the smiths' guild soon. Your brother wanted to discuss priorities for weapons and armor. A fire's likely built there."

"So long as Makta's busy at her forge, I'll accompany you."

Emra laughed softly, studying the bruise on the side of his face. "I'm not certain what your history is with her, but she claimed you deserved her wrath. I've known you long enough to believe her."

Patak gaped in mock outrage. "You would side with *her*, Em? Whatever have I done to deserve your ire?"

She grinned, unable to maintain a pretense of anger with him. She strode toward him and gingerly touched the bruise that marred his handsome features. "You know I could never be upset with you."

"Then perhaps it's best you stay clear of Makta." He tilted her chin upward with one finger and gazed down at her, desire in his blue eyes. Their lips met. She lost herself in his embrace for some time.

Finally, she stepped back with a smile. "I'd best go. I'll expect more of that from you later."

His grin was mischievous. "Count on it, Em. I'll meet you at the guild hall, provided it's safe and Makta-free."

With an amused shake of her head, she made her way out of the room, into the foyer, and toward the exit door. Her cloak was hung on a crooked peg beside the door, while Patak's was tossed unceremoniously on the floor beneath it. She stooped to pick it up and hang it on the unoccupied peg. He'd be looking for it before he ventured outdoors.

A light snow had begun falling by the time she stepped outside. She drew the hood of her cloak up to protect her face from the frigid air and glanced toward the forges. She spied Makta near its heart, clad in a heavy leather apron as she hammered her latest blade into shape.

Emra knew Makta and Patak were once lovers and understood from their tense interactions that theirs had not been an amicable split. She prayed that whatever had transpired between them would not interfere with the army's operations—or create a wedge between herself and the man she loved. Patak did not wish to speak of his time with Makta, and she would respect his privacy unless the matter became pertinent. She believed he'd tell her his story in time.

Tearing her gaze away from the forges, she strode quickly toward the smiths' guild hall and the promise of warmth it held. As she pushed open the door and began shaking the snow from her cloak, the ethereal figure of Aeon materialized before her. She stiffened as she studied the god's feline features; with charcoal gray fur and blue-white eyes, Aeon cut a striking, yet eerie figure. His cat-like ears twitched as he smirked with amusement.

"Your general is within. I have asked him to summon the remainder of your officers. There is a matter we must discuss."

She nodded as unease twisted her gut. Aeon's presence within her camp did not bode well. "What is this about?"

His furry tail lashed the air in either agitation or amusement, she was uncertain which. "I'll explain once the others arrive. Come. You're cold."

He disappeared into the room Vardak had set up as his command center, where the hearth was ablaze. The warmth was inviting, yet she was reluctant to follow his lead. Aeon was often considered a harbinger of strife and suffering, and few people sought his guidance. Even the Felenes found their patron god's presence uncomfortable.

She hung her cloak near the exit door, braced herself, then followed Aeon toward the hearth. Vardak stood near the hearth and nodded to her as she approached, while Aeon seated himself on the far side of the room.

"Is Patak coming?" Vardak asked quietly. He was on edge, though she knew he'd never admit it. He liked Aeon's intrusion even less than she.

"Yes. Makta's at the forge, so he has no reason to avoid this place."

Vardak snorted. "For all his bravado, he's certainly terrified of her. It's typical for Patak."

Emra lifted her eyebrows in question, but before Vardak could elaborate, Danian and Maryn trudged inside. Maryn was grinning, but his expression quickly faltered as he took note of the divine presence within the room. He made his way toward Vardak and muttered darkly under his breath, while Danian leaned against the wall nearest the door, unconcerned by the cold.

Moments later, the exit door opened again, this time to admit Patak. He opted to keep his cloak fixed in place even as he moved to stand near the hearth alongside Emra. He shivered visibly, though she was uncertain if his chill was the result of the weather or Aeon.

"Why is he here?" Patak whispered.

"Your guess is as good as mine. He wouldn't say."

Patak frowned, concern etching his brow. "Was blessing the forges yesterday not enough?"

She shrugged, but her attention was diverted as the door opened once more. The two Airess entered, followed by Ravin, Aziarah, and Radosan. Neither wizard nor mage appeared affected by the cold, and she assumed they both possessed one of the relics young Badolo had manufactured. She smiled faintly; the boy's skill was remarkable. Perhaps if she survived the war, she could mentor him further. In her first incarnation, she'd been a Yellow wizard, after all.

Aeon rose to his feet as the others entered the room. Without preamble, he began another blessing ritual, one Emra recognized only from history books and legend. Her eyes widened at the realization—Aeon was offering his unconditional protection to everyone gathered within the room. She studied the faces around her; most appeared confused, but Ravin was clearly frightened. He understood the implications inherent in the god's actions.

"Em, is he…?" Patak whispered in her ear.

She glanced up at him and nodded once, her body rigid with fear. "It's a protection ritual."

He blanched. "Why? There must be a reason for this."

Aeon concluded the blessing and fixed his blue-white eyes on Patak. "There is a very good reason I've come, Patak. I do not offer absolute protection to mortals without great need—or a dire cause."

Emra's stomach clenched in terror. In her past lives, Aeon had never deigned to grant her divine defense. His actions could mean only one thing.

"Has he broken free?" her voice came out in a strangled rasp.

Aeon shook his head. "He remains caged—for now. One of the Soulless summoned a powerful magic in the depths of the night, a magic necessary to weaken his prison. It was successful, and he has shielded the tower and its inhabitants from our divine sight."

Emra stared at the floor, stunned. She was only dimly aware of Patak's arm as it encircled her waist while her thoughts raced. For all her power and experience, she'd never entertained the notion that the Soulless would succeed in breaking their master free. The Nameless' tale and the threat it posed was supposed to be a mere tale to frighten children into behaving. It was not meant to become reality.

"You believe they will succeed." Ravin's voice echoed through the room.

"He has grown powerful, as we knew he one day would," Aeon replied. "There is little else we gods can do until he breaks free of his prison. We are sworn against engaging in mortal conflicts—and this war remains a mortal affair until the Nameless' return. We may act within the bounds of our vows, which allows us to provide guidance and bless mortals as we desire. Blademon and I have blessed your forges, while Solsticia and Minora have given aid to the mages. Ukase works with the rogue Murkor, while Flariel provides fire for your smiths. These things cannot directly sway the tides of battle."

"You didn't answer my question," Ravin growled.

Aeon hesitated, pausing to study each mortal around him in turn. Finally, he said, "We do not know if he will escape his prison, but the events of last night make it far more likely."

"I know well enough how Blademon's blessings work," Vardak said evenly. "Have you granted your protection to others?"

Aeon's expression was unreadable. "Several Murkor and…several Serpentus."

Emra snapped her chin up to meet Aeon's gaze. "Serpentus? Please don't tell me she—"

Aeon held up one furred mitt, and she fell silent. He glanced between Vardak and Patak, then said, "Dranamir has performed the ritual for a second time. The human prisoners taken during the Murkor campaign in Balotica are no longer human."

She clapped one hand over her mouth as bile rose into her throat. Patak grew rigid beside her, but it was Vardak who spoke next.

"My ancestors suffered greatly by her hand. I will make certain the Serpentus are welcome in the Stronghold once she has been destroyed." The ferocity in his tone was startling; she'd never heard him speak in anger before.

"You cannot face her, Vardak," Ravin replied, "but I can."

Aeon nodded at Ravin knowingly. "Yes. Minora's designs have led you here for this purpose."

Ravin glowered and looked away, but said nothing more.

"If the Nameless god breaks free, you will know." Aeon shook his head sadly. "Emra, I would like to speak with you privately now that this business is concluded." He gestured toward the door to the smaller chamber Blademon had used on his previous visit, then strode across the room and ducked inside.

Patak withdrew his arm, but she grasped his fingers tightly in her own for a moment. "I doubt this will take long."

He nodded, and reluctantly she made her way toward the other room and Aeon.

As soon as she entered, he said, "Close the door. The others should not overhear what I must say."

Heart thudding in her chest, she complied. Aeon paused to gather his thoughts while her own became a frenetic whirlwind of questions and fears. Why had he singled her out? What did he want of her? What more could the gods ask of her weary soul?

"Emra, I am prepared to grant your request on the condition the Tower of Obsidian is destroyed," Aeon said, bringing the chaos in her mind to an abrupt halt.

She stared at him for several seconds, uncomprehending. "Do you mean I'll finally be granted a respite from this wretched cycle?"

He smiled sadly. "If you recall, I tried to persuade you to follow a different course. The cycle is of your own creation."

"I know, but I would like it to end."

"Yes." His smile broadened. "If the tower is destroyed, I will grant your request."

"Is it not enough to defeat the Soulless once more? Why the tower?" She demanded.

"Solsticia's son can provide you with the answer to your question," he replied. "I will not. Speak with him, and perhaps you will understand."

Aeon faded from sight to leave her alone within the small room. She sighed heavily and opened the door to find Ravin was already gone.

CHAPTER TWENTY-TWO

EXALTATION

"It is time." Garin's voice echoed across the room as he studied each of the other Soulless in turn. A faint smile curled his pale lips while a zealous light shone within his eyes. He paced the length of the room in front of the oval mirror in its twisted frame as he gauged their reactions.

Dranamir's pulse accelerated with the pronouncement, and she straightened from her position leaning against one of the room's glass cases. They had all spent countless years working toward this moment, honing their skills in preparation for this auspicious night. Every piece was finally in place, the hours and years of toil and strife about to come to fruition.

Her gaze flicked toward the dark mirror behind Garin, but there was no sign of the Nameless within. Disappointment flared into sharp anger. If it were truly time, why hadn't Garin called to their master?

Beside her, Kama crossed his arms and sneered down his long nose. "Patience, Dranamir."

She clenched her fists and glared at the tall Kamshati. "Out of us all, *I* have awaited this moment the longest. Do not council patience, Kama. I've waited long enough."

"And of us all, I have sacrificed the most," Garin replied ominously. "Savor the anticipation, Dranamir. We will be rewarded accordingly once our master is freed."

"We will, indeed," Dranamir sneered. The Nameless had promised her a place at his side, as his second, his confidante, and greatest champion. For all his bluster and the brand he bore, Garin could not boast the same.

Unperturbed, Garin turned to examine the array of items beneath the mirror. There was a large urn, decorated with gemstones and gold filigree that Alyra had brought with her; it was the elixir she'd crafted during the recent new moon. Next to it was a wide cuff made of green and gray snakeskin, Dranamir's contribution and the means for the Nameless god to assume control over the Serpentus. A pair of enormous swords, crafted of the black metal favored by the Murkor leaned against the wall. Kama had them designed specifically for the Nameless' use on the battlefield. They were too heavy and unwieldy for any mortal warrior, but in the hands of a god, they would prove deadly. Garin's gift was nowhere to be seen.

Dranamir frowned at Garin's back, angered that he believed himself above making a proper offering to their god. Certainly, he was responsible for performing the ritual that would ultimately tear the walls of the Nameless' prison asunder, but their god was not one to be trifled with. The ritual alone would not be sufficient to appease his thirst for power, but if Garin failed to please him, it was one less Soulless rival she must contend with. She would not miss his patronizing ways nor his false sense of superiority.

After several moments, Garin knelt before the mirror and closed his eyes. "I will begin."

Dranamir sensed as he tapped deeply into his magical power and began to weave a complicated pattern of malevolent energy. The pulsation of the magical currants thrummed through the room, invisible, yet potent. Her ears popped as the pressure changed, while her skin crawled in response to the disquieting sensation. In all the years she'd spent mastering her own magical abilities, she'd never encountered anything to compare with Garin's display.

Strands of magic connected him to the mirror on the wall, at first merely sensed, then as his work progressed, they became tangible threads of shadow. The mirror's surface flickered to life, and the Nameless god's yellow eyes appeared within, alight from within by anticipation.

At long last…

The Nameless' voice thundered through the room, a shockwave greater than the magic Garin continued to summon. Dranamir clutched the edge of the glass case behind her in a desperate bid to remain upright as the unseen onslaught to her senses continued. Across the room, Alyra fell to her knees, weeping. Kama braced himself and kept his footing.

The image in the mirror abruptly changed to reveal a tidy, coastal town comprised of sandstone buildings with colorful tiled roofs. The architecture was clearly Kamshati; each structure sported arched doorways and panoramic windows. Beyond the town, an expanse of calm, blue-green water stretched to the western horizon and beyond. As she watched, the water became agitated, then rapidly receded from the sandy shoreline. Moments later, a towering wave appeared, rushing toward the settlement at breakneck velocity. People began to emerge from the buildings, running from the sea's unexpected fury.

The mirror flickered to reveal the yellow eyes once more. The Nameless god laughed darkly before he disappeared into its depths.

Another image replaced him, this time revealing an aerial view of the Gray Mountains. Dranamir was uncertain of the exact location they were being shown, but she recognized the dark entrance of a mine shaft below. The image shuddered violently. When it stilled once more, a great crack had opened in the earth between two of the mountain peaks. A cascade of snow and boulders careened along the nearby slopes, burying everything in its path. The mine shaft was covered in several feet of debris.

The eyes reappeared, and this time the shadowy outline of the Nameless god's face could be seen.

The seals are breaking. I will be freed.

Another flicker, another image, this time looking skyward. It was evening, the sky a velvet backdrop to thousands of unfamiliar stars. Broad-leaved trees framed the image, strange and unfamiliar to her. Dozens of fiery streaks shot through the sky to explode in a violent shower of sparks overhead. The trees shuddered, then broke like brittle twigs from the force of the explosion.

The images within the mirror's twisted frame began to change rapidly with each successive image. Scenes of destruction accompanied distraught visages of people, those undoubtedly affected by the devastation the breaking of the seals wrought upon the land. Storms raged, fires erupted, the earth cracked and heaved.

The legends stated the other Immortals had lent portions of their own power in the creation of the Nameless god's prison, a safeguard against his ability to break free. Yet over the span of centuries, her god had devised a means to do just that. She gazed at the chaotic scenes captured within the mirror's twisted frame, exultant by the fact that he would soon grace her with his physical presence for the first time.

The eyes reappeared in the glass, aglow with a fierce light.

Give me the Twilight Stone. It is time.

Garin rose unsteadily to his feet and stumbled toward the mirror. He reached into a pocket to withdraw the talisman, a chunk of smooth onyx carved in the likeness of a wolf. Even from her position across the room, Dranamir noted his fatigue. His hands shook, sweat beaded upon his brow, and his pale skin was nearly colorless. Despite his exhaustion, Garin carried out his orders while his magic continued to rage around them.

He pressed the Twilight Stone against the mirror's surface. The glass rippled as the talisman disappeared within. The Nameless god laughed.

The mirror shifted again and again, each time displaying a new scene of mayhem and death. A tremor rocked the foundations of the tower as an image of the Wasted Land and the far perimeter of the Murkor encampment came into view. The ground split along the northern edge of Blackstone Chasm, cutting a jagged rent into the landscape. The crack stopped paces from the camp's perimeter, where a mass of milling and agitated Murkor could be seen. Amongst them, several Serpentus stood silently, expressions unreadable.

As the image shifted again, the tremors ceased. Dranamir regained her footing and stared at the yellow eyes within the mirror's confines in awe. Until that moment, she'd been unaware the destruction playing out on the glass occurred in real-time.

The shadowed face trapped within the dark pane smiled grimly. **Garin. Place your hands upon the mirror and receive your greatest reward.**

Without hesitation, Garin obeyed. Dranamir watched, a flare of jealousy coursing through her as the small man prepared to accept their master's first gift. She was the first, his chosen. Garin should not be honored over her.

Garin placed his hands on the dark glass. The eyes on the other side winked out of existence while the mirror shattered. Shards of glass tinkled upon the tiled floor as his magic abruptly came to an end.

Dranamir sensed a change in the room, a presence far greater than her own, but only the four Soulless remained. She was certain the presence belonged to the Nameless god, though he remained elusive to her sight. Frustrated, she clenched her jaw and narrowed her eyes in Garin's direction.

The small man had not moved since the mirror disintegrated with his touch, but now he straightened and moved awkwardly, as though unfamiliar with his own limbs. Slowly, he turned to face the others, and as his eyes opened, Dranamir's previous anger evaporated. The eyes that looked at her from within Garin's pale features were the same yellow eyes they'd seen within the mirror. Her unspoken prayers had been answered.

"It will take some time, weeks perhaps, before I regain the strength to shed this flimsy shell," he said. "I branded Garin long ago for this very purpose. I required a vessel, an obedient servant that would not balk when the time came." A dark chuckle issued from his throat. "Garin sought power above all else. He accepted the brand without hesitation, and now I have consumed his very essence."

For the first time in her life, Dranamir knelt before an entity of her own volition. He alone was deserving of her respect—there would never be another.

He turned toward the objects gathered beneath the mirror. He picked up the snakeskin cuff, a cruel smile on his lips as he secured it to his left wrist. "The Serpentus are a fine gift, Dranamir."

Her heart fluttered in her chest with the compliment. "Thank you, my lord."

"The weapons, too," he continued. "It's a pity I am forced to wait before I might wield them."

Kama muttered his gratitude from where he knelt not far away. Unlike Dranamir, he kept his head bowed, but whether in deference or fear, she was uncertain.

He stooped to pick up the jeweled urn and carefully removed its lid. He inhaled deeply, then took a tentative sip. "Yes, this will do nicely." He gulped more of the elixir without pausing for breath, then turned to face Alyra with a satisfied smile. "You have also done well."

"Thank you, master," Alyra replied through tears of elation.

He stretched his arms behind him and drew another breath, his borrowed body seeming to stretch and grow rapidly with the motion. "Ahhh. Perhaps my strength will return more quickly than I've anticipated."

The yellow eyes scanned the room, then fell upon her. "Dranamir, come here."

Her pulse thundered in her ears as she stood and made her way toward the Nameless god. She would obey, no matter his command. Though he occupied Garin's body, already he'd increased in stature and now stood taller than she did.

A pleased smile creased his face. "I must take you to the temple," he said in a low tone. "Only there can I fulfill my vow to you."

She nodded, her mouth suddenly dry. She'd waited years for this moment, decades… An unforeseen fear gripped her belly as she wondered if she would live up to his expectations.

He glanced at Kama and Alyra, who continued to kneel on the floor. "Go about your duties. We shall return in time."

His arm encircled her waist. Immediately, she felt as though they were plummeting to a great depth at a rapid speed, then just as abruptly, the sensation vanished. She blinked in wonder at her new surroundings. They were within the heart of his temple, steps away from the dais and its silvery mirror.

He turned to look directly into her eyes, and she felt heat rush through her body at the desire she saw in his gaze. He traced her jawline with one pale finger. "You've kept your purity throughout the years. I promised to make you my queen if you did, and I do not break my word."

She trembled with anticipation, her breath quickened, and her pulse accelerated to a wild pace. She understood what he demanded of her, and she would give it willingly. Since the day he'd first reached her through the void, she'd been awaiting this moment, this exaltation.

"I am yours."

He grinned knowingly. "Yes. I have never encountered another soul as purely murderous as yours, Dranamir. It is a beautiful thing to behold. I have long desired you."

"I have awaited this moment since the night you spoke through my dreams," she whispered. "I am ready."

He touched the side of her face, a tender gesture at odds with his dire reputation. "Good."

CHAPTER TWENTY-THREE

FURY AND FLAMES

Ravin jolted awake, certain something was amiss. All was quiet in the warehouse the wizards had taken as their temporary headquarters, but the air was cloying, oppressive. He felt along the floor near his blankets in search of his cloak and boots, while soft snores and quiet breathing filled the darkness around him. He located his boots and pulled them on, then realized Badolo's relic was within his trouser pocket. The cloak was unnecessary.

He rose and carefully picked his way through the sleeping forms of the wizards, drawn toward the wide windows that lined the front room of the building. Once he was out of the designated sleeping area, he created a magical light to illuminate his path. His sense of unease continued to deepen as he peered through the frosted panes toward the forges in the plaza beyond.

A sliver of moon hung in the sky, wreathed in thin clouds. The plaza was empty, save for a pair of watchmen on patrol, the city silent as most of the temporary inhabitants slumbered. Nothing appeared out of place, yet he couldn't shake the sensation that something was terribly wrong. He frowned in consternation and wondered if this was another of Minora's undesired machinations.

Abruptly, the ground trembled beneath his feet. He threw one hand toward the window sill in order to keep his balance as the tremor passed, then glanced over his shoulder as murmurs erupted in the sleeping quarters. Dust continued to rain from the rafters long after the earth grew still. He returned to the other room and scanned the faces of those shaken awake.

He motioned to Tavesin, who was sitting upright with a puzzled expression on his young face. The boy grabbed his cloak and pulled it around his shoulders as he made his way toward Ravin, rubbing sleep from his eyes.

"Ravin, what—?"

The floor rocked beneath them again, cutting off his words. Ravin grasped the door frame to prevent himself from falling as the building shook around them. The ceiling groaned ominously. The heavy beams overhead began to crack and splinter.

"Taven, shield!" Ravin cried out.

He prayed the boy understood his intent, but he had no time to explain as the roof began to collapse. Wooden beams and stone tiles tumbled around them as the walls began to crumble. Ravin knelt reflexively, his arms over his head, as he erected a shield around himself. His defensive magic was sufficient to protect him, but it was paltry compared to Tavesin's ability. He squeezed his eyes shut and hoped Tavesin would be able to spare the others from harm as the earth's assault on their dwelling continued.

When the quake finally subsided, Ravin opened his eyes to find the building littered with rubble. One of the walls had toppled and most of the roof was caved in, but none of the wizards were injured. Beside him, Tavesin crouched with his eyes closed tightly in concentration. A brilliant blue shield enveloped the area.

Ravin smiled and grasped the boy's shoulder. "Taven, it's over."

Tavesin startled, but released his shield. He turned to scan the room, eyes wide with shock. "What happened?"

"You saved many of your colleagues," Ravin replied quietly.

"I know, but what *happened*, Ravin?"

"An earthquake." Slowly, he rose to his feet and became aware of shouts from elsewhere in the city for the first time. "I'm going to find Emra and learn how she fares."

"I'm coming with you." Tavesin glanced at the others, then the gaping hole where the roof used to be. His face paled in the soft glow of Ravin's light. "What's that?"

Ravin followed his gaze. Streams of fire crossed the night sky, trails of ash and debris in their wake. His mouth suddenly dry and heart racing, he looked away and sought Radosan. "I need to find Emra. I fear your skills will be needed by others before the night is over."

Radosan nodded silently and began to gather his belongings.

Ravin turned to Tavesin, who watched him intently. "Come. If events are unfolding as I suspect, I may need your shield a second time."

Tavesin followed him silently as they picked their way through the rubble toward the plaza. The forges appeared unscathed by the violent upheaval, though several nearby buildings leaned precariously and threatened to fall. The smith's guild hall looked to be undamaged, but as his gaze traveled to the opposite side of the plaza, his heart sank. The smaller buildings—one of which Emra had taken for herself—were flattened.

Without a word to Tavesin, he broke into a run and intensified his magical light as he neared the downed structure. He sensed magic in use nearby. He prayed it was hers, that she'd managed to protect herself and Patak from the devastation. He closed his eyes briefly, pinpointed the magic's source, then began to carefully lift debris away from the site. Tavesin joined him a moment later. Together, they stacked the rubble in a heap on one side of the plaza and held it in place with their magic.

It took several minutes before Emra became visible. Her arms encircled Patak's bare torso, and the two were shrouded in a thin, silvery shield. As soon as the remainder of the debris had been relocated, her shield vanished, and she turned to face them.

"How does the mountain fare?" she rasped.

"The mountain?" Ravin echoed. "It was an earthquake—"

She shook her head wearily and clutched Patak's arm as they made their way toward him. "Earthquakes are often precursors to the mountain's eruption," she said before her words were swallowed by a wracking cough.

Ravin nodded. "I see. Taven and I will see about the mountain. You need Radosan to have a look at you."

She grimaced. "It's merely dust…in my lungs." She coughed again with a shake of her head.

"Em, he's right." Patak glanced worriedly at her, then met Ravin's eyes. "I'll make certain she's seen by a healer."

Ravin watched the pair for a moment as they made their way toward the demolished warehouse, his thoughts upon Adalin. Once he assessed the damage the quake had wrought and made certain the nearby volcanic peak was at peace, he vowed to return to Delucha. He suspected the devastation was not limited to Daesan, but prayed he was wrong.

"Ravin?" Tavesin's voice cut through his reverie.

He shook himself from his thoughts and managed a smile for the teenager. "It'll be faster if we travel through the Aethereum."

Tavesin nodded and created a portal for them both. Once inside, Ravin led him to the city's outskirts and the base of the trail he'd ascended toward Flariel's shrine. From within the magical realm, nothing appeared amiss, but he knew it would take time to manifest the results of the night's events. Abrupt changes in the physical realm were never immediately reflected within the magical one.

He hesitated as he gazed toward the peak, illuminated starkly by the Aethereum's unearthly glow. "I don't know what we'll find, Taven. Be ready for anything."

Tavesin nodded but said nothing.

"Do you have your relic?"

Another nod. Ravin smiled, relieved at the news, then created an exit portal.

Smoke assaulted his senses as they stepped onto the trail at the mountain's base. His eyes watered and his lungs wheezed in response. He coughed and squinted toward the summit. A red-orange glow illuminated the column of smoke from behind, while a geyser of molten fire shot skyward from the cone.

He sent a blast of air through the smoke that blocked their view, temporarily displacing it. The glow was the result of a river of magma that cascaded down the mountain's flank. It was headed directly toward their location and the city.

"Shit." Ravin glanced at Tavesin warily; preventing the stream of lava from wreaking further havoc on Daesan was beyond his capabilities alone. "Taven, we can stop this. We can save Daesan, but we must link to do so. Do you understand?"

He loathed asking Tavesin to sacrifice more of his lost childhood, but there was no one else who possessed the strength to help him. And with the Moon's Eye to bolster his power, Tavesin was one of the strongest magic wielders Ravin had encountered, excepting himself. A link—a shared magical bond—was temporary, but he feared what Tavesin would uncover about his past. The boy had endured enough heartbreak and bloodshed for a lifetime; he hated himself for adding to the tally.

"I've never linked with another wiz—mage before," Tavesin replied quietly. "I've read about it, and I think I understand how it works."

"Link with your relic first," Ravin instructed, his gaze fixed on the lava flow as it drew ever nearer.

While he awaited Tavesin's response, he withdrew the eagle-shaped talisman he'd acquired in the depths beneath Delucha's palace from his pocket. The talisman's innate power would prove useless against their molten foe, but he could still use it to enhance his own for a time. The magic trapped within the golden stone sang through his veins as he connected to it. He was only dimly aware of Tavesin's next words.

"I'm ready."

"I'll initiate the linkage. While we're connected, you will... You will likely see pieces of my past I'd rather not speak of," Ravin explained with a cough. "I'm sorry, Taven, but it cannot be helped."

"I know." Tavesin's voice was forlorn, yet determined. "We can't stop the fire without linking. I'm ready," he said again.

Ravin drew an unsteady breath. "Follow my lead, Taven. I will guide you as best I can."

He opened himself and sought Tavesin. When the boy responded, their combined magic—and that of the relics—collided with enough force the air was driven from his lungs and he lost his balance. He gasped and rose unsteadily to his feet while Tavesin did the same.

He stared at Tavesin, stunned, for several seconds as he was inundated with the boy's thoughts and memories. Tavesin was far stronger than he'd anticipated. It was little wonder he'd been singled out by Minora. Ravin had connected with another only twice in his life, but never had the other been graced with the magical prowess the dark-haired boy possessed.

He cleared his throat and shook his head in an attempt to focus. "Gods, Taven. That was…unexpected."

"It isn't always like this?" The echo of a dozen questions followed his words, sensed rather than spoken through their bond.

"No. But we…We can discuss this later." He turned to face the mountain once more and was alarmed to find the fiery sludge was nearly upon them. "Lend me some of your strength, Taven. And if the fire draws too near, shield us both."

"What will you do?"

Ravin grimaced. "I'm going to create a rainstorm."

Momentary panic flooded their link as Tavesin understood what he intended to do. Taking control of the weather, even for a short time, required vast amounts of power. If Ravin had misjudged their combined might, it was likely he'd be consumed by the process and find himself at Aeon's gates within moments.

Tavesin's initial panic quickly subsided to be replaced by a steely determination and a firm resolve to place his trust in Ravin. Ravin swallowed the wave of unanticipated emotion the boy's reaction evoked within him. He could not afford to dwell on the experience with the mountain's threat imminent.

He drew on his power, the talisman's, and the reservoir Tavesin provided to begin weaving a complex tapestry of magic in the smoke-filled sky above. He silently prayed to Maelstrom for forgiveness as he forced thick clouds to coalesce above Mount Daesan. The last thing he needed was to draw the ire of the storm god in his desperate attempt to spare the army's temporary stronghold from obliteration.

Fat drops of rain began to fall through the sky, at first in a mere trickle, then in a deluge. The water hissed and steamed where it met molten rock, but still, the lava continued to inch forward.

Ravin braced himself and commanded more power through the talisman and his bond with Tavesin. The rain shifted to sleet, then to a thick, blanketing snow. Tavesin cried out as Ravin stumbled, but awash in the blaze of magic, Ravin was deaf to the warning and blind to his surroundings. Nothing mattered except the protection of the city and the boy at his side. He would sacrifice himself to the cause if it meant Tavesin and the others lived. He would give his life to ensure Adalin remained safe in Delucha.

Abruptly, much of his power source vanished. He fell to his knees, his own magic depleted. He panted for breath as Tavesin came to stand in front of him, fury in his blue eyes.

"You tried to kill yourself."

Ravin shook his head, too exhausted to explain his motive. "Is it done?"

Tavesin crossed his arms and stepped aside to allow him to view his handiwork. The mountain continued to smoke and spew ash, but much of the fire was gone. The lava was frozen and coated with snow only paces away from their location. Relief surged through him, and he managed a strained smile.

"We did it."

Tavesin continued to frown. "You didn't tell me how to break the connection, Ravin," he accused. "I had to figure it out myself. You almost *died.*"

Ravin tried to rise, but his limbs refused to cooperate. He collapsed forward on the sodden earth. He closed his eyes, seeking the solace of sleep.

"Ravin!" Tavesin's shout roused him. The boy knelt at his side as his previous anger transformed into unabashed concern. "Don't sleep. Not yet."

"Tired…" he mumbled.

"Ravin, no!"

His eyes closed of their own accord. His last thought was of Adalin as darkness enveloped him.

When he awakened, he expected to be greeted by the sight of jeweled gates and Aeon's wily countenance, but instead his eyes gazed upon sturdy wooden beams aglow in firelight. He blinked several times, disoriented, and slowly sat up.

A hearth blazed nearby, and beside it stood a long table littered with papers and maps. A window across the room afforded him a view of the forges. It was daylight, and a number of smiths were at work, though fewer than on previous days. He was in the smiths' guild hall; the table held Vardak's correspondence. He'd been placed in the general's study.

"You're awake."

He turned toward the room's single door and the speaker. Emra leaned against the door frame, a relieved smile on her lips. A thin cut marked her forehead, but she appeared otherwise unharmed.

"Did Patak take you to see Radosan?" Ravin asked. His voice was hoarse, and he realized his throat was parched.

She snorted. "After the scare you put us through, your first question is about *my* welfare?"

He shrugged. "I did what needed to be done. Your role is far more important than my own." He cleared his throat and groaned. "I could do with some water."

"I'll fetch you some. Radosan will no doubt return before I do."

"Emra," he said before she disappeared into the other room, "how long?"

Her blond eyebrows lifted in question. "What do you mean?"

"How long was I asleep?"

"Four days. Every wizard in Daesan was aware of what you did, and Tavesin has given us the details." She crossed her arms. "He's angry with you."

"I suppose I'm deserving of his ire." Ravin sighed. "If you see him, tell him I'd like to speak with him… If he'll allow it, that is."

"I understand why you acted as you did, Ravin, but I'm in agreement with Tavesin. Your actions were incredibly reckless."

Ravin met her gaze with a pointed look of his own. "It was the only way."

She nodded. "Perhaps, though Maelstrom was not pleased."

A cough escaped his throat. "He was here?"

"As were Flariel and your mother. Blademon as well, though he hasn't left. The eruption was no coincidence, Ravin, but I suspect you knew that." Emra studied him carefully, gauging his reaction. When he made no reply, she said, "It was but one of many disasters that night. The Nameless god has broken free."

CHAPTER TWENTY-FOUR

ACCEPTANCE

They were trapped, and he was to blame. The Kal's instructions told Sal'zar to seek the Moraine Mines, to hide in the dark tunnels beneath the Gray Mountains until they were summoned. But he'd chosen the route they followed away from the tower, he'd selected the mine entrance, and he'd decided which cavern would serve as their base camp. All of their plans had gone smoothly until four nights ago. Now they were trapped beneath leagues of rock, the tunnels on either side of their camp collapsed, and there was no one to blame for their current predicament but himself.

He sat apart from the others, his gaze fixed on a chunk of reddish rock on the cavern floor. There was nothing of interest in the rock; it was simply there, the sole object in his field of view. He stared at the rock while he considered his options, though they were few.

He'd led over one thousand Murkor away from the tower and the Soulless' clutches to the safety of the mines. When the ground began to quake, he'd feared the worst. Chips of rock had rained down upon them as their subterranean world groaned with the strain of the forces that threatened to rip it apart. When the first tunnel collapsed, it was a minor setback, an inconvenience. There was still a second exit to the cavern. They would be safe.

Then another violent tremor shook the earth, and he feared the cavern itself was about to cave in. Without taking the time to consider his actions, he drew on his magic and erected a protective barrier around the camp. Both the shield and the cavern withstood the assault, but the second tunnel had crumbled. The Murkor lived, but he wasn't certain how long they might last, cut off from the outside world and supplies.

Several of the alchemists had attempted to blast through the rubble to clear a path, but neither tunnel yielded to their efforts. They were entombed beneath the mountains, doomed to inevitable death by either air loss or starvation, and he was to blame. If Sal'zar had chosen a different path, a different mine shaft, a different cavern…

He looked down with a sigh and closed his eyes. Even his magic was useless to aid them. He'd studied defensive techniques and healing methods while in the tower, but little else. Barriers and shields could do nothing to penetrate solid rock.

He wished he could speak with Jal'den. His partner always knew what to say when Sal'zar fell into the depths of despair, knew how to cheer him and refocus his attention on what must be done. But Jal'den was with the Soulless' army and he couldn't risk contacting him now. He'd rather risk starvation than allow the Nameless god's thralls to learn of their location—or of his connection to Jal'den. As much as he needed Jal'den's counsel, he refused to place his partner or the others in such danger.

Their survival was tenuous at best, and unless he came up with a plan for escape, they would be with Aeon soon. Yet ideas continued to elude him.

Footsteps neared his location, but he ignored them. He preferred solitude to the accusatory glances and frustrated whispers he'd been greeted with since they found themselves trapped.

"Sal'zar, sir," a voice said quietly to his left.

Sal'zar did not look up and chose not to respond for several seconds. When the speaker scuffed his boots against the cavern floor, Sal'zar sighed heavily. "Yes?"

"Sir, Ukase is here."

His head snapped up as hope surged through him. Ukase's arrival could herald their salvation. He adjusted his hood and scanned the dim cavern. He spied Ukase on the opposite side, near one of the collapsed tunnels, but the patron god of the Murkor people was not alone. Another figure, feminine and clothed in an array of flowering foliage, towered beside him. Dus'tanne.

Sal'zar was on his feet in an instant. "Have they come to liberate us?"

"I pray that is the case, sir," the soldier replied earnestly. "Ukase asked for you by name but has said nothing more that I'm aware of."

He smiled beneath his hood for the first time in days. "If nothing else, he brings us hope."

He made his way across the vast cavern toward the pair of gods, a lightness in his steps that had been absent since he'd fled the tower. Ukase's iridescent gaze locked onto him well before he reached the midpoint of his journey. Sal'zar forced himself to breathe evenly in an attempt to still his nerves. He'd encountered Blademon once before, but from a distance; he'd never been forced to speak directly with one of the gods.

He recalled the lessons his father had taught him early in his life. Show deference. Be respectful. Speak only when addressed. Show humility. Every Murkor child was schooled in the proper etiquette used when speaking with the gods, though few were ever granted an audience.

In his younger years, he longed to be singled out, to be noticed, but after he met Jal'den his worldview changed. Jal'den was charismatic, a born leader. Sal'zar preferred the isolation of his laboratory and the meticulous process of his alchemical creations. He'd come to accept his own nature, but this business with the Kal had pushed him into a leadership role he believed himself wholly unsuited for. And now the gods had arrived; their presence renewed his hope, yet induced a level of anxiety he could scarcely conceal.

He knelt before Ukase and his vine-garbed sister, then bowed his head low. He continued to breathe evenly, despite the tremors in his hands, and said nothing until Ukase acknowledged him.

"Sal'zar, the Kal will be pleased to know you still live." Ukase's voice rumbled through the cavern.

Sal'zar peered upward but remained kneeling. A dozen questions circled his mind, but he feared to ask any of them, lest he manage to offend the god. Instead, he waited, trembling and uncertain.

"There are many things we must discuss," Ukase said in a softer tone. "It seems we will have little privacy here, but that can be remedied."

Ukase clapped his hands together, and silence enveloped them. Startled, Sal'zar looked up, then glanced over his shoulder. The other Murkor continued to mill about in the cavern, but he could hear nothing of their conversations. Confused, he returned his attention to Ukase, whose blue lips quirked in a knowing smile.

"You cannot hear them, and they cannot hear us." Ukase motioned for him to stand. "Our conversation may take some time, Sal'zar, and the ground is rather unforgiving on one's knees."

"Only if you lack the skill to manipulate it," Dus'tanne quipped from behind him. "I will leave you to your discussion, brother. I must repair this tunnel."

Sal'zar's spirits lifted with her words. "Then we can be free of this place, sir?"

Ukase held up one hand, seeking his patience. "In time. For now, you are safe here. Dus'tanne will open the tunnel so you are no longer trapped, but it is best for your people that you do not leave the mines yet. The Soulless have not discovered your location, and we must ensure it remains that way."

Sal'zar nodded, relieved their whereabouts remained hidden from the Soulless.

"I've spoken with your Kal," Ukase said. "I know of his plan and your role in it. Before the cataclysm rocked the world, Aeon watched the final moments of Aran'daj."

Sal'zar's heart stuttered. "The commander… Is he…?"

"He refused to deny his knowledge of what the Soulless now deem 'rogue' soldiers," Ukase replied. "Aeon manipulated events as best he could. Aran'daj was granted a final statement and a swift death. His soul has been given a place of high honor in the Underworld."

Sal'zar looked down, frustrated and deeply saddened that Aran'daj had given his life for the Kal's scheme. Jal'den had spoken highly of him. "And Jal'den?" he asked in a pained whisper.

"Your partner has been named Commander. I know this is difficult news to bear, Sal'zar, but I cannot take any messages to him on your behalf. It is *imperative* that you do not attempt to contact him until this war is ended. Do you understand?"

Sal'zar swallowed the lump forming in his throat and managed a nod. "What have the Soulless done?"

Ukase was silent for a time, his expression troubled. "That is why I've come, Sal'zar. Were you aware they worked toward freeing the Nameless god?"

Fear clutched his heart in an icy grip. "Yes."

"They have succeeded, and we can no longer observe their actions as we once did. The Nameless god blocks our divine sight." Ukase studied him for a moment as he grappled with the news. "This is why you cannot contact Jal'den. The Nameless has threatened your people with a fate to rival the builders of old if they disobey his orders. I have spoken with your Kal. The only reason the Murkor people have not been destroyed is that he managed to convince the Soulless you and the others acted alone. He supports you in spirit, Sal'zar, but he cannot openly condone your actions. If he does, you will all die."

Sal'zar looked down, stunned and terrified. "What can we do?"

"You will remain here for a short time. Aeon plans to pay you a visit and grant some of you his greatest blessing. We are preparing to face our fallen sibling, while you must prepare to face their followers." Ukase paused, and his eyes raked across the bustling cavern beyond. "There is an army gathering, one you have faced previously, in Delucha. It is in your best interest to ally with them."

Sal'zar shook his head helplessly. "How can I, when we are ordered to remain here?"

Ukase chuckled. "When Aeon returns, he will bring a mage along for the purpose of cementing your alliance. He is human, and I believe you have encountered him once before."

"Was he in the tower, sir?"

"No, Sal'zar. Solsticia informed me you met in the Aethereum, a realm of her design that she monitors closely."

Sal'zar nodded slowly. He recalled the morning he'd found himself in a landscape that mirrored the Wasted Land, but the light was distorted and pained his eyes in a way even sunlight did not. He'd been homesick and inexplicably found himself transported to the entrance of the Underground Caverns. Each time he attempted to enter the cavern, he was repelled by an unseen force. A man with brown skin and strange eyes appeared, then gave him the knowledge to extract himself from the magical plane.

"He never gave his name, sir, but I remember him."

"He is Ravin De'vor. Once he is recovered, Aeon will bring him here to meet with you." Ukase eyed him meaningfully. "He has aligned himself with Fireblade's wielder and is a bitter enemy of the Soulless. I suspect the two of you will have much to discuss."

"Will the humans accept us, sir?"

Ukase smiled broadly. "They already have, Sal'zar. You and the 'rogues' here will be welcomed."

CHAPTER TWENTY-FIVE

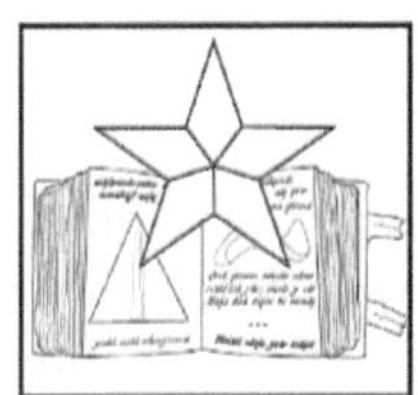

ANCIENT SCHEMATICS

Tavesin looked up from his reading to gaze out the tiny window his new room sported. He was one of only a handful of wizards given a room on the upper floor of the smiths' guild hall after their previous dwelling collapsed. The room was tiny, only large enough to accommodate his blankets, satchel, and a single chair. He didn't mind the cramped quarters, much preferring the privacy the room afforded when compared to the warehouse. He suspected he'd been given the room at Emra's insistence in return for his part in Daesan's defense against the recent eruption.

He sighed and focused on the plaza below. It was nearly midday; the smiths were at work, Blademon's towering form amongst them. From his current vantage point, the god of war didn't seem as intimidating as he did up close. Tavesin wasn't privy to the reason why Blademon remained in Daesan after the other gods departed, but the god's presence gave him a measure of comfort. They would not be forced to face the Nameless without divine assistance.

He tore his gaze away from the window and returned to his study of Morganus' journal. The pages before him spoke of the black tower's construction, centuries before the Soulless claimed it for themselves. As Ravin had indicated, the Enlightened once stood for noble and just causes—the founders of their council had never intended for their tenants to become corrupt, nor were they supporters of the Nameless god.

He considered the recent events within his own council and wondered if the wizards would have fallen to depravity if the former

Radiant had remained in power. Tavesin remained incensed at Berasin's decision to ignore the missing apprentices and lie to their families when they disappeared. The families deserved to learn the truth.

He glowered at the page and flipped it over to reveal detailed schematics of the black tower. Each floor was labeled meticulously. Tavesin recalled the tower's wide foyer and the spiral stair that led from the entrance all the way to the tower's apex from his visit while in the Aethereum. His memory of the tower's top floor was clearer; the glass cases filled with magical objects, the terrifying relic hanging from the wall with its searching, black tendrils, and the star-shaped box he'd absconded with.

Idly, he wondered if the box now gathered dust in the Shining Tower's restricted area. It was an Aethereal relic, one that granted its user the ability to enter the magical realm even if they lacked the innate power to do so. The star-shaped box would have proved useful to them at present, but it was not his place to suggest it. Besides, neither he nor Ravin had the time to teach someone the ways of the Aethereum, and the Drakkon mages were equally unavailable. The Drakkon had volunteered to act as impartial messengers between Emra and the various leaders of the Five Kingdoms and beyond, and Tavesin scarcely interacted with them now.

He studied the schematics carefully and noted a strange symbol drawn beneath the tower's base. It was hexagonal in shape, and a single eye was drawn within. The eye was round and slit vertically by a dark pupil, reminiscent of a reptile's. Tavesin frowned at the symbol, but nothing on the page explained its meaning.

He turned the page to reveal another diagram accompanied by a set of detailed instructions. The diagram showed the tower, and forming a triangle around it, a trio of symbols. The bottom-right point of the triangle was marked with a "T," the top point a circle, and the bottom-left a teardrop. As he pored over the instructions, his pulse accelerated.

It revealed how the tower might be destroyed.

He startled as a knock sounded on his open door. He closed the journal and looked up to find Emra studying him from the corridor. "Ravin's awake. He'd like to speak with you."

Tavesin nodded and tucked the book under his arm as he stood. "I need to speak with him, too."

She lifted her eyebrows in silent question. "I thought you were angry with him."

He shrugged. "I am, but that doesn't matter. The duchess said he's a fool with a big heart and that I should forgive him."

Emra laughed as he fell in beside her and made his way toward the stairs. "He won't be pleased you paid her a visit without him, you know."

"When we were linked, I saw…" Tavesin cut himself off to chew on his lower lip. Ravin wouldn't appreciate his private thoughts being made public. "I had to tell her what happened, Emra. In case he didn't wake up."

She patted his shoulder. "I understand. He's still in Vardak's study. Radosan ordered him to remain there until he's recovered some of his strength." She turned to face him at the base of the stairs, her expression somber. "If you had waited any longer to break your connection, it's likely he would be dead. You saved his life, Tavesin, though I don't believe he realizes it."

He shrugged again. "I wasn't going to watch him die."

"And for that, we are all in your debt," she replied. "Go, Tavesin. He'll be pleased to see you."

Uncertainty gripped him as he trudged through the foyer, the larger meeting room, and Vardak's study beyond. He didn't know what he ought to say to Ravin, though he wanted to share his latest discovery from within Morganus' journal. A discussion about the night of the earthquake and their temporary bond would prove awkward, at best.

The door to the study was propped open. As Tavesin stepped inside, he saw Ravin swathed in a blanket near the hearth, his eyes closed while Radosan knelt beside him. Ravin's face was gaunt, his dark hair a tangle of unkempt curls, but he was alive. Radosan's hands moved inches above Ravin; his eyes were closed as well, and Tavesin could sense the healing vibrations of his magic as he assessed Ravin's injuries.

Radosan rocked back on his heels with a satisfied nod and flicked his gaze toward Tavesin in acknowledgment. "You'll recover well enough, but I advise you continue to rest for a few days," he told

Ravin. "I'll have a meal brought to you, and fresh water. Avoid using your magic if you can. You need to regain your strength."

Ravin nodded absently and sat back. As he opened his eyes, he noted Tavesin in the doorway and managed a strained smile. "I hope I'm allowed visitors, Radosan."

Radosan chuckled and rose to his feet. "Of course. I'll fetch your meal." Radosan gave Tavesin a warm smile as he passed.

Tavesin lingered in the doorway as words continued to elude him. What should he say? He'd glimpsed portions of Ravin's memory that the mage had kept hidden for years, he'd been privy to some of Ravin's private thoughts, and he knew with certainty that Ravin was in love with the duchess. He admired Ravin's resolve and the heroism he'd shown on the night of the cataclysm, but he felt cheated; Ravin had intentionally omitted critical information, and Tavesin had nearly watched him die as a consequence. He remained bitter, but perhaps Ravin would provide an explanation for his actions.

"Taven, I'm glad you've come."

Tavesin nodded and stepped into the room. "Adalin said you're a fool," he blurted angrily as he seated himself against the wall facing Ravin. His face heated with embarrassment; he'd meant to keep his visit with the duchess to himself until he was certain Ravin wouldn't be upset by the news.

To his surprise, Ravin chuckled. "No doubt she did. Is she well?"

"Yes. Delucha wasn't affected by the breaking of the seals." He paused to chew on his lip. "You aren't mad?"

Ravin laughed. "Why would I be upset with you, Taven? I'm certain you know what I feel for her." When Tavesin nodded, he said, "Then you must realize I'm grateful you spoke with her. I'd planned to visit her once we were finished that night, to make certain she was well. I wasn't anticipating the need to halt the mountain's eruption."

"Flariel wanted to thank you when she was here," Tavesin replied somberly. "She lost control of the mountain when the Nameless broke free. She's the one that brought you here. I wanted to, but I… I gave you too much of my own power. Even with my relic, I couldn't open a portal. I was scared. I thought you were dying." Tears pricked his eyes, but he could not stop the flow of words now that they'd been unleashed. "When Flariel appeared, I asked for her help. She brought us here. I thanked her, but I was so angry… I didn't want to stay with you. I left. I'm sorry."

He drew a shuddering breath and looked away, ashamed by his admission. He realized his anger was the byproduct of his own selfishness and the fear of facing the Soulless without Ravin's guidance. He considered Ravin a mentor and a friend—after losing Arra, he couldn't imagine coping with another, equally devastating blow.

"Taven, I should be the one apologizing to you," Ravin said quietly after a time. "I should have told you how to break our link if something went wrong, but there was too little time. In my hubris, I believed I could control my own power as well as yours. It was too much."

Tavesin stared at him sullenly. "You almost *died*, Ravin, and I didn't know what to do. I don't like feeling helpless."

"You're right, and Adalin was right. I'm a gods-damned fool, and I should never have placed you in such a position. My arrogance nearly cost me my life, and without your intervention, it would have." Ravin looked down and ran one hand through his hair, further mussing the unruly strands. "I owe you a great debt, Taven, and I pray you will forgive me one day."

"Ravin, I—"

A tap on the doorframe interrupted him, but he was grateful for the intrusion. He glanced across the room to find Radosan had returned with the meal he'd promised to deliver. Tavesin fell silent as the Sect Master entered and placed a tray of food on the floor next to Ravin.

"If you're hungry after you've eaten this, I will fetch more. I'll just be outside. Call should you need anything." Radosan exited and closed the door softly behind him.

Tavesin watched Ravin silently for several moments, while Ravin tore off a chunk of bread and began to devour it.

"Ravin, I don't want to be angry any longer." He sighed and shifted his eyes to look into the hearth's flames. "I understand why you did it, why you believed you could wield so much power. I know about Minora."

Ravin swallowed audibly and he looked down, his expression unreadable. "Have you told anyone?"

"No. It's not my place to say."

Ravin closed his eyes briefly as relief rippled across his features. "Thank you. I don't want Adalin to learn of my situation. She would only question the validity of my words, of what I feel for her." His smile was pained. "I have a plan for freeing myself from Minora's schemes. Perhaps once it's done, I will tell Adalin the truth."

Tavesin nodded. The talk of Minora reminded him of the primary reason he'd come, though he was pleased they'd sorted out the more troubling aspects of the conversation first. "Ravin, I've found something important in the journal Minora gave me."

"Show me."

Tavesin stood and crossed the room to settle himself beside Ravin, while Ravin reached for another chunk of bread. Tavesin opened the book in his lap and flipped through the pages until he located the instructions for the tower's destruction.

He pointed at each symbol in turn. "If I understand this correctly, we'll need another mage's help."

Ravin studied the page thoughtfully while he chewed. "Yes. According to this," he said, pointing at a line in the instructions, "the 'T' indicates a mage bearing a relic of immense power. Morganus surmises a peace talisman would suffice."

"That would be your position, then." Tavesin leaned back and tilted his face toward the ceiling while he considered their options. "The teardrop shape must be the Moon's Eye. The shape is identical, and we've already been told that it's necessary."

"The third mage must stand atop the tower," Ravin continued. "Gods, that leaves us with few options. Do you believe Aziarah would assist us?"

"I don't know," Tavesin admitted. "Since the former Radiant was deposed, she's kept her distance." He swallowed a wave of grief. "Even from me."

"I'll speak with her," Ravin promised. "This matter is too important to allow petty politics to stand in the way." He paused to scan more of the page. "It speaks of a seal beneath the tower, placed there by the first of the Soulless. This is the second time we've come across the notion that a floor exists beneath the tower, but I know nothing of it."

Tavesin frowned, then brightened as he recalled the previous page. He flashed a grin at Ravin and turned the page. "If I understand this correctly, we must perform the ritual on the other page in order to destroy the seal and access the lower level." He pointed at the strange hexagonal shape. "I was planning to ask you about this. I don't know what it means."

Ravin frowned. "I don't recognize the symbol, but I know someone who will—and she's promised to help us as she can."

"Solsticia?" Tavesin asked hopefully.

Ravin chuckled. "You glimpsed far more through our bond than I anticipated. Yes. Once Radosan allows me to go about my business again, I'll pay her another visit."

CHAPTER TWENTY-SIX

NEW RULES

Dranamir awakened alone for the first time in over a week. Every facet of her being ached, and her energy remained depleted, despite her recent sleep. Slowly, she pulled herself into a sitting position to assess her injuries. Her hands and feet were unmarked, but every inch of her gray skin was mottled with dark bruises from shoulder to ankle. Some were the purple-black of the newly-acquired, others were ringed with yellow-green, a sign they were several days old.

She'd always known his treatment would be rough—he was the death god, after all—but the days of agonizing ecstasy had certainly taken their toll. She would have been surprised at the extent of her injuries if she weren't on the brink of collapse. He'd drained her magical power each time he'd lain with her in order to promote his own regeneration. The elixir hadn't been enough to sate his hunger.

She staggered to her feet and braced herself against the nearest sculpted pillar that stood sentinel within his temple. She required food, water… She hadn't eaten since he'd taken her here, and he was unconcerned with the needs of mortals.

She scanned the room and the silvery mirror on the nearby dais, seeking her clothing. She spied it not far away, but knew immediately it would be of no use to her. The dress she'd been wearing upon her arrival was in tatters, torn to ribbons by the Nameless god in his frenzy to possess her.

She'd denied countless men throughout the years, killed many more for their perceived advances, simply to save herself for the god she was devoted to. But she had been wholly unprepared for his many demands. He was violent, impatient, uncompromising, and yet she would give herself to him again and again. Her life had always belonged to him and no other.

She grasped at her magic and was stunned when enough of her spark remained to create a portal. She must return to the tower. Her wardrobe would provide a means to hide the bruises; she could take a meal, and bathe. She stumbled into the refuge of the Aethereum but did not linger. An encounter with Ravin in her present state would be her last. She lacked the energy to defend herself. Even Alyra could have bested her.

The thought soured her stomach as she transported herself into her private quarters within the tower. It took her several attempts to form an exit portal. She'd never been so thoroughly drained as she was now. She must not allow the others to witness her present weakness.

Her room was as she'd left it, the door closed and locked from within. She staggered to her wardrobe and assessed her reflection in its mirror. Her face was unblemished by the Nameless' many assaults, but shadows ringed her eyes and her cheeks were sallow.

A glint caught her attention, and she became aware of the intricate jewelry she wore. He'd placed it around her throat before he'd left the temple for other pursuits, a symbol of her status, he'd said. She'd been too exhausted to appreciate the gift, had merely nodded, then drifted into a dreamless sleep. Now she examined the piece carefully in the glass.

It was an intricate choker that covered her throat and flared out at its base to encompass the tops of her shoulders. Numerous strands of tiny black pearls intertwined, forming a lattice pattern across her skin. Above the hollow of her throat, a single square-cut ruby the size of her thumb hung suspended in the web of pearls. The ruby's facets reflected the room's light to dazzling effect. It was beautiful.

"Do you like it?"

His voice startled her. She spun away from the mirror to find him lounging against the wall near her door. He no longer wore Garin's face; he'd altered his features at some point during the past week, though she could not recall when. The small man's shell had been discarded, and in its place, the Nameless god towered at his natural height, exuding malevolent power. He'd adopted the gray features and crimson eyes of the Soulless, assumed a muscular build, and sported short, dark hair. The face he now wore was striking, yet embodied danger and ferocity. Clad in dark leather, he cut a dashing figure.

Dranamir trembled with anticipation, her mouth dry as she truly studied him for the first time. Her left hand brushed the base of the choker in response to his question. "Yes."

A knowing smile graced his lips. "It suits you. It suits *my queen*."

She ignored the unsatiated hunger in his tone. "Do the others know?" she asked, turning to scan the contents of her wardrobe.

He chuckled. "I've summoned them to the temple. I will present you then. But first," he said, pushing away from the wall, "you must regain your strength."

She glanced toward him and noted he held a crystal goblet, half filled with a dark liquid. As he approached, a pungent, herbal aroma wafted toward her. She recognized the scent, the faintly oily sheen the liquid possessed.

"Your elixir?" she prompted, stunned by his gesture.

"This is all that remains, but I have no further need of it." He grinned and held the goblet to her lips. "Drink, Dranamir. My queen must radiate power, even amongst purported allies."

She obeyed. His power was immense, and she'd learned long ago that the price of defiance often meant death. The elixir was warm, almost soothing despite its unpleasant odor and acrid taste. She drained the contents of the glass and felt a tingling sensation slowly spread through her from core to limbs. Within moments, her energy returned and the depleted reservoir of her magic was refilled, but the elixir's power did not cease there. Her power continued to increase; her once smoldering flame ignited into a deadly inferno that threatened to consume her unless released.

She gasped and shuddered as she grappled with her newfound power. The Nameless stood before her, his crimson eyes twinkling with amusement. After several long moments, she found a means to subdue the raging tide of magical energy within her. Only then did she understand the enormity of what he'd done.

She fell to her knees and gazed at him, reverent.

He grinned and reached toward her. "Rise, Dranamir."

She accepted his hand and rose to her feet, her eyes locked upon his. "This gift. It is—"

"It is exactly what you require," he replied. "What good is a murderous queen without the ability to inflict death from afar?" He smirked. "Now your power nearly rivals that of my sister's son. You have earned my favor, Dranamir."

His hand caressed the side of her jaw. "Prepare yourself. The others will arrive in the temple soon, and we have much to discuss."

He vanished, and she was left alone once more. She turned to face the wardrobe again and noted with a measure of satisfaction that the elixir had healed her bruises. Her gray skin was once again unblemished, pristine, *perfect*. She smiled wickedly at her reflection before selecting a flowing red gown in the same shade as the ruby at her throat.

Alyra would envy her appearance—and her power. For the first time since she'd met the intolerable woman, Dranamir finally held the upper hand. In spite of Alyra's former beauty, her voluptuous figure, and her voracious sexual appetite, the Nameless god had chosen *Dranamir*.

She dressed carefully and ran a comb through her hair, taking care to ensure her outward appearance commanded respect. And with the recent amplification of her magical ability, her presence would induce fear. Alyra's fear, Kama's fear, the terror of the Enlightened. Her life's work had finally come to fruition.

She returned to the temple and was startled to find herself once more alone with the god. He stood atop the silvered mirror, hands clasped behind his back as he studied her.

"Come here, Dranamir."

She strode toward him and knelt upon the steps near his feet, her gaze fixed on the polished surface of the mirror and his reflection within. He began to pace as a low chuckle emanated from his throat.

"The others will arrive in a moment," he told her. "Remain there until I command otherwise. Your new power will come as something of a shock to them both, and I plan to make the most of it."

"Of course." She kept her head bowed in deference while her pulse thrummed with anticipation. She yearned to see the shock on Kama's angular features, the dismay and outrage on Alyra's.

The Nameless stopped pacing moments before she heard a pair of footfalls on the obsidian floor behind her. She remained kneeling as their god instructed and was rewarded when he halted the others at the base of the steps. She heard a shuffle as they knelt in kind. A grim smile crossed her lips as Alyra gasped in sudden shock. She resisted the urge to smirk at the other woman over her shoulder.

"As you can see, I've decided to become the patron of the Soulless," the Nameless began. Dranamir could hear the grin in his tone. "There are no other species worthy of my divine attention."

"We are greatly honored, my lord," Alyra replied breathlessly.

He ignored her unconcealed attempt at flattery. "I have summoned you here for several reasons. First, there is to be a reorganization within your hierarchy. Kama, Alyra, your duties will not change, but you will now report directly to my chosen consort."

He bent to extend one hand toward Dranamir. With a malicious smile, she grasped it, rose to her feet, and allowed him to position her at his side. Kama's piercing stare was unreadable, though she detected a rigidity in his posture that indicated he was furious. Alyra was unable to hide her outrage and openly gaped. Dranamir's smile broadened. Finally, the bitch would serve *her*.

"Why?" the word escaped Alyra's lips in an anguished wail. "Why her?"

The Nameless laughed darkly. "You were never worthy of my full attention, Alyra, nor would you have survived it. You are weak, but you serve your purpose well enough."

Aghast, Alyra looked down. "I beg your forgiveness," she mumbled through the tattered curtain of her hair.

Emboldened by her elevated position and Alyra's despair, she said, "May I?"

The Nameless arched one dark eyebrow in amusement. "Certainly, but don't kill her. I still have a use for her talents."

"No, master, please." Alyra scrabbled backwards as tears began to leak from her eyes. "Please, no. What have I done to displease you?"

Dranamir advanced upon her while the Nameless chuckled from behind. "Nothing, my dear," he replied, "but an example must be made. Without it, Kama might believe himself capable of rising against her, against *me*. I cannot abide a mutiny on his part, can I?"

Alyra's face crumpled at his words. She ceased her futile efforts to put distance between herself and Dranamir. Dranamir smirked at Kama as she strode past, but he wisely kept his head down and his thoughts to himself. She gazed at Alyra while elation coursed through her veins. She'd awaited this moment for years. No, *decades.*

She'd long ago determined what she'd do to the once-beautiful woman with the corrupted face if granted the opportunity. The Nameless god's order echoed in her mind; she could not kill Alyra, but she could certainly make her wish for death. As she reached for her power, she was disappointed when Alyra chose not to harness her own in defense. It seemed she'd given in to the perceived punishment and would not fight. It was a shame, but one Dranamir could exploit.

She ignited Alyra's pain receptors. With her newly granted power, she could trace those fragile points within the other woman's brain along myriad twisting pathways throughout her body. She set every nerve fiber she encountered ablaze, then imbued her magic within them to administer further injury indefinitely.

Alyra screeched and tore at her skin even after Dranamir had released her magic. Every movement, every breath, every blink of her crimson eyes would send an agonizing jolt of pain through Alyra's body. The effect was permanent.

Dranamir sneered and turned on her heel. Alyra's screams faded into sniffles as Dranamir resumed her position alongside the Nameless god.

"I've always admired creativity," he stated as he placed one hand on the small of her back. "Now that you all understand the new rules of my little game, I have a final bit of news to share."

Alyra staggered to her feet while swiping tears from her eyes. "I am…your willing…servant, master," she gasped.

Dranamir grinned maliciously, pleased at the effect her magic had wrought. Alyra would act the willing pawn; both women knew Dranamir could have done much worse.

"As am I," Kama intoned without looking up. He continued to kneel in deference to the Nameless god, though Dranamir suspected he now properly feared her as well.

"You will continue with your previous assignments," the Nameless said again. "However, be prepared to act on a moment's notice. The others have blocked my sight, and I am no longer capable of observing the enemy's army. Of course, I have blocked their view of this area. Your movements will likewise be shielded from the unwanted intervention of the gods." His smile was grim. "I will relish the day when my foolish siblings attempt to make war with me a second time."

CHAPTER TWENTY-SEVEN

A BID FOR FREEDOM

Ravin stood before the familiar wooden door, poised to knock, yet hesitant to do so. Two weeks had passed since his last visit, ten days since Mount Daesan's eruption, and during that time, he'd been forced to rely on a teenager to deliver his messages. Tavesin was a kind soul and asked few questions when it came to Ravin's personal life, though Ravin believed the boy learned far more during their linkage than he'd let on. He'd ferried a few messages between Ravin and Adalin while Ravin remained abed in recovery.

Ravin believed himself well enough to make the journey to Delucha days ago, but Radosan had urged caution. Grudgingly, he'd acknowledged the healer's advice. Sitting idle was not a skill he excelled at, and he loathed the self-perception of uselessness. He yearned to act, to *do*. After days spent waiting, his request was finally granted.

He immediately fled the confines of the smiths' guild hall through a portal and made his way to Delucha. There was no one he wished to see more than Adalin, and the realization unnerved him. He'd never before needed anyone in his life as much as he did her. Standing empty-handed before her door after two weeks away left him feeling decidedly inadequate, yet he'd failed to consider his options before he arrived.

He sighed, disappointed in his lack of foresight. He hoped she would understand.

He rapped lightly on the door, a series of five taps in a pattern they'd established before his departure with the army. Rapid footfalls from within greeted his ears, and he smiled. Adalin wrenched the door open to beam at him. She wore one of her riding outfits, and her dark hair was swept up in an elaborate, braided bun. Her blue eyes sparkled in the shaft of sunlight from the corridor's single window, and his heart constricted at the sight. She was beautiful.

"Ravin," she breathed. "You're here."

He shrugged and offered her an awkward smile. "I wish it could have been sooner."

She stepped aside and motioned for him to enter. "Tavesin told me of your…antics. You saved many lives." She closed the door behind them, a note of melancholy in her tone.

"But?" he pressed; he knew there was more she wished to say.

"He told me you nearly killed yourself, that you would have if he'd been unable to sever the bond you'd formed." She crossed her arms and looked away, unable to meet his gaze any longer. Tears shone in her eyes, and his heart crumpled. "After everything you've worked toward, why take such a risk?"

"If it meant Emra and her followers survived to face the Soulless' army, it was justified. *She* is the most important figure in this fight. Without her, all will be lost, and I…" His voice cracked, and he drew an unsteady breath. "I didn't want to imagine that future for you. If my sacrifice meant you would live and thrive after the war, I would do it again."

She crossed the space between them rapidly, her expression contorted by grief, and when she raised her hand to strike him, he closed his eyes in acceptance. Her palm connected with the left side of his face in a stinging blow. He'd put her through days of anguish; he would not deny her this outlet.

Her hand fell to her side as she began to sob. Her reaction was a final confirmation of her unspoken feelings for him, and he smiled in spite of himself. He gathered her into his arms, holding her close while she wept into his shoulder.

"I'm sorry," he whispered. "Tavesin said you'd called me a fool. I cannot blame you."

She sniffed and wiped at her eyes but didn't pull away. "You are. A brave, noble, arrogant fool that nearly crushed my soul when I heard news of what you'd done." She reached up to gingerly touch the side of his face. It continued to sting from where she'd slapped him. "Gods, Ravin. Promise me you'll never do anything so reckless again."

He dropped his gaze, his heart heavy. "I will not make a promise that I'll be forced to break, Adalin."

"Then promise me you'll visit as often as you can, you gods-damned fool."

He smiled. "That, I can do."

Impulsively, he drew her closer and bent forward to rest his forehead against hers. She met his gaze with a dazzling smile, her previous frustration and grief temporarily forgotten.

"Adalin, I want this. *Us.* If I survive the war, I won't return for a mere visit." He wanted to kiss her, but felt it wasn't the proper time. Instead, he said, "If we succeed, I'll come back for you, and you'll never be rid of me."

She laughed softly. "I rather like the sound of that. I'll be certain to save a few bottles of mead for the occasion."

"As will I."

Ravin startled at the voice, though he recognized it immediately. He dropped his hands and stepped away from Adalin with an aggrieved sigh, while the duchess, flustered, spun around to face their unwanted guest. Solsticia leaned against the room's window, head bent low to avoid the ceiling. Ravin scowled at her, irritated by the interruption.

"Who are—?" Adalin's words died on her lips, and her eyes widened with surprise. She bowed low and stammered an apology.

"Do not apologize, my dear," Solsticia replied gently while her eyes studied Ravin. "Won't you introduce us properly, Ravin?"

He crossed his arms and complied while his temper soured further. "Mother, this is Adalin Nantess, Duchess of the Mers. Adalin, this is Solsticia, who apparently doesn't know the meaning of privacy."

Solsticia chuckled while Adalin said, "Oh, Ravin…" The duchess shook her head in mock annoyance, then extended her hand toward the celestial goddess perched on her window sill. "It is an honor to meet you."

Solsticia accepted her hand with a smile. "Likewise. Any woman with the fortitude to put my son in his place and capture his heart in the process has earned my respect."

Ravin's face flushed, and he looked pointedly at the floor. "Why are you here, mother?" he growled.

"Your young protégé approached Flariel's shrine this morning. He has several concerns regarding the contents of the journal, and feared to wait for your recovery any longer." Solsticia eyed him critically. "One of the Drakkon mages accompanied him on the journey, which is fortunate considering much of the path leading to the shrine was destroyed."

Ravin sighed, his shoulders slumped in defeat. In his enthusiasm to see Adalin, he'd forgotten his promise to Tavesin regarding the strange symbol depicted in Morganus' schematics of the tower. The duchess truly had stolen his heart—and his senses.

"He understands why you chose to travel here first," Solsticia continued. "I suspect he understands your desire even better than you, Ravin. I've come to escort you to my palace. He and the Drakkon are there. We must discuss his findings—and your role in what must be done."

Ravin nodded but turned to Adalin, regret like a stone in his gut. "I'm sorry our time was cut short."

"As am I. I'll make good on my promise if you make good on yours." Unshed tears shone in her eyes. It required an effort of will to force himself to look away.

"I will," he vowed as he stepped toward Solsticia.

Solsticia gripped his hand. A tumultuous sensation of falling, spinning, tumbling engulfed him as darkness shrouded his vision. It lasted but a moment, then he found himself in a large courtyard adorned with marble statuary. A vast expanse of darkness stretched overhead, dotted with millions of stars, far more than he'd ever witnessed in the evening sky. He looked up at Solsticia with questions in his gaze.

"Welcome to the Sky Palace," she said with a wave of her hand. "I was forbidden to take you here previous to this day, but I've long wished to share my home with you. After your selfless act in Daesan, I'd like to believe the others are finally willing to accept you."

"Did you know how they'd react when you chose to lay with my father?" The question spilled from his lips unbidden, laced with a lifetime of rage. If she were mortal, he'd curse himself and the unfairness of the query, but she was a goddess. Surely, she would have known.

"No, Ravin, I did not." She sighed and beckoned him to follow her. "Most of my siblings have at one time or another borne mortal children. None were gifted with magic, as you are."

"I fail to understand the significance," he hissed as they passed through an arched doorway into a tapestry-lined corridor. "Many people are born with the ability to wield magic."

"Yet none rival you in power. Magic is celestial, Ravin, and I am its goddess. You are my son." The anguish in her tone tempered his rage. "If I'd known what they would force upon you—upon us both—I would have chosen a different path. I will never bear another child if it means their fate belongs to Minora's weavings and Aeon's whims. Your life has not been what I'd hoped for you, Ravin. What you were forced to endure…" Her voice cracked with emotion, but she tossed her head and pressed on. "The centuries of unabated loneliness you faced while grappling with your own madness… I begged them to end your suffering, but they would not relent. Minora was not finished with you. *Is* not finished with you, and my heart crumbles with each painful reminder."

He sighed and raked one hand through his hair. "Can anything be done, mother?"

She was silent for a time as they wended their way through another corridor and past a number of closed doors. "Perhaps, but my words will do nothing to persuade the others. Only your actions can."

He nodded as a plan began to form in his mind. The gods needed him in order to thwart the Nameless' plans and return him to his cage. It was his only bargaining chip, the only leverage he might utilize in his bid for true freedom. He must play his hand carefully and make his demand at the optimal moment. If he succeeded, he would no longer be Minora's unwitting pawn.

"Ravin?" Solsticia asked over her shoulder, concerned.

"I'm fine, mother, merely considering my options." He smiled to himself; he would wrangle a vow from the very gods who had scripted his fate.

"I believe I know what you're considering. Don't do anything rash—she won't tolerate it."

He smirked at her back and chuckled dryly. "She may not have a choice."

Solsticia whirled to face him, golden eyes wide with surprise. "You would…?" She shook her head as a bemused smile crossed her face. "You would. I should have known, but I'll pretend it's the first I've heard of it when you decide to broach the subject."

Ravin grinned as they continued their journey. His mother's intuition unnerved him, but he was pleased she planned to act as his ally. As furious as he'd once been with her, he supposed he could forgive her past choices if she helped him thwart Minora's future schemes.

She paused in front of a pair of double doors engraved with an array of stars. "The others—Tavesin, his Drakkon friend, and all of my siblings—are within. Tavesin may be overwhelmed. He'll require your guidance."

"Which Drakkon accompanied him?" Ravin asked. "Aziarah gave strict orders to her people to avoid 'entanglements' with the wizards."

"Trozyen."

Ravin nodded in understanding. Trozyen was the Drakkon mage who had helped Tavesin hone his shielding ability into the unparalleled force it now was. He was young, yet more powerful than the elders of his people who accompanied the army. It seemed Trozyen maintained his friendship with the young wizard, despite his orders to the contrary.

"I'm aware of his orders, Ravin," she continued, "but he was not forbidden 'entanglements' with the gods."

Solsticia threw the doors wide and escorted him inside. A long table occupied the center of the room, the other gods encircled it, but it was not the sight of the world's deities that drew his gaze. The far wall and the ceiling were a single pane of crystalline glass, beyond which was an unencumbered view of the heavens. The room overlooked a vast, luminous, blue-green orb swirled with white and mottled in swaths of brown; their world, far below.

Solsticia's hand brushed his elbow, drawing his attention. She gestured to an open seat next to Tavesin, who appeared smaller than he was amongst the towering gods. "I never tire of the view," she whispered, "but there will be time to admire it later."

He made his way to the indicated seat while Solsticia strode to the head of the table where the view of the star-strewn expanse served as her backdrop. Ravin smirked at the symbolism and wondered if she always chose the location to address her siblings.

"Now that everyone is present, we will begin." Solsticia's gaze fell upon the marble-sculpted features of Minora. "We were led to believe all traces of his name were destroyed, Minora, yet this book not only *names* him, it includes his sigil. Explain yourself."

Blademon rose to his feet from the other end of the table, his eyes ablaze with righteous indignation. "You've kept this from us, sister," he growled ominously.

Minora's sculpted features revealed no emotion and when she spoke, her lips did not move. "It was a necessary precaution. If you believed the traces vanished, then so would *he*." Her tone was calm, forthright, unruffled.

"I fail to see why this information needed to be preserved," Ukase thundered across from her. "It puts us all in danger. If he learns mortals possess this information, they will *all* be destroyed."

"And our chance of corralling him once more will evaporate," Blademon snarled. "Do you work against him, or with him?"

"Peace, brother," Armistral interjected. He placed one hand on Blademon's forearm, and his twin seemed to relinquish some of his anger. "Allow her to speak."

Ravin observed the exchange warily while praying their disagreement would not spark an internal schism. The Nameless god could not be defeated unless the remainder of his siblings were aligned.

"In his hubris, the Nameless believed only we Immortals could unravel his power," Minora began. "Morganus uncovered his fatal error. He tied his power—his *godhood*—to a physical seal and secreted it away beneath the tower that now stands as the symbol of his followers. The seal's location is shielded from divine interference, but *mortals* may enter the space."

Ravin stared at the immobile features of Time's Guardian as a chill ricocheted along his spine. This was the reason she'd commandeered his fate—she needed him, needed his power in order to destroy the Nameless' threat for good. She'd directed his life to reach this pinnacle of her schemes, and he was helpless against her directives.

His mouth was dry and his throat rasped as he spoke. "That's why you need me."

Minora's marble face swiveled in his direction. "Precisely."

"And his *name*?" Solsticia pressed, anger driving an edge into her tone.

"Ravin cannot access the space without it," Minora replied evenly. "I had no choice but to preserve the knowledge."

"I understand why I am required," Ravin interrupted, "but please, spare Tavesin this horror. War is no place for a child."

When Minora next spoke, her tone was amused. "By the boy's own admission, you have both studied the ritual required to open the sealed chamber. It requires *three* mortal mages with great magical prowess. Discounting the Soulless, there are *only* three such mages alive. The three of you."

Ravin clenched his jaw in momentary frustration, but he knew she was right. He looked away helplessly, his ploy to release Tavesin from Minora's grasp in tatters. When Minora began to speak again, he rose from his seat as a sudden rage grasped him.

"I will not stand for this!" He struck the table with his fist and glared across the table at the statuesque goddess.

Minora leaned back slightly, the only indication she was stunned by his words. "Tell me, Ravin: What can you possibly do to alter your present course?"

He pounced upon her words as the opportunity he'd been seeking and grasped the talisman in his pocket. He drew upon its power, allowed the energy to cascade through him unchecked. He felt his essence begin to fracture and tear, the fibers of his being scorch and fray. He would allow the relic to consume his soul to prove his point, but he knew the gods would step in before death claimed him. They were desperate, they needed him, and they would set him free.

"*Enough!*" Minora shrieked, horrified. "You will ruin everything!"

Ravin released his hold on the talisman and collapsed into his chair, weakened by the magic's assault. Radosan would have his head when he returned to Daesan, but he'd proven his point.

"What do you want?" Minora demanded.

Ravin flicked a glance at Solsticia, who nodded once in understanding. "If I do this and risk Tavesin's life in the process, I expect something equally precious in return." His voice came out in a strained rasp.

Radosan would be furious, as would Adalin when she learned what he'd done, but Minora had forced his hand. He would recover again, given time.

"Name it." Minora crossed her sculpted arms as she awaited his reply.

"Freedom. *True* freedom. I want to live a life of my own design."

"He has played your game long enough," Solsticia added. "Allow him this, sister. If he fails to break the Nameless god's seal, it will be punishment enough. If he succeeds, grant his request."

"He will always be a danger if left unchained," Maelstrom rumbled.

"He suffered centuries of agony in the soul-stone," Aeon countered. "I am with Solsticia on this matter."

The debate lasted several minutes, but Ravin knew within moments that he'd won. He closed his eyes, listened to the gods' discussion, and smiled. Only when Minora spoke his name did he reopen them.

"Ravin, it has been decided. *If* you succeed, I vow to grant your freedom. You will weave your own thread through time's tapestry, as all other mortals do."

"Thank you."

"I believe we are finished," Solsticia said. "I will transport the mortals to Daesan."

Ravin remained seated as the gods around them began to vanish from sight. Beside him, Tavesin chewed on his lip, contemplative, while Trozyen appeared shocked at the events that had unfolded.

"Taven?" Ravin asked once only Solsticia remained. He suspected the boy was once again angry with him, and he supposed he deserved it after forcing himself to the brink a second time in as many weeks.

Tavesin glanced at him, a sudden mischievous glint in his eyes. "I know why you did it. I won't tell the duchess if you don't."

Ravin tipped his head back and laughed, relieved by the unexpected commiseration. "We have a deal."

CHAPTER TWENTY-EIGHT

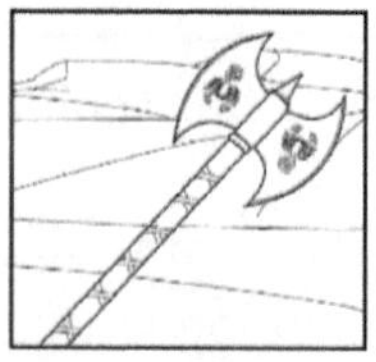

BLADEMON'S ARMY

Vardak stood aside as his study was once more commandeered for use as an infirmary. He kept to the corner of the room, observant of the commotion around him, yet apart from it. It was the business of the mages, the wizards, and the celestial goddess that granted their abilities.

Solsticia fretted over Ravin's weakened condition, while Tavesin disappeared to fetch Radosan. Trozyen approached him hesitantly once he was certain his services would be of no use to the injured mage, and Vardak led him toward the larger room beyond.

"What happened?" Vardak asked. "Just this morning he was given the healers' blessing."

Trozyen shifted uncomfortably and adjusted his leathery wings. "We were summoned to the Sky Palace, to a meeting with the gods. Things became heated between Ravin and Minora. I'm afraid I don't understand the source of his anger, nor did I fully comprehend what they discussed, but Ravin made a spectacle of himself." The young Drakkon looked away, his scaly features troubled.

"That doesn't explain his injury," Vardak replied.

Trozyen sighed. "He drew upon the talisman's magic. It was a vast amount of energy, and I could sense it was burning him from the inside out. He did nothing to temper its flow—I've never witnessed a mage wield so much power and simply let it begin to consume them." He swallowed hard, shuddered, then grimaced. "He did it to force the goddess' hand on a matter that I fear only he can explain. The gods demand we perform a ritual to subdue the Nameless, but we can't complete it without Ravin. He knows this, and used himself as a bargaining chip. You will have to ask him for details, Vardak."

Vardak studied him carefully. Trozyen was distressed by what he'd witnessed, unsettled, afraid. "I'll speak with him once he's alone."

"Thank you. And if she should ask, tell Aziarah I was summoned by Solsticia." Trozyen managed a weak grin. "She's still angry with the wizards, and I don't want Tavesin to be blamed for my involvement."

Vardak nodded. "I will."

Trozyen turned to leave, hesitated, then glanced over his shoulder. "And Vardak? I'd steer clear of *all* the gods if I were you. Our meeting was…tense."

Vardak remained within the guild hall until Radosan arrived with Tavesin trailing in his wake. Radosan paused to greet him but did not linger; his brow was furrowed with concern, and it was clear he didn't wish to delay Ravin's healing. Whatever had transpired in Solsticia's palace was grave, indeed.

He made his way to the exit, plucked his cloak from the peg beside the door, and skittered outside into the tepid winter daylight. The day wasn't as cold as most of its predecessors had been since his arrival in Daesan. The nearby forges bustled with activity, and he gazed longingly at the scene for several moments. He could step no closer than his present location without drawing Flariel's misplaced ire; rather than venture toward the familiarity of the scene, he forced himself to turn away. His path led him from the city center and toward its western outskirts.

He desired conversation. With Patak a constant at Emra's side, he sought Maryn's company. Maryn's command post was housed in a ramshackle building blocks away from the western wall, but the structure had managed to withstand the recent earthquake and sported an intact, if leaky, roof.

As he entered, he was unsurprised to find Maryn and a trio of others huddled around a table near the roaring hearth, engrossed in a game of dice. Maryn nodded to him with a sly grin.

"Care to join us, General?"

Vardak chuckled with a shake of his head. "Patak still owes you a tidy sum. I'd hate to indebt my family further." He removed his cloak and settled himself near the fire. "I'm content to watch."

Maryn snickered. "Learn from his example," he said to the others. "Don't engage a foe that cannot be beaten. It's futile."

His words were met with laughs and good-natured grumbles, but at the conclusion of the round, it was clear the wily Felene had bested them. Maryn grinned impishly as he collected his winnings and the others dispersed. Tucking his coin purse away, Maryn sat down on the hearth ledge near Vardak.

"Something's on your mind, Vardak."

Vardak shrugged and forced a grin. "I just witnessed three men ruthlessly bested by their captain. You're relentless."

"I have to pay for my daggers somehow, and they knew the risks."

"How many do you have now? A dozen?"

Maryn laughed. "I have enough to see us through this war." He peered at Vardak knowingly while his ears twitched in unspoken agitation. "I knew the moment you stepped inside that you needed to talk. Something's happened."

"My study is being used as an infirmary again, and I've grown weary of Ravin's company." He sighed. "Something has happened, but I don't know the details. I'm not certain I want to."

"It was my understanding Radosan cleared him earlier today." Maryn's tail swished in aggravation.

"He did, then Ravin was carried into my study by Solsticia, nearly as weak as he was after the eruption." Vardak shrugged. "I simply needed a reprieve. There are days I'm busy from dawn to dusk, yet I feel as though I've accomplished nothing. This business with magical injuries is incomprehensible to me. I needed some time away."

"And I've suggested you needed that for weeks. Gods, Vardak, everyone sees how diligent you've been, the hours you've spent building what we have and training new recruits. You deserve a break now and again."

"A part of me thinks it's a risk I should avoid," he replied. "So much relies on *me*, my decisions—"

Maryn sprang to his feet and motioned impatiently. "I know *exactly* what you need. Follow me."

Vardak frowned, uncertain what Maryn planned, but he'd come to his friend seeking a diversion, an escape from the tedium after all. He threw his cloak around his shoulders and followed Maryn outside.

Maryn beckoned him forward, and together they traveled the short distance to the city's western gate.

In the snow-dusted fields beyond, a unit from the Santinian cavalry charged in formation. At a shouted command from their leader, the group wheeled as one and rushed in another direction. Vardak watched silently, impressed by the ease in which the mounted soldiers transitioned.

Maryn smirked up at him. "Do you see, Vardak? The army will run itself for a few days without your hand to guide it. Allow Emra to fill in while you rest. It'll give her something to do besides moon over your brother."

Vardak snorted. "I should not have encouraged Patak to follow that path. Even if I don't tell our people, Makta will."

Maryn crossed his arms while his tail lashed of its own accord. "If you want the truth, I think she's good for him, like it or not. He's become more grounded."

"I know." Vardak continued to watch the cavalry while he considered his next words. "I promised Patak I wouldn't stand in his way after the battle in Delucha. I plan to keep my word, but he may be exiled from the Stronghold. It wouldn't be the first time one of our people fell in love with a human, and each time the result was the same." He sighed and looked down. "I want to see him happy, but I don't want to lose him, either."

"You admire him," Maryn stated.

"Yes. I always have, though I doubt it's safe to admit it to him. His ego would become intolerable." Vardak chuckled sadly. "I can do nothing but pray the Warleader will make an exception for him. Emra is no ordinary woman."

Maryn snickered. "Such is the way of siblings. You're lucky you only have two."

Vardak lifted his eyebrows in silent question.

"Felene women often birth six to eight children in a single litter," Maryn continued. "I was one of seven, and my mother had two litters before mine. We have large families. I find it peaceful in your northern lands. There is much less family drama to contend with."

"You've rarely spoken of your family, Maryn."

He shrugged. "I took the post as a guard in Cynda to escape them. Half of my sisters were at war with the others—or what passes for war amongst our kin. There was much public shaming and snobbery involved. It was tiresome."

Vardak nodded. "I imagine it was. You've seen how my people deal with such problems. You were present when Makta arrived."

Maryn began to laugh. "Oh, if my sisters were like her, that would have been a sight. The whole town would have erupted into a brawl! Imagine the coin I could have made on the betting." He paused to compose himself, then said, "There is more I'd like to show you. Come."

Dusk was falling when Vardak returned to the smiths' guild hall. He'd spent the remainder of the day in Maryn's company, simply observing the workings of the army around them. They'd discussed many things, but few related to the war and their reason for being in Daesan. It seemed a weight had been lifted from his shoulders; he felt better than he had in weeks. Perhaps a break was warranted now and again.

The foyer was unusually quiet as he entered and hung his cloak on its customary peg. He could discern voices through the ceiling, where some of the wizards had taken up residence, and the crackle of a fire in the adjacent chamber. The room was empty when he entered, and the door to his study on the opposite side stood ajar.

He knew he must speak with Ravin; he'd postponed their meeting long enough as it was. He crossed the room, then paused just beyond the threshold as Ravin spoke to an unseen visitor.

"He's not here." The mage's voice was weary and strained. "I've no energy for an interrogation."

There was a pause, then a voice Vardak knew well made a reply. "No, you don't, but it seems he's arrived as I expected."

Vardak drew a breath and made his way into the study to face Blademon. The god was aware of his presence; there was no purpose in lingering outside. Ravin sat near the hearth, several rolled blankets cushioning his back. His face was haggard and drawn, but he was awake. Blademon stood in silhouette before the room's only window, arms crossed and expression unreadable.

"I hope your day with the Felene has rejuvenated your spirit," Blademon stated. "It may be the last respite you have for some time."

Vardak suppressed a groan and nodded. "I take it you have news."

"Yes, and a plan. It involves both of you," he replied with a pointed glance toward Ravin. "Your threats to Minora have caused us a delay we cannot afford, but we must adapt to the present situation."

"It was the only way," Ravin growled.

Blademon scowled. "Perhaps, perhaps not, but it is the way you've chosen." When Ravin said nothing in response, he continued. "The Nameless blocks our sight, but we have reason to believe he's further empowered one of the Soulless. The signs are there, if one knows what to seek. He has recovered more rapidly than we'd anticipated, which brings me to the reason for my visit."

Dread writhed in Vardak's gut, but he kept his voice even. "You want us to march."

"Yes." Blademon studied him, his expression unyielding. "We cannot delay any longer. Flariel has agreed to clear the passes, and Maelstrom will alter the weather to hasten your journey. I have come to oversee the army, Vardak. This is no longer a battle of mortals alone. You will act as my second."

Vardak saluted, an ingrained response, though he could not hide the swelling of pride at Blademon's words. It was a position of great honor. He would do his utmost to live up to war god's expectations.

A twitch of a smile crossed Blademon's features before he leveled a steely gaze at Ravin. "Your role is to act as a liaison between our army and the rogue Murkor. As Solsticia was quick to remind us, the Aethereum was constructed for *you*, and *you* are its true master. It is unsafe for anyone else to travel through that realm until we know for certain what the Nameless has done. Therefore, this task falls to you."

"Where are the Murkor located? I cannot simply enter the Aethereum and *know* their whereabouts, unless they happen to be within the magical realm. And that is very unlikely." Ravin leaned his head back against the rolled blankets and closed his eyes. "Radosan has condemned me to another week abed, as well."

"As I stated previously, your spat with Minora has cost us precious time," Blademon growled. "As soon as you are well enough to use your singular gifts, Aeon or Ukase will arrive to escort you to the Murkor camp. They will rendezvous with us on the eastern side of the mountains."

"When do you plan to depart?" Vardak asked as an endless list of unfinished tasks began to inundate his mind.

"In three weeks," Blademon replied. "I have spoken with Sevic, as well. He is aware of the Murkor army and their role in this matter. They will march from the Stronghold at my signal, and if we are fortunate, both armies will unite with ours on the date of my choosing. I suggest you inform Emra and her various captains this evening. I will take command on the morrow."

"Yes, sir," Vardak replied.

Blademon nodded once, then vanished.

"Well," Ravin said into the ensuing silence, "this certainly changes some things."

CHAPTER TWENTY-NINE

THE ROGUES MARCH

"Sit still," Sal'zar instructed in as calm a tone as he could muster. The soldier on the mat before him squirmed and turned his hooded face away as Sal'zar unwound the soiled bandage from his arm. Each evening with this patient had been the same; how a man with an aversion to his own blood had been selected for the soldier's caste was baffling.

He inspected the cut carefully, noted the blue skin at its edges was no longer inflamed, and the injury itself was beginning to knit together. This soldier refused to allow him to use his healing magic on the wound, no matter how many times Sal'zar assured him he would not be harmed in the process. It left him with traditional methods; poultices and soaked bandages, treated by himself and the other alchemists to promote mending and reduce scarring.

"Your wound has closed," he said. "You should not require bandages any longer."

Slowly, the soldier turned his head to peer down at his exposed arm. "The others healed faster," he muttered.

"The others didn't shun me," Sal'zar replied bitterly. "This is the best I can manage for you."

He nodded tersely. "Thank you. I will go."

Sal'zar suppressed his heavy sigh until the soldier was beyond earshot, then allowed it to explode from his lungs. He wished everyone were as understanding of his unique talent as Jal'den was. Perhaps he'd feel less drained with each encounter, less resentful, more optimistic. At least most of the people injured during the earthquakes and subsequent tunnel collapses were fully recovered, he reminded himself. It had been an eventful three weeks.

He rose and stretched his arms behind him, tired despite what seemed an early hour. It was impossible to track time within the confines of their cavern, but he believed it was not long after sundown. He wished for just one of the illuminated crystals that adorned the Murkor home; they dimmed and flared subtly according to the position of the sun outside and allowed his people to gauge the time. They had none here. Without the calculated passage of time, he was adrift, detached from reality.

His gaze swept across the cavern. He took in the bustle of activity, most centered around the makeshift sparring ring the soldiers had set up on one side. A pair of black-clad soldiers circled one another within, their blades swathed in leather to prevent damage to the weapons and unnecessary injury to one another. Around the perimeter, dozens more gathered to observe the match. Some cheered, others jeered, bets were exchanged.

Sal'zar shook his head with a sigh; he'd never understood the fascination with such displays of violence. As Jal'den was fond of reminding him, it was one of many reasons he was better suited to the alchemists' caste.

"Your people are coping, Sal'zar." The low voice behind him momentarily startled him, but he calmed as he recognized Ukase's basso tones.

He turned around and bowed swiftly, and only when he began to straighten did he realize Ukase was not alone. A brown-skinned human with a mop of curly, dark hair accompanied him. Sal'zar met his piercing, golden eyes with a stiff nod. Though he'd been anticipating this meeting, he was uncertain what to expect, and his limited experience with humans did little to ease his discomfort.

"Ravin, this is Sal'zar," Ukase stated. He eyed the pair carefully for a moment while each sized up the other. "You know what you must do," he said to Ravin before he promptly vanished.

"This is not our first encounter," Ravin began. "You have access to the Aethereum."

"Yes," Sal'zar replied uneasily. "I don't believe I properly thanked you for your assistance that day."

"I would teach you more of the magical realm, given time, but I must be certain of something first." Ravin crossed his arms and frowned. "I understand the ways of your people well enough, and what I must ask of you is…improper, but there is no other way."

Sal'zar's pulse accelerated as he prepared to defend himself against the human. "What do you seek?"

"I need to see your forearms to make certain you were not branded."

Sal'zar released a sigh, relieved it was a simple request and one he was willing to accommodate. He pushed up his sleeves and allowed Ravin to examine the network of familial tattoos that decorated his skin. A faint smile touched Ravin's lips as he visibly relaxed.

"Thank you. I had to be certain." Ravin tilted his head, his expression thoughtful. "Ukase told me you were fully trained, that you'd undergone your initiation rites. How did you escape the tower unscathed? They always brand their members, willing or not."

Sal'zar looked down. "They tried, but the magic failed. Dranamir wanted to kill me for it, but Garin intervened. My immunity was not of my doing."

Ravin's expression darkened at the mention of the Soulless. "You're fortunate Dranamir was overruled. She's murdered others for lesser offenses."

"I know." He forced himself to meet the human's eyes. "Garin is tied to their god in a way I don't fully understand, and he acted as the Nameless' voice to the others. I don't know why he spared me, but I'd like to believe it was for this purpose. My people are weary of the endless cycle of subjugation, century after century. The Kal's plan for us seemed the only means to achieve our freedom."

It was more than he'd intended to say, more than he should have said, but he could not take the words back now.

"I understand the desire for freedom," Ravin replied quietly. "Better than you might realize, in fact. The gods sent me here to assist you. I will do my part." His gaze drifted away from Sal'zar to scan the cavern. "I won't fault you if you don't trust me, but know this—I am no friend of the Soulless."

Sal'zar nodded and glanced over his shoulder to find they'd begun to gather an audience. The human's presence was both a novelty and a source of palpable tension for the Murkor. He faced Ravin again, and when he spoke, his voice carried across the cavern to the onlookers. Any doubts about Ravin's purpose needed to be quashed before rumors began to spread.

"We've been awaiting orders from Ukase. He has brought you here, so I believe you speak the truth. How do you plan to help us?"

Ravin managed a smile. "I may have come here with Ukase, but I was sent by Blademon. He commands both the human army and the Scorpion Men. He seeks an alliance with your people, as well." Ravin shrugged uncomfortably. "I am no diplomat, but I will do my best to convey your people's needs to the rest. If you would join us in the fight against the Nameless god, I can provide you with directions to Blademon's proposed rendezvous point."

"If you are not a diplomat, why were you sent?" some called from the crowd.

Sal'zar turned to face the others and stepped backwards to stand alongside Ravin. "He is a mage. One more powerful than the Soulless."

Ravin glanced at him uncertainly as whispers erupted around them. "Was that wise?" he whispered.

"It's better they learn the truth now," Sal'zar replied. "After the business with Shan'tar, then the Soulless, we know little of other magi. I don't want them to learn what you are at a critical moment, only to rise against us."

Ravin scowled at the cavern floor. "Then perhaps I ought to mention I am Solsticia's son."

Sal'zar grinned beneath his hood. The admission fit several pieces of the puzzle together in his mind—the reason Ravin was chosen, the vast amount of power he could sense in the man, his strange, yet beautiful eyes. He held up his hands for silence, and after a few moments, the others quieted.

"Ravin is not only a mage," he stated, "but the son of the celestial goddess herself. He *can* help us, and I believe we ought to accept Blademon's offer of alliance. The Kal would agree if he were able, but as each of us knows, he cannot openly support our cause any longer. We wish to see our people freed. We wish to see them spared the terrible fate the Nameless god had promised. I believe this is the only way."

Hundreds of voices rose to echo off the cavern walls. Some shouted questions, some cheered, others made demands. It would take time to sort through the complicated mix of emotions he'd stirred within them, yet he had hope for the future for the first time in months.

"For an alchemist, you certainly know how to inspire your people," Ravin said in a low tone. "I've met a few of your kind before. They are always reticent. At first, I believed you were the same."

Sal'zar chuckled, pleased with the unusual compliment. "Perhaps it is why the Kal chose me to lead them. Or perhaps my partner's personality is beginning to affect and alter my own."

"Is your partner here?" Ravin asked.

Sal'zar shook his head sadly, pained by his knowledge of Jal'den's unfortunate role. "He is our army's latest commander. At the Kal's insistence, he remained behind with the others. He didn't want to, and I didn't want to leave him."

"I'm sorry." Ravin looked away, his expression troubled.

"There is nothing to be done about it now," Sal'zar replied brusquely, pushing his emotions aside. "I must speak with the others about this alliance you've proposed. It will take some time."

"Ukase encouraged us to accept this alliance on his previous visit," Sal'zar stated for at least the tenth time since the debate had begun. "Blademon leads the armies. We've been granted the freedom to choose our path, and I believe we ought to join them."

"And what of the Nameless' threat to our people?" The speaker's hands marked him as Ram'anaz. "If we are discovered, he will destroy us. He will murder the others still at the tower, and leave our home caverns a place of ghosts. We are safe here."

"You delude yourself," another replied. Sal'zar could not see the speaker's hands. "Ukase shields us. Our patron will protect our path, no matter which we choose."

Sal'zar glanced toward the cavern wall where Ravin sat, his back to the rough stone and his eyes closed. He appeared to be asleep, but Sal'zar suspected it was a ploy. The argument had raged for hours without a resolution; he could not fault the human for succumbing to boredom.

He turned back to the others, determined to put an end to the useless bickering. They'd wasted too much time.

"Enough!" He shouted and rose to his feet. "We'll do nothing if we do not make a decision. I plan to join the gods in this fight. Those of you who wish to join me are welcome to follow. Those who wish to remain here can do so. I'm finished with this debate."

He turned on his heel and strode toward Ravin, who hastily regained his feet. "I cannot speak for the others, but I will join you in this matter. The Nameless must be brought to heel." He shot a heated glare over his shoulder. "Those who decide to follow me will begin the journey to the location within the hour."

A flurry of activity greeted his final words, and he believed more Murkor would join his march than would remain behind. Relieved, he faced Ravin with a smile the mage would never see beneath his hood.

"I believe most of us have chosen to follow Blademon's proposed course."

Ravin nodded. "The others will be pleased to hear it. While you were discussing your options, it gave me some time to consider your situation."

Sal'zar stiffened, uncertain what the man before him was about to say.

"Blademon knows your partner well, if I'm not mistaken. Emra's general met him in battle outside of Delucha."

"Yes. Blademon's other…student." Sal'zar shifted uneasily and looked away.

"You told me he didn't wish to stay behind, that he did so on your Kal's orders."

Sal'zar peered up at him. "That's true."

"It's inevitable that they meet on the field a second time. In fact, the Nameless will be expecting it." Ravin's golden eyes studied him carefully. "I will mention your connection to the Murkor commander to Vardak. I suspect he'll be willing to subdue your partner in battle rather than kill him. I cannot make a true assurance this will be the case, but it is all I can offer at present."

"You offer us hope," Sal'zar replied, overwhelmed by a wave of emotion. "If Jal'den can be spared, I will owe you a great debt."

Ravin shook his head. "You will owe me nothing. Go. Your people will soon be ready, and they'll need you to lead them." He withdrew a folded slip of parchment from his pocket and pressed it into Sal'zar's hand. "These are Blademon's instructions. I'll return to our own camp to report."

"Thank you," Sal'zar whispered.

Ravin paused, one hand lifted in the air. "Did they teach you the art of learning magic through observation, Sal'zar?"

When he nodded, Ravin grinned. "Then pay close attention. I will open a portal into the Aethereum. You have the same gift, and you should be able to replicate it. Once in the other realm, you can travel quickly from one place to the next, as long as you can properly visualize your destination. Create a second portal to exit."

"I understand." His heart leapt at the opportunity; the ability to travel swiftly might prove invaluable.

"Seek me if you need anything, Sal'zar. Watch carefully."

Ravin waved his hand at the empty air, and as he did so, Sal'zar sensed the brief flicker of magic he'd employed. A luminous blue oval appeared in the air near Ravin's fingertips. Sal'zar smiled.

"I will find you if the need arises," he promised the mage. "It is comforting to learn not all humans are monsters. Thank you."

Ravin's smile faltered at his words, but he nodded. "I pray some of our actions can make up for the crimes the Soulless have committed against your people. We are not so different, you and I."

He watched Ravin disappear through the portal, then turned to face the cavern. A renewed sense of purpose suffused his movements; determination fueled his steps. He gathered his belongings and made his way through the throng to the tunnel Dus'tanne had cleared for them a week ago. As the others began to fall in behind him, he grinned beneath his hood.

"We march!" he bellowed as he stepped into the tunnel.

He knew if Jal'den could see him in that moment, he'd be proud.

CHAPTER THIRTY

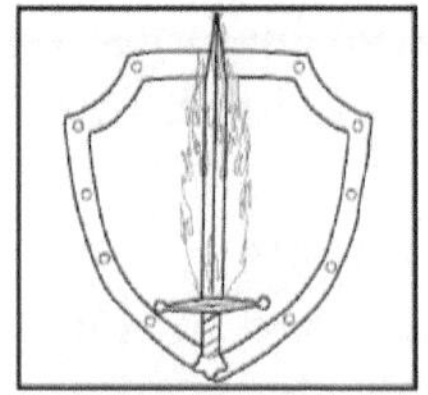

A CONVERGENCE OF MIGHT

"I didn't realize there were so many of them." Patak shook his head, overwhelmed by the number of wizards that continued to emerge from the portal on the slope below. He crossed his arms and shifted, his arachnid legs tapping an uneasy cadence on the parched earth.

"We knew they were coming," Emra replied. She placed one hand on his forearm with the hope her touch would calm his nerves. He stilled at the contact and looked down with a smile.

"We did."

"And the Shining Tower possesses the largest number of magical folk anywhere in the world." She smiled up at him. "When the new Radiant agreed to join us in this fight, he offered every Gray and Green their order could spare. But there are many others, too." She pointed at a pair newly emerged from the Aethereum as they paused to make their obeisance to Solsticia, who stood sentinel at the portal. "They are both Blues, like Tavesin."

Patak snorted. "How do you know what Sect they belong to from this distance, Em? They all appear the same to me."

She laughed lightly. "I can sense their innate abilities, their attunements, if you will. Any trained wizard can do the same."

"Hmm. And what of those like Ravin? He's no wizard."

"No, he certainly isn't."

She frowned and gazed at the portal. Solsticia was responsible for maintaining both openings, but her son, several of the Drakkon, and Tavesin were within the Aethereum, ferrying the wizards through to safety. The Soulless could access the magical realm at any time, a point

Ravin had brought up extensively as they'd discussed arrangements. The gods had ordered them to avoid the Aethereum only weeks ago, now they'd changed their stance out of desperation. They needed the wizards' assistance, and it was the quickest means of uniting their forces. Ravin had not been placated, but he'd eventually relented.

"Em?" Patak asked uncertainly.

She forced a strained smile. "Let us hope they remain undiscovered. Ravin's power is unrivaled in the Aethereum, but the Soulless are ruthless."

He chuckled uneasily. "And you didn't answer my question."

"No, I suppose I didn't. Any mage can judge another's abilities and aptitudes. It is why many of the wizards are hesitant around Ravin, despite his alliance with our cause. He's refused their vows, yet wields greater power than any of us."

"Do you fear him?" Patak asked, his tone contemplative.

"I did at first, but after seeing him work with Tavesin, I believe his heart is in the right place. He's not a danger to us—only to himself, it seems."

"Well, he's gone almost a month without another incident," Patak replied. "Perhaps he's finished goading the gods."

Emra shrugged. Ravin refused to speak of how he'd sustained his second grave magical injury. She believed Tavesin knew the cause and Ravin's reason for incurring it, but the boy proved more loyal to his mentor than he did to anyone else and would not share what he knew. It was at once comforting to realize the two most powerful wielders of magic had formed such a strong bond, yet disconcerting. Together, they were nearly unstoppable, for good or ill.

"Ah, that must be all of them." Patak breathed an audible sigh of relief as several Drakkon emerged from the portal, followed by Tavesin and Ravin. "Gods, there must be two hundred of them."

Sensing his discomfort, she reached for his hand and laced her fingers through his. "We're not all bad, are we?"

A wicked grin creased his face. "That depends on your definition of 'bad,' Em."

"In that case, you're terrible." She returned his grin with one of her own. "Perhaps we return to your tent, and I'll demonstrate for you."

The yearning in his gaze was answer enough, but he suddenly straightened and muttered a curse under his breath. "My brother has the worst fucking timing."

She turned to follow his gaze. Vardak was climbing the hillside toward them.

"He likely has news from one of the scouts," she told Patak. "I ought to hear this. We can make time for ourselves later."

He crossed his arms, nonplussed, and shot a scowl in Vardak's direction. She understood his frustration; since leaving Daesan, they'd scarcely had a moment to themselves.

Vardak met his brother's glare with an impassive stare. "I'll make this quick, since it's clear I've interrupted something." He cleared his throat and focused on Emra. "Some of Danian's scouts have returned. The Murkor are in position. We should encounter them before mid-afternoon tomorrow."

"This is good news." She glanced at Patak, whose expression had softened somewhat. "I'd hoped to meet with them once we draw near. I'd like you both to accompany me."

"Blademon suggested the same," Vardak replied. "The Murkor are unused to humans. The gods won't state it explicitly, but I suspect the Murkor were ordered to join us here. They'll be distrustful of us—and of you, in particular."

"I'm well aware of their concerns," she replied with a faint smile. "Ravin has kept me apprised of their movements and his meetings with their leader."

At Ravin's name, Vardak sighed and raked a hand through his hair. "Yes, Ravin. I suppose I ought to extend the invitation to him, as well. The Murkor will likely be expecting him."

"You still don't trust him." Emra eyed him with concern. "He's been an immense help, Vardak."

Vardak shrugged uncomfortably. "I know, yet I cannot shake the impression that he operates according to his own agenda." He shook his head. "My thoughts don't matter. I'll speak with him and leave the two of you to your evening."

"My brother is right," Patak said once they were alone.

"Perhaps," she replied, "but Ravin's allegiance is a risk I feel we must take. And the gods seem to trust him. Who are we to argue with their judgment?"

He sighed. "I pray you're right."

Impulsively, she took both of his hands in her own. She would not allow another interruption to spoil what might prove to be their final evening together. She was certain once they united with the Murkor and the Scorpion Men, Blademon would urge them forward at a grueling pace. The gods wanted to be rid of their forsaken brother as much as she wanted to be rid of the Soulless. This night was an opportunity to forget her present concerns for a time, and she was not about to waste it.

"Let's not worry about the gods, your brother, Ravin, or this damned war for one night. We both know our futures will become uncertain with the dawn. Come."

A slow grin spread across his handsome features. "Then let us make the most of the night."

Emra awoke near dawn as shivers racked her body. She sat up and peered around the tent while clutching the tangled blankets to her torso. Patak was near the exit, a mere silhouette in the semi-darkness as he strapped on his armor. He paused as she began to stir, his blue eyes locked on her form.

"I tried not to wake you, Em."

"You didn't. I'm cold." She chuckled softly and reached for her clothing. "You're usually not awake before I am."

He shrugged and tugged on his gauntlets. "I'm on edge. I always am when I know a battle is on the horizon. And it's only a matter of time before the rest of my people arrive." He averted his gaze to study everything in the tent but her. "Sevic won't be pleased with…*us*."

Her heart wrenched at the anguish in his tone. "Patak, I thought we were past this." She pulled on her tunic and rose to begin donning her own armor. "For all your bravado, you're still concerned over what they'll think."

"I can't help it, Em. It's one thing to make light of exile when I'm hundreds of leagues away from home. It's another matter entirely when I know I'll be forced to explain myself in a few hours." He crossed his arms and scowled at the floor. "I may be spared an interrogation until after the Nameless has been dealt with, but knowing Sevic, there *will* be one. I shouldn't be treated like a common criminal simply because I've fallen in love with you."

She crossed the tent in an instant and reached up to touch his face. He wouldn't meet her eye until she adjusted her position to stand directly in his vision.

"You are no criminal, Patak."

She rose up to her toes and kissed him. He resisted for a moment, then returned it with ravenous passion that stunned her and caused her knees to weaken. When she stepped back moments later, she was breathless. His expression was filled with an unspoken desire that threatened to stir the residual cinders of the previous night into a raging inferno within her. She didn't trust her voice to remain steady and was relieved when he spoke first.

"You're right," he said, his voice rough. "This cannot be a crime. And if I'm proven wrong, you're worth any punishment the Warleader metes out." He grinned, then turned to retrieve his weapons from their resting place against the side of the tent. "I'll meet you outside."

"I won't be long," she promised.

She finished donning her armor, then rolled the blankets into a bundle while her thoughts whirled. In several of her lives, she'd found love, found a partner that understood her and remained at her side long after the conflicts she'd been born to fight were ended. In all of her pasts, those others had been human. Her attraction to Patak was a first, a beautiful anomaly in an otherwise scripted existence. She prayed they would both live to see the conclusion of the Nameless god's senseless war.

She buckled on her sword belt, reassured they would survive with the Fireblade at her side, grabbed the rolled blanket and her satchel of belongings, then ducked outside. The air was warmer on the eastern side of the mountains, though it was still cool as the dawn approached. Her gaze drifted to the horizon, aglow with shades of crimson, a harbinger of strife and struggle.

Patak appeared at her side to study the sunrise. "My people have a saying about mornings such as this."

"What is it?"

"The world mourns the fallen when the sky is painted in blood."

She shuddered as a wave of memory overcame her. Another warrior had once uttered the same phrase to her in another life, on the eve of a much different battle, as they prepared to face Garin on the plains of Santine. That warrior had also been one of the Scorpion Men, the greatest general of the day, Katya.

Emra shook her head and tore her gaze away from the rising sun. "You aren't the first of your people to speak those words in my presence."

"Vardak?" he asked as he turned to begin dismantling their tent.

"No. It was…long ago."

He chuckled. "I should have known. You always grow still when you're lost in memory."

She peered at him, surprised. "I do?"

"Yes, Em, you do." He smirked at her, a mischievous gleam in his eyes. "There are times I wonder if I'm speaking with *you*, or with one of your past selves—but I wouldn't change it for all the gold in the world."

She smiled, grateful once again that she'd met him. He'd changed her life, her perspective, her existence for the better. "I should see to Fyrmane," she said quietly after a time. "He'll be indignant that I've waited this long to get his breakfast, and I need to ensure he's ready for a long ride."

Patak nodded and continued his work with the tent. "I suppose I ought to make certain I'm prepared for a long run. I can't have your steed making me look inadequate when we meet with the Murkor." His grin faltered, and he sighed. "Or my people."

"We'll get through this, Patak," she assured him. "I promise."

An hour past mid-day, the Murkor camp was sighted. Word came minutes later that the Scorpion Men were near as well, and it was likely the three armies would converge at the same time. Blademon joined Emra at the head of the column, Vardak at his side, while Ravin appeared through a portal nearby.

"We will strike out ahead of the rest," Blademon stated, his steely gaze pausing to study each of them in turn. "The Murkor were hesitant to join us after freeing themselves from the Soulless' grasp, and we must provide them with assurances that they and their people will be treated fairly in all matters." He eyed Emra fiercely. "They have little faith in humans, though the mage here has done much to win their trust."

Ravin crossed his arms with a glower, but remained silent.

"I suggest you ride with Emra," Blademon told Ravin. "You'll be unable to keep up on foot, and I would like to monitor this first meeting carefully. I won't have you magicking yourself ahead."

Emra mounted Fyrmane, who danced and snorted as Ravin reluctantly approached. She knew the big bay could sense the man's magic, and though he accepted Emra, he was rarely friendly with anyone else. He'd made an exception for the Scorpion Men, but no others.

"Easy," she said, and patted his neck. "He's no threat to you, and we must follow orders."

Fyrmane shook his head and snorted again, but stilled his hooves.

"He doesn't like me," Ravin stated as he edged toward Fyrmane's side.

"To be fair, he doesn't like any human other than Em," Patak replied.

Ravin glowered, then pulled himself into the saddle behind her. "You can tell him I don't care for horses, either. Perhaps he can sway my opinion." In a quieter tone, he muttered, "Adalin will never stop asking to ride once she learns of this."

Emra laughed. "The duchess is fond of horses?"

Ravin groaned as she kicked Fyrmane into a trot to keep pace with the others. "She used to have a stable full of them before she was forced to leave her late husband's estate. She loves the beasts, and I… I have little experience with them."

"I imagine her horses were much gentler than this brute," Emra replied. "He was bred for war." She stroked Fyrmane's neck affectionately, and he arced his neck to stand taller in response.

"He has a high opinion of himself," Ravin said with a chuckle.

Beside them, Patak snorted. "You've seen nothing of Fyrmane's ego. Believe me."

They fell silent as the path arced between a pair of low hills and the Murkor encampment came into view. Soldiers garbed and hooded in black patrolled the perimeter, armed with weapons forged of their coveted poisoned metal. An expanse of tents sprawled across the land at the foot of the mountains; she calculated there must be over a thousand Murkor present. The camp itself was still, with the exception of the sentries, but that was to be expected during the daylight hours.

"If this was but a portion of the Murkor army, how many remained behind with the Soulless?" she asked of no one in particular.

"This was a full third of their army," Ravin said from behind her. "But that was before the reinforcements arrived from their homeland, and prior to the…induction of the Serpentus into their ranks."

Patak growled ominously. "They need to pay for what they've done to those prisoners."

"Yes," Ravin agreed in a fierce tone. "Dranamir and I have an old score to settle as it is. I will not allow her atrocities to go unpunished."

As they reached the perimeter, one of the sentries greeted them and spoke with Blademon in his own tongue. For all her experiences, she'd never learned the musical language of the Murkor. She glanced at Patak, who grinned and began to translate.

"He says they've sent for Sal'zar, who seems to be the leader of this group."

"Yes, he's the alchemist mage," Ravin confirmed. "I've spoken to Vardak about him at length. I only pray he'll make good on his word to me."

"If my brother has promised you anything, he'll follow through," Patak replied. "Even if he doesn't trust you, he'll keep his word."

It was several minutes before another Murkor approached. He was tall and thin, garbed in a lurid shade of green that marked him as an alchemist. He bowed low to Blademon, then swiveled his hooded head as he studied the others. Ravin dismounted and strode forward to greet him, and the alchemist's shoulders visibly relaxed.

Blademon made introductions and immediately began to seize control of the camp's operations. "Vardak will speak with your military leaders and establish command here. You will follow his orders as if they come from me."

Beside her Patak's eyebrows rose. "Fucking gods, he's actually making good on his promise to Vardak," he whispered, stunned.

"Your brother has proven himself time and again," she replied. "Will the Murkor follow him?"

"If Blademon has ordered it, they will. The Murkor are more devout in their worship of the gods than any other people I've known."

A commotion erupted on the far side of the camp, and Blademon chuckled. "It seems Sevic's people are near, as I've planned. Come, all of you. We must speak with the Warleader."

A pained sigh erupted from Patak. "Shit. Shit. *Shit.*"

Emra reached over to touch his armor-plated shoulder. "We're in this together, Patak. I doubt he'll have the time to accost you until after the battle has ended."

Patak shrugged away from her and would not meet her gaze. "You don't know Sevic. Yes, you met him during your brief stay in the Stronghold, but you don't *know* him, Em."

He fell silent as they passed through the Murkor camp. Emra wished there was something she could say to him. She desperately hoped to ease his mind, to assure him all would be well, but she knew too little of the Warleader to accurately gauge his temperament, as Patak had pointed out. His unspoken pain wrenched her heart, but there was little she could do to interfere.

Sevic saluted Blademon from afar as they approached. Silver flecked his temples, and his tanned skin was creased from years spent patrolling beneath the unrelenting desert sun. His gaze was fierce, hard as iron, and unyielding as steel. He sported plate mail nearly identical to Vardak's, and a pair of swords were strapped across his back.

Sevic greeted Vardak, and once it was established that Vardak would command the Murkor in battle, Sevic accepted his role in Blademon's scheme. When Ravin was introduced, Sevic eyed him suspiciously but said little, his natural distrust of magic wielders apparent. He saluted Emra when Blademon mentioned the Fireblade.

"My ancestors pledged their blades to you in ages past," Sevic stated. "I will uphold their vow, though I dislike the news that your camp harbors so many wizards."

Ravin rolled his eyes in exasperation. "Without us, there is no hope of truly defeating the Nameless god."

"My nephew speaks the truth," Blademon stated, startling Ravin with the familial acknowledgment. As Ravin gaped at him, he said, "We each have an important role to play. I suggest you leave your prejudice behind, Warleader."

"Of course." Sevic saluted. "If that is all, I must attend to my people and establish our camp."

"There is one further matter," Vardak replied. "If you happen to find yourself engaged with the enemy Murkor commander, make an attempt to subdue him. He is not in his position by choice."

Sevic's eyes narrowed, but he nodded. "I will spread the word."

"What was that about, I wonder?" Patak whispered. Ahead, Sal'zar thanked Vardak and Sevic departed.

Emra studied the alchemist carefully. "Perhaps there is more at play than we know, Patak. At least Sevic did not launch into the interrogation you've been dreading."

"A delay for the inevitable," he replied dryly. "Once he speaks with Makta, I've no doubt I'll be summoned."

Vardak turned toward them with a pensive expression. "I've spoken to Makta," he said. "She's agreed to say nothing until the battle is over."

A slow grin crept across Patak's features. After a moment, he rushed Vardak and wrapped him in a fierce embrace. "Gods, little brother, I wish you'd said something sooner."

Vardak shrugged. "I haven't had the opportunity, but I'm glad you're pleased."

Blademon cleared his throat. "Now that the armies have converged, I suggest you each take some time to prepare yourself for the days to come. By my estimation, we will arrive at the tower in three days' time, but if the Nameless learns of our whereabouts, we may be forced to engage the enemy sooner. Rest while you can."

CHAPTER THIRTY-ONE

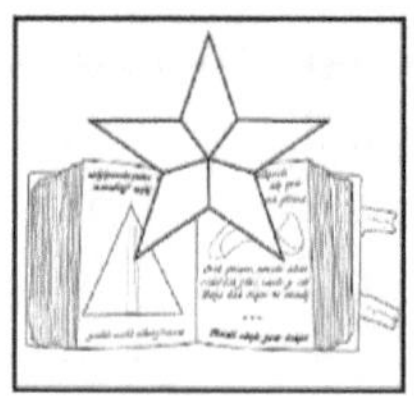

ON THE BRINK

"What do you suppose the Nameless looks like?" Rostin asked. "None of the stories describe him, and when I've asked, none of the wizards seem to know."

Tavesin chewed his lower lip and trudged on, uncertain how to answer his friend's question. Instead, he studied the landscape and was relieved when the black tower remained out of sight. They'd been marching for the better part of four days since their rendezvous with the Murkor and the Scorpion Men. Each step drew them closer to battle, nearer to the Soulless and the cruel god they served.

The Wasted Land stretched before them, seemingly endless in its barren expanse. The afternoon sun scorched the earth, and after weeks spent shivering in the winter cold of Delucha, Tavesin was unused to the heat. Once the sun set, however, the heat would quickly dissipate and they'd be forced to seek the warmth of a campfire once more.

"The stories don't describe him because the gods erased every ounce of his identity," Badolo replied, sparing Tavesin the temptation of divulging the secrets he'd gleaned from Morganus' book. "But he is a *god*, Rostin. If he chooses to change his appearance, I'm certain he can. After all, Blademon did not always wear the form of the Scorpion Men."

"Hmm." Rostin glanced down at the sword he wore at his hip. "I suppose my blade won't do much good against *him*, but I plan to take out a few of his minions."

Dread threatened to engulf Tavesin at Rostin's words. He swallowed his rising panic and averted his gaze.

As a Blue, it was his duty to protect the wizards on the front lines of battle, the Grays such as Rostin. But as the most powerful of his order, Tavesin was required to follow through with the gods' command to destroy the Tower of Obsidian; he would not be granted permission to stand at Rostin's side. His overzealous friend would be in danger, yet he was forbidden to assist. He prayed Rostin would be paired with someone half as capable as he was with defensive magic.

"I hope you're not planning to run head-long into the enemy lines," Badolo replied. There was an edge to his tone, an anxiety that Tavesin shared but could not muster the courage to voice.

Rostin snickered. "No. We've all been given orders to follow Emra's lead, and I've been assigned to the rear guard. I'm to protect the Greens and the Airess healer."

Tavesin breathed a sigh of relief. "Good."

"Good?" Rostin demanded in a hurt tone. "Don't you have faith in my abilities, Taven?"

"It's not that." Tavesin shrugged uncomfortably as he struggled to explain himself. "You weren't on the wall in Delucha. You didn't see the battlefield, the blood…" He shook his head, pained that his friend had misunderstood. "I may have already lost Arra. I don't want to lose you as well."

Rostin's shoulders slumped, and he seemed to deflate. "I understand. I'm sorry. We're all on edge, and the tower hasn't even been sighted yet."

"Promise you'll follow orders, Rostin." Tavesin was unable to mask the tremor in his voice. "And you, too," he said to Badolo.

"I will if you do the same," Rostin replied, while Badolo nodded emphatically.

"I have no choice," Tavesin said in a hollow tone. "But my orders don't come from Emra, as you both know."

Rostin cracked a grin. "As I said, promise to follow your own orders, Taven. If you and Ravin don't bring that tower down, we're all dead."

Tavesin frowned and looked away, unsettled by the reminder. His role was critical to the gods' scheme, and there was no one with the power to fulfill his part should he be captured or killed. His gaze swept across the ranks marching ahead of them; soldiers, cavalry, humans,

Scorpion Men, Murkor, wizards, Drakkon… So much of their fight relied on Blademon's cunning, and the ability of their army to divert the Nameless god's attention long enough for the trio selected by Solsticia to uncover the seal locked within the tower's sublevel. He believed they could prevail, but he did not entertain the delusion that success would come easily.

Rostin nudged him with an elbow. "I was jesting, Taven."

"Your words are truer than you know." Tavesin scanned the eastern horizon for what seemed the hundredth time that day, but this time, his eye was drawn to a tiny, dark splotch directly ahead of the army's path. His heart leapt into his throat; though they had not yet received word regarding the tower, he knew with certainty it was what he'd just spotted.

Badolo gasped beside him. Tavesin glanced at the other boy to find he'd followed Tavesin's gaze. "Taven, that's it, isn't it?"

"What?" Rostin asked.

Tavesin pointed toward the smudge far ahead. "You wanted a battle, Rostin," he said in a voice made tight by fear. "I believe you're about to get one."

The remainder of the afternoon passed in a flurry of activity as the various regiments were called into formation. Leaders were drawn into final discussions of tactics, wizards and Drakkon were dispersed amongst the rest, rations and water skins were distributed, and soldiers readied their weapons and armor. Rostin was ushered to the rear guard, where the healers planned to set up their tents and pavilions, while Badolo was sent to accompany several wizards assigned to the Murkor ranks. Tavesin was left alone to seek Ravin and Trozyen.

As Tavesin searched, the gods began to appear on the field. The four elementals gathered around Blademon while Armistral made his way toward the healers. Ukase appeared within the Murkor ranks, and Aeon sought out Emra amongst the cavalry. Tavesin knew he'd find Ravin if he located Solsticia, but the celestial goddess was slower than her siblings to appear. He continued to seek the golden-eyed mage while more of the Immortals arrived.

He located Trozyen first, near the rear of a human contingent. The young Drakkon offered him a strained smile and nodded in greeting. "Aziarah said I ought to find you and Ravin, but I haven't seen him."

"I've been looking for him too." Tavesin scanned the ranks of soldiers as his heart sank. It would be impossible to locate Ravin amongst the thousands gathered unless Solsticia appeared.

A deafening clang resounded across the field before Troyzen could make a reply. It was followed by several others, struck in a timed cadence, a signal to the soldiers. Dread gripped his belly as Scorpion Men responded with a staccato beat of their own, striking weapon hilts against shields. Murkor drummers joined them, while most of the human soldiers stood at attention.

Tavesin peered up at Trozyen while his heart pounded in time with the Murkor drums. "Is this the beginning?"

Trozyen shook his scaly head. "It is a signal for attention, but I fear the battle won't be far off."

The cacophony diminished as abruptly as it had erupted. The ensuing silence was thick with anticipation, dread, resolve. Tavesin was frozen as fear gripped his limbs and quickened his breath. The devastation he'd witnessed in Delucha replayed in his mind. He didn't want to relive that night, and he was certain what awaited in the hours and days to come would prove far more terrible than everything he'd endured previously.

But he'd continued on his path for Arra. Though it had been more than two months since their last meeting, he clung to the hope that she still lived. He prayed the gods—and the Soulless—would allow him the opportunity to search for her before he was forced to topple the tower. He couldn't bear the thought that his journey had been made in vain.

Blademon's voice rumbled across the field, drawing his attention. Blademon was too distant for Tavesin to see clearly, though he could make out the war god's towering figure as he paced before the front lines. Despite the hundreds of soldiers between them, his words were distinct, as though Blademon stood only paces away.

"Each of you has traveled to this place for your own reason, yet each of you has chosen to fight a common enemy. The denizens of the black tower, that scar upon the horizon, have long proven a bane to this world, but previously, we gods have had no reason to become involved."

Blademon paused to study the image of the black tower in the last rays of the setting sun. Tavesin could not discern his expression from his position, but he imagined the god's face was twisted into a fierce scowl. When Blademon spoke next, his voice was thunderous.

"Our promise to remain apart from mortal conflicts has allowed our fallen brother to reclaim much of his former power. With his return, our world is in peril. We cannot abide his thirst for death, for blood, for an end to all we know. The Nameless god must be stopped. He believes himself immune to your struggle, but he has miscalculated. He has discounted the valor and strength of the mortals who inhabit this world."

"I believe I finally understand why every general in history is known for one speech or another," Trozyen muttered to Tavesin. "They emulate the war god."

Tavesin smiled, amused by the Drakkon's words, but it was another voice that responded from behind them. "You have to admit, he inspires the soldiers."

Tavesin spun around with a grin. "Ravin!"

He fell silent as he noted the mage was not alone. Solsticia stood beside him. She gestured for silence, and Tavesin returned his attention to the speech unfolding ahead.

"...we will *not* allow the Soulless to continue their reign of tyranny. We will not allow those who call themselves Enlightened to perpetuate the falsehoods of the Nameless god. And we will not tolerate that god's desire to see all of creation fall into ruin. They must be stopped—and we shall be the spear that devastates their schemes. We shall be the resolute breaker that shatters their tide of darkness. We shall prevail!"

His final words were met with shouts, cheers, and a raucous cadence from the Murkor drums; the sound was deafening. Tavesin clapped his hands over his ears. He turned to face Ravin and Solsticia once more, but could not form his questions until the clamor began to fade. Slowly, he dropped his hands.

Ravin grimaced. "If the enemy was unaware of our present location, there's no doubt they know of it now."

"The soldiers expect a few words to raise their spirits," Solsticia replied. "Blademon is merely serving his purpose, as he must."

"We were searching for you, Ravin," Tavesin interrupted before the mage could form a retort.

"I suppose you were. I wanted to see Adalin one last time." He averted his golden eyes, and though he made an effort to shield his emotions, Tavesin recognized the anguish in his expression. "What matters is that I'm here now."

"Yes," Solsticia agreed. "The three of you must be prepared for my signal—or Minora's. One of us will indicate when the time has come to begin the ritual. But first, the Nameless god must be sufficiently weakened. If we begin too soon, he will destroy all of you without hesitation."

"I need to find Arra," Tavesin blurted.

Solsticia smiled kindly. "Yes, I'm aware of your desire to see her freed. I will alert you if an opportunity to do so arises, Tavesin, but I cannot promise one will."

He clenched his jaw and looked down as he battled with anger and despair.

"Does the girl live?" Trozyen asked quietly.

"I don't know," Solsticia admitted. "The Nameless god has blocked our sight since his return. She may live, but you must prepare yourself for the worst."

Tavesin closed his eyes with a heavy sigh before sudden inspiration struck him. He snapped his head up, a wild hope swelling within his chest. "Aeon would know if she's dead."

The goddess smiled once more. "He would, indeed. I will speak to him before the battle begins. If she lives, I will do all I can to ensure you are granted the opportunity to free her. As I stated before, I cannot promise one will come. And do not attempt to enter the tower without my signal, for if you do, he will make certain it is your final act in this world."

Tavesin nodded grimly. "I understand, but I've come here for Arra. I will do what I must to rescue her."

"Your loyalty is commendable, and your determination admirable, but you would be wise to heed my words." Solsticia turned toward

Ravin. "As his mentor, I expect you to keep watch over him. Do not encourage foolishness, for I'll make certain Minora learns of it."

Tavesin blanched at her words. He would be forced to await her signal or risk destroying Ravin's bid for freedom. He respected Ravin, admired him. He would not become an instrument of the mage's forced servitude to the gods.

He slumped his shoulders in defeat. "I won't act without permission," he promised. "I will not harm a friend."

CHAPTER THIRTY-TWO

THE NAMELESS GOD'S WAR

Dranamir swept across the obsidian floor, furious at Kama's unannounced arrival in the Nameless god's temple. She seized her power, fully prepared to strike him a vicious blow he would never recover from, while her eyes radiated her raging displeasure. The tall Kamshati bowed low in deference to her.

"Before you take my life, you should be aware the enemy army has been sighted."

Her anger receded to a simmer as she eyed him coldly. "Where?" she demanded. "Our master must know of this development."

He compressed his lips into a thin line and nodded tersely. "It's why I've come. His orders to Alyra and myself were to refrain from coming here unless summoned, but this news could not wait."

Dranamir narrowed her eyes and leaned toward him to hiss in his ear. "I asked you a question, Kama. Where are they?"

A baleful light emanated from his crimson eyes, but he did not rise to her bait. She scowled, disappointed he gave her no reason to inflict pain or shed blood.

"Within visibility of the tower," he replied evenly. "The army does not come alone. Some of the gods accompany them. The Serpentus scouts reported Blademon's presence, Aeon's, and Ukase's. I'm certain the others will appear before long."

"I will inform him."

She spun on her heel before he could say anything more and marched toward the mirror inset on the temple's dais. Behind her, Kama let loose a string of curses, most directed at her. She smirked; if he continued, she'd kill him in the same fashion as Jannyn. She relished the thought of hearing Kama's screams as he writhed in agony before her. One day, his usefulness to the Nameless god would come to an end and she would pounce on the opportunity to destroy him. It was no less than he deserved.

She knelt at the mirror's rim and placed her hands on its cool surface. She glanced over her shoulder to shoot Kama another glare and ensure he remained at a respectful distance before she silently summoned the Nameless god to his temple.

His essence coalesced into the now-familiar gray countenance she'd come to desire. An imperious smile touched his lips as he beckoned for her to rise and accompany him across the room. Kama knelt and kept his eyes fixed upon the glassy floor.

"I assume this means you bring news, Kama."

The Nameless god stopped several paces away from his subject and pressed his palm possessively against the small of Dranamir's back. She smirked at Kama, standing taller in response to the god's touch.

"I do, sir." Kama reiterated what he'd told Dranamir, and to her dismay, the god dropped his hand and stepped away from her side.

"We have prepared for this moment." A fervent light glowed within the depths of the Nameless god's eyes. "Call the army into formation. The Murkor and the Serpentus are both adept with combat during the night. We shall make use of their natural predisposition. Go, Kama—there is little time to waste."

"Of course." Kama rose, bowed a final time, then disappeared into a portal.

The Nameless grinned at Dranamir. "You, my dear, shall summon the Enlightened. Order Alyra to oversee those few with healing abilities and prepare the tower for an influx of wounded. You shall take command of the rest, but do not strike until I signal you to do so. There is something I must do first."

She began to bow, but he arrested her movement with one arm. "No. You bow to no one. You are my queen." He caressed the side of her jaw with an arrogant smile. "Go. I will join you in the lands above soon. My siblings will rue the day they allowed me access to your soul."

A chill coursed through her as he stepped away. He'd once favored Garin and showed no qualms at using the man as a vessel to be consumed and tossed aside when convenient. She stilled her features and created a portal, then prayed she would not suffer a similar fate. Perhaps his words were simply meant as an acknowledgment of her power, but she could not be certain.

The Nameless god thrived on death. Even she could not hope to be immune from his insatiable lust for destruction indefinitely.

She pushed the thoughts aside and made her way to the tower's foyer. With Ravin inevitably near, she could not risk lingering in the Aethereum long, nor could she allow herself to become distracted. Even with her enhanced abilities, she knew he could overpower her if he wished to—and in the Aethereum, his magic was unparalleled.

As she exited the Aethereum, she stepped into a hive of panicked activity. News of the enemy's approach had reached the Enlightened in the tower. She pursed her lips in disdain and strode toward the meeting room, enacting the magical summons to the council once she was inside. Yet again, Alyra had proven herself inept at controlling their floundering subordinates.

She paced across the dais at the front of the room, impatient and craving blood. The Nameless god's orders echoed through her mind, and she forced her destructive desires into the background. They were not to attack until he signaled, and she certainly would be unable to justify the slaughter of Enlightened so near the onset of battle. The bloodshed must wait.

Nervous Enlightened began to stream into the room. Moments later, Alyra emerged from a portal nearby, her agonized body bent and her movements sluggish. Dranamir smirked, pleased with her handiwork. It was little wonder the Nameless had relegated her to assisting the wounded; she would be useless on the field.

"Dranamir! I never believed I'd say this, but I'm pleased to see you here." Alyra winced and hobbled toward her. "Has the master—?"

"Yes," she snapped. "I'll address everyone once they arrive."

Alyra nodded. "I was never very good at organizing for battle."

Dranamir snorted but made no further reply. Dranamir had worked tirelessly for years during their first campaign, had crossed the Gray Mountains, stormed both Delucha and Santine, and had dragged the might of her army to face the wizards at Dar Daelad. None of the other Soulless had managed such success.

All of her work had proven futile when she'd fallen to Morganus' surprising strength. Alyra became Soulless after her demise, only to fall months later, their army scattered and plans in ruin for centuries. Alyra's failure at conquest was only one of the reasons Dranamir despised her.

As the final stragglers entered the room, she enhanced her voice and began to speak. "The Nameless god commands us to join the coming battle. Anyone with healing skills, however meager, are to remain here with Alyra. Prepare to receive the wounded. You are to heal any who come here—even the Murkor—so I suggest you put aside any prejudice you may have."

She crossed her arms and sneered at those below. "The rest of you will follow my lead. We are to refrain from attacking until the Nameless god indicates it is time. He has something of a surprise planned for the enemy, I believe." A cold smile crossed her lips as she imagined scores of soldiers abruptly falling dead at the god's whim. "You have your orders. Go."

She descended from the dais and strode through the room as the Enlightened sprang to their feet and began to comply. She cared not where Alyra chose to set up to receive the wounded, nor did she wish to waste any more time in the woman's presence. Her place was outside with the army—and the Nameless god.

She emerged from the tower as the last rays of the sun disappeared behind the horizon. The Murkor army was some distance away, yet she could see the dark mass of hooded figures stood in formation, prepared to strike as commanded. Interspersed amongst them were the Serpentus, marked from afar by their taller stature and distinctly human faces.

Beyond them stretched barren wasteland… And then she spied the smudge near the horizon line that indicated the movement of a large force. The enemy was too distant to make out, yet she was certain they were on the march. She wondered if Kama meant to meet them halfway, or if he would allow them to approach and engage first. The Nameless had only ordered him to prepare the soldiers for battle, but perhaps he had something of a plan.

Without waiting for the others to follow her lead, she marched toward the rear flank of the army, where her talents would be best utilized. The journey took little time. She could hear others traipsing along behind her, accompanied by brief snatches of tense conversation. Most of the Enlightened were untested in combat, skittish, fearful. She would ensure each complied with the Nameless god's command by any means necessary. They would fight for his cause, or die by her hand.

Kama noted her approach, crossed his arms, and scowled with displeasure. He stood with the young Murkor commander and several violet-garbed drummers at the rear of the formation. He spoke in a low tone to the commander, who bowed swiftly before striding toward the front lines. She raised her eyebrows at the exchange.

"All is ready," he informed her. "You and the others should remain here. Allow the soldiers to engage them while you attack from afar."

"I'm aware of my role, Kama." She fixed him with an icy stare. "Alyra should be prepared to receive wounded by the time the fighting begins. She knows what is at stake if she fails."

"Did he give you any further instruction?" Kama asked.

"Nothing more than you overheard. I am to await his signal before we attack. I may be his present favorite, but he does not share his every thought with me."

Kama grunted. "I find that difficult to believe, Dranamir, but I will accept your word. For now."

They remained in place well into the night. As the hours drew on, Dranamir grew increasingly impatient, but it seemed the enemy was content to make them wait. The Nameless god did not show himself either, and her frustration intensified. If she'd been in charge of the army as she'd been in the past, they would have engaged the enemy upon sight and annihilated their threat before dawn began to paint the sky.

As it was, she was forced to bide her time, bottle her rage, and obey the Nameless' orders. Despite all he'd given her, she resented him for the delay.

She grew weary and eventually succumbed to her body's desire for sleep, only to be awakened what seemed moments later by Kama's rough hands. She glared at him fiercely before she realized the sky had lightened significantly. She rose hurriedly and brushed dust from her garments while scanning the lands to the west.

The enemy loomed nearer, visible in the pre-dawn light. Rank upon rank of human soldiers filled the arid land. Scorpion Men and Drakkon accompanied them, along with the hooded forms of the rogue Murkor. Her blood boiled at the sight of the traitors who had struck a bloodless blow to their forces. She would make certain they would pay dearly for their troubles.

Her eyes traveled further, and she spied the gods towering amongst the mortal soldiers. All twelve were present in a show of solidarity against their Nameless brother. Dranamir's heartbeat quickened as she realized this fight would be like none in her experience. The gods had chosen sides, twelve with the enemy to the single powerful deity that stood with them. Yet his purview was over death, disease, destruction. The mortals would be hard-pressed to survive the Nameless god's war.

Malicious laughter echoed from within the chasm. She shifted her gaze from the enemy army to watch as the Nameless god emerged from the obsidian depths, a fervent light in his eyes and a smirk upon his lips. The pair of swords Kama gifted him were crossed behind his back. He studied the opposition in silence for a time, then his voice boomed across the parched land for all to hear.

"Welcome, my brothers and sisters. It's been far too long since last we spoke."

Amongst the enemy lines, Blademon surged forward to stand at the head of the army. "Choose your words carefully, brother, for they may be your last."

The Nameless god tipped his head back and roared with laughter. "Arrogant as ever, I see." He made a sweeping gesture toward his own army. "I've gathered my pets, just as you've gathered yours. Shall we dance?"

His voice thundered through Dranamir's skull in the same instant. **It is time, my dear. Do what you do best.**

She grinned wickedly and signaled to the Enlightened, her murderous gaze fixed upon the Murkor traitors.

CHAPTER THIRTY-THREE

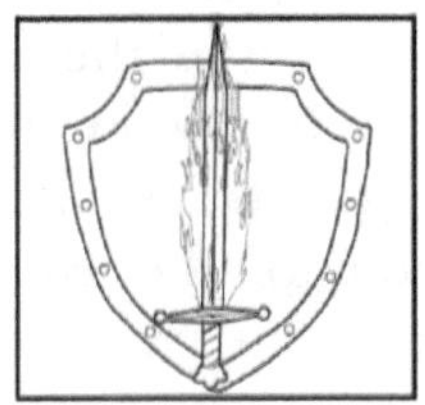

FIREBLADE'S RAGE

"Fuck. Is he—?" Patak grimaced and looked up at Emra where she was perched atop Fyrmane.

"It seems that way," she replied, her eyes locked on the distant form of the Nameless god.

The legends had spoken of him as the patron god of the builders, and he'd once worn their form. No longer. It seemed he preferred the corrupted, gray features of the wicked souls he'd bound to himself over the passage of the centuries. The Soulless were terrible in their own right, and now they'd won themselves a patron.

"Will that change anything?" Patak asked in a strained whisper.

"I doubt it. We're to follow Blademon's commands, and he'll adapt his strategy as required."

She continued to scan the enemy forces arrayed before them while she spoke. There were several thousand Murkor, and at least a thousand of the enslaved Serpentus. Behind their lines were scores of Enlightened, but their numbers were small compared to the wizards that bolstered their own army. She could not make out which forms belonged to the Soulless, but she harbored no doubts they were present.

Patak shrugged, checked the straps of his shield for what seemed the hundredth time that morning, adjusted its position on his arm slightly, and sighed. "I don't like it, Em."

"Nor do I, but we must not lose faith. He is but one god against twelve, and our army outnumbers his." She reached out and patted his shoulder. "Trust me when I say we'll get through this."

He grunted and pulled his mace free of his belt, blue eyes scanning their ranks. "Some of us will, but many more will not."

She suppressed a sigh and resisted the urge to inform him such was the way of warfare. It would do nothing to alleviate his anxiety, and most of the others—her guards included—were unaware of the blessing Aeon had bestowed upon the army's leadership in Daesan.

"Patak," she hissed in warning, "we're not alone."

"After all they've put my brother through, and Ravin as well, forgive me if I don't implicitly trust the gods to preserve us," he replied bitterly. "He'll expect something in return for his apparent altruism. They always fucking do."

"We can worry about that later," she replied.

"I'd rather not have to worry about it at all."

"Welcome, my brothers and sisters. It's been far too long since last we spoke." The Nameless god's voice echoed across the plain, clear despite the distance between them and his position near the chasm.

Beside her, Patak stiffened. "This won't end well for most of us," he growled in a low tone meant for her alone.

Blademon charged forward to stand at the head of their army. "Choose your words carefully, brother, for they may be your last."

"Then we will do all we can to ensure as many of our people survive as we can," she told Patak while the gods continued to verbally spar. "We cannot allow the gods' war to destroy our world."

He nodded once. "You're right, Em. I stand with you, now and forever."

Magic crackled across the sky, signaling the beginning of the Shadow Council's attack. Blademon issued a series of commands, a staccato cadence produced as the hilt of his massive sword struck his shield. Ahead, soldiers surged forward toward the onrushing Murkor and Serpentus. Emra studied Patak as he listened. He understood the orders hidden within Blademon's signal; it was the same method his people employed on the battlefield.

"We're to move north and flank the enemy, following Danian's cavalry." He turned to eye each of her guards and the pair of blue wizards assigned to her unit. "Our orders are to protect Emra with our lives if we must. Blademon hopes the cavalry will provide an opening for the Fireblade." He offered her a grim smile. "Strike a deathblow to the Soulless if you can."

The bulk of the cavalry remained in place to the north, though as she watched, the first ranks of horsemen began to charge toward the enemy lines. She motioned for the others to follow her lead and nudged Fyrmane toward the rear of Danian's unit. The bay tossed his head with anticipation while she prayed he would not spook as the hiss and sizzle of magic continued overhead. She struggled to maintain the eager beast's speed as she sensed his desire to join the battle.

Patak kept pace with the horses easily and flashed her a knowing grin as they neared the rear of the cavalry. "Your steed will need to move faster if he means to outpace me."

She chuckled, surprised once again that Patak could find a means to make her laugh when circumstance scarcely allowed for humor. His optimistic and upbeat outlook was a refreshing reminder of what might be if they survived the Nameless god's onslaught.

She reined in Fyrmane and motioned for the others behind her to do the same. "Patak, how long are we to wait?"

He shrugged. "Either Blademon will signal us again, or we wait for an opening. It's your call, Em."

She studied the cavalry as they charged toward the Murkor lines in a wedge formation. If they created an opening in which she could attack, she'd need to capitalize on the brief window of opportunity. She could not do so from too great a distance, and the gods might prove too preoccupied to signal them a second time. Her gaze shifted toward the rim of the chasm where the Nameless god towered above his subordinates. The other gods surrounded him in a loose half-circle, but there seemed to be little activity amongst them. Relying upon them was a risk she was unwilling to take.

"We will charge after the cavalry." She drew the Fireblade from its scabbard and held it aloft; its edges ignited at her touch. "Ride!"

Fyrmane lunged forward at her words. She guided him with her knees as she prepared to engage the enemy ahead. Danian's unit was driving through the initial Murkor defenses, but the taller Serpentus were putting up a valiant defense. The cavalry began to slow, and she motioned with her free hand for the others to do the same.

Her gaze flicked toward the chasm in time to see the Nameless god tilt his head back as raucous laughter spilled from his lips. He gestured dismissively toward the bulk of the wizards who remained safely behind the front lines. She followed his motion to watch with horror as more than a dozen were stricken and fell dead.

She narrowed her eyes. As rage coursed through her, she gripped the Fireblade's hilt more fiercely. "He must pay for that," she hissed.

"Let's hope Ravin and the others are up to the task," Patak growled in response.

Directly ahead, a sudden gap appeared in the enemy lines. She shot Patak a meaningful look and urged Fyrmane toward it while Patak banged out a signal on his shield, a warning to those of their army to remain clear of her path.

The gap widened before her. Emra leaned forward and aimed the sword's tip toward the hooded Murkor and armored Serpentus within her view. Some distance beyond them, she spied several humans in common garb; Enlightened, she suspected. She adjusted the point toward the location of the magic wielders and released a volley of fire that forced Patak to slow slightly and skitter farther from her side.

The wall of flame rushed forward, slicing through enemy soldiers too slow to evade its path. Soldiers screamed and fell, the sickly-sweet odor of burned flesh assaulted her nostrils, yet more of the enemy rushed forward to fill the brief opening she'd created in their lines. Magic rained toward them from above. One or both of the Blues behind her erected brief shields, though they paled in comparison to their youngest counterpart's performance in Delucha.

Briefly, she wondered how Tavesin fared and prayed Ravin and the Drakkon would see him safely through the battle. His childhood had been shattered in Delucha, yet his desire to continue refused to waver. He would grow to become an impressive adult should they prevail in their fight against the Nameless god.

She sent a second wall of flame toward the enemy. They were near enough now that she could hear the sizzle and pop of the fire as it seared bodies and maimed limbs. The second attack reached the nearest of the Enlightened; one who faced another direction was cleaved in two, while the woman nearby was engulfed as her skirt ignited. She shrieked and dashed past several Murkor, who tracked her progress toward the tower from beneath their hoods.

A more powerful magical attack roared toward her, sensed more than seen or heard. She had only moments in which to react as the dark wave of energy consumed her group and left several of Danian's soldiers unseated from their mounts, either unconscious or dead. She nudged Fyrmane out of its path, ducked, and erected her own meager defensive shield as the magic threatened to consume them. The Blues put forth a valiant effort to further protect her and those nearest her location.

The Blues' shield hissed before disintegrating with a thunderous boom. She glanced upward to find no further magic assailed them, then twisted in her saddle to assess the condition of the others. Her human guards were unharmed, though shaken, while the pair of wizards offered her nods.

"Where is Patak?"

She scanned the area frantically but could not locate him. She turned to the others again as panic gripped her heart with its icy talons. "Where is he?"

And then she spied him, some distance away from the group and surrounded on three sides by Murkor. She nudged Fyrmane in his direction, intent on rejoining him. Fyrmane picked his way gingerly through the still smoldering earth at her urging, though she sensed he was uneasy doing so. Her horse's concerns could be dealt with later; she needed to reach Patak before he was overwhelmed.

A mail-clad Serpentus darted in front of her, her green eyes fierce as she slithered forward, a sword held ready to strike in each hand. It was the first true glimpse Emra had of the Soulless' latest atrocity. The woman appeared human from the waist up, but her body was otherwise serpentine. A leather collar encircled her throat, which Emra recognized from her first campaign centuries ago. The half-serpent woman smirked at her scrutiny and lunged forward.

Emra twisted in her saddle to block one strike with her shield and the other with the Fireblade. She was stunned to find the Serpentus stood as tall as the Scorpion Men; she was nearly eye-level with her attacker from atop Fyrmane.

Two of her guards rushed forward to strike the Serpentus while she engaged Emra. An axe struck her midsection just below the base of her mail, spattering blood and gore across those nearby. The woman gasped as she fell, then smiled as the axe was wrenched free from her abdomen.

"Thank you…for freeing me."

Emra shuddered and pressed on; the woman's final words and blissful expression were unsettling. Patak was surrounded. She and the others cut their way toward him while he battled Murkor and Serpentus alike. His mace struck several deadly blows while his tail arced time and again toward his enemies. She knew his venom would be depleted soon, if it wasn't spent already.

She released another wall of flame toward the enemy, cutting off those who would further surround Patak. One of the Murkor nearest him looked up as she bore down on him. He braced himself and shouted something in his own tongue, only to be cut off as Fyrmane reared and kicked him savagely into the flames. He was replaced by another Serpentus, this one wielding an axe.

"Good timing, Em," Patak panted in greeting.

She parried a blow from the Serpentus, shifted her blade slightly to leave him momentarily unbalanced, then bashed her shield against his skull. He crumpled and lay still, unconscious.

"I was not about to leave you out here alone," she replied. "We need to fall back. We'll be cut off here, and I can only conjure flames so long before I grow weary."

He nodded as the other guards took their places around her. They began to back away from the enemy lines and toward the relative safety of the cavalry, when another wave of dark energy thundered across the field in their direction. One or both of the Blues erected a shield, but it splintered on impact. Emra raised her own magical shield, a feeble barrier against the onslaught of vile magic that washed over them.

She turned her attention to their latest attacker, a tall Kamshati with grayish features and crimson eyes. She clenched her jaw, determined to withstand his assault. She'd bested him once before and she would do so again.

As his magic ebbed, she aimed the Fireblade at his withered heart. "Your time is up, Kama."

She pored as much energy as she could muster into her weapon and unleashed it at her Soulless target. A flicker of defensive magic enveloped him only to falter and fail in an eyeblink. She heard Kama roar, though whether it was in surprise or anguish, she did not know. Flames engulfed his position. Even if he survived, she was certain he was not unscathed.

She turned toward the others to assess the damage his magic had wrought. Two of her guards were sprawled on the parched earth, blood leaking from their eyes and ears, their unseeing gaze fixed upon the cloudless sky. The two wizards were unharmed, as were several others. When her eyes found Patak laying face-down and unmoving, a wail burst from her throat.

She dismounted and rushed to his side before she realized she'd moved. He'd been granted Aeon's protection. If the wily god had failed to keep his bargain and Patak was dead, she would strike him from the earth just as they planned to do with the Nameless. She would not accept his fate.

Gently, she turned him over, oblivious to the swirl of battle around them. Her remaining guards formed a defensive ring, providing her a few precious moments with the man she loved. Her hand found the gap between his helm and breastplate, her fingers sought his neck, pressed carefully into his warm flesh… She was greeted with a weak pulse.

"He's alive," she rasped. "We must take him to the healers. I will not leave him here."

"I can levitate him," one of the Blues said, "but we must hurry. My energy wanes, and Ela cannot shield us alone for long."

They were some distance away from safety, but she would not leave Patak to the ravages of battle. "I will cut down anyone who attempts to stand in our way."

"We stand with you," one of the guards stated. "And we stand with our captain."

Later, she could scarcely recall the events following their departure from the field. She was told the enemy soldiers who found themselves caught in her path were dispatched to Aeon's realm without hesitation.

Nothing slowed her rampage, no one stilled her resolve, and the Fireblade raged.

It wasn't until they reached their camp and the healers that she became aware of their progress across the field, that they'd reached their destination, or that the sun was beginning to set. Patak was taken directly to Coreyaless for care, and she went with him, reluctant to leave his side. She'd shed enough blood for one day.

"He bears the signs of a death curse," the Airess informed her uneasily. She knelt at Patak's side while she examined him carefully for injury. "Aeon's protection spared his life, but I do not know if he will ever awaken. There is nothing I can do but keep him comfortable, Emra. I'm sorry."

She swallowed her anguish at the words, bottled up the smoldering hatred she held for the Soulless, and used her fury to strengthen her resolve. If Kama was not dead by her previous strike, she would make certain he entered Aeon's dark realm before the battle was done.

She knelt beside Patak and clasped his unmoving hand while she struggled to maintain her composure. He was her future, her foundation, the source of her joy. Tears stung her eyes, but she blinked them away. Those who followed her command could not be allowed to watch her unravel. She would grieve later.

"You're a warrior, Patak," she whispered. "Fight this. *Please.* For me. I can't…I can't lose you. Not like this."

On the far side of the battlefield, the Nameless god roared with unmitigated fury. She squeezed Patak's hand a final time and reluctantly rose to her feet.

"I'll return for him once this is finished," she told Coreyaless. "But now, I must return to the field. The fight is far from over."

CHAPTER THIRTY-FOUR

ALCHEMICAL MAGIC

Sal'zar was unused to the cacophony of battle, the screams, cries, shouts, the clash of metal upon metal. The stench of blood and entrails, the tang of urine, and the cloying odor of sweat assaulted his nostrils. He was near the rear of the Murkor formation led by Blademon's chosen, yet as they pushed forward, the unpleasantness of the conflict became appallingly clear.

Dead Murkor sometimes obstructed his path. Whether they fought for the Nameless god or against him, Sal'zar could not determine. He struggled to maintain his composure; he'd become an alchemist to avoid battle, to remain safely ensconced within the confines of his laboratory while others fought and died in the lands above. He cursed himself a fool a thousand times over for his insistence on accompanying Jal'den when he was deployed to the wizard's army. He should have remained in the caverns at his partner's request like any sensible Murkor would have done. If he'd listened, he would never have been taken to the tower, never been forced to part from Jal'den, and would have remained blissfully unaware of the horrors a battlefield had in store.

Yet here he was, storming toward scores of his own people and the enslaved Serpentus at the behest of the Kal and the gods. It was not the life he'd envisioned for himself, but it was the life he must lead—and his only hope of reuniting with Jal'den one day.

He fingered the row of vials at his belt as he ran, his calloused fingers identifying the contents of each by touch alone. He may not be a warrior, but he had his own array of weapons. Some were typical alchemical compounds, and some were of his own design.

His magic had been honed for healing and defense, and he'd keep those around him safe as well as he could. His people had suffered too much at the hands of the Soulless already, and more Murkor blood would be spilled before the end of the war than that of any other group. He would use his skills to prevent as many deaths as he was able.

Behind him, the drummers spurred them on. Ahead, Blademon's chosen urged them forward, his tall form easily visible above the mass of dark hoods, his axe a blur of silver and crimson as he battled their foe. Sal'zar noted with some relief that most of those they faced at present were Serpentus, though he grieved for their situation as much as his own.

Driven by the Nameless god's orders, the Serpentus fought relentlessly without regard for their personal welfare or those around them. Many battled valiantly and many fell, their tortured forms released to Aeon's realm, where Sal'zar prayed they would receive a warm welcome and a respite from the horrors they'd endured.

Their group pressed forward as the morning stretched into afternoon. He remained near the rear, his purpose to shield his comrades from magical assaults while he hurled various vials into clusters of the enemy, invoking a brand of chaos of his own design. Some of his vials contained combustibles that would explode or erupt in flame on impact. Others produced smoke to limit visibility, and a select few were used to invigorate his allies as their bodies began to tire and fatigue set in.

Some considered him a wonder; others feared his abilities. His focus remained on their enemy, unconcerned by their reactions. The only opinion that mattered to him was Jal'den's, who was undoubtedly somewhere deep within the fray, his blade just as bloody as his counterpart's axe. Sal'zar swallowed a wave of bile at the notion. How many Murkor had Jal'den been forced to kill when his heart was not in the deed?

It was mid-afternoon when Sal'zar's attention was drawn toward the north, where towering lines of flame streaked through the opposition. He recognized it as the Fireblade's work. Though he'd been introduced to the relic's owner, he'd said little to her. His first impression had been of a stern woman with a steely resolve, born into battle and tempered by the centuries into a formidable opponent. He prayed the magical flames would not find their way to Jal'den, that his partner would somehow be spared.

He watched as terrible magic cascaded across the battlefield, then moments later, the Fireblade erupted once more in response. He tracked the progress of the flames silently with his eyes and nearly shouted with glee when he witnessed their intended target suddenly engulfed. The tall Kamshati with his corrupted features roared in agony, the sound clear even from Sal'zar's position.

The flames ceased abruptly, but Kama remained. He fled toward the tower, clutching the mangled remains of his left arm to his chest. Sal'zar could not be certain, but he believed Kama's arm had been severed just above its elbow. His clothing smoked and steamed as he disappeared within a knot of Serpentus soldiers.

Sal'zar slowed his pace until he was abreast of the drummers. "Signal to Vardak. I must speak with him."

The nearest bobbed his violet hood in acknowledgment, but said, "He won't like the interruption, Sal'zar."

"It's imperative that I speak with him," Sal'zar pressed. With Kama injured, he believed there was an opportunity to press forward, nearer the tower and its depraved inhabitants.

The drummer shrugged and changed his cadence subtly. "Don't expect him to arrive immediately. He's much like Jal'den."

"I know."

Sal'zar returned his attention skyward to survey the streams of magical energy raging overhead. A bolt of blue-white fire exploded directly above his unit as it collided with a wave of vibrant orange. He threw a shield over their location as molten sparks began to rain from the sky. He noted belatedly that the sun was beginning to sink behind the mountains, marking an end to the first day of fighting.

The gods continued to tussle amongst themselves near the chasm's edge, seemingly oblivious to the struggles of the mortals around them. Sal'zar believed Ukase had spoken true when he'd claimed the gods meant to end the conflict with the Nameless for good, but after a wearisome day on the field, they'd made little progress. The Nameless god remained; arrogant, defiant, vicious, unyielding.

As the drummer had indicated, it was several minutes before Vardak fell back to his position. Sweat slicked his brow, gore spattered his armor, and though weariness was evident in his expression, he appeared unharmed.

"You wished to speak?" he asked in the Murkor tongue.

Sal'zar nodded, then related what he'd witnessed of Kama's injury and rapid retreat. "If he is wounded, it provides us with something of an opportunity."

"Perhaps." Vardak studied him shrewdly for a time, then said, "You've spent time within the tower. What do you propose?"

"We should aim to strike him before he recovers his energy. Kama is powerful, though not as strong as Dranamir. His death would be a great blow to the Nameless god."

Vardak shifted his attention forward to study the movement of the enemy ranks. The Murkor soldiers were showing signs of fatigue, but their Serpentus counterparts fought on relentlessly. Sal'zar pitied them; their actions were dictated by the Nameless god, who saw them as little more than fodder for his enemies' blades.

"I believe I know what we can do." Vardak motioned to the drummers, then pointed ahead. "Adjust course, there." He turned toward Sal'zar. "You will accompany me. I require your insight."

Sal'zar bobbed his head nervously. "I'm no soldier—"

Vardak flashed a brief grin beneath the grime and gore that stained his face. "We won't move to the front, Sal'zar, only to the middle of the unit. I cannot direct both the drummers and those on the front lines from here."

"Of course. I see."

Sal'zar kept pace with Vardak as they moved forward. The unit adjusted its position according to the tapped commands from the drummers, and soon the front lines formed a wedge formation. The sounds of combat were greater from his new position, and Sal'zar gripped one of his dwindling supply of flasks with fingers made clammy by fear. This was Jal'den's element, but he must endure. It was his idea that had landed him at Vardak's side, after all.

"Relax," Vardak said quietly. "I gave my word that I'd do all in my power to make certain you reunite with your partner. That vow includes making certain *you* survive, Sal'zar."

He released his grip on the flask and nodded again. "I know little of battle."

"And yet you were with the Murkor army when the Soulless arrived. Why?"

Sal'zar swallowed, then lifted his gaze skyward to trace an arc of green energy as it blazed across the darkening sky. "For Jal'den."

"I understand."

Vardak fell silent for a time as their group edged forward, deeper into the throng. They were nearing a group comprised almost entirely of Murkor. Vardak's fingers flexed along the haft of his axe as he studied the enemy lines.

"It seems he is near." Vardak pointed a short distance south, where combat was more heated.

Sal'zar followed his hand and noted the nearest human unit was engaged with a dense throng of Murkor. The arc and slash of a broadsword caught his eye. His heart constricted painfully; he was certain the blade was Jal'den's.

"He lives," he whispered.

"He received the same training as I did," Vardak replied. "I'd expect nothing less." He lifted his axe into the air. Moments later, the drummers adjusted their cadence.

Sal'zar peered at him uncertainly. "What—?"

"In order to keep my promise, we must make our way to him," Vardak replied. "This is as near to the tower as I can risk bringing you. Can you strike at them from here?"

Sal'zar swallowed nervously and glanced toward the tower. They were much nearer; he could make out the figures of the Enlightened in the dusky light. He'd expected Vardak would charge their unit toward the mages and strike them directly, but it seemed he'd been wrong in his assumption.

"I have no offensive magics," he stated, a note of helplessness creeping into his tone.

"I believe the enemy mages grow tired," Vardak replied. "The attacks have grown less frequent of late. If there is anything you can do to carry out your plan, do so, but I will not risk your people's lives unnecessarily, Sal'zar. You must act from here."

Reassured that Vardak had his people's best interests at heart, he braced himself and studied the silhouettes near the tower further. His eyes were better suited to the darkness than to the daylight, and he could discern a number of details that had previously been hidden from him in the sun's harsh glare.

A row of Enlightened stood between the rear of their army and the tower; he recognized most of them, but saw nothing of the Soulless at first. As he continued his survey, a petite figure emerged from the tower and staggered toward the others. He recognized Alyra's buxom figure easily, even from a distance. A puzzled frown crossed his lips as he studied her movements. She staggered and limped, as though in great pain. Perhaps if he could not draw Kama away from wherever he'd gone, it might be possible to engage Alyra. She was the weakest of the Soulless; her power paled in comparison even to his own.

"I cannot see Kama, but I can see Alyra," he said to Vardak. "Either is a worthy target. I will fall back to minimize any magical attacks that may strike you or the others." He didn't mention he feared for Jal'den's welfare, as well, but it was forefront in his mind.

"Gods be with you, Sal'zar." Vardak clapped him once on the shoulder, then skittered forward nearer the front lines and the group of Murkor led by Jal'den.

Sal'zar stopped moving to allow those behind him to pass him by. He kept his eyes fixed on Alyra's position, watched as she made the slow journey to the line of Enlightened to kneel some distance away from them. Something on the ground had drawn her attention, though he could not see what it was.

He waited until the drummers marched past him before he shielded himself. He could not attack her directly, but he could prevent her from conducting her business. He'd learned a few tricks from some of the Blue wizards during their march through the Wasted Land. He erected a semi-solid barrier directly in front of Alyra and smiled when she leaped backward. He made no attempt to hide the source of his magic from her and hoped she'd realize who was responsible for the interruption.

He watched as she spun slowly to face him across the field, her hands clenched into fists at her sides. Moments later, she created a portal and vanished inside.

He considered following her into the Aethereum, but was uncertain if Dranamir lurked within. She was not a foe he was prepared to face outside of the Initiate's circle. His indecision was rewarded within seconds, however, when another portal opened steps away from his position. Alyra limped outside, her corrupted features twisted into a malevolent glare.

"*You*," she hissed.

"Yes."

"I defended you from the others' cruelty. I *taught* you," she continued, seething. "And you would prevent me from tending to the wounded."

Sal'zar remained motionless, even as he sensed her seize her magical power. He strengthened his shield and awaited her first strike. He could endure her attacks; he'd done so before.

"Why have you betrayed us, betrayed your people?" She demanded.

He smiled beneath his hood. She was unaware of the Kal's scheme, which ensured Jal'den would remain safe for a while longer. "The Serpentus are unnatural. You and the others destroyed their lives."

Rage billowed within his chest. He would speak no more. He pored energy into his shield and launched it toward her in a flurry, his actions too swift for Alyra to form a proper defense. She was thrown several paces backward by the force of his strike, where she lay crumpled on the parched ground. He reformed his shield and marched toward her as his fingers sought a vial of fire serum.

He was surprised to hear her sobbing as she gingerly rose to her feet. "*Dranamir* is solely responsible for the Serpentus. She threatened me with the same fate if I tried to stop her." Alyra wiped at her eyes. "I believed our master would protect me, but he favors her now that Garin is dead."

Sal'zar understood she was stalling, attempting to distract him with conversation in order to catch him by surprise. He filed her words into memory, but made no response. He must strike her again before her apparent schemes bore fruit.

He threw another shield around her, nearly encircling her in its shimmering walls. Her eyes widened, then narrowed in suspicion. She opened her mouth to speak again, but before her words were uttered, he flung the vial of fire serum toward her. His aim was true, and the vial landed at her feet, shattering on impact.

"Sal'zar, what is—?" she began.

Her words were lost in a wordless shriek as fire erupted from the vial and blazed upward in a column, the flames contained within the shield. He held one hand over his nose and mouth to block the stench of burnt flesh that wafted toward him. Alyra continued to scream as her hands battered at his shield ineffectually.

His stomach roiled and bile rose into his throat. He'd never killed someone directly, and he found the notion made him ill. Her screams continued for some time. Only once she fell silent did he disintegrate the shield he'd used to trap her. The flames continued to burn, even as the charred mass within their heart grew still.

He pressed his hand against his mouth with more force, hoping the action would prevent him from vomiting the meager contents of his stomach. He continued to stare at Alyra's remains for some time, unable to tear his eyes from the terrible deed he'd committed. Soulless or not, Alyra had been a living being, and he'd taken her life.

A roar thundered across the battlefield from the area of the chasm. He looked up to find the Nameless god's eyes scanning the area in which he stood, fury painted across his gray features. Panicked, Sal'zar created a portal into the Aethereum and darted inside. He prayed the Nameless could not follow him there, prayed he'd escaped undetected, prayed he would not be forced to test the bounds of Aeon's blessing.

He took a moment to catch his breath once within the magical realm, then decided his skills were best utilized away from the direct fighting. He'd seen enough bloodshed to last a lifetime, and did not wish to destroy any other lives if he could manage it. He traveled to the area where he recalled the healers had set up and exited the Aethereum amongst their hastily-erected pavilions.

Sal'zar cast a wary glance toward the chasm. The Nameless god's attention was once more upon his siblings; it seemed he'd escaped the Nameless' wrath unscathed. Relieved, he stumbled toward the nearest pavilion to find the leader of the Green wizards at work tending the wounded.

Sal'zar knelt beside him. "I'd like to help."

The man smiled and gestured at the row of wounded. "Some were struck with the black metal of your people. Perhaps you know of a cure for the toxin?"

"Yes." Sal'zar beamed beneath his hood. "I am more useful here than on the field. Thank you." He paused, then said, "I don't know who ought to learn this, but Garin and Alyra are both dead."

The Green nodded. "I'll ensure our people learn this news."

Sal'zar scanned the tent and made his way to the nearest wounded soldier, a human. Here, he could truly help. He'd tried to deny Jal'den's concerns since the day he'd enlisted his services to the army, but now he realized his partner had been correct. The battlefield was no place for him—but tending the wounded was a task he excelled in.

CHAPTER THIRTY-FIVE

SEEKING RAVIN

The first day of the battle raged by without any sign of Ravin. Dranamir was furious; she'd hoped to draw him out, to revel in her newfound power and wipe the ever-present smirk off his dark features a final time. She knew he was somewhere nearby, knew with a certainty that belied reason that he would never miss this battle.

Yet he remained elusive, his tell-tale signature nowhere in the flurry of magical energy that clashed and sparked overhead. *Where was he?*

She'd depleted much of her energy throughout the long day, and as the sun sank behind the mountains far to the west, she knew she must rest soon or risk collapse. But Ravin's unknown whereabouts terrified her and she feared leaving herself vulnerable even for a few moments. Perhaps it was all a part of his dark machinations. He'd observe for hours, gauging her energy level, watching it wane, then appear when she was on the brink of exhaustion. The tactic was dishonorable, but typical of his character.

She scowled toward the enemy lines. Her own army was falling back, pressed ever nearer to the tower and the chasm's dark ledge by the sheer number of their adversaries. For all their work with the Murkor and her gift of the Serpentus, it was still not enough. Even the Enlightened, vicious as they were, could not match the volley of magic hurled in their direction from the wizards. And the Nameless god had done little since the battle's onset to assist in their cause.

She swallowed a wave of bitter anger. Her god was vastly outnumbered but had thus far managed to hold his own against the other twelve Immortals. She wished there was a way to assist him, to distract one or more of the others, opening an avenue of opportunity in which he could strike. Perhaps he'd even destroy Ravin in the process and spare her the trouble.

Nearby shouting and a commotion amongst the Enlightened drew her attention. Irritated by the interruption in her thoughts, she spun toward the sound, prepared to strike down the source. She raised her hand and channeled her magic, only to gape at Kama's appearance as he collapsed to his knees amongst the others.

His grayish skin was blistered and burned, his clothing singed and blackened, the hair on the left side of his head burned to stubble. He clutched his left arm to his chest with a grimace; in the failing light, it took her several moments to realize the limb ended in a charred stump, just above where his elbow should have been. His baleful eyes met hers with a ferocity she'd never encountered from him previously.

"It was…the Fireblade. Fetch…Alyra," he snarled through gritted teeth.

One of the others began to race toward the tower, but Dranamir stopped him. "*I* will find her."

She strode away to the stunned silence of Kama and the others, yet accompanied by the symphony of bloodshed from the battle beyond. She smirked, amused by their reaction. She had her own reasons for entering the tower, and summoning Alyra to Kama's side was a convenient excuse to disappear for a time. She must rest if she hoped to face Ravin on equal footing, but she could not allow the others to learn the depth of her present exhaustion. Even wounded, Kama could present a challenge to her authority if he wished to, and with the Nameless god distracted, she could not rely on his orders to stay the feral Kamshati's hand.

Alyra and the handful of healers assigned to assist her had set up in the meeting room. Dozens of wounded lay within, many tending to themselves as the Enlightened were kept busy with the most serious of injuries. There were too few healers to meet the influx of bloodied Murkor and ravaged Serpentus, but it was not Dranamir's concern. They served their purpose in the Nameless god's war.

Alyra knelt beside a Murkor with a vicious gash across his torso. Dark blood soaked his black garments where they were pushed up around his shoulders. Even wounded, the Murkor were too stubborn to remove their hoods. Dranamir shook her head in disdain; their behavior was unfathomable.

"Alyra, you're needed outside." She stopped to stand over the Murkor and kicked at his boot. "This one can wait."

"No, he can't, Dranamir." Alyra sighed but did not look up from her ministrations. "He'll die if I leave him now."

"*Kama* may die if you don't." She crossed her arms and smiled cruelly. "This blue-skinned pawn must make do on his own for a time."

The Murkor muttered darkly under his breath as Alyra tottered to her feet. Dranamir sneered at him and seized her power.

"I have no patience for insolence."

She struck him forcefully across his injury with a blast of air crafted to feel like a hammer's blow. The Murkor cried out in agony and clutched at his abdomen as fresh blood erupted from the wound.

"Dranamir," Alyra gasped. "We need all who can serve."

She snorted. "He'll wish I killed him outright before the night is done. Go to Kama. *Now.*"

Alyra grimaced and began to make her way toward the exit, each step a study in pain. Dranamir smirked at her back as she examined the results of her handiwork, still poignant weeks later. She shifted her gaze back to the Murkor.

"Alyra's pain is also of my doing. Be grateful yours was brief."

She strode toward the dais, intent on overseeing the healers while Alyra was otherwise engaged. She had no means of assisting them, but perhaps her presence would be sufficient to prompt them into greater action. She seated herself on the same chair she'd occupied while creating the Serpentus, smiled to herself at the memory, and allowed her weary body to relax. The Nameless god would understand the reason for her absence on the field.

She drifted to sleep while scowling at the others in the room, only to be awakened moments later as the Nameless god bellowed outside. His rage surged like a tidal wave through her skull. She gasped at the raw hatred his essence exuded.

She staggered to her feet and raced toward the exit, oblivious to the wide-eyed stares she drew from the other Enlightened as she passed. She must learn what had occurred to draw the Nameless god's ire. Overseeing the healers in Alyra's stead no longer mattered. Her exhaustion was of no further consequence. She would fight until she dropped if her god demanded it.

The sun had fully set while she'd been within the tower. Twilight blanketed the land. She could make out the individual silhouettes of the Enlightened, the slumped form that belonged to Kama, but Alyra was nowhere to be seen. Dranamir's lips twisted into a bitter frown. Alyra had always been inept, but she'd never completely shirked her duties. The implications were troubling.

She turned to look within the tower once more and shouted for the nearest of the healers to accompany her. Kama required assistance, and with Alyra nowhere to be seen, one of the others must tend his wounds. A pair of Enlightened scrambled to obey her summons, and she led them to Kama's location wordlessly. As they set to work, she studied his burned countenance in the dusk light.

"Where is Alyra?" she demanded.

"Interrupted," Kama replied hollowly. "One of the enemy—a wizard no doubt—blocked her as she began to tend me."

Dranamir lifted her gaze to peer across the shadowy forms of Murkor and Serpentus, illuminated periodically by the erratic displays of magical crossfire arcing over the battlefield. It was growing too dark for her to make out individual figures, but she imagined Ravin amongst the enemy, his golden eyes ablaze as he cut Alyra down. She doubted anyone else would have been brazen enough to strike at one of the Soulless directly.

"I do not see her."

Kama snorted. "Surely, you sensed our master's rage not long ago? Or perhaps you only heard his roar, since as his gods-damned pet, he's decided to spare you the worst of his fucking wrath?"

"Keep talking, Kama," she replied in a dangerous tone. "Our master won't care if you lose your tongue."

"Aeon fucking take you," he swore. His charred face twisted in momentary agony as one of the healers touched the stump that had once been his arm. "And you," he hissed at the offending healer, who blanched.

"Where is Alyra?" Dranamir repeated impatiently. "You did not answer my question."

Kama met her gaze with a baleful one of his own. "She's dead."

Dranamir crossed her arms and nodded thoughtfully. She harbored no grief for the other woman's passing; instead, she felt a sense of relief that her long-time adversary had finally met her demise. A twinge of frustration accompanied the sensation. She would have liked to be the one to destroy Alyra, or at least bear witness to her end.

"She had her uses, you know," Kama rasped, his tone laden with pain.

"Such as warming every man's bed she came across?" Dranamir sneered. "She was a hindrance, useless to us, and useless to *him*." She gestured toward the Nameless god, where he continued to struggle against the combined might of his siblings.

"You're heartless, Dranamir."

"I am but a product of my upbringing," she replied dismissively. "By the time our master found me, my heart was long dead, but he has given me purpose where no others could."

She watched as the Nameless god was engulfed in flame and staggered as the earth shifted precariously beneath his feet. He danced around the tongues of fire to strike a blow upon Blademon's massive shield. A ripple of laughter echoed across the darkening landscape, only to be abruptly cut off as Cirrus and Hydralene combined their efforts, encasing him in a thick shell of crystalline ice.

Dranamir sensed his rage, his frustration, his determination to break free. While he struggled, his words thundered through her mind, shattering her thoughts.

You tire, but you must not rest. Seek Solsticia's blasted spawn and end him. I must weaken my most powerful sister.

She stumbled and fell to her knees, stunned by the desperation she'd sensed in his orders. It was several moments before her awareness coalesced once more and she could form a cohesive thought. When she opened her eyes, she was inches from Kama. He eyed her suspiciously, but waited for her to speak.

"I must find Ravin." She rose unsteadily.

"I haven't sensed him since the onset of the battle." Kama grimaced as one of the healers touched the raw skin of his scorched shoulder and the mangled flesh began to knit together.

"He'll be within the Aethereum," she replied. "Even I cannot risk facing him there."

Kama shrugged, then winced at the gesture. He scowled at the charred stump of his arm. "As you've been quick to remind us for months, you know him best. I'm certain you'll find a means to disarm him."

She fixed him with an icy glare. "After I've dealt with Ravin, I'll return to deal with *you*."

"I doubt *he* will approve," Kama replied. He tilted his chin toward the chasm, indicating the Nameless god. "Even his fucking favorites aren't free, Dranamir. Or have you already forgotten what he did to Garin?"

She snarled, turned on her heel, and stormed away to leave Kama alone with the healers. She would not confide in him; she would not admit her own misgivings about the Nameless god or his plans, nor would she allow him to see her weakness. Weakness meant death, and Dranamir had no intention of dying so soon after her resurrection.

Her furious gaze darted across the distant silhouettes on the battlefield. Hooded Murkor clashed with Scorpion Men and humans, while Drakkon darted into the fray from above. Serpentus fought and bled with a fervor that could only be mustered by the Nameless god's unyielding orders and their inability to break free of his hold. Magic continued to cascade through the sky, though much of it now issued from the enemy lines. The Enlightened were outnumbered, but perhaps not outmatched.

She ground her teeth in frustration and opened a portal. If Ravin was within the Aethereum as she suspected, she had only moments in which to locate him before she lost the element of surprise. Catching him unaware was her only hope of destroying him without great cost to herself.

She steeled herself and entered. The sudden silence within the magical realm was unnerving after the hours spent working to the chaotic symphony of battle. She cast her senses as wide as she was able. There was nothing. No one. Surely if Ravin were within, he'd be nearby.

Puzzled, she traveled across the landscape to a point she suspected was at the heart of the enemy's reserve forces. She sought Ravin's energy signature once more, but again, she encountered nothing. The man had always been a source of ire, but she'd always believed him predictable. *Where was he?*

She returned to a safer location near the tower and exited the Aethereum. Ravin would have appeared to goad her if he were within; she was keenly aware of his ability to locate anyone in the realm from anywhere he happened to be. Since he'd failed to materialize, he must be in the physical realm.

Her gaze swept across the night-darkened plain. There was but one option left to her—she must strike at a vulnerable group, land a devastating attack, and hope her actions were sufficient to draw Ravin into the fray. Her eyes sought the distant shadows that marked the enemy's support structure; the healers, the craftsmen, the youngest of the wizards.

She channeled her power and launched a powerful attack toward the location. It was at the limit of her range, and with true night beginning to blanket the land, her magic blazed across the sky like a malignant beacon. Ravin would be forced to acknowledge her once the army's lifeline was destroyed.

Her satisfied smile twisted and soured as her magic neared its target. A brilliant, glimmering shield erupted, encasing the area in its protective bounds. She recognized the work as coming from the same wizard who had thwarted so many of her attacks in Delucha. Ravin had been with the wizard then; perhaps it was the same now.

She sent another volley of magic, this time directing it toward the wizard's location. She gasped and staggered as her energy waned and faltered. She considered returning to the tower, not to rest, but to retrieve a relic to bolster her power as another shield sprang to life and her latest attack was thwarted.

She lifted her hand to create another portal, but was stopped. She sensed the Nameless god's will overpower her mind, his fury and desperation as he seized control. Her heart fluttered in panic; he'd never taken advantage of the bond he shared with her previously.

There is no time. Find him *now*.

She resisted his command, much as a moth resisted a spider's web. Her fatigue meant nothing to him, her fears were inconsequential, his will was imperative.

You cannot subvert my command, Dranamir. Seek him and kill him without further delay. I will not tolerate your insubordination.

A jolt of pain raced along her spine, and she shrieked as her feet began moving of their own accord. Magic flowed from her fingertips as she watched, trapped within her body, an observer to the marionette she'd become.

She struggled to regain control, only to be rewarded by his dark laughter. **You will obey me. Have I made myself clear?**

A snarl escaped her lips as she sent him a furious mental acknowledgment.

Another laugh rang through her psyche as he relinquished control. **I may favor you, my queen, but you are not above punishment. Kill Ravin, and I may see fit to reward you instead. In the meantime, I will grant you this.**

Knowledge flooded her mind, and with it, a means to replenish her energy without sleep or the use of a relic. She smiled grimly, placated by his gift, and continued her march forward.

CHAPTER THIRTY-SIX

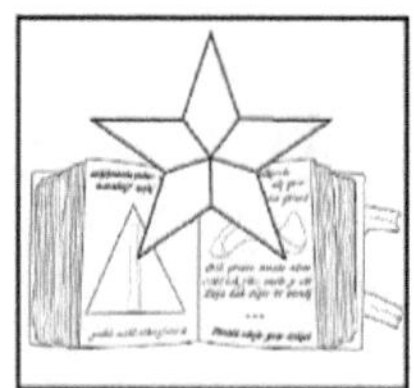

RESCUE

"That was fast thinking. Thank the gods you chose Blue."

Tavesin glanced at Ravin, unnerved by the mage's uneasy tone. "I hope your mother won't be upset that I disobeyed her."

Ravin forced a chuckle. "I think she'll understand. If you didn't react to her attack as you did—"

"Her? Do you mean Dranamir?" Tavesin interrupted sharply.

"Yes. I recognize her energy signature, which is why Solsticia forbade me from attacking. I suspect her reasoning was the same for you. You were with me at Delucha, and Dranamir is no fool." Ravin raked a hand through his dark hair and sighed. "I cannot sit by and watch her continue in this manner, Taven. I must do something, and I fear I am the only one with the power to stop her."

A brilliant flash illuminated the battlefield, drawing Tavesin's attention away from Ravin. White light, piercing as the sun, yet brighter than noon on a summer's day, enveloped the Immortals at the chasm's dark ledge. Tavesin squinted into the glare in an attempt to make out what the gods were doing. He could see nothing of them from within.

The battlefield stilled and grew silent as thousands paused in their combat to gaze in terrified wonder at the spectacle. Behind them, a number of Greens emerged from the tents to learn the source of the light and the sudden silence that had descended over the land. A tall figure came to stand at Tavesin's side, but he could not force his eyes to look up at the newcomer.

"That… That is mother's doing," Ravin whispered reverently. "But why?"

"A diversion."

Tavesin spun away from the spectacle to peer up at Minora's statuesque features. The goddess' unmoving countenance seemed to be focused upon Ravin, who crossed his arms and frowned at her.

"Is it time, then?" Ravin demanded.

"No, Ravin. He is not yet weakened enough to risk a strike at the tower." She swiveled her neck in Tavesin's direction. "This is an opportunity for you, Tavesin, and perhaps the only one you will receive. Go into the tower and find her."

Tavesin's heart swelled with hope. "Arra?"

"Yes. Do not go alone. Enemies remain within those dark walls."

Tavesin looked to Ravin, but Minora shook her head. "No, Tavesin. He must face the Soulless who presently threatens you." She lifted her hand to gesture toward the silent figure on his other side. "You are familiar with the tower. You will accompany him."

Tavesin frowned in confusion as Minora disappeared from sight, then turned to face the figure she'd indicated. He swallowed as he looked up at the shadowed face within its hood, the glint of pale eyes within its depths reflecting Solsticia's light. The lurid green he wore indicated an alchemist, but it was the magic Tavesin sensed emanating from him that brought understanding. This was the leader of the rogue Murkor; the one Ravin had met with weeks ago, the one who could enter the Aethereum. The Murkor who could wield magic.

"Tell me of Arra," he said in a soft tone, his words accented by a musical lilt. "Perhaps I know where she is held."

Tavesin glanced uncertainly at Ravin, who gestured, indicating this was Tavesin's business. "I must deal with Dranamir. The gods be with you both."

"And with you," the Murkor replied.

"Ravin, wait." Anxiety clutched at Tavesin's heart; he'd never imagined entering the tower to save Arra without Ravin at his side. He trusted the Murkor because the gods did, but he was not Ravin.

Ravin must have sensed something of his internal conflict, for he paused to place his hands on Tavesin's shoulders. "This is not how I'd planned for this to play out either, Taven, but this is the opportunity we've been given."

Tavesin nodded glumly and dropped his gaze as the brilliance of Solsticia's power abruptly faded, leaving the world in darkness. He was momentarily blinded as his eyes attempted to adjust to the sudden gloom.

"It may be your only chance to free her, Taven. Go. Sal'zar can help you, and he's stronger in magic than you realize." Ravin stepped back and glanced at the battlefield. "I'll find you once I've finished with *her.*"

Tavesin watched as Ravin's form disappeared into the darkness. His strides were purposeful, his expression grim. Tavesin drew a shuddering breath and turned to face the Murkor—Sal'zar, Ravin had said.

"We should use the Aethereum," Tavesin mumbled uncertainly.

Sal'zar nodded and opened a portal, then shifted as though uncomfortable. "Ravin has taught me the basics, but I am no expert in his realm. The Soulless did not know of this talent of mine, or if they did, they chose to ignore it. I was beneath them, less than deserving of the same attention they spared for the humans."

Tavesin chewed his lip, uncertain how to respond to Sal'zar's bitter words as they stepped into the Aethereum. He'd never encountered a Murkor before Delucha, and he'd certainly never spoken to one. Sal'zar seemed intelligent, and his actions to lead his people away from the Soulless and to Emra's army were admirable and brave.

"They were wrong to treat you that way," he said. "Is that why you decided to leave?"

Sal'zar adjusted his hood to pull it lower over his eyes. "It was the smallest of reasons," he replied. "My people do not want the subjugation we've endured. When the Soulless returned, they threatened our Matriarch and our Kal—our leaders. I had no desire to train in magic, but I was given no choice. I was…collateral. I learned much while in the tower, but my hope has always been that I might use my knowledge against them. Minora ordered me to help you, but I would have offered to do so all the same."

Reassured by the kind words, Tavesin offered Sal'zar a tentative smile. "Thank you. Ravin promised he would help me save her, but the gods…" He sighed and looked down. "I don't know if she still lives. Garin took her. He hurt her, tortured her. I…When I last saw her, she told me goodbye." He swallowed a threatening sob and forced himself to continue in a strangled tone. "Arra is my friend. I promised I'd rescue her, and I have to try."

"Garin was a brutal man." Sal'zar held out his hand. "There were rumors he'd taken a human girl to his quarters, a hostage of sorts. We should begin our search there."

Tavesin nodded and clasped the offered blue fingers in his own. "Take me there. *Please*."

Tavesin felt the familiar shift as Sal'zar transported them through the magical realm. He found himself within the black tower for the second time in his life, facing a rather plain door. They stood somewhere along the vast, winding staircase. Steps descended to innumerable levels below them and disappeared in a dizzying spiral far above. It was silent within the Aethereum, save for the sound of his rapid breaths and the frantic beating of his heart.

He cast his senses through the area and was unsurprised to note several strange presences nearby. He glanced at Sal'zar warily. "We're not alone."

Sal'zar nodded. "I know. We must move quickly." He pointed to the door. "This leads to Garin's quarters. It was often sealed during my time here, but perhaps with the Soulless distracted, we can successfully breach his room."

Tavesin closed his eyes and probed for evidence of the seal, but he could sense nothing. He knew little of such magical constructs, only the scraps of information the wizards had imparted to him during his training.

"Ravin knows how to dismantle seals. I don't." He hated the helplessness he heard in his own voice, but he was unable to mask it as fear gripped him in its icy fist.

Sal'zar stepped forward and tentatively tried the door knob. "I cannot sense it any longer. Perhaps it has been removed." He pushed the door inward before Tavesin could stop him.

"Sal'zar, no!" he hissed, certain the Murkor had just sprang a trap designed specifically for them.

Garin was a brutal, uncompromising sort, and Tavesin was certain he'd taken Arra as bait. She had never been his target. It was Tavesin the small man had sought, Tavesin who had garnered his ire, Tavesin who had unwittingly thwarted him not once, but twice.

Sal'zar shrugged and stepped aside, revealing the empty chamber beyond. The room was far smaller than Tavesin had expected, large enough for a single bed, a narrow bookcase, and a small table. A trunk was visible at the foot of the bed. Relief washed over him as he realized they were alone.

"I thought…I thought…." His panic began to subside, and he shook his head. "I thought it was a trap."

He squared his shoulders and stepped inside. He felt less exposed inside the room, though his senses continued to indicate others were within the Aethereum. They could easily be traced to Garin's room if the others happened to take notice of them. He glanced at Sal'zar, who closed the door behind him as he entered.

"I don't know what we will find here," Sal'zar admitted. "There is little to indicate she is here from within this realm, and I was never invited into another's private space."

His pulse thundered through his veins as he drew an unsteady breath. "We have to search, Sal'zar. Are you ready?"

Sal'zar shrugged. "Like you, I know shields and defenses. I know healing. I will protect you as I can."

Tavesin ignored the thread of unease that wormed its way through his gut. Shields could do much against an enemy, and he'd learned a few methods of repurposing his magic for attack, but he couldn't deny they would be vulnerable. Without Ravin's attacks and expertise, they were at a disadvantage should Garin or one of the others appear.

"Are you ready?" he asked.

When Sal'zar bobbed his head, Tavesin waved another portal into existence. Together, they stepped through into darkness.

Sal'zar released a relieved sigh. "There is no one here."

Tavesin remained still as his eyes slowly adjusted. He could see little beyond the dark silhouettes of the furniture. "You can see?"

Sal'zar laughed softly. "My people are used to the darkness of the caverns. We are nocturnal by nature. It is daylight that pains my eyes most."

A rustle issued from beyond the bed, and Tavesin froze, heart in his throat. "What was that?"

Sal'zar stepped around him and made his way toward the source of the noise. Tavesin heard his boots on the hard floor, then a sharp intake of breath. "Oh, gods…"

Tavesin sensed Sal'zar channel his magic, and a moment later, soft light illuminated the space. Sal'zar knelt at the end of the bed, his hooded head bowed low as he continued to manipulate what Tavesin recognized as healing energies.

"Tavesin, come here." Sal'zar did not look up from his work.

The words served to drive him forward. Tavesin stumbled across the room, then fell to his knees beside Sal'zar as he took in the sight revealed on the other side of the bed. Arra lay sprawled across the floor, her broken and mangled legs splayed at unnatural angles. The fading remnants of bruises marred her fair skin. Her reddish hair was a tangled and matted mass, a twisted halo around her head. The tattered remains of her clothing were filthy, soiled by blood, grime, and feces. It was clear she hadn't been able to move from her present location in weeks. Her body was frail and emaciated, as though she'd gone without nourishment for just as long.

Painful, wracking sobs erupted from Tavesin's throat, unbidden. She'd been captured because of *him*. This was his fault. If he'd only heeded Hasnin's warnings about the Aethereum and been braver that final night on the rooftop, Arra would have been safe. But he'd continued to venture into the magical realm unchaperoned, he'd drawn Garin's ire, and he'd failed to be there for Arra when she needed him most. Now, he'd come too late.

Arra remained motionless through the blur of his tears, but Sal'zar continued to work.

"We must take her back to our camp," Sal'zar said softly after a time.

"We're too late." Tavesin hung his head as a fresh wave of tears spilled down his cheeks.

"No, she still lives. Look." Sal'zar pointed toward her chest, the faint rise and fall that indicated breathing. "She is weak, but it is not too late. We can save her."

Tavesin wiped at his eyes and nodded. "We should hurry."

"Yes." Sal'zar stopped channeling and gingerly scooped Arra into his arms. "I will follow you while I watch over her."

Tavesin opened another portal and led Sal'zar through. Garin's chambers remained empty, a small comfort to his aching heart. He gripped Sal'zar's elbow and transported them out of the tower, away from the depraved followers of the Nameless god and the horrors they'd inflicted within the dark confines of its walls.

They emerged from a final portal in time for Tavesin to see the onset of what he assumed must have been Ravin's confrontation with his ancient foe. Soldiers from both sides were in rapid retreat as violent blasts of magic careened across the landscape. He forced himself to turn away from the spectacle and focus on Arra. He'd failed her before, but he would not do so again.

He followed Sal'zar into the nearest pavilion. Coreyaless knelt beside a wounded Murkor soldier, binding his arm with long strips of cloth. Danness was beside her, an array of herbs and tools before him. He looked up as they entered, his eyes wide at the sight. He whispered urgently to Coreyaless.

"Finish binding his arm," she stated firmly after she cast a brief glance at Arra's still form, cradled in the alchemist's arms. She rose and motioned for them to follow her to the opposite side of the tent.

A strangled cry broke free of Tavesin's lips as he spied Patak's unmoving form amongst the rows of wounded. Coreyaless indicated Arra should be placed on the empty mat alongside the wounded warrior. She crouched at Arra's side and began to examine her with deft fingers.

"This is your friend?" she asked without looking up.

"Yes. Arra." He glanced at Patak once more. "What happened to him?"

"An attack by the Soulless," Coreyaless replied briskly. "He will live. Arra's condition is much more serious. Many of these injuries were never treated. Her legs..." Coreyaless shook her head, compassion and grief warring across her pale features. "She may never walk again, Tavesin, but with the wizards' help, she may yet live."

"I will—" Sal'zar began, but she cut him off.

"No. You must tend those afflicted by that vile poisoned metal your people prefer." She looked at him sharply. "I do not know the cure for that particular toxin. I can tend the girl. Send one of the Greens here to assist me."

As Sal'zar turned to go, Tavesin grasped his arm. The alchemist tilted his head in question, but said nothing.

"Thank you. I owe you a debt I'm not certain I can repay. You helped me…when no one else could." Tavesin blinked away tears and dropped his hand.

"It was the right thing to do," Sal'zar replied. "If I see Ravin or your Drakkon friend, I will tell them you're here."

Tavesin sank to his knees near Arra and watched Coreyaless as she began to clean the grime from Arra's skin. He whispered prayers to the gods and hoped fervently she would survive. His fragile psyche would shatter if she died from the result of his carelessness.

"I believe you found her just in time," Coreyaless said after a few moments' silence. "She has been tortured, abused, starved… If she wakes, Tavesin, you must be prepared. She may not be the same girl you once knew."

He looked down, unable to meet her gray-eyed gaze. "I wanted to find her sooner, but even Ravin believed it wasn't safe. This… It's my fault."

"You are a fool if you believe that."

He peered up at her, and Coreyaless shook her head with a frown. "This was the work of the Soulless, Tavesin. I suspect they allowed her to live in the hope that you would do as you wished and attempt a rescue. I may not be privy to the details of what you and Ravin have planned, but I know this: You are vital to our victory. The Soulless are cruel, but they are not stupid. They would have recognized what you represent, and if you'd followed her, you would be dead, and Arra with you."

Coreyaless rocked back on her heels and sighed. "You have done the right thing, Tavesin. Sometimes the right path is not easy, nor does it bring happiness. But she *lives* because of your actions. That alone is worth celebrating."

He nodded, though he could not bring himself to believe her words. Only Arra's survival could hope to assuage the guilt that threatened to consume him, and only her forgiveness could mend the festering wound her capture had wrought within his soul.

CHAPTER THIRTY-SEVEN

A FATED BATTLE

Turning his back on Tavesin at Minora's request proved to be one of the most difficult acts Ravin had been forced to commit. He'd given the boy his word numerous times, promised he'd be there when Tavesin ventured into the black tower to seek Arra's whereabouts. He was certain Minora had dictated this aspect of his life, just as she'd orchestrated the rest. His resentment for her grew as he strode away from the promises he'd voiced for months, festering into bitter hatred.

Yet he knew Dranamir must be dealt with. There was no one else powerful enough to face her. It must be him, and it must be now.

A jagged bolt of lightning rent across the night sky to strike near the chasm's rim, while a surge of storm clouds whirled into existence overhead. The earth shuddered in response as thunder crashed, deafening in its proximity. Ravin studied the cluster of gods in the brief flash, noting Minora had returned to assist them. The Nameless god's expression was twisted with malice. His attention was focused solely upon his siblings.

Ravin looked away as the image was enveloped by darkness. He pressed forward, past the reserve lines of soldiers and wounded limping their way toward the healers. The cacophony of battle grew louder as he neared the rear ranks engaged with the enemy. There was no further sign of Dranamir, though he knew she would be somewhere near the fray.

He frowned. Perhaps she'd paused in her attacks to murder one of the Enlightened for insubordination, or merely for exhibiting a perceived weakness. She'd carried out such acts countless times before.

Regardless, her break, whatever it's reason, was an opportunity for the others.

He prayed Tavesin and Sal'zar would enter the Aethereum and complete their task safely; he would never forgive Minora if something happened to either of them due to her meddling. Tavesin's childhood had been shattered in Delucha, but that battle was nothing compared to what they'd witnessed here. If he survived to carry out the tower's destruction and Minora upheld her vow to release him from her grasp, Ravin would do all in his power to ensure Tavesin's life was better than what he'd endured thus far.

He drew an invisible shield around himself and fingered the talisman in his pocket as he neared the true fighting. Dranamir remained quiet, her thirst for blood either sated for a time, or her energy depleted to a dangerous level. He doubted the former and discounted the latter. Until he located her, he must be prepared for anything.

Ahead he spied a bloody scene between a number of human soldiers and towering Serpentus. His first true glimpse of the unfortunate souls told him they'd once been human, much like the Scorpion Men before them. His stomach churned, its meager contents threatening to spill forth. It was Dranamir's handiwork; he could sense her corruption upon them like a rotten stench that no amount of cleansing could eradicate.

Another brilliant flash illuminated the sky overhead, though whether it was due to magic or Maelstrom's fury, he did not know. In that brief moment of stark light, he saw the leather collars that adorned the Serpentus' necks, and he knew what he must do to garner her attention.

He created thin threads of energy and shot them toward the offensive devices at the nearby Serpentus warriors' throats. He snapped the threads like tiny whips; a crackle of energy accompanied each strike, and the collars fell free, severed neatly alongside each buckle. The affected soldiers stiffened and dropped their weapons instantly, hands raised in a gesture of surrender. There were perhaps three dozen in total; he would seek others and free them as he crossed the field.

Confused shouts erupted from his allies. Ravin pushed his way through the throng to address the nearest officer. He recognized Maryn at the head of the group, his orange fur dark and matted with gore.

"They are no threat to you any longer," Ravin said in the Felene's ear as he came to stand alongside Maryn. "I will attempt to free others as I have these. For now, have some of your men escort them to the healers. Most are wounded, some gravely."

Maryn eyed him warily, but nodded. "As you say, mage."

Maryn began calling orders while others moved forward to defend from further attack by the nearby Murkor. The Serpentus would be treated by the healers and word would be sent to Vardak if he could be found within the chaos of the battlefield. Ravin lingered while he scanned the area for more Serpentus. His actions were certain to draw Dranamir's ire, and he would spare as many souls as he was able from their otherwise horrific fate. They would be forever changed—he could not undo what she'd done to their bodies—but he could grant them freedom from the Soulless' relentless control.

"What did you do to them?" Maryn asked once he'd finished.

"I did nothing to *them*." Ravin pointed at the nearest broken collar where it lay. "The collars, however, are what controls them. I've seen their like before."

Maryn's ears twitched in agitation as he eyed Ravin with greater suspicion. "I'm still not convinced we should trust you, but I suppose I must set my misgivings aside and put faith in the gods' judgement." He sighed. "I'll spread word through the ranks about the collars. Perhaps we can turn a few more of them to our cause in the process."

Ravin nodded tersely. "You don't have to trust me, but I *am* on your side. And theirs," he added with a pointed look toward a passing Serpentus. "They are captives. This fate was not of their choosing."

Maryn crossed his arms. "Be that as it may, they've killed many of our people this day. Their sudden surrender will not be accepted by everyone, no matter what they've been forced to endure."

"Then take them to Sevic or Vardak," Ravin snapped. "*Their* people will understand, even if these others do not."

Without waiting for another reply, he strode away. The handful of Serpentus he'd freed had not been sufficient to draw Dranamir's attention to his location, and he meant to end her before Tavesin returned from his errand. She'd caused enough suffering and anguish during her lifetime, and his own quest for vengeance was long overdue.

He shoved several Murkor forcefully away from his location with a sweep of his arm as he continued across the battlefield. The more he cast magic, the higher the likelihood Dranamir would come for him. She knew his energy signature, just as he recognized hers.

When a group of Serpentus darted toward him, he used the same whipcrack of energy to free them from their servitude. When the human soldiers nearby failed to comprehend their surrender, Ravin took charge. Most had suffered multiple wounds and had been forced to continue the battle despite severe injury. Once freed, some were unable to remain upright as pain overwhelmed them and had to be assisted away from the field.

Ravin's fury continued to mount with each atrocity he faced. Dranamir had much more to answer for than his own torture and death. She'd distorted the very essence of an imprisoned populace not once, but twice during her tenure as Soulless, subverting the natural order and destroying numerous lives. She'd struck at Tavesin in Delucha, and again this night, a crime he would make certain she paid for with her life. He'd grown protective of the boy and wanted Tavesin to have the opportunity he himself had been denied. The opportunity for a life of normalcy and peace. Dranamir threatened his chances, and Ravin meant to stop her.

A blast of red-orange light arced skyward not far from his position, the tell-tale signature of his quarry fouling its essence. He smiled grimly, strengthened his shield, and shouted for those around him to move away. Most heeded his warning before the blast struck, but several failed to react in time. Those unfortunate enough to be caught in the attack's epicenter were crushed by its force, their broken bodies flung backward in a circle of destruction.

Another flash of lightning shot across the sky, and Ravin narrowed his eyes as he spied Dranamir in the brief illumination. Cold drops of rain began to fall as she stalked toward him, a malevolent glow in her crimson eyes. He smiled grimly in response. She'd come, as he'd known she would.

He grasped the talisman and linked with its power, intent upon finishing the battle swiftly. Dranamir undoubtedly possessed a relic of her own, though he knew nothing the black tower might harbor could rival his. Energy coursed through him, straining to be released, but he paused. He would force her to strike first. Given her nature, he didn't expect to wait long.

She continued to march forward, her long, dark hair billowing into a writhing halo around her head. Bright flares crackled and sprang to life at her fingertips. She flung them in his direction forcefully. They ricocheted from his shield and careened into the ground.

Ravin frowned. Her attacks were powerful, yet she struck sparingly. It was unlike her. Was she under orders from the Nameless god to capture him, as Garin had once intended to do? He flicked a glance toward the Immortals, but could see little of their present combat through the storm.

When he turned to face her once more, Dranamir stood a stone's throw away, her arms crossed and her lips twisted into a sneer. "Why do you hesitate?" she demanded. "I've been awaiting this moment since I learned of your return."

"I should ask you the same."

Ravin studied her in the darkness. When they'd last stood this near, she'd still been fully human, her skin a healthy pink, her eyes a soft hazel. She could have been beautiful if she wasn't merciless and cruel. Now, her skin was a foul shade of gray, reminiscent of a corpse, her eyes a baleful crimson. Only her dark hair retained is previous luster. Her new form seemed a physical manifestation of her twisted psyche; she'd always been murderous and cold.

"Perhaps I merely wish to toy with you, before I kill you again," Dranamir stated. "I have been favored by the god I serve. He will lend me his might if I ask it of him."

Ravin snorted and directed a powerful beam of energy toward her in response. When it struck her shield, he pored more magic into the attack. Her shield became visible, flickered, shattered. She erected another, but not before his magic enveloped her in a blaze of white light. She shrieked with rage from within as he took the offensive.

He struck again and again, battering her defenses and testing her strength. Her power faltered and waned, and he realized belatedly she'd come to face him without a relic to bolster her. He was stunned by her lapse. He wondered if in her hubris, she'd believed the favor of the Nameless god alone would suffice to best him. He would make certain she learned the enormity of her error before she departed for Aeon's realm.

As his attack faded, soldiers on both sides began to make a hasty retreat at the behest of their commanders. Ravin smiled grimly, pleased this long overdue confrontation would have fewer casualties than he'd anticipated. The farther the others were from the magical onslaught, the better.

Dranamir glared at him from within a reinforced shield. Her dark eyebrows had been singed away in his attack, but she appeared otherwise unscathed. Without breaking eye contact with him, she thrust her left arm toward the backs of several Murkor and one Serpentus. As one, they were pulled toward her, but before they reached her location all but the Serpentus began to writhe in agony.

Ravin gaped at her, horrified and stunned into inaction. He'd never witnessed such magic utilized before. She siphoned their energy, replenishing her own waning stock with the lifeforce of her captives. By the time he realized what she'd done, her victims were dead, sprawled at her feet in a tangle of blue limbs and serpentine scales.

"I no longer require trinkets to be a match for you," she snarled.

He sensed Dranamir seize the full force of her power. Frantically, he pored more energy into his defenses; she wielded more magic than he recalled her possessing. He remained stronger than her while linked with the talisman, but she was driven by desperation and madness, a dangerous combination.

The earth rumbled beneath his feet. He looked down as a fissure rent the earth and raced toward him, gouts of flame erupting from within its dark maw. He leapt aside an instant before the attack reached his position. He hit the unyielding ground and rolled to kneeling with a grimace. A geyser of molten rock fountained from the tear in the precise location where he'd been standing. He rose to his feet, panting, while Dranamir cackled with glee.

"Even with your little toy, you cannot stop me, Ravin."

He kept his features carefully neutral. If she learned he possessed no mere relic, but a talisman, he would lose the advantage her arrogance presently provided him. He would let her believe she could best him, perhaps feign injury, then strike with a fury she'd never anticipate.

He squared his shoulders. "Perhaps not, but I will gods-damned try."

Her lips twisted into a sneer as she launched another blazing volley of molten energy in his direction. His shield withstood the onslaught easily, but he dissolved it momentarily as she prepared for the next strike. For his plan to succeed, she must believe he was tiring, weakening.

He reformed it as a brilliant beam of energy lanced across the darkness toward him, scorching the rain-soaked earth in its wake. The precipitation evaporated into steam before it reached the deadly missile. This would be a true test of his defenses. The only person he was certain that could thwart the attack with a shield alone was Tavesin, but he was not about to get the boy involved with Dranamir.

He braced himself, strengthened his shield, and in the last moment channeled his energy directly into the earth. Rocks shot skyward from the ground only to be pulverized by the force of Dranamir's attack. The earthen obstacles served to diminish its power before it struck him, but his shield still took the brunt of the attack. It shimmered and threatened to dissolve of its own accord as he scrambled to bolster it. Searing white light engulfed him for countless seconds as he grappled to maintain his defenses. Dranamir's newfound strength was phenomenal.

He grimaced as the light began to fade around him. A lesser mage would have been killed instantly by her attack, shields or no.

As his eyes readjusted to the darkness, he noted Dranamir swayed on her feet. The attack had taken much of her stolen energy, but a maniacal grin was plastered across her face. Her gaze was fixed beyond him, toward the chasm where the gods continued to battle.

He smirked; she thought him finished, dead.

He drew deeply from the talisman's energy reserves as he pounced upon the moment. She was distracted, exhausted. He must act now, or risk her killing more innocents to fuel her rampage. He mimicked her previous attack, but added his own flair to the flow of energy. Magic coursed through him like tendrils of fire seeping from every pore, only to ignite the very air between himself and his ancient nemesis.

He sensed her scramble to form a shield, sensed it shatter a heartbeat later. She began to scream, but the sound was muted by the flow of energy that roared through him. It was several seconds before he realized her screams had ceased.

He relinquished his link with the talisman and allowed the energy to dissipate into the night. Behind him, the Nameless god's anguished roar echoed from the chasm's walls while Maelstrom's storm continued to thunder overhead. Ravin remained still for several moments, his breathing rapid and shallow, his limbs heavy with sudden fatigue. Sweat and rain slicked his face and soaked his clothing.

When his eyes adjusted to the darkness once more, he saw little more than a pile of charred bone where Dranamir had last stood. He created a portal and stumbled into the Aethereum, much of his energy spent in the final moments of his battle. He could return to the healers and rest for a time before the gods required his services again.

Dranamir's long reign of atrocities was finally at an end.

CHAPTER THIRTY-EIGHT

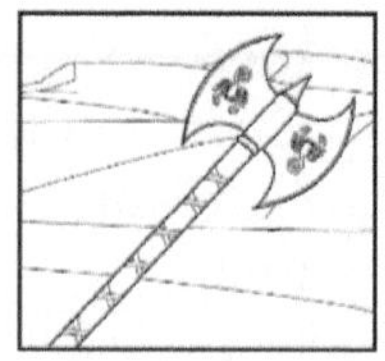

THE MURKOR COMMANDER

Vardak assessed the Murkor soldiers he'd been assigned to lead into battle as dawn began to paint the sky once more. Despite the lengthy fight the previous day, most appeared in good spirits. There were fewer of them than he'd charged into the fray with; dozens were dead, and more were wounded severely enough they could not continue another day. Sal'zar had also disappeared from the ranks, as his skills were needed by the healers. He was no fighter, in any case.

A few hours' rest had done much to rejuvenate those who remained. He'd been rattled the previous night by the magical duel that unexpectedly unfolded upon the battlefield and had called a hasty retreat. The soldiers welcomed the break, though many remained on the perimeter to watch in stunned silence as the golden-eyed mage faced off against one of the Soulless.

Vardak had been reluctant to fall back. He'd been so near to reaching Jal'den, to perhaps fulfilling his promise to Sal'zar, and the interruption stalled his progress. In retrospect, their retreat toward safety had saved more lives than if he'd continued to press the attack. The landscape was scarred in the wake of the magical battle, rent and charred by the celestial forces that had been summoned.

He glanced over his shoulder toward the array of pavilions the healers now operated from. Ravin was somewhere within, recovering from the ordeal. Vardak didn't understand the workings of magic, but he'd gleaned enough from the wizards to know that Ravin's feat was extraordinary, one he should not have walked away from unscathed. And another of the Soulless had been eradicated in the process. That news alone served to bolster morale throughout the ranks.

His gaze swept across the landscape to land at the chasm's ledge. The Nameless god continued his struggle against his brethren, his actions decidedly more desperate with this dawn than they'd been on the last.

"As usual, I find you scowling at the landscape." Maryn snickered half-heartedly and came to stand at his side. "When do you expect Blademon to signal us again?"

Vardak shrugged. "Any moment, I suppose. How are the…Serpentus?"

He grimaced at the word, the teachings of his childhood regarding his own people's creation forefront in his mind. Maryn had taken responsibility for the defectors and ensured they were offered proper treatment after the night's retreat from the field, while Vardak had gone to check on Patak's condition. He knew he should have introduced himself to the Serpentus, but his brother was of greater concern.

"Most of those we escorted will survive." Maryn twitched his ears in agitation. "I've heard the tales of how your people came to be, Vardak. I didn't believe the Soulless would attempt such a thing a second time. It's gods-damned barbaric."

"At least some of them are now free."

Vardak looked across the muddied landscape toward the black tower, the scores of hooded soldiers clustered at its foot. Amongst them remained more Serpentus, unfortunate slaves to the Nameless god's sadistic schemes. Many had been killed during the previous day's battle and more were wounded, but would be forced to fight on heedless of their injuries. He wasn't certain which portion of their plight angered him more—the loss of their humanity, or the subversion of their will. They were hapless pawns to the Nameless god, useful yet sacrificial, unable to break free of his control.

The histories claimed his ancestors had suffered a similar fate. He vowed to keep his promise of sanctuary when the war was over and done. They were kindred spirits, wrought by magic, forged by battle, captives to their unfortunate fates. He would speak with Sevic and demand the Serpentus be granted welcome in the Stronghold, if it came to it. He suspected the Warleader would understand his desire and might even offer the same without his prompting. The Serpentus had suffered enough, and the Scorpion Men would offer them refuge.

But first, they must survive the remainder of the Nameless god's war.

"Will you join the human contingent again?" Vardak asked of Maryn.

Maryn's orange tail swished. "No. Emra plans to lead that unit on foot today, along with her guards. She's out for blood. If only the rest of us could be so fortunate as Patak. He's found a woman who will tear down the very foundations of the world to avenge him," he added wistfully.

"Do you miss your people? Your homeland?" Vardak asked. They'd discussed the matter previously, but Maryn always shrugged and laughed his misgivings away.

Maryn offered him a wry grin. "I may return to the jungles one day, but not yet. Today, my place is here."

"You've been a good friend."

Maryn snorted. "Do not start speaking in that gods-damned manner, Vardak. We'll get through this."

"Are you willing to place a bet on that?" he countered.

Maryn's grin widened. "Always. Thirty silvers says you'll not only live, you'll go home a hero to your people. Your brother as well."

"I'll gladly pay that sum if your words are proven true." Vardak's smile faltered. "I pray Patak will recover. There's been no change."

"Your brother may be a terrible gambler, but he's an impressive fighter, Vardak. He'll pull through."

"I hope so."

He sighed and looked down, his thoughts on family. Patak, injured. Travin, soon to be a father, safely away from the combat where he tended his forge and his wife. Their mother Zaria, aged, yet still fierce, likely lending her skills to aid in the defense of their homeland in the south.

Maryn nudged his elbow. "Vardak, we cannot wait for Blademon's signal any longer."

He snapped his head up at Maryn's words. Serpentus were forming ranks across the field, and behind them came scores of Murkor. He glanced toward the gods, but none of them paid the mortals any heed.

He gestured to the violet-garbed drummers behind him to come forward.

"Relay to the others that we must engage. The Serpentus are priming for another assault." He studied the Nameless god's army, shading his eyes as the sun burst above the horizon. "Get word to Sevic that I plan to move toward the Murkor commander. Tell him to flank from the south after we engage, and have Danian's cavalry do the same from the north. And Emra…" He shook his head. "I don't know what she means to do, but inform her of what *we* plan. I'll pray she doesn't strike our own with that gods-damned accursed sword."

As the drummers began to pound his commands in a string of rapid beats, he turned back to Maryn. "They'll be charging soon."

"I know. I stand with you, my friend. *General.*" Maryn grinned. "We're a far cry from where we began, aren't we? Our meeting in Cynda Village seems years ago."

He unsheathed his axe with a nod. "Indeed, it does."

"Sir," a Murkor said from behind, "I can see Jal'den. The…commander."

"We make for him," Vardak replied. "I will engage the commander—those with him are your responsibility." He hefted his weapon skyward, another signal to the drummers. His muscles protested the action, sore from the previous day's combat, but he ignored his discomfort. "We move!"

Murkor surged forward to the steady tempo of the drums. To lines of soldiers arrayed themselves in front of his position, though he knew before they reached the enemy forces, he'd once again stand at the forefront of the unit. It went against his nature to allow others to defend him, though given his placement within Emra's army, he was certainly entitled to it.

Maryn kept pace with him as they marched across the sodden landscape, muddied in the aftermath of Maelstrom's furious outburst from the previous evening. They were forced to veer in their course as they neared the sight of Ravin's battle; a long fissure rent the land, deep and wide enough to cause serious injury if an unwary soldier stumbled into its maw.

Vardak clenched his jaw as he surveyed the damage left in the mages' wake, thankful he'd called the retreat the night before. Many of the Murkor that now followed his command would have been caught in the magical crossfire. His decision, reluctant though it had been, was proven the correct one in the light of day. It eased his conscience to know he'd spared the lives of some Murkor, even though he'd slain countless others amongst the Soulless' army. Their people had suffered more than most since the onset of the conflict.

Vardak pushed past several Murkor and into the front line as the armies prepared to clash anew. His position was not far from the Murkor commander, though a number of Serpentus darted ahead of the ranks, spurred on by the Nameless god's thirst for blood. Most sported injuries that appeared to have been left untended during the night.

Beside him, Maryn shouted, "Remove the collars, and they'll stop their fight!"

He nodded. A moment later, his axe blade met the sturdy shield of the first Serpentus he would face that day. It was a woman he noted, as he shoved her forcefully and swung his axe blade up to parry her mace. A gash ran from her hairline toward her left ear, the dried remains of her blood caked on her skin. Her armor was spattered with gore and mud from the previous day. The Nameless had not afforded the Serpentus the opportunity to care for their gear—or for themselves.

Rage for their unfortunate plight simmered within. No person should be forced to endure such indignities.

She hissed a warning, the sibilant sound at odds with her distinctly human face. He side-stepped, slipped his axe from her mace, and swung toward her shield. The blade bit deep into the wood, splintering it.

Beside him, Maryn darted forward. He nimbly evaded a wild swing by the Serpentus, while Vardak drew her attention once more. He parried her mace once, twice, while Maryn struck from the side. A brief flash of sunlight reflected from his dagger as he arced it toward her throat. She jerked from Vardak, prepared to strike at the smaller Felene as his blade cut through the leather collar.

She gasped and lowered her arm, eyes wide. Vardak shifted his focus to the nearest enemy Murkor and pushed past her while Maryn instructed her to seek the healers. If he could spare others of her kind, he would, but he feared more would lie dead at his hands than not. The thought soured his stomach, but there was little more he could do for them.

He battled his way through another pair of Murkor, toward the distinct flash of the steel broadsword he knew belonged to Jal'den. Jal'den had promised him they'd meet again when they'd fought in Delucha. Vardak had left the field the victor that day, but he was uncertain how their next battle would unfold. He'd promised Sal'zar he would spare the commander's life if he were able, but the soldiers on both sides expected a show as Blademon's chosen clashed.

A burly Murkor appeared in his path, the last defender before he reached Jal'den's position. He wielded a battle axe akin to Vardak's, though it was forged of the black metal. The Murkor struck first, his blade arcing low toward Vardak's torso. Vardak skittered backward as the axe blade whistled a hair's breadth from its intended target.

Without pausing to allow his adversary to recover, he charged forward, utilizing his superior speed to cover the distance in a flash. His axe caught the Murkor above the elbow, severing the arm cleanly. The Murkor howled in shock and pain as he dropped his weapon. The detached arm continued to clutch the haft, even as its owner scurried away.

Vardak's gaze met the dark hood of the Murkor commander as Jal'den wrenched his blade free of his latest victim, a fellow Murkor. The hood swiveled toward him. Jal'den raised his sword, prepared to face Vardak a second time.

"Take command," he told Maryn without looking away from Jal'den. "I must deal with him."

"Of course." Maryn's voice was strained as it rose to be heard over the surrounding cacophony.

Vardak inched forward, uncertain what he might do to convince Jal'den to surrender. He suspected that Jal'den, like him, would balk at the notion. Soldiers on both sides backed away, giving the pair space as they began to circle, an eddy within the bloody tide.

CHAPTER THIRTY-NINE

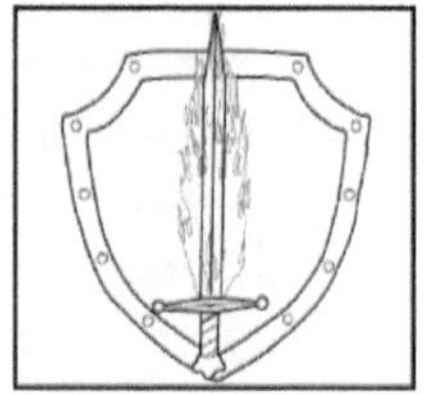

AVENGING FLAMES

"I bring word from Vardak, lady."

Emra turned to face the speaker, a green-clad Murkor smaller in stature than Sal'zar, yet with a similar timber to his voice.

"What is it?" she asked. "They're prepared to strike, and we must be ready to meet them."

The green hood bobbed in acknowledgment. "Yes. He plans to charge the commander's position—Jal'den's. He's asked the Scorpion Men to flank south, and the cavalry north."

"And what of my group?"

The alchemist looked down. "He said you must do as you will, but he hopes your…ah, relic won't pose a problem for our own forces."

Emra chuckled. "He doesn't like my blade. Nor do I, for that matter, but it's a tool that must be utilized."

She glanced at the others around her, keenly aware of Patak's absence. Her heart wrenched at the memory of his still form sprawled in the healers' pavilion, physically unharmed, yet unresponsive. She drew a breath to stifle her pain. She must focus on the task at hand.

"We will meet the enemy head-on," she stated. "If you spot the remaining Soulless, I must know immediately. I intend to finish what I started yesterday."

Drums began to sound from the south; Vardak and the Murkor had begun their charge. She turned to the alchemist who had delivered Vardak's message. "Will you remain with us?"

He hesitated as his head swiveled between the movement to the south, the enemy to the east, and her. Finally, he said, "I will never catch up to my own people. Yes, I will accompany you."

"I, for one, welcome your skills."

Emra donned her shield and withdrew the Fireblade from its sheath, her eyes on the advancing enemy forces. Her group would make for the thickest knot of Serpentus warriors; they seemed to be guarding the remaining Enlightened. Where there were Enlightened, there would be Soulless.

She lifted the blade, its tip pointed skyward as flames cascaded along its length. She'd faced Soulless in battle life after life. Her soul craved relief, an end to the centuries-long cycle she'd forced upon herself. With an end to the Soulless and their Nameless master's plans, Aeon would grant her peace at long last, but what good was such peace without Patak to share the remainder of this, her last life, with?

Bitterness twined with fury and flowed through her veins. She would avenge him. If he never awakened again, at least she would have this final act of retribution on his behalf. Any Soulless still alive would wish it otherwise before the day was done.

She began to march forward, determination fortifying her steps. Her guards and the hundreds of human foot soldiers behind her kept pace as they closed the distance between themselves and the enemy. The single Murkor with them remained at her side, small glass vials in his blue hands. He may not have magic on his side, but the contents of his flasks often proved just as deadly.

She watched as Vardak's group engaged the Murkor, watched as the other units north and south began to swarm toward the enemy on both sides. Her target—the greatest number of Serpentus, and beyond them, the Enlightened—loomed nearer with each step. She increased her pace, eager to deliver justice to those who had maimed the man she'd come to love. The soldiers with her rallied, pressing forward at her side. She would make certain the Soulless would rue the day they'd allied themselves with the Nameless god. And Kama, if he still lived, would further regret his decision to strike Patak.

As they neared the ranks of Serpentus, Emra knew she could not in good conscience wield the Fireblade indiscriminately as she'd done the previous day. Vardak's message echoed in her mind; she would never risk her allies, but the Serpentus were captives to their present fate. Ravin had freed enough of them the previous night to allow her to understand their story.

"Remove the collars if you can," she called over her shoulder, a reminder of her previous orders. "If you cannot, then may Aeon grant them peace."

On foot, the Serpentus towered over her, most as tall as the Scorpion Men. Clad in armor, spattered with gore and sporting untreated wounds, they were an intimidating sight, made more so by the serpentine nature of their bodies from hip down.

Most faces she did not recognize, but there were several she'd encountered the previous day that haunted her memory. Fellow soldiers, knights, *friends*, captured during the Soulless' campaign in Balotica then twisted into their new and loathsome forms. Until Ravin's acts had set some of them free, she'd never realized they were compelled by the devices that encircled their throats. She mourned the deaths she'd caused within their ranks, even as she began to wage war against them anew.

"Shields up," she commanded as the space between her force and the Serpentus dwindled to mere paces.

She braced for impact as she continued to charge forward behind the shield she'd acquired upon knighthood. The white snow leopard of Balotica rose on its hind legs, its fangs bared against a background of blue. The Fireblade flickered in her other hand as the sword responded to her unspoken desire to see the Soulless cut down. There were too many Serpentus at risk; she could not engage with the relic's magic without endangering them. Instead, she would wield it as an ordinary blade as its smith creator had intended, long years before she'd acquired and repurposed it into the magical device it now was.

Her blade met that of the first Serpentus in her path, a hulking man with the muscular arms of a smith. He struck with such force that the bones in her arm jammed painfully at the elbow. She bared her teeth and shoved with her shield, to little effect. He was easily as tall as Patak, yet far stronger—and compelled to attack without regard for his own welfare, she reminded herself.

In her periphery, she noted an object sail over the heads of the nearby soldiers to land paces behind the brutish Serpentus she presently faced. She wrenched her blade free of his while he swung toward her head. She ducked behind her shield and rocked backward from the force of his blow. As he prepared to strike again, Emra lunged forward, leading with her shield.

Dark plumes of smoke suddenly erupted from a point behind the Serpentus, obscuring those behind him. She smiled grimly, pleased to have the alchemist's assistance, though the smoke did little to affect her present foe. If she could somehow remove his collar, he'd abandon the attack, but she could see no safe means of doing so. He was too strong and she'd never learned the sort of magic Ravin utilized.

She parried another blow, blocked another attack, swung the Fireblade toward his midsection but pierced nothing but air. He was as swift as he was powerful.

He reared back and prepared for another powerful swing, his sword clutched in both hands. She raised her shield and braced herself, but the impact never came. Warily, she lowered the shield to find the Serpentus before her sprawled on his back. His eyes stared sightlessly at the sky. At his side, one of the soldiers wrenched an axe free from the Serpentus' torso, now cleaved nearly in two. He nodded to Emra briefly before turning to face his next foe.

Without the soldier's intervention, she would have remained on the defensive against the unfortunate Serpentus, outmatched and outmuscled. She shook her head and blinked sweat from her eyes as she sought her next opponent.

The line of soldiers had advanced while she'd struggled against the enormous Serpentus, carving their way through the enemy as they made slow progress toward the Enlightened. Magic once again crackled through the air above while the earth rumbled and shook with the gods' wrath. Emra risked a glance toward the chasm, but it seemed the standoff between the deities continued without any noticeable change.

She pressed onward with the others. More Serpentus fell than were freed of their imposed servitude, but she rejoiced with each soul they spared. By the time the sun was nearing its zenith, she was weary, coated in grime and sweat, and her blade dripped with the blood of the fallen. They were nearer the tower, nearer the Enlightened, yet more soldiers rushed to block their passage. Murkor appeared between the

Serpentus, and a few wayward humans who had either defected or remained near the rear of the enemy's ranks previously.

With the aid of another soldier, she dispatched a tall Murkor, the Fireblade slicing easily through his leather armor. He toppled with a strangled gasp as his blue hands sought unsuccessfully to keep his entrails within. The alchemist with her darted forward and tossed a small vial to the fallen soldier. She watched as the soldier fumbled with it, his hands slick with blood, then tipped the contents into his mouth.

"Poison," the alchemist informed her as he turned away. "He will not suffer needlessly."

It was an act of compassion, one she'd never considered during the thick of battle. The Murkor people continued to surprise her with their unexpected kindness.

"Did you know him?" she asked.

He shook his head. "He is Murkor. None of us wished to fight for the Soulless, but most of us were unable to escape that fate. I do what I must and help those I can."

"If everyone were so noble, there would be no premise for war. Our world would be better for it."

"Sometimes conflict is necessary to bring about great change," he countered. "You, of all people, must understand that."

She fell silent and resumed the rhythm of combat as the alchemist disappeared into the ranks behind her. She'd fought, bled, and channeled her way through scores of battlefields with the understanding that her actions would one day bring peace. Yet the cycle had continued, haunting her existence century upon century. There was but one way to ensure the lands were freed from the devastation and terror of the Soulless for good.

She looked to the chasm once more, observed the gods battling their Nameless counterpart, and prayed for their success. The Nameless god's fall was the only means to achieve lasting peace and an end to the Soulless' tyranny.

Her hand tightened on the Fireblade's hilt as she faced the enemy soldiers once more. An opening appeared between her people and the Serpentus. Time seemed to slow as she was afforded a view of the Enlightened, casting their magics across the field. At their forefront, she spied the gray countenance of Kama.

His left side was blistered and scarred, the skin raw from their previous encounter. His left arm hung useless at his side, reduced to a mere stump. His hair and beard were gone, singed away by the fire she'd unleashed upon him, but his angular features were recognizable even from afar.

She stormed forward, heedless of her guards or the other soldiers. Kama was responsible for Patak's current state. Kama was responsible for countless deaths and numerous atrocities, all committed in the name of his monstrous god. He would torment the world no more.

Serpentus lunged toward her as she leveled the Fireblade in Kama's direction. His crimson gaze was elsewhere, but there was no room for niceties when dealing with the Soulless. She would strike while the opportunity remained and deal with the Serpentus who swarmed toward her afterwards. She'd failed to kill him the previous day, a mistake she would not repeat.

A small part of her understood her actions would be seen as reckless, but she pushed her misgivings aside. She had little left to lose.

Flames erupted along her sword's length as she aimed it at Kama and the Enlightened beyond. She channeled her power through the blade, felt the searing heat of the flames as they burst forth to blast their way across the earth. Kama turned his head an instant before he was engulfed by the magical fire, but his reaction came too late. Screams greeted her ears; Kama's, those of the Enlightened, and some from the unfortunate Murkor caught in the magic's path.

She poured more energy into the attack until Kama's screams ceased, and she was certain he was dead. She relinquished her magic then and dropped her arm to her side, her brow slicked with fresh beads of sweat. Many of the Enlightened had fallen, their bodies burned to ash alongside Kama.

A hard blow struck the side of her skull as she surveyed the damage she'd wrought. Darkness swiftly encroached upon her vision as she stumbled and fell to her knees. A pair of Serpentus loomed over her, prepared to strike the life from her body. In her blind determination to seek retribution for Patak, she'd momentarily forgotten them—a grave mistake.

She was uncertain if her destiny was to die on this battlefield, surrounded by Serpentus and Murkor, but she could not fight the blanket of darkness that swept over her consciousness. In her last moments, she prayed that Aeon would be true to his word. She prayed for an end to the cycle of rebirth, an end to the wars, an end to her long years of struggle.

In that moment, she was at peace. Kama was dead. Patak was avenged.

CHAPTER FORTY

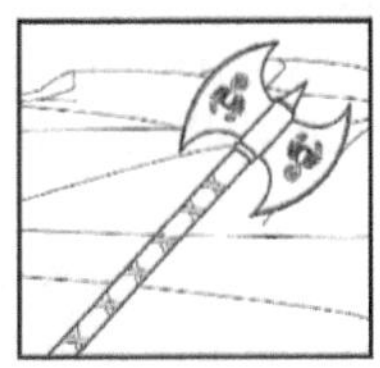

A DECEPTIVE BATTLE

Vardak broke the pattern of circling first. He charged forward with a wordless roar, his battle axe primed to meet the Murkor commander's steel blade. Blademon's mark branded both weapons, gifts the war god had presented them with at the conclusion of their training. Vardak anticipated Jal'den would move to block his attack, a maneuver he could have easily thwarted if he'd wished to. He did not.

The clang of their blades rang through the air upon impact. Vardak attempted to peer into the black hood, to glimpse something of his adversary's expression, but he was met with only shadows. He grimaced, frustrated that he'd still not devised a plan of action. That they must fight was inevitable, but he hoped to keep his promise to Sal'zar. Jal'den must survive the encounter, and Vardak must appear the victor.

"I told you we would meet again," Jal'den growled from within his hood.

"It seems your shoulder has healed," Vardak countered in the Murkor tongue.

Jal'den tilted his head momentarily, then freed his blade and swung. Vardak parried the strike and shifted his axe to hold the sword in place. He bent toward Jal'den in a show of menace, but said, "Your partner asked that I take you back alive."

Jal'den struggled to free his blade and snarled. "If you've spoken with Sal'zar, then you know what you ask is impossible. We must fight. One of us will die."

Vardak released his hold on the sword and backed away. There must be a way to convince Jal'den he was wrong, but if words failed to sway him, Vardak could attempt to overpower the commander and incapacitate him. He would not spill Jal'den's blood a second time if it could be avoided.

"There *is* another way," Vardak persisted as he parried Jal'den's next strike. An idea had begun to form in his mind, one that was both feasible and would yield the desired outcome, if only he could persuade the commander to consider it.

Jal'den growled and wrenched his blade free. "I fail to see it."

Another strike, another parry. Vardak shoved Jal'den away, the force of his action sufficient to cause the commander so stumble. Jal'den regained his footing and considered him as they began to circle once more. Vardak noted the way Jal'den adjusted his grip on his blade's hilt, the careful manner in which he moved his feet. The commander was preparing his next attack.

He held his ground as Jal'den rushed toward him again, braced his legs for the impact, and met the commander's strike with another parry.

"We can make a show of this fight," Vardak said through gritted teeth. "The Soulless will know nothing of the truth, if you would only listen."

Jal'den growled low in his throat, slid his blade free, and spun in a deadly arc. Vardak skittered backward and swung his axe. The weapons met with another resounding clang.

"Say your piece." Jal'den forced the axe blade upward slowly. Vardak sensed he could have easily shoved him away, but the commander did not. "I'm no stranger to making a farce of battle for the benefit of the gods-forsaken Soulless."

"We'll give them a show," Vardak said again, "but you must allow me to appear the victor. I will take you prisoner. You'll be safe."

Jal'den snorted and shoved him away, clearly affronted by the notion. "It goes against my gods-damned nature to yield."

Vardak chuckled grimly as their blades met once more. "I know."

He considered their previous battle in Delucha as they continued to trade blows and evade strikes. He'd been unaware of the Kal's scheme then and would have killed Jal'den if the opportunity had presented itself.

The morning grew warmer as their fight became more heated. Vardak wasn't certain if Jal'den would agree to his terms, nor if he fought merely for the benefit of those around them. The soldiers on both sides of the conflict continued to give them space as they struggled against their own opponents.

Vardak risked a brief glance toward the chasm to note little between the gods had changed. Jal'den took advantage of his momentary lapse and leveled a blow to his torso. The flat side of his sword struck Vardak's plate mail with considerable force, and he gasped as the air rushed from his lungs. He grimaced and shifted his axe to strike Jal'den's hip with its haft.

Jal'den's laugh was breathless as he limped backward. "You asked for a fucking show."

"Then you agree?" Vardak panted. He was certain at least one of his ribs was broken. He ignored the jagged pain that lanced along his side as he braced himself for the next strike.

"Your terms are…better than certain death."

Vardak grunted as their blades met once more and the impact sent slivers of agony along his rib cage. Perhaps he'd broken more than one rib.

"Allow me to end this. Soon." Vardak grimaced at the unspoken admission of his injury.

Jal'den bobbed his hood once. "I believe I understand."

Jal'den spun away, but Vardak pressed forward, keeping the distance between them to a minimum. His side began to throb, punctuated by searing pains each time he swung his axe. Despite his previous words, Jal'den refused to give in until he was satisfied with their display of force. Vardak clenched his jaw and swallowed the agony each parry brought with it.

Finally, Jal'den stumbled, providing Vardak an opening that none of the onlookers might question. Jal'den had eroded Vardak's patience to its breaking point. He brought the flat end of the axe haft down upon Jal'den's hooded head with enough force to render him unconscious, ending the fight in an instant.

He stood over the commander's fallen form for several moments as he regained his breath. More of his unit were nearby; some merely watched to see what he would do next. Maryn had taken the bulk of their force forward during the tussle, and he was left with several Murkor. He motioned to a pair of the onlookers.

"Help me get him back to our camp." He motioned to another and grimaced with the movement. "Get word to Maryn. I will escort our prisoner myself."

Vardak scowled as Danness assisted in the removal of his armor. Though the Airess' touch was gentle, the motion sent white-hot bolts of pain through his side. Coreyaless stood, her hands planted on her hips, her expression vexed as she studied him.

Vardak looked away as she began to examine his rib cage. Dozens of wounded were arranged in rows within the pavilion. Some were well enough to sit upright, while others lay upon mats with more grievous injuries. He and Jal'den had not been taken to the same pavilion as Patak, though he'd requested it. The haggard Green he'd spoken to indicated there was no more space within, and he must go elsewhere.

His gaze scanned the space once more before it settled upon the still form of the Murkor commander at his side. Jal'den's wrists and ankles had been bound as a precaution, though he remained unconscious. Guilt gnawed at Vardak; he'd expected Jal'den to awaken long before they reached the healers' pavilions.

"Sal'zar will tend to him," Coreyaless stated. "I may not understand every aspect of the Murkor culture, but I know it would be improper for me to examine his head wound. Neither he nor Sal'zar would appreciate my intrusion."

Her fingers pressed against his side as she continued the examination. "Two are certainly broken, and you'll be bruised for some time. I can bind the ribs to prevent further damage, but you must allow them time to heal." She arched one pale eyebrow knowingly. "I suggest you remain with the rear guard."

He groaned. "I'm needed in the fight."

"And what good would you be to those who follow you if you're dead?" She shook her head, exasperated. "Do as you will, *General*, but you're more useful alive. Think on that."

He rolled his eyes. "Cracked ribs will not keep me from the gods-damned battle. There is too much at stake."

"It seems I won, after all." Jal'den chuckled groggily and began to stir.

Vardak turned to face him as Coreyaless set to work with her bandages. "I believe Sal'zar has been sent for," he said in the Murkor tongue.

Jal'den began to nod, then groaned. "Good. My fucking skull feels as though it's about to cave in. Was that final strike truly necessary?"

Vardak shrugged and immediately regretted the action. "You broke my damned ribs."

"I thought you wanted our fight to appear authentic." Jal'den struggled into a sitting position and stared at the bindings on his wrists. "And now I must play the part of captive."

"I could think of no other way to honor my promise. I'm sorry."

Jal'den snickered. "Only Sal'zar could have managed to wrangle such an outcome. It's a relief to know he's safe."

"Lift your arms, Vardak," Coreyaless cut in sharply. "I may not understand what the two of you are discussing, but I need your focus for a moment. And he'll need to pay attention, as well." She nodded toward the pavilion's entrance and the green-hooded figure striding toward them.

Vardak did as she asked and kept his attention on Coreyaless as Sal'zar knelt beside Jal'den. They began to speak in the Murkor tongue, but he feigned disinterest in their conversation to provide them the illusion of privacy.

"Gods, *ama*, what happened to your head?" Sal'zar whispered.

Vardak winced at his words while Coreyaless continued to bind his ribs.

Jal'den snorted, but any further response was drowned by shouting near the door. Vardak shifted his attention to find several of Emra's personal guards entering, with her seemingly lifeless form between them. Radosan accompanied them and gestured that she should be placed in the open space next to Jal'den.

He was on his feet before he realized he'd moved, his gaze fixed on the procession as they passed. Even Coreyaless paused in her work to watch while fear drained the color from her cheeks.

"Who is she?" Jal'den asked quietly.

Sal'zar pointed at the Fireblade gripped in her hand. "She is *anaj'elai*."

Vardak was unfamiliar with the term, but Jal'den understood its meaning. His dark hood swiveled silently as she was laid on the mat at his side. Dried blood was caked around an impact wound near Emra's right temple, but she appeared otherwise unharmed.

"Vardak, please sit down."

He turned to face Coreyaless once more. "She lives?" he asked as he settled himself to the mat.

"She would not be here otherwise," Coreyaless replied. "Head wounds are fickle things. She may recover, as your, ah, prisoner has done. But she may not, even with Radosan's care." She tied off the bindings and nodded. "Try to keep yourself from further harm. We've enough to tend to as it is, and more are brought every hour."

He nodded and began to don his armor. Though the ribs still protested his movements, the discomfort was manageable. "I'll do what I must to finish this," he replied.

"As will we all, Vardak. I've others to see to. Gods be with you." She rose and made her way to Emra's side, where she spoke quietly with Radosan.

As he rose and hefted his axe in preparation to leave, Sal'zar stood. "Vardak, I must thank you. I wasn't certain you would keep your word."

Vardak smirked at Jal'den. "He didn't make it easy."

CHAPTER FORTY-ONE

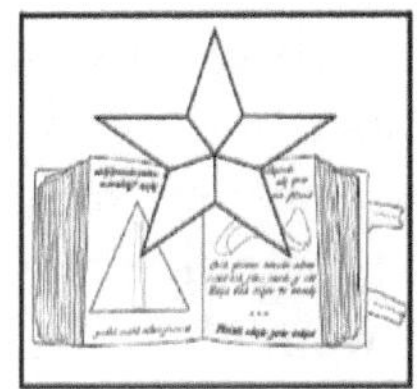

THE FINAL LINK

The battle had raged for seven days, with little progress on either side as far as Tavesin could see. The gods continued to attack the Nameless near the chasm tirelessly, yet the Nameless seemed immune to their machinations. Countless were dead on both sides; soldiers, wizards, Murkor, humans, Drakkon, Scorpion Men, Serpentus. Each night, weary soldiers piled the dead on the outskirts of the battlefield where great pyres were lit. Fire was more efficient than burial, and time could not be spared for grave-digging, besides.

Vardak had returned several times from the battle, battered but not seriously wounded. Many of the Grays, Rostin amongst them, fared similarly. Tavesin dreaded each morning when the soldiers were dispatched, knowing one of his greatest friends marched with them. He feared his friend would depart and never return.

Others fared much worse than Rostin. Emra lay in one of the healers' pavilions, alive yet unresponsive since she'd been carried from the battlefield. Patak's state was much the same, though more puzzling according to the Greens. The Warleader of the Scorpion Men had been slain, surrounded by Serpentus as they launched one of their many assaults. His mantle was passed to his niece; Makta was a smith, but a fearsome warrior in her own right. The Gray Sect Master had been killed the previous day.

And Arra... She was weak, battered, broken, and refused to speak with anyone other than Coreyaless. Tavesin had attempted to visit her twice, but was escorted away by one healer or another. She did not wish to see him. The news threatened to crush him, to catapult him into oblivion. He'd given his all to rescue her. The rejection hurt worse than anything he'd yet endured.

Tavesin attempted to bolster his spirits by considering the casualties from the other side, but it did little to alleviate the black depression that threatened to consume him. Hundreds of Murkor were dead, and scores defected to their side every day. If Sal'zar was to be believed, his people never wanted to fight for the Soulless or the Nameless god. They were victims as much as the rest.

The Serpentus fared worse. Though many had been freed of their magical shackles, many others remained enslaved to the Nameless god, and even more lay dead. Those who had been liberated and were well enough to fight often did, yet each day was a struggle as they attempted to regain their identities. Few of them spoke to anyone save the Scorpion Men.

He'd learned from Ravin that all the remaining Soulless were dead. He knew what had happened to Dranamir and Kama, and learned of Alyra's fate—and her admission that Garin was dead—from Sal'zar. A part of him wished to know how Garin had been killed, but it was silenced by his overwhelming relief at the knowledge that Garin was dead.

The days dragged on, and the number of dead continued to rise. The gods seemed to have forsaken their purpose, their focus solely upon the Nameless. They'd been promised a signal, yet nothing came.

He spent his days near the healers' pavilions, summoning shields when the enemy's magical attacks drew near. Ravin was often nearby, biding his time under orders from his mother, though Tavesin suspected he'd rather be in the midst of the fray. Trozyen, too, stayed close, while the rest of his people pushed forward with the soldiers or attacked from the air.

Tavesin was weary of the long days and sleepless nights, the unending conflict, the blood, the death. If he survived to see the end to the Nameless god's war, he would never again join the ranks of an army. Perhaps he would leave the Council of Auras entirely and return home to Rican Mer. He'd once yearned for adventure, but he'd endured enough to last several lifetimes since embarking on the journey to Dar Daelad with the wizards. It had been just over a year ago, but seemed a decade.

He was no longer the same naïve boy, dazzled by the prospect of magic and the sights of the city. He simply wished to return to the life he'd once led, the family he'd left behind, the simplicity of the village he called home.

Tavesin watched as streams of fire lanced from the sky to strike near the chasm and the Nameless god's position. Thunder rumbled a warning overhead, as it had done countless times during the past week when Maelstrom concentrated his fury against his wayward brother. The earth rippled beneath his feet, while a fierce wind began to gust, stirring dust into the air. Brilliant light burst suddenly from Solsticia's position to outshine the afternoon sun.

Tavesin coughed as dust swirled around him and the wind whipped at his cloak. The gods were once more on the offensive.

Ravin appeared at his side moments later, one brown hand shielding his eyes as he studied the Immortals. "It cannot be much longer. Gods-damn it all, we've waited long enough!" He looked around their location and scowled. "Where's Trozyen?"

"I'm here." The Drakkon mage landed lightly on the ground on Tavesin's other side. "I thought to gain a better view from above the dust, but it's just as thick up there. I cannot risk flying too high with the storm."

Ravin's scowl deepened. "We cannot afford to prolong this battle much longer. How many must die in this gods-damned chaos? Unlike them, *we* do not have the luxury of time, nor the ability to withstand grievous wounds indefinitely." His heated gaze landed on the cluster of Immortals near the chasm.

Tavesin stared at the ground between his boots as a fresh wave of melancholy enveloped him. They were at the mercy of the gods, helpless to act and forced to endure, while awaiting a signal that had begun to seem more like a broken promise with each passing day.

Ravin's hand gripped his shoulder and he peered up at the mage.

"Things are grim, but I speak out of frustration," he said. "We must hold onto the sliver of hope that remains, Taven. Do not give up yet."

Tavesin shrugged away from his touch with a sigh. "I want to go home." To his own ears, his voice was small, pitiful. His previous resolve eroded with each blood-soaked hour that ticked by, unbroken by the promised signal that never manifested.

Ravin's expression was compassionate. "I know how difficult this has been for you, Taven. I was once in a very similar position. I would like to help, if only you would allow it."

Tavesin shook his head and turned away as tears stung his eyes. There was nothing more Ravin could do for him; he knew he must overcome his despair alone. Ravin would never understand how deeply Arra's refusal to see him had cut, how agonizing it was to learn the one person he'd set out to save could not stand to look upon his face. He'd failed her, even as he'd saved her life.

They fell silent. The sun dipped toward the mountainous horizon line as another day neared its conclusion. The gods continued to strike at the Nameless in force, but from their distant vantage point, Tavesin could see little change. The cadence of Murkor drums changed as soldiers were recalled to recover and prepare to fight anew with the next dawn. Tavesin's hope waned, flickered, and threatened to evaporate entirely.

It was as the last rays of the sun vanished behind the Gray Mountains that Solsticia appeared before them. Her golden eyes brimmed with compassion as she studied the trio before her. The dying embers of his hope rekindled as he looked up at the beautiful goddess expectantly. He prayed in silence that she'd come as their signal. He could not stomach the idea that her arrival was yet another empty promise that would go unfulfilled.

"The Soulless are dead and the Nameless god is weakened," she stated. "It is time. Uncover the seal." She turned to Ravin. "You alone possess the power to destroy it, Ravin. Once it has been revealed, the responsibility of ending this war falls to you."

Ravin smirked. "If you're concerned I might fail, mother, perhaps you should consult with Minora."

Sadness descended over Solsticia's features like a veil. "I will ensure she keeps her vow, Ravin. But first, you must finish this." She vanished before any of them could make another reply.

"We must link, then enter the Aethereum," Trozyen said. "From there, we've all determined our positions and know what must be done."

Tavesin nodded, morose. The only time he'd linked with anyone was on the outskirts of Daesan, the night Ravin had stopped the lava flow from entering the city. He feared linking again; his only experience had been one of terror, forced to watch helplessly as Ravin drew upon too much power and nearly killed himself in the process.

"Tavesin, this time will be much different."

Ravin's hands gripped his shoulders firmly, and reluctantly, he looked up.

"The link is merely part of the ritual," Ravin continued. "You've read Morganus' book cover to cover—you know this. We each have a role to play, and yours will be to use the Moon's Eye to strike the tower from the north. We will be aware of one another while linked, but there will be no sharing of power. You have nothing to fear."

"Do you promise?" Tavesin asked warily.

"Yes, Taven. You have my word."

He studied Ravin's expression for some time. He appeared genuine, and Tavesin could find no reason to doubt him further. Finally, he said, "I believe you."

Relief spread across the mage's features. "Good. We must begin, and I'll be with you every step of the way."

Ravin nodded to Trozyen. A moment later, Tavesin sensed the magic of both intertwine as they linked, then Ravin's eyes sought his once more. "Are you ready, Taven?"

"Yes."

He allowed his own power to join theirs and was once again astonished by the sheer volume of magic Ravin was capable of wielding. Trozyen was an equal to Tavesin; his energy signature was distinct, though it was overshadowed by Ravin's.

We can speak across a great distance in this manner, Trozyen's voice echoed in his mind.

Tavesin gaped at the Drakkon. "How did you—?"

Trozyen frowned at Ravin, but responded through the link. *You said you taught him of the linkage.*

Regret flooded Tavesin's mind, but it was not his own; it was Ravin's. *I showed him how to link, but as you are aware, we had little time in which to act in Daesan. And I was…incapacitated for some time afterward.*

Aloud, Ravin said, "I will mind-speak again, Taven. You've learned the skill to unravel the workings of magic, and this is but a simple feat. Pay attention, then respond if you are able. Our communication will be crucial during the ritual."

Tavesin nodded uneasily. "I'm ready."

I know you can hear us, Taven.

Ravin's eyes remained locked on his own, and he found it unsettling to face the mage, to hear his voice, though his lips did not move. As Ravin had indicated, it was a simple trick, one he could easily replicate now that he understood what the others had done.

Yes? He sent uncertainly.

Ravin smiled proudly. *You're a quick study. Come.*

Ravin opened a portal and stepped inside. Tavesin scurried after him while Trozyen brought up the rear. The Aethereum was eerily silent compared to the noisome scene of battle that played out in the physical realm. Out of habit, Tavesin cast his senses through the area, but sensed no one else within.

We each know our place, Trozyen sent. *I will observe and await your actions.*

Tavesin swallowed a sudden wave of anxiety and nodded as the Drakkon vanished. Through the linkage, Tavesin could sense his location, somewhere in the sky above the tower's roof. Trozyen's portion of the ritual would occur last.

He chewed his lower lip and faced Ravin, who offered him an encouraging smile.

Out of everyone, you have studied Morganus' book the most, Taven. Your part comes first, but I have every confidence in your abilities. Ravin continued to smile. *Minora chose you well.*

"I will do my best," he whispered aloud. What he needed to say next was meant for Ravin alone. "When you destroy the seal, what will happen? And I don't mean the tower, Ravin. What will happen to *you?*"

Tavesin sensed Ravin's uncertainty, his fear and regret through the linkage. "The honest answer is I don't know, Taven. If I fail to return…" He drew a breath and took a moment to compose himself. "If I fail to return, there is a small puzzle box amongst my personal possessions in the main healers' pavilion. Take it to the duchess for me."

Tavesin clenched his jaw in an effort to stave off tears. He could sense Ravin's unspoken anguish through their link, and it threatened to overwhelm him. "I will."

"Thank you." Ravin turned to face the tower. "And Taven? Whatever transpires tonight, know that it's been an honor to guide your path."

CHAPTER FORTY-TWO

THE TOWER OF OBSIDIAN

Ravin traveled to his position without waiting for Tavesin to reply. He could sense the boy's grief and concern through the link, but there was nothing more to say on the matter. It was his task to destroy the Nameless god's seal, but what might happen to him afterward was an unknown. There was a chance he would walk away unscathed, but an equal one that the tower would collapse upon his head. Or perhaps the seal itself would react adversely to his attack, and his life would be forfeit as he sought to destroy it. It was a creation of the death god, after all.

He positioned himself along the lip of the chasm due south of the tower. The Aethereum shimmered and shuddered west of his location, in the same area the Immortals stood in the physical realm. With the exception of his mother, he'd never encountered one of the gods within the magical plane. He was uncertain if the instability he noted was the result of their battle, her proximity, or the work of the Nameless god. Regardless of its source, he knew their time was likely limited.

Taven? He sent through the link. *Are you in position?*

He knew Tavesin was in place before the boy sent his response, but Ravin's words were meant as reassurance. Tavesin was edgy, nervous—and with good reason. They had but one opportunity to complete the ritual before the Nameless god became aware of their scheme. The magic involved was both complex and unique, of ancient stock that none of them were familiar with. Minora had wagered everything on their abilities, and her siblings had allowed the blood of thousands to paint the land before their singular opportunity to end the Nameless god's brief tenure arose.

He, Tavesin, and Trozyen stood on the precipice; one misstep would bring ruin and devastation to the world. But if they succeeded, the Nameless god would be vanquished. Not merely imprisoned, as he'd once been, but utterly powerless.

It was this understanding that had forced him to divulge to Tavesin the existence of the puzzle box. If he did not live to see the next dawn, he would have Adalin know the true depth of his feelings for her. Within the box was a letter, one he would destroy if he survived, and a sapphire ring, which he would deliver himself, if he was able. He'd meant every word he'd spoken to her on the day his mother had interrupted their conversation. He would make a life with her if he lived to see Minora's vow to him fulfilled.

I am here, sir.

Tavesin's words stirred him from his thoughts. He closed his eyes briefly and braced himself for what must be done. *Begin, Taven. You know what to do.*

He sensed Tavesin link with the Moon's Eye through their connection. An abrupt surge in magical energy accompanied Tavesin's use of the relic, and a heartbeat later, he felt Tavesin's manipulation of the celestial powers at his command.

Gods! Trozyen sent, his astonishment clear through the link. *I knew the relic was powerful, but I was not expecting…this.*

To his credit, Tavesin ignored the Drakkon's words and continued to work, methodically following the ancient instructions first penned by Morganus the White. Ravin smiled to himself, pleased he'd been given the opportunity to act as Tavesin's mentor, however briefly. Since their meeting in Delucha, Tavesin had endured hardships beyond any a boy of fourteen should have dealt with, yet he'd persevered. Ravin believed, given time, Tavesin would once again thrive.

A delicate golden filament of energy bloomed into existence and twined itself around the tower's dark expanse like the tendrils of a vine. It glowed softly, its warm light at odds with the Aethereum's stark illumination and the tower's inky surface.

It worked! Tavesin's astonishment was evident in his tone.

Ravin chuckled. *Yes, as I knew it would. You're a power to be reckoned with, Taven.*

Your part is next, Ravin. I stand ready, Trozyen added.

Ravin glanced toward the shifting, shimmering mass near the chasm and prayed they would remain undetected by the Nameless god. He wanted to believe they could trust his mother, that she'd waited to signal them until the precise moment he would no longer be a true threat. Yet the larger part of him remained skeptical and wary of the gods' interference in his life.

Solsticia was the messenger, but Minora pulled the strings and forced him to dance as she desired. Had she promised him freedom, knowing his life would be forfeit in the process? Her ends would be achieved, his perceived threat would be finished, and her vow would be upheld. There would be no loose ends, no outcry, no further blood to stain her marble hands. Only his own.

Ravin pushed his thoughts aside. No matter the outcome, the seal must be uncovered and destroyed. The Nameless god could not be allowed to continue sowing the destruction he craved. He would accept the consequences of his predetermined performance with the understanding that he no longer acted for himself alone. He fought to give Tavesin a better future and to offer Adalin the chance to live out her life in happiness—with or without him. He was no longer a man consumed by revenge.

Ravin grasped the talisman in his pocket for what might prove to be the final time. He drew upon its power, channeled the energy, and wove it into a vast network of interlacing threads. The threads grew and expanded, grasped the tower in their invisible tendrils, then interlocked with those Tavesin had laid in place. A silver glow blossomed from the tapestry he'd woven. He sensed each strand as it locked in place.

He gazed, awestruck, as the black tower began to shiver from its foundations. He wondered if the same effect was visible in the physical realm, and if the Nameless god was in a position to put an end to their ploy. The shimmering near the chasm appeared unchanged, but that meant little.

Trozyen, he sent through the link, *my part in this strange magic is done.*

I see it. This is remarkable. Wonder accompanied the Drakkon's words. *Pray that I am as capable as the gods believe I am, and that I can accomplish what I must, as the two of you have.*

Solsticia chose you over Aziarah for a reason, Tavesin replied. *I believe you can do this.*

Trozyen chuckled, though Ravin could sense his unease. *There is but one way to know for certain, isn't there? Pray for my success.*

Trozyen's piece of the ritual took less time to channel but was no less potent in its design. A brilliant beam of light shot from his position in the sky to strike the tower's apex. Where each of the gold and silver filaments gripped the tower's sides, fissures appeared. The cracks widened and spread while the stone itself rumbled in protest.

"Ravin, you cannot access the seal from here."

He spun around at the urgency in the tone to find Minora paces away. Behind her, the shimmering near the chasm intensified.

"Go to the physical realm. Enter the tower. *End this.*" Her marble features betrayed nothing of her emotions, but her words were frantic. "He knows what you plan."

"Protect the others," he replied, his thoughts on Tavesin.

He traveled to the tower's base before summoning a portal. *I must go,* he sent through the link before he disconnected from it. His next actions would either save the world or see him dead. Perhaps both. Tavesin did not need to experience what came next, regardless of its outcome.

As he stepped from the portal, he was stunned to find no one stood in his path. He turned slowly to look over the battlefield and the chasm beyond to find a broad, crystalline dome had formed over the tower. Enlightened and Serpentus battered at the dome's exterior, but it seemed they were unable to penetrate its surface.

The Nameless god broke free of his siblings then, his malevolent gaze locking upon Ravin as he strode forward. Cold sweat broke out across Ravin's brow and his pulse accelerated painfully. The Nameless was capable of striking him down from afar, yet he seemed intent upon closing the distance between them before he struck. Momentarily frozen, Ravin stared as the death god stalked toward him.

Solsticia appeared between the Nameless and the dome, her dark hair swirling in a wind Ravin could not feel. A golden network of starry points erupted in the space between the two gods, the work of his mother. She glanced over her shoulder, golden eyes wild with panic.

"Ravin, you've run out of time. *Go now!*"

Her words freed him from his paralysis. He spun away from the scene, certain if he failed, his mother would suffer terribly for it. As would Tavesin, Adalin, and so many others.

He stumbled into the tower's foyer, empty and silent within the dome. A fissure had opened in the tower's floor, the jagged crack revealing another level far below. A set of crudely-hewn, narrow steps ran from the foyer along one side of the fissure to descend toward the room the Nameless god had kept hidden for millennia. An orange glow permeated the space and glittered from the fissure's obsidian walls.

He glanced toward the open doors of the tower's meeting hall as he strode past. Within were row upon row of wounded soldiers; Murkor, human, and Serpentus. A handful of green-robed alchemists worked amongst them, but he spied none of the Enlightened. He hesitated briefly, then jogged toward the room.

"This tower is going to collapse upon your heads," he called. "I suggest you flee while you can."

An intimidating roar broke the relative silence of the tower, and he sensed the Nameless god was undeterred by his mother's defenses. He sprinted toward the fissure and its dizzying stair. Too many had fallen to the death god's schemes. There would be no more.

The steps were rough and uneven beneath his feet. The obsidian wall on his right was jagged and adorned with sharp angles and razor edges that tore at his clothes and his hands. The tower shook as the Nameless god continued to bellow outside, his enraged cries growing louder with each moment. Ravin dared not look back.

He pressed forward, nearer to the source of the orange glow with each step. Lacerations, the result of his body brushing too near the obsidian wall, oozed blood, but he ignored his injuries. They were minor. He'd endured worse at Dranamir's hands.

The glow coalesced into a tangled web of individual strands. They were not the result of magic as he understood it, but were formed from the Nameless god's very essence. If Minora's information was correct, the Nameless god had protected this space from his siblings—but he'd never considered the possibility of a mortal finding their way here.

Ravin stumbled down the last of the steps and stood before the threaded mass. It hung in the air, while energy pulsated through each of its filaments. Ravin moved toward it, but was repulsed by an unseen field.

He frowned in frustration and glanced toward the tower's foyer, high above. Blademon stood sentinel at the top of the stairs, a sword in each hand and his stinger primed to strike. Before him stood Minora, Cirrus, Flariel, and his mother. The Nameless god roared, and Ravin spied a glimpse of his grayish countenance between the shoulders of the others. The gods were defending his position, buying what time they could.

"By forsaking my name, you've already failed." The Nameless god's words echoed through the fissure as he began to laugh mirthlessly. "I cannot be undone. The power you once stripped from me has become your undoing."

Ravin turned away from the scene with a grin. The barrier could be breached by a mortal, and the Nameless god had inadvertently forced Ravin to recall its key. His mind raced back to the discussion in the Sky Palace, the words spoken before he'd made his desperate bid for freedom. Minora had preserved the Nameless god's identity within the writings of Morganus.

He braced himself, uncertain what the result would be with the Nameless god so near. "Necronus holds no power here."

A sound like the rending of fabric tore through the air in front of him. Above, the Nameless god continued to laugh, seemingly oblivious to the destruction of the barrier. Ravin stepped forward, no longer repelled, and studied the tangle of pulsing, orange threads. Morganus' book had provided no details on what must be done to destroy the seal.

He risked another glance toward the gods and found Solsticia was turned toward him. Her golden eyes pleaded with him to hasten his mission, but he shrugged helplessly. The seal was not a construct of magic, and though he'd breached its protective shield, he did not know how to proceed.

"Do it now!" Minora screamed as the Nameless god struck her with a fierce backhanded blow. She crumpled beneath him and disappeared from Ravin's view.

"You are my son, Ravin," Solsticia whispered, though her words found his ears over the surrounding din. "Your power is unrivaled. In your heart, you understand what must be done."

He nodded once and turned as tears began to leak from Solsticia's eyes. He gripped the talisman and closed his eyes, allowing its power to flood his veins. The same magic he'd summoned to kill Dranamir would serve him again. This time, however, he could not hold back, could not spare an iota of his own magical essence in reserve.

He focused his energy on the heart of the glowing mass and unleashed it to a chorus of the Nameless god's screams. There was little chance he would survive the outpouring of magic, but for the first time since his resurrection at Garin's hands, he was content. The world would be better without the Nameless god's influence. Tavesin would grow up and thrive. Adalin would mourn him, but she would move on to live a life of her own design. Even the young Deluchan queen, murderer that she was, would survive to bear Jasom's child. Perhaps the child would one day become the benevolent monarch her kingdom deserved.

The tower began to crack and tremble violently around him. He continued his attack, even as he felt the familiar sensation of his being as it began to tear and fray. The magic would consume him, but the Nameless god would fall. His death would save countless others. He no longer harbored any regrets.

His ears rang with the noise of the tower's demise. Great blocks of obsidian sheared off and broke free of the walls to rain down upon his position. The Nameless god roared in agony a final time before his voice was abruptly silenced. The orange glow subsided as the threads dissolved into nothingness.

Ravin fell to his knees then pitched forward. Blood trickled from his nose. His eyes sought Solsticia's in the moment before darkness and exhaustion consumed him. It was over; he was spent. He could fight no more.

"Mother... Give my love...to Adalin."

CHAPTER FORTY-THREE

AEON'S GATES

Dranamir sensed the others nearby, their magical essences like beacons in the endless night. She was disembodied, blind, but aware. She knew her body had perished during the battle with Ravin, but true to his word, the Nameless god had preserved her being. Hers, and those of the others.

Nearest her position, she sensed Kama. He brooded, fury and bitter disappointment a palpable force that emanated from his being. He'd been alive when she'd battled Ravin, but it seemed he'd fallen in the end. Or perhaps he'd succumbed to the burns and the loss of his arm, unable to recover from the Fireblade's wrath.

She attempted to speak, intent upon gloating over his failure, but found she had no voice. No mouth with which to form her words, nor tongue to deliver them. She was as mute as she was blind.

She floated away from Kama's dour presence and neared another, consumed by madness. Elation warred with blackest hatred, while giddy ecstasy coursed through its core. Dranamir was uncertain which of the former Soulless it was, but she would learn by examining the others. The emotional turmoil exuded by the being threatened to consume her if she drew too near. She flitted away to avoid inadvertent contact.

Cold fury greeted her from the next being. Jannyn sought vengeance, and he wished her dead—again. She could sense his malice from afar, like an acrid taste she was unable to cleanse from her tongue.

His presence in this dark place told her much; he remained in the Nameless god's favor, and perhaps she'd been too hasty in her judgement of him. Every shred of evidence indicated Jannyn had betrayed them in Delucha, yet his soul remained tethered to their god. If his treachery had been true, the Nameless god would have severed his cord and dispatched Jannyn to Aeon's realm.

Aeon would not hesitate to mete out harsh punishments for a fallen Soulless. An eternity of damnation would await should they find themselves suddenly detached from the Nameless god. It was his power that thwarted the natural cycle of their souls, his divine intervention that spared his truest servants from Aeon's grasp.

She'd found Kama, Jannyn, and the other caught in the throes of insanity. There were no further presences imprisoned in the dark. She considered the circumstance of Garin's demise. The Nameless god used his body as a conduit to break free of his ancient bonds and utilized Garin's power to further his own. Garin's essence was likely annihilated in the process. Which left only Alyra.

Dranamir would have sneered if she retained lips. Alyra had always been the weakest of their number. She'd been killed while Dranamir rested in the tower and Kama lay injured on the battlefield. Who had struck her down, and why had the remnants of her psyche devolved into madness?

She moved toward the chaotic cloud of emotions once more, then stopped herself. She'd sensed the insanity was dangerous previously; it was best to keep her distance, despite her curiosity. When their time came to return to the world above, would Alyra prove more of a hindrance than in the past, or would the Nameless god simply cut her loose to face her fate in Aeon's realm?

She focused inward to study the connection that tied her to the Nameless god. It remained, though it was no longer whole. The edges frayed and threatened to snap, then rapidly wound together once more.

Panic surged through her as the cord began to unravel a second time. Such an occurrence could not be. It was an impossibility. Only the Nameless god himself could sever the connection he shared with his Soulless, yet he was not present to do so. Other forces were at work, beyond his control.

The realization terrified her.

As she examined the diminishing connection to her god further, an abrupt searing agony shot through her. Each nebulous molecule of her body shrieked in unison as pain consumed her. Its magnitude was far greater than what she'd endured as Ravin vaporized her physical body, for it was prolonged and intense. She would have screamed if she'd retained her voice. She sensed the others nearby, writhing in their own anguish.

After moments that stretched into eternity, the pain ceased as swiftly as it had begun. With the sudden release, the cord tethering her to the Nameless god snapped, and in the same instant her essence was driven forcefully from its dark abode.

She crashed into unyielding stone, no longer nebulous nor blind. She was once more in her body, though she appeared ethereal in form. She studied her hands for a time, stunned at the change in coloration. The gray hue that had infused her skin was gone, replaced by her former, healthier pink shade.

It wasn't right. It shouldn't be.

Truly terrified for the first time in decades, Dranamir lifted her gaze to study her new surroundings. Pale gray stone shot through with veins of white and gold was underfoot. The stone formed a domed cavern. At the far end from her present position were a pair of magnificent gates, wrought in gold and decorated in a dazzling array of colorful gems.

Her heart plummeted. She stood before Aeon's gates, a sure sign the Nameless god had been defeated.

She spun around to survey the cavern behind her, irrational hope that she might escape Aeon's divine wrath guiding her steps. The cavern wall loomed, unbroken. Her only path forward was to approach the beautiful gates and beg for mercy from the Underworld's master.

She faced the gates again. While she'd been turned in the other direction, Alyra and Jannyn had appeared. Alyra knelt, sobbing into her dark hands. Like Dranamir, her original form had been restored. Her dark hair was once again lustrous, her beauty evident even in her grief.

Jannyn stumbled forward, his form hale and portly. He exuded a strength in his original form that he'd lacked as Soulless. He knelt beside Alyra, whispered to her, then offered his hand. She wiped at her eyes and clasped his pale fingers in her own, her dark eyes locked on his face.

A pang of jealousy shot through Dranamir as she watched the pair. They would face Aeon together, accept their punishment together. She would have no such luxury. She'd spurned everyone who offered their assistance—everyone save the Nameless god himself. He was Immortal and would not appear at his youngest brother's ornate door.

Kama appeared steps away from her then. He sported the bronzed skin common to those of Kamshati heritage, and like Jannyn, he possessed a bearing of physical strength he'd previously lacked. His dark eyes locked on the gates ahead, then moved to study Jannyn and Alyra. A frown of regret crossed his lips even as he strode purposefully forward. He was prepared to meet his fate at Aeon's hands.

Dranamir remained at the rear of the cavern as the others approached the golden gates. They had each committed atrocities on a scale previously unheard of in the world's history, yet Dranamir believed hers would warrant punishment more severe than the others. Once she'd committed her life to the Nameless god, she'd never looked back, never hesitated to carry out his orders, and never believed she'd find herself severed from him. All of his promises had come to naught.

Aeon himself appeared as the others reached his gates. His dark Felene fur was matted and mussed, but his blue-white eyes were stern. He crossed his arms and eyed the trio before him with disdain, but he did not speak.

"Dranamir."

She spun around at the sound of her name, whispered with desperation. The gray countenance that faced her with its striking features and crimson eyes appeared as insubstantial as she and the others. His eyes were wide with terror as the reality of their situation—and his presence outside his brother's realm—began to sink in.

"This is impossible," she said as her voice rose with panic. "This cannot be!"

"I've…miscalculated. Severely." He raked his hands through his dark hair while his eyes darted about the cavern as though seeking an escape.

"You are a god. Why—?"

He pressed one finger against her lips. "In my hubris, I thought to ensure my immortality by separating it from myself. It lay protected beneath the Tower of Obsidian for generations, undisturbed. I shielded it from my siblings' touch in the days before they imprisoned me so long ago. Only a mortal could have hoped to destroy it, and then, only if they were in possession of my name."

"But they've stolen your name," she protested. "This should not be!"

He shook his head with regret. "Minora preserved it, to my great shame. And together, with Solsticia, they manipulated one man's fate to ensure my demise. I am a god no longer, Dranamir." He grimaced and dropped his eyes.

She spun away from him, stunned into silence. Her savior, her guide, her protector… He was no more. He was only a man, and like all men before him, he must face Aeon with his death. She lifted her gaze to take in the gleaming gates and their towering, dark-furred master. The other former Soulless were gone from the cavern.

When he next spoke, his tone brimmed with fury. "I did not believe Solsticia's whelp could wield such power. At least I can take solace in the knowledge that he no doubt resides beyond those gates. Even you, with the enhancement I bestowed upon you, could not have hoped to survive."

"I believed him dead twice," she replied hollowly. "I was wrong on both accounts."

"In this matter, I am certain." His arm encircled her waist for what she suspected would be the final time. "Come, my queen. I will not force you to face my brother alone."

She nodded but made no reply. There was nothing he could say to redeem himself. He had failed her; his many promises lay shattered and broken like the countless bodies of the mortal soldiers on the battlefield far above.

As they began to step forward, she lifted her gaze to meet Aeon's. His blue-white eyes glowed with a baleful light, narrowed into near slits as he assessed the pair. It would not matter what the Nameless god might say on her behalf—her punishment would be one of the most severe the Underworld's caretaker would ever mete out.

Anger consumed her. She wrenched away from the Nameless' grasp and marched forward. She'd dedicated her life to him, committed unspeakable atrocities in his name, yet she refused to let him overshadow her in this, her final act. She would face Aeon alone, as would he. She would answer for her actions and retain the last shred of dignity she possessed.

Aeon's lips quirked into a bemused smile at her action, but his eyes focused on the Nameless god. "It seems even your truest allies now shun you, brother."

Words spilled from her lips, unbidden. "I do not *shun* him," Dranamir hissed. "I will always revere him. He was once my savior, and I owe him a debt I can never repay."

"Such misplaced devotion," Aeon replied, compassion in his tone. "Do you not deny your crimes eclipse those of all the other Soulless combined?"

Dranamir shrugged. "It's true. Denial is useless."

"It seems you have a stronger constitution than this *man* who was once a god." Aeon swished his dark tail in agitation. "He would share the responsibility for his own actions with you, the woman in his thrall. Yet you have thwarted his final scheme." Aeon paused to study her for a moment, then nodded to himself. "You will face the wrath of every soul whose life you unrightfully claimed, Dranamir. This afterlife will be wholly unpleasant for you."

"Aeon, she acted on my orders!" The Nameless god's plea rang through the cavern.

Aeon chuckled. "Yes. And for that, you will face the wrath of every soul whose life you claimed, and every soul who met their end at the hands of your Soulless. You are a god no more."

CHAPTER FORTY-FOUR

KINDRED SPIRITS

When the semi-transparent dome appeared over the black tower, Vardak's waning hope swelled. He was uncertain what had occurred to cause it, but he suspected magic. And with such magic, he prayed the gods had finally given the signal to Ravin and the others to accomplish the daunting feat they'd been tasked with.

He caught but a fleeting glimpse of the dome before his attention was drawn back to his present opponent. A weary Murkor who wielded a short sword in his only hand charged toward him, but rather than shout insults or curses, the Murkor sang a prayer in his people's tongue. Soldiers on both sides wished for an end to the fighting.

Days had passed since he'd last departed the battlefield unscathed. His injuries were minor compared to many others, a fact he attributed to his advanced training with Blademon. His ribs were healing, albeit more slowly than he wished. Coreyaless admonished him each evening with a terse reminder he would never mend without proper rest. But the Nameless god would never give them rest so long as he remained standing.

The dome's appearance drew the Nameless god's attention immediately. He bellowed wordlessly and charged away from the chasm, heedless of the other gods' pursuit. The one-armed Murkor skidded to a halt and turned to observe the gods, no longer concerned by Vardak's proximity. For his part, Vardak lowered his axe and called to the drummers to sound a retreat. Perhaps it was premature, but he sensed the events about to unfold within the tower would prove far more prominent than anything on the blood-soaked plains beyond.

The Murkor glanced at him, his head tilted in question.

"This fight is no longer in our hands," Vardak stated in the Murkor tongue. "Pray that whatever has drawn the Nameless to the tower brings a swift end to the war."

The Murkor shrugged and turned away. Vardak busied himself with the withdrawal of his dwindling troops. Too many lives had been lost on both sides during the past week, and many more in Delucha and Balotica beforehand. He would spare those he could from further strife, with or without Blademon's blessing.

The war god was preoccupied, in any case. Blademon appeared at the tower's entrance, his swords ready as he prepared to block the Nameless god's advance. Vardak paused in his retreat to watch as the other gods joined him. In his rage, the Nameless was undaunted, fearless, and fiercely determined. He charged forward and shouted a challenge to his siblings, and brandished his own pair of dark swords.

Vardak prayed for the success of the gods' mad plan. He hoped Ravin, Tavesin, and the young Drakkon would achieve what they'd been tasked to do. If they failed… Vardak shook his head and turned away from the scene. He didn't want to dwell upon what might happen if the Nameless god prevailed.

By the time he'd crossed the charred expanse that marked Ravin's battle with the Soulless, most of the gods had disappeared inside the tower. Though they were hidden from his sight, the rage-filled bellows of the Nameless god continued to roll across the battlefield. Vardak halted amongst a cluster of human and Murkor allies, then turned to face the tower once more.

The dome that now encased it had become occluded. Its surface seemed to thicken of its own accord. The glittering black walls of the tower remained visible behind it, though blurred and hazy as the magical energy surrounding it seemed to strengthen. The Nameless god's furious shouts suddenly transformed into shrieks of panic, then to wails of agony.

As the pitch of the Nameless god's vocalizations changed, the first of several tremors rocked the landscape. Vardak widened his stance and dug his legs into the earth to keep his footing, but many of the bipedal species around him stumbled and fell. A moment later, a low rumble issued from the tower, and the dome rapidly collapsed upon itself.

He stood frozen, unable to tear his eyes from the spectacle that unfolded in the distance. Despair threatened as he watched the dome disintegrate, the last tatters of his dying hope extinguished. The dome had been a promise of hope, and with its destruction, he feared the Nameless god had won.

Additional tremors shook the land, more powerful than the last. Then, inexplicably, the tower began to crumble. Great blocks of obsidian broke free to crash into the hard-baked earth. The enemy soldiers near the tower's base scattered in several directions as they sought to escape the destruction. Vardak spied a large knot of Serpentus nearer his location cease their pursuit. Several ripped the collars viciously from their necks, a sign their forced tie to the Nameless god was severed.

He allowed hope to surge through him then. The Serpentus—*all* of the Serpentus—were freed. The meaning was plain to him: The Nameless god was defeated. The war was at an end.

Murkor who had continued to battle for the Nameless god's side threw aside their weapons and knelt on the blood-soaked plain in a show of surrender. Weary warriors from both armies cheered as the dark beacon that marked the Nameless god's last bastion of power toppled.

Vardak remained still and silent as he watched it fall. No one emerged from the wreckage of the tower—not the gods, not Ravin or Tavesin, nor their Drakkon counterpart. It was likely the gods had vanished once the fight with their brother was over, but he feared for the others. Trozyen and Tavesin were both young, with the bulk of their lives ahead of them. And while he'd often been wary and mistrustful of Ravin, the mage had proven himself a staunch ally during the past week. His gaze remained locked on the tower's remains long after it became clear no one would be emerging from the ruins.

Aziarah landed softly beside him. "Some of my people have offered to scour the wreckage for survivors."

He nodded but did not look at her. "There may be Murkor or Serpentus inside. With the Nameless god defeated, they'll have no further reason to attack." He omitted his concerns regarding the trio responsible for the dome's appearance, but Aziarah intuited what plagued his mind.

"I will seek Tavesin and Trozyen personally," she said. "It's possible they're safe within the Aethereum."

He lifted an eyebrow in question. "And Ravin?"

Aziarah was silent for a time. "It is my understanding the gods chose him to complete the ritual that caused the tower to collapse. He was likely within."

"I see." He studied the tower for several seconds, then turned to face her. "If he is within, perhaps your scouts will locate him."

"I pray for Tavesin's sake he lives," she replied with a frown. "I'm certain the boy is well. Ravin would have given his life to protect him. I may not like the man, but he's done right by Tavesin." She spread her wings in preparation for departure. "Vardak, your interim Warleader is on her way."

He nodded as Aziarah sprang into the air once more. He'd been expecting a visit from Makta at the battle's conclusion. As Sevic's only living relative, she'd been nominated Warleader in his stead until a proper conclave could be arranged to discuss their people's next leader. Her age would be a detriment to her claim, but Vardak would champion her cause to the elders when they returned to the Stronghold. She'd done a remarkable job with maintaining order after Sevic's death.

He continued to study the impromptu celebration that had erupted on the battlefield, even as others began to seek more wounded amongst the piles of dead. He prayed Aziarah would locate the mages and find them all safe.

"Vardak." Makta's voice was steady, calm in the face of the rampant destruction.

He turned to face her. She was clad in leather armor that left her arms bare. Both sported dozens of cuts and abrasions, but she appeared otherwise unharmed. A sword was strapped across her back while a smith's hammer hung from her belt. Her expression was melancholy.

"Makta." He saluted her.

"I'll have none of that," she said wearily. "We both know my role is only temporary. Our people will look to someone else. Someone with battle experience and a mind for strategy. I have neither." She sighed. "I've been speaking with several of the Serpentus, Vardak. There is… We are obligated to offer them refuge. Our ancestors shared their plight."

"Yes. I assumed you would ask them once the war was ended."

He studied her, uncertain why she hesitated or why she sought his approval for the act. The Serpentus were kindred spirits of a sort. To his mind, there was no question of offering assistance, a place to call home, somewhere they would be welcomed. It was the duty of the Scorpion Men to take them in, if that was the path they chose for themselves.

Makta looked away, her expression pained. "I am Warleader only until we return home, Vardak. This decision… I cannot make it alone. I am not my uncle. I need… I need your support in this. Our people look to *you*, Vardak, whether you realize it or not."

He shook his head. "I am younger than you are, Makta. My word will mean nothing to the elders."

She snorted. "Patak always said you were blind to the obvious. Your age is irrelevant in this matter. You were trained by Blademon himself, then chosen as his second during this campaign! Don't you see? Even if the conclave doesn't name you Warleader, your word means a great deal. So I will ask you again: Will you back my decision to offer sanctuary to the Serpentus people?"

"Of course. I am of the same mindset." He ran one hand through his hair and sighed. "I hope they'll name someone else Warleader. I'm not certain I want the post."

She smirked. "My uncle said the same, you know."

He shrugged uncomfortably. "Perhaps we ought to speak with the Serpentus and make a formal offer to them."

"You're avoiding the issue, Vardak."

"I'll deal with it *if* it arises," he replied. "The Serpentus need us now. There are hundreds of wounded who could use our aid. More pyres need to be built and set aflame. I must send word to the Murkor leader. Messengers need to be dispatched across the mountains… This talk of Warleader can wait."

Reluctantly, she nodded. "Very well. But you cannot push it aside forever. There will come a time when it must be addressed, and I want you to know you have my backing."

He grimaced as they began to make their way toward the healers' pavilions in the distance. She was persistent in her determination to see him take up Sevic's mantle. "As I said, I will deal with it when the time comes."

Makta led him inside one of the pavilions, where she sought a Serpentus man whose torso was swathed in bandages. Another was wrapped around his head. His lower body was coiled while he rested his forearms on the lip of the ring. Vardak was stunned at the flexibility of the man's spine. For his part, the Serpentus followed their progress toward him with soft brown eyes but said nothing.

"Owen," Makta said as they came to stand in front of him, "this is Vardak."

Recognition lit his eyes, and he straightened to offer his hand in greeting. "It's a pleasure to finally meet Emra's general and Blademon's other chosen."

They shook, and Vardak said, "You are the leader of your people?"

Owen snorted. "Leader is too strong a word for what I am. I am—I *was* a knight. One of only a handful captured and taken to the Murkor caverns. I… I don't believe the others survived this war."

"I'm sorry," Vardak replied somberly.

Owen shrugged, then grimaced and glanced down at his bandages. "Gods, I hope I heal soon. But back to the matter at hand—as the only person of rank left to us, the others have begun deferring to me. We don't know what the future might hold for us, and who am I to decide what path we ought to take? I'm still struggling to come to terms with what she did to us. It was not enough to strip our humanity. We were made slaves, as well. So many good people were killed needlessly, simply because we were unable to resist the demands of the Nameless god and the Soulless."

Vardak settled himself into a seated position. "Your tale is akin to our ancestors'. Makta and I have spoken, and I believe we can help—if you and the rest of your people are amenable, that is."

A faint smile crossed Owen's lips. "I'm listening."

Vardak glanced at Makta, who indicated he should continue, despite her rank as interim Warleader. He kept his misgivings to himself and focused on the matter at hand.

"Our people can offer refuge," Vardak said. "When we return to the Stronghold, the Serpentus are welcome to join us. It may take some time to secure lodgings for all of your people, but I'm confident our elders will make certain it's done."

Owen's smile broadened. "Thank you both. I'll speak with the others. It is a far better solution than anything I've come up with so far. And as you've said, our peoples share a similar history. We are kin, of a sort."

"I will send word to the Stronghold of your decision once it has been made," Makta promised. "No matter what your people choose, know that we will be allies."

CHAPTER FORTY-FIVE

PROMISES

It was a struggle to open his eyes. The lids felt insurmountably heavy, his body was weak, and his head pounded with each beat of his heart. But he was alive. Impossibly, inexplicably *alive.*

Ravin's lids fluttered open. He lay on his back atop a soft mattress, while thick goose-down pillows supported his head. Thick blankets covered him. The ceiling above was constructed of smooth, white stone.

He blinked in confusion. His last memories were of the black tower collapsing around him as the last dregs of his energy were spent on the Nameless god's destruction. By all accounts, he should have been dead. But this place, unfamiliar as it was, did not belong to Aeon, nor was it anywhere near the battlefield.

He pushed himself into a sitting position while his weakened muscles protested the action. He was in a small room, adorned only with a single chair placed near his bedside. On one side was a door, on the other, a large window. Beyond the glass, he could see a dark expanse broken by myriad pinpricks of light—stars, if he was not mistaken.

He smiled to himself. He was in the Sky Palace. His mother had managed to save him from the fate he'd believed was inevitable. Perhaps there were some perks to being the son of a goddess, after all.

The door opened moments later. He turned, expecting to find his mother. Instead, Minora hovered near the door, her statuesque features unreadable. Ravin suppressed a groan as he studied her. He was certain she was there to discuss his future, and part of him anticipated she would renege on her vow.

Minora took an uncertain step toward the chair. "Ravin, we must talk."

He nodded and immediately regretted the motion. His aching head felt as though it would split at any moment.

"My sister—your mother—told me you'd accepted your death in the tower." Minora sat down carefully and rearranged her skirts. "When the Nameless god was vanquished, I knew the expenditure of energy on your part was phenomenal. No one else could have accomplished what you did, Ravin. I'll admit, my designs were for your life to end that day, but I heard your final words, just as the others did. It was never my intent that you should fall in love, yet you have."

Ravin leaned back against his pillows and crossed his arms. "What does Adalin have to do with this?"

"With the small amount of freedom I granted you, you defied some of my designs, though you did not know it. Your planned friendship with Adalin Nantess was never meant to grow into anything more. Yet it has." Minora's marble gaze was fixed upon him. "Armistral demanded I change my final design for you, Ravin. And Ukase stated your death was unjust. I'd promised you freedom, after all. He said my trickery and manipulation were deplorable."

Ravin looked down as he absorbed her words. "In my last moments, I knew I could not survive. I'd given everything." He peered up at her. "It wasn't my mother who saved me from the tower. It was you."

"At the behest of the others, yes." A reedy sigh escaped her chiseled lips. "I stalled time long enough to reach your location. With the Nameless god's death, the safeguards he'd placed there were destroyed. I brought you here to recover."

"And Tavesin?" he demanded. "Is he safe?"

"Yes. He and Trozyen returned to the camp after the battle was over. Your mother spoke to them. They know you live and are eager for your return."

He closed his eyes and smiled. "I'm relieved they're both well."

Minora was silent for a time. A rustle of fabric told him she'd risen to her feet, and he opened his eyes. She stood at the foot of his bed, facing him.

"I'll not endure the disfavor of my siblings, Ravin," she said. "I promised I would grant your freedom once the Nameless god was dead. My words were not false—your soul would have been freed in Aeon's realm. But since I've been forced to alter your life's course from my intended design, you now live."

Ravin clenched his fists beneath the blankets as anger and frustration competed for prominence within him. "I believe I've proven myself worthy of freedom," he replied coldly.

She sighed. "Yes. Even Karmada has demanded I release you, and she rarely favors mages. Truly, it is the reason I came here today. My siblings are in agreement—whether it is for your mother's sake or your own, I do not know—but you are, from this moment forward, the master of your own destiny."

He expected to feel different, to sense the release of his invisible bonds, but there was nothing. He lifted his eyebrows in question as he continued to assess his inner workings.

Minora laughed softly. "The threads of your life as I wove them were still yours, Ravin. You'll find yourself unchanged."

A light tap issued from the door. When Minora spoke, amusement was in her tone, though her marble features remained untouched by her mirth. "No doubt that is your mother."

Minora crossed the room to open the door. Solsticia was not alone in the corridor beyond; Ravin spied both Armistral and Aeon with her. Aeon's presence he could understand, but Armistral's was a mystery. The god of peace and love, Blademon's twin, would have little reason to pay him a visit.

"It is done," Minora informed them. "I'm certain you are aware that I have kept my promise to him—and to you."

"Yes," Aeon replied as Solsticia pushed past her sister and into the room. She seated herself on the vacant chair and smiled at Ravin fondly.

"I'm pleased you're awake, Ravin." She reached toward him and brushed an unruly curl of dark hair from his forehead.

He flinched away from her touch, wary of her intent. "Minora tells me I'm free. She planned for me to die in the tower. Did you know?"

Solsticia dropped her hand, her expression pained.

Aeon came to stand at the foot of his bed, while Armistral occupied the space between himself and Solsticia. "None of us were privy to Minora's design," Aeon replied.

"It was only at the end, as the Nameless god's life was snuffed out, that we realized you could not survive without our intervention," Armistral added with a flutter of his golden wings. "I would not stand for her manipulation. In that matter, she erred."

Near the door, Minora harrumphed in displeasure. "When Solsticia birthed him, we all agreed he posed a threat to the balance of this world. He could not be allowed free will until he properly proved himself."

"He *has* proven himself, sister," Aeon replied in an acid tone. "You would have seen him dead for it. He deserves the opportunity to make a life of *his* choosing after everything he has done for us—and for the world below." He turned to Ravin and made a half-bow. "If we'd been unable to convince Minora to spare you, I would have given you a place of great honor in my realm. I will one day, but not yet." He flashed a mischievous grin.

Ravin closed his eyes as he listened to the gods' discussion. He wasn't certain how long he'd been asleep before he'd awakened in the Sky Palace, but the short span of time he'd been alert proved draining. He was exhausted.

"We must give him time to rest, to heal," Solsticia said, sensing his ebbing energy levels.

"Of course," Armistral replied. "I came only to state my reasons for advocating on Ravin's behalf. I felt he should know."

Ravin forced his eyes open once more. "I don't understand."

Armistral smiled, pleased with himself. "You knew before you entered the tower what awaited you, even as most of us did not. With your final breath, you asked Solsticia to speak to Adalin on your behalf, and in that moment, I understood what drove you. You did not enter the tower because we ordered it, nor did you go seeking revenge—as I'd always believed you would. No, you acted as you did for *love*. Such an act is rare and beautiful. I would not stand idly by and allow you to die, and we gods have the means to alter the course of fate. You will live, Ravin, and it is my fervent hope you will make a life with your duchess."

Ravin turned toward Solsticia with a tired grin. "I hope you've procured the mead you promised us, mother."

CHAPTER FORTY-SIX

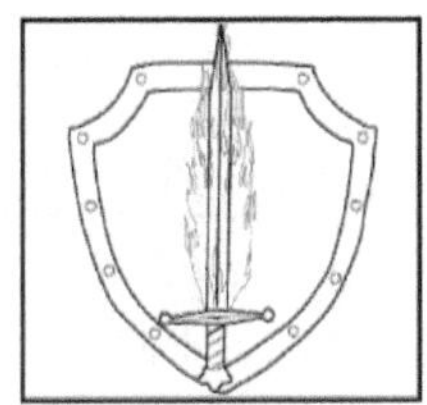

LOOKING TOWARD THE FUTURE

"Fucking gods, not again."

Patak's laughter roused Emra from the depths of a dreamless sleep, but she lay still and listened to his banter.

"You're a terrible liar, Patak," Maryn replied. "This game requires a knack for deception, which you do not have. Pay up."

"At this rate, I'll need to beg my brother for coin again," Patak grumbled good-naturedly.

A card game, then. Maryn was right; Patak was unable to conceal his emotions and his excitement. Emra opened her eyes and began to sit up, but Patak turned and beamed down at her even as he shook his head.

"Lay still, Em. You've been unconscious for days."

"All the more reason to be up," she muttered. "The soldiers will need me, and—"

He silenced her with a knowing grin. "You've done your part. Lay still. I'll fetch one of the wizards."

He rose and left her alone with Maryn, who began shuffling the deck of cards. "The battle's over," he informed her. "It has been for several days, and he's not left your side since he awakened himself."

She frowned. She'd lost too much time. "Since we're alive and the pair of you were gambling, I suspect our side has won?"

"Better. The Soulless are gone for good, as is the Nameless god." Maryn smirked. "Care to play a hand while your beau is off seeking a healer? You're a more worthy opponent."

She stifled a laugh. "I suppose it can't hurt—too badly. You have a reputation, Maryn."

He snickered. "Let's find out if it remains untarnished. You'd never play me before."

"You never asked." She managed a grin. "Patak lost enough coin to you for the both of us, in any case."

"Ah, but think of the riches I'd have if I *had* asked." He began to deal and placed her cards where she could reach them without sitting upright. "The game is Triples. Do you know the rules?"

"That depends. Do you play standard or Santinian?"

"Standard, of course. Leave the nonsense to your cavalrymen."

His words sparked another question. "Fyrmane. How does he fare? I was—"

Maryn held up one furred mitt. "Vardak asked one of his people to look after your mount, since it seems he wouldn't allow anyone else near him. Since Patak awakened, he's taken up the duty himself. For a species who cannot ride, the Scorpion Men have certainly taken a liking to Fyrmane."

Relieved, she picked up her cards. "Fyrmane will be incensed when I'm able to see him next. He's liable to disown me."

"I suspect he'll be pleased to see you—after he's made his displeasure known," Patak replied from her other side. "Radosan will be here soon."

She smiled up at him. "Thank you. Fyrmane would thank you too, if he were able to speak."

Maryn placed his first card and eyed her quizzically. When Emra played her card, he began to snicker.

"Given Patak's expression, your choice in cards is puzzling."

She laughed. "As we both know, Patak, for all his charm, is not a brilliant strategist."

"Perhaps not when it comes to games of *chance*," Patak replied with a grin. "Games of the *heart*, however…" He shrugged casually and allowed his words to trail off.

Maryn groaned. "If it's going to be like this, I think I'm better off playing against someone else. Someone whose partner doesn't activate my gag reflex." He placed his second card and sat back expectantly.

Emra studied her remaining cards while shielding them from Patak's sight as much as she was able. Footsteps drew her attention after a moment, and she looked up to find Radosan standing at the end of her mat. She glanced at Maryn regretfully.

"Perhaps we can finish this later."

Maryn chuckled. "Perhaps. And if we deal Patak in, he'll be less likely to cause your hand to lose." Maryn collected the cards and disappeared, undoubtedly to find another victim and take their coin.

Radosan knelt beside her as the watch commander left. "How do you feel, Emra?"

"Well, considering Patak mentioned I've been asleep for days."

"It has been ten days," he confirmed.

Radosan began channeling his magic; she sensed the healing energy before it met her skin. Unlike much of the magic she'd witnessed on the battlefield, his was pure, soothing, *comforting.* She allowed her eyes to drift shut as he examined her for any further injury. Her body relaxed despite her desire to rise and be about her business. And she was certain there were dozens of matters requiring her attention after her prolonged sleep.

"I can find nothing amiss," Radosan said after a time. "You'll be weak for a while and will tire easily until you can rebuild your stamina. Don't go anywhere alone."

"She won't," Patak promised.

She pushed herself upright. "What happened on the field?" she asked of Radosan. "I recall attacking Kama, and then…something struck my head. I remember nothing else."

"From what I've pieced together, you killed Kama, but left yourself vulnerable to the nearby Serpentus," he replied. "Your guards fought them off, but you'd taken a significant head wound. Your skull was fractured," he amended. "We repaired the damage to your bones, but few have ever been gifted with the means to mend an injured brain."

Patak took her nearest hand in his own. "No one was certain you'd be the same when you awakened. *If* you awakened."

She squeezed his fingers gently. "I can assure you, I haven't changed. Now that I've been given leave to go about my business—"

"*Slowly*," Radosan cut in. "You must not overextend yourself, Emra."

She sighed. "Very well. I'd still like to speak with Vardak and Ravin."

Radosan looked down, and Patak chewed his lower lip uneasily. She knew something was amiss without voicing the question.

"Patak?" she prompted.

"My brother is well, and he'll be pleased to see you," Patak replied. "Ravin is… I don't know, Em. Solsticia brought news that he is recovering in her home, that he's alive, but we've heard nothing more since the tower fell."

"The tower has *fallen?*" She gaped at him.

He managed a wary grin. "Yes. You'll see it once we're outside."

"What Maryn said is true then," she whispered. "The Soulless can never return, nor can their master."

"Exactly." Patak's grin widened. "I suspect you'll want to meet with Aeon soon?"

She nodded. "He has a vow to keep, but that can be discussed later. First, let's find your brother. I've been lying about too long already."

Patak offered his arm as she pulled herself to her feet. A wave of dizziness overcame her, and she gripped his arm to steady herself. It passed swiftly, to her relief, though Radosan eyed her knowingly.

"I'm fine," she assured him. There were undoubtedly countless others who required his services more than she did.

"Make certain she rests when needed," Radosan said to Patak. "There is no cure for stubbornness."

Patak chuckled. "I will, and believe me, I can handle stubbornness. I grew up with Vardak, after all."

They picked their way through the pavilion. Emra was relieved to find fewer mats were occupied than had been during the battle. Those who remained in the care of the healers sported the most severe wounds, or had succumbed to disease as a result of their injuries.

Patak led her outside into the light of a brilliant morning sun. A proper camp had been erected while she'd lain unconscious. Humans and Drakkon moved about, interspersed with Scorpion Men. A large swath of the campsite was quiet; she assumed the tents belonged to Murkor, who were once more acting on their natural, nocturnal schedules. She spied only one Serpentus amongst the city of canvas.

Beyond the tents lay the battlefield, deceptively barren from a distance. Past it, she could see jagged blocks of obsidian strewn across the parched earth, the remnants of the tower. She studied the scene for a time, uncertain what she should feel. Her ages-long battle was finally at an end and the Soulless were no more. She should have been elated, yet a deep melancholy permeated her core.

There had been too much death, too much suffering, too much pain. Though the war was over, her memories remained.

They traveled to the center of the camp, where her pavilion had been set up. Instead of the usual crew of her personal guards standing watch outside, she found Danian in the midst of a dice game with Maryn, while a pair of Scorpion Men she did not recognize looked on. Maryn had wasted little time in securing his next opponent.

Maryn flashed a grin in their direction as they neared. "Vardak's inside." He smirked. "As is Makta."

Beside her, Patak groaned. "I should have known."

"She's not so bad," Emra replied in a lower tone meant for his ears alone. "I understand you have a past, Patak, but don't let it interfere with the present."

"She's interim Warleader now," he replied uneasily.

She understood his unspoken concern. Makta held the power to exile him for his attachment to her. He'd made no secret of their relationship when Makta joined them in Daesan.

They ducked inside the pavilion to find Vardak issuing orders to a pair of messengers, both Scorpion Men. Makta stood to one side, her arms crossed as she observed silently. She nodded a greeting as Emra and Patak entered, but said nothing until Vardak finished speaking. The messengers were each given sealed scrolls before they departed with a brief salute.

Emra smiled. She recalled Vardak's reluctance to accept his position as her general, but he'd excelled. Now, he led the camp without her guidance—and his people looked to him rather than Makta, it seemed. A slow grin crossed his face as he took in her presence.

"Emra, it's good to see you're awake."

"We have capable healers." She gripped Patak's arm tighter as she stumbled. "I'm still a bit weak, it seems."

Makta skittered forward, her eyes on Patak, though she spoke to Emra. "You're in good hands. I would know."

Patak stiffened. "Makta, now isn't the time—"

She chuckled. "And when would be, Patak? This matter must be addressed, and we've put it aside long enough." To Emra, she said, "I'm certain he's informed you of my present role."

Emra sensed curiosity in the other woman's demeanor, but there was no animosity. She nodded slowly. "He has."

"Then it is my duty to…assess the situation." Makta grinned at Patak, a mischievous glint in her eyes. "As interim Warleader of our people, it is my solemn duty to deny—or approve—your unspoken request to partner with a human."

Patak tensed further at her words. "You torture me, Makta."

She tossed her head back and laughed. "It may be my last opportunity to do so, Patak. It was always fun to watch you squirm."

Vardak crossed his arms, clearly tired of the banter. "Makta, we've discussed this. Tell him, before he grinds his teeth into dust."

Makta shot him a disapproving frown. "Very well. Since your brother insists, this is what I—*we*—have determined. The law disallowing our people to pair with those of other races is ancient, Patak. It was borne of an era when we were too few, and our enemies many. In order to survive as a species, such unions were forbidden." The mirth faded from her eyes to be replaced with sorrow. "As much as it pains me to see you choose this path, I will not seek your exile. Rather, one of those messengers who just departed carries my judgment to the Stronghold, even now. I suspect yours will be the first of many such unions in our future."

Patak stared at her, stunned and unblinking for several moments. "You've accepted…? We can remain together?"

Emra squeezed his arm in reassurance, while Makta said, "Yes. Vardak and I have agreed that the old rules are no longer relevant. I'm glad you've found happiness, Patak. We may have had our disagreements, you and I, but you were always a good man."

Patak turned to beam at Emra. "I know we haven't spoken of the future, Em, but I hope this pleases you as much as it does me."

"It does." She grinned an instant before she rose up to her toes and kissed him. Startled, he resisted for a moment, then leaned in with a throaty chuckle.

The sound of a throat clearing near the entrance interrupted the moment. Emra felt her face flush as she stepped away, and she stumbled once more. Patak caught her in one arm while she regained her balance. Grudgingly, she admitted Radosan's warning must be heeded, though she'd rather enjoyed his affection. A brief dizzy spell was worth the price of her joy.

A pair of red-hooded Murkor stood at the entrance. Vardak moved past her to greet them in the musical Murkor language. Emra glanced at Patak in question.

"They are the Matriarch and Kal's personal guards," he whispered. "I suppose our kiss was ill-timed. I didn't know they would arrive today."

"The Matriarch and Kal have come here?" she asked, but it was Makta who answered.

"Yes. We sent word at Sal'zar's request the day after the battle was finished. They've come to reunite their people. Vardak has agreed to facilitate the negotiations between Sal'zar's faction and those who remained with the Soulless' army."

"Vardak?" Emra asked pointedly. "But you are Warleader, Makta."

Makta chuckled. "My post is temporary. His is not."

"I'll explain later," Patak promised. "For now, I think we ought to leave my brother to his discussions. You're unsteady on your feet, Em."

"I've been worse," she replied with a glower. "But I will heed your words. You promised Radosan to watch over me after all, and I *am* rather hungry."

He grinned, then turned to Makta. "Good luck with the Murkor, and… Thank you. For everything."

"Take care of her, Patak," Makta replied in a thick tone. "If you don't, you *will* answer to me, whether I'm Warleader or not."

Patak led her to a makeshift mess tent where they both ate. She was forced to admit she felt better afterwards and was steadier on her feet. Patak smirked knowingly, but for once, kept his thoughts to himself.

It was dusk as they approached the small tent Patak claimed was his own, but the familiar silhouette sitting near its entrance was unmistakable.

Aeon sat with his legs crossed, the Fireblade resting across his knees. His blue-white eyes glowed softly in the failing light as he tracked their progress. He remained seated as Emra made a half-bow in greeting.

"Ukase informed me you were awake," he said. "He presides over the Murkor affairs at present."

"I planned to speak with you once I reached a temple," Emra replied. "I was not expecting you to seek me out."

Aeon chuckled. "No one ever does. Even the Felene people believe my appearance is the harbinger of foul luck—more so than Karmada's."

Emra shook her head, amused. She'd come to know Aeon better than most mortals during her many lifetimes, and while his words were true, she knew the common assumption about his presence was mere superstition. He heralded foul tidings no more than any other god.

"I don't subscribe to that folly, Aeon. You know this."

"That I do." He paused to examine the sword, ordinary in appearance while in his possession. "You know why I've come, Emra. I gave you my solemn word. Should the Nameless god be permanently dealt with, I will put an end to your long cycle. In exchange, I would have your blade."

"Why?" she asked. "The sword was not part of our original agreement."

"The sword—and all it stands for—is an important relic in this world's history." Aeon smiled wistfully. "I will preserve it, for one day its services may be required again. But do not fret, Emra. Your soul is free of me, and free of *it* from this moment forward."

"I fail to understand how anyone *else* might use the Fireblade." She crossed her arms and eyed him uneasily. "It was tied to my soul alone."

"My eldest sister is the goddess of magic," he replied with a sly grin. "Another can be chosen, should times demand a new wielder. I don't believe our world will require it, for even Minora does not foresee a need to preserve the Fireblade. Perhaps I am merely sentimental."

He rose to his feet and nodded to both of them. "I bid you goodnight, Emra. Make the most of your final existence." He flashed a grin at Patak. "You've already made a good start."

CHAPTER FORTY-SEVEN

ROGUES AND PRISONERS

Sal'zar approached the command pavilion with measured steps as he grappled with his inner turmoil. He'd asked for this meeting between himself, the Matriarch, the Kal, and Daj'ven, the soldier who had taken command of the Murkor army after Jal'den's capture. Though amenable to negotiations with the Scorpion Men, humans, Serpentus, and even the Drakkon, Daj'ven had made a point of avoiding Sal'zar and those labeled rogues since the battle ended. Sal'zar had given up trying to reason with him, which was the purpose behind the requested meeting.

A pair of Scorpion Men and four crimson-hooded guardsmen stood sentinel outside the command tent. They watched his approach with disinterest and waved him inside without question. He was expected.

The center of the pavilion was occupied by Ukase. The Matriarch and Kal were seated on the god's right, while Vardak stood with Jal'den on his left. The Kal nodded to Sal'zar in silent greeting. Jal'den did the same, though Sal'zar suspected he would have signed something more if his wrists had not been bound. He remained Vardak's prisoner. Daj'ven was nowhere to be seen.

Ukase gestured to the space nearest Jal'den. "Sal'zar, please join us. Daj'ven has been summoned as well. Once he arrives, you will both be granted an opportunity to speak. This rift between your people must be mended."

Sal'zar nodded and took his position beside Jal'den, who whispered, "This will be over soon, *ama*. Relax."

Sal'zar glowered beneath his hood. Jal'den, ever the optimist, could see nothing foreboding in their future. Sal'zar knew Daj'ven would attempt to lay much of the rift's blame upon Sal'zar and their deceased former commander, Aran'daj. Daj'ven was not privy to the Kal's schemes to subvert the Soulless and understandably believed they'd acted against strict orders. He'd done his best to impart his misguided opinion on every Murkor that had remained a part of the Soulless' army, despite the prevailing belief that none of them wished to serve the Nameless god or his corrupted associates.

Sal'zar prayed the Kal would explain his role in the matter and lift the cloud of suspicion that hovered over Sal'zar and those that had been chosen to flee with him. Yet Sal'zar wasn't certain the Kal would speak of his plot; by doing so, he risked losing the long-standing faith of his people.

When Daj'ven entered moments later, Sal'zar stiffened. He could sense the soldier's animosity as he crossed the tent and came to stand in the open space between Sal'zar and the Kal. Daj'ven kept his focus on Ukase and the Murkor leaders, but spared a brief nod for Vardak and Jal'den. Daj'ven did not acknowledge Sal'zar, as though he were an insect and beneath notice.

"We shall begin," Ukase stated, his voice a low rumble. "It is my belief that the origin of your present rift stems from plans set in motion many months ago, plans that arose when the Soulless were resurrected." He motioned to the Kal. "While some of the parties present are aware of portions of your scheme, there are others who were kept in ignorance. Explain."

The Kal bowed his copper hood, and Sal'zar noted the downward slope of his shoulders, an indication of great sorrow. "When the Soulless returned, one of their number, the Kamshati, traveled immediately to the caverns. He demanded an audience with us. The soldiers at the entrance would have denied him entry, but he killed one of them to make his power known. The others felt compelled to obey."

"We met with him outside the cavern," the Matriarch confirmed in a reedy, aged voice. "He informed us the Soulless were in command of our army at the chasm. I protested—our people had suffered enough under the wizard's rule, and I did not wish to see further grief spread amongst us. He laughed."

"He called forth a magic to ensure we complied," the Kal continued. "A sickness that has ailed our great Martriarch these many months. The Soulless stated she would survive so long as our people continued to serve him. If we subverted them, the disease would worsen and eventually kill her. He insinuated it would spread to her successor and continue its deadly cycle to ensure our continued obedience. Under such a threat, we could do nothing but cave to his demands."

Sal'zar watched the pair in shocked silence. The Kal had told him nothing of the circumstances surrounding the Murkor people's conscription, but to threaten the Matriarch was unthinkable. Without her guidance, Murkor society would flounder and devolve into chaos.

"But I formed a plan," the Kal continued. "The threat was to her alone. If she was not privy to *my* scheming, I believed the disease would not worsen. It was a terrible gamble, yet one I was compelled to make. Our people have been used too many times throughout our history, to our great shame. The time had come to assert ourselves."

"He told me nothing of what he'd done until I felt the sickness lift," the Matriarch added. "That was perhaps ten days ago. I knew immediately the Soulless was dead."

The Kal turned his copper hood to face Daj'ven directly. "You have been deceived, Daj'ven, but not by Sal'zar. He acted upon my orders, as did those who went with him. Even Jal'den was aware of my plot, though I forced him to remain with the Soulless' army. I feared our overlords would grow suspicious if he disappeared along with the rogues."

Daj'ven looked down. When he spoke, his voice was hollow. "If you'd only informed me—or any of the others—we would have gladly assisted, sir. This is…" He shook his head helplessly. "This was not the news I'd expected to hear when I was summoned."

The Matriarch strode toward him and placed one hand on his shoulder. "The ruse was necessary. Our Kal gambled not only with my life, but with the lives of all our people. The fewer who remained aware, the safer we were from the Soulless' wrath."

Daj'ven nodded but did not look up. "I believe I understand."

"Daj'ven," the Matriarch stated firmly, "you cannot continue to harbor ill-will toward Sal'zar and the others. Our people were in a difficult situation, and the Kal did what he believed necessary to remedy it. Even your former commander, my grandson…" Her voice broke, and she took a moment to compose herself. "Aran'daj was part of the Kal's plan, may Aeon bless his soul."

She dropped her hand and made her way back to the Kal's side, her head hung in grief. Daj'ven turned to Sal'zar then.

"I cannot fault you for acting on the Kal's orders, though I still fail to understand what business you had with the enemy *in their tower*." Daj'ven's final words were like acid.

Sal'zar shuffled uneasily, uncertain what to say. To his relief, Jal'den spoke, sparing him from an awkward response.

"Sal'zar is blessed with the Ability, Daj'ven. When the Soulless learned of his gift, they forced him into the fucking tower," Jal'den snarled. "You do not understand the suffering he endured while there. The Soulless—and the other humans—were not kind."

Daj'ven was silent for a time, his hood shifting between Sal'zar and Jal'den as he contemplated his next words. "Ability? As in magic?"

Sal'zar shrugged uncomfortably. "Yes."

To his astonishment, Daj'ven laughed. "I believed you spent your time in the healers' tents to avoid run-ins with us. But you were there to help."

A small smile crossed his lips, though the others could not see it. "Yes," he said again. "The Soulless wanted us to learn terrible magics, but I… I could not stomach it. I focused my training on healing and defense instead."

Jal'den chuckled. "Ever the alchemist," he whispered, "focused on the betterment of our people despite what you faced."

"Given Sal'zar's position in the tower," the Kal said, "I was obligated to bring him into my schemes. He provided invaluable information to me—and Aran'daj. With it, I believed my plan would succeed. It has, though our people suffered great losses during the fight. It pains me that Murkor killed Murkor, but I could see no means of avoiding it without greater repercussions."

"It seems we have reached an accord," Ukase stated. "Daj'ven, you will inform your faction of the proceedings today. Leave nothing out. The Murkor people must understand the forces at work in order to properly reunite." He turned to Sal'zar. "And you will spread word amongst those deemed rogues. They will be welcomed by the others."

"Thank you." Sal'zar made a half-bow, and Daj'ven did the same.

"This brings us to the other matter." Ukase peered at Jal'den. "You were captured as commander of the Soulless' army, Jal'den, and have remained prisoner to the general since the fighting ended."

Jal'den bowed his head. "Yes, sir."

"The Kal admitted you remained with the Soulless upon his orders," Ukase continued.

"I did."

Sal'zar sensed Jal'den's discomfort and uncertainty. While neither knew what Ukase's judgment might be, Sal'zar hoped it would prove favorable. He recalled his partner's rage when he was ordered to remain behind and the pain they'd both endured with yet another forced separation. Since their *ujar'havel* ceremony, Sal'zar could count the number of weeks they'd been allowed to spend together on one hand.

Ukase shifted his gaze to Vardak. "He has proven an amicable prisoner, has he not?"

Vardak hesitated and glanced at Jal'den. "I met him on the battlefield in the hope I could take him alive, though it took some convincing before he agreed to my terms. Sal'zar approached me not long after our forces converged. He asked that I do all in my power to ensure Jal'den not only survived the battle, but would be treated well. I've upheld my end of the bargain."

Jal'den peered at Sal'zar. "I haven't properly thanked you for that."

Sal'zar tilted his head and smiled beneath his hood. "There will be time later."

"Indeed," Ukase agreed. "It is my belief the commander should be freed."

Vardak bowed and began to unravel the knots used to secure Jal'den's wrists. Sal'zar noted with some amusement the bindings had been loose, their presence a mere formality. Jal'den could have slipped them off if he'd wished.

"Thank you for overseeing this affair," the Kal said to Ukase. "It seemed appropriate, given our circumstance."

Ukase nodded once, then faced Daj'ven and Sal'zar. "You both have important tasks to carry out. I bid you a good evening." He vanished, leaving the five Murkor alone with Vardak.

Daj'ven walked to the exit with the Matriarch and Kal, but paused on the threshold to glance at Sal'zar a final time. "I will speak to the others tonight."

"As will I," Sal'zar promised.

Vardak clapped Jal'den on the shoulder as he began to make his way toward the exit. "I suspect the two of you would like a moment alone."

Sal'zar stared at his boots as Vardak departed, uncertain what to say now that he and Jal'den were alone for the first time since he'd left with the rogues. A thousand different words swirled through his mind, but nothing was sufficient to properly express his emotions. He'd missed Jal'den during their long separations, feared for his safety, prayed for their reunion. Now that their time together had finally arrived, speech failed him.

"I always believed you'd succeed," Jal'den said into the silence. "And you have. You've done more for our people than that little shit Daj'ven realizes."

Sal'zar looked up then. He smiled as he took in Jal'den's face; his hood was pulled down to fall around his broad shoulders. Jal'den smiled in the knowing way he often did, a glint of mischief in his pale blue eyes. A thin scar marred his scalp above his right ear, a new addition since their last private meeting. Sal'zar brushed his fingertips along the ridge of raised flesh.

"You were hurt."

Jal'den chuckled. "That was nothing, *ama*. Vardak did worse—as you know."

"Jal'den, I—"

"You don't have to say anything, Sal'zar. The war is over. I'm freed, you've been cleared of suspicion… It seems to me that we've finally been granted what we've always wanted." Jal'den's smile broadened. "Time together."

Sal'zar shook free of his green hood. "It should have happened years ago."

"Yes, but now our future is open. There is nothing left to keep us apart."

Sal'zar returned his smile. "Not even the gods, my *ama na jalan.*"

CHAPTER FORTY-EIGHT

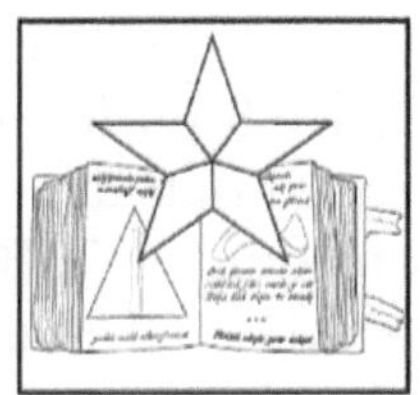

A NEW POST

"There you are."

Tavesin looked up from the book he was studying to find Badolo standing on the other side of the table. The younger boy flashed a grin.

"Rostin said you'd be in your study, but I knew I'd find you here. Some habits don't change."

Tavesin shrugged. "It would take too long to carry so many books upstairs."

He didn't mention that he was still unused to having a private study, as befitted a wizard, nor that he preferred the serene atmosphere of the Shining Tower's library. It was a familiar space, comforting, unchanged by the ravages of the Nameless god's recent war. It brought a sense of peace to his wounded soul to sit amongst the tomes and immerse himself in their secrets.

They'd returned to Dar Daelad nearly a month prior, and despite his misgivings, Tavesin decided to remain part of the Council of Auras. Ravin would hear of no other path for him, but promised to remain in contact. Ravin kept his word, and Tavesin settled into a routine that felt deceptively *normal*. In fact, it was one of Ravin's theories that presently had him scouring ancient books within the library.

"It's fortunate you're here, then," Badolo replied with a grin. "You're late for your ceremony."

Tavesin blanched and scrambled to his feet, while Badolo chuckled. He'd lost track of time. Again.

Together, the pair hurried from the library and made their way to the nearest curved stair. His ceremony was to be held in the tower's garden. Since spring had begun to warm the earth, the outdoor setting would be pleasant—so long as he was not reprimanded too harshly by Mari El'Vero or Aziarah for his delay. They bounded down the stairs and across the tower's expansive foyer toward the exit.

By the time Tavesin stepped outside, he was winded. He paused for a moment to catch his breath, while Badolo pointed toward the grove where he'd first met Vardak. That day seemed years ago, rather than mere months. He wondered what the warrior was doing with his time, now that there were no wars left to fight.

"They're in the grove, Taven," Badolo panted. "Mari thought it would give us more privacy, and the Drakkon didn't want to enter the tower. Aziarah is still bitter."

Tavesin nodded in understanding. "I can't blame her. Let's go."

They walked toward the grove of trees at a slower pace. By the time Tavesin had pushed through the last of the branches to enter the clearing at the grove's heart, he was no longer short of breath. Mari El'Vero stood on one side, garbed in her ceremonial blue Sect Master's cloak. Across from her were a trio of Drakkon. Tavesin grinned as he spied Trozyen, who smiled and nodded in greeting. Between Mari and Aziarah was Virano Rinsahk, the recently-elected Radiant, clad in gray to mark his former Sect. He, too, wore his ceremonial cloak; it shimmered in a variety of colors as he moved.

Several others were seated nearby, and Badolo moved to join them. Tavesin's former mentor, Hasnin, was present, as were several of the Whites who had shaped much of his training. Rostin sat alongside Hasnin, and beyond him…

He gasped. "Arra?"

She smiled shyly, then dropped her gaze as color blossomed across her cheeks. The bruises she'd suffered at Garin's hands were gone, and it appeared the healers had repaired much of the damage to her legs and hands. She remained too thin, but was no longer skeletal as she'd been when he and Sal'zar rescued her. Tavesin was relieved to see she was physically recovering from her ordeal.

She'd refused to speak with him numerous times before their return to the tower, and he'd given up on the hope of rekindling the friendship they'd once shared. Her presence here was unexpected and left him reeling. Had she forgiven him for his role in her capture?

Would she be willing to speak with him after the ceremony's conclusion?

"Tavesin, are you ready to begin?" Mari's voice was soft, yet it carried easily across the clearing.

He forced himself to look away from Arra and clasped his hands behind his back to prevent himself from fidgeting. The ceremony was merely a formality, yet he was edgy, in part due to his late arrival. Virano's expression was stern and Aziarah's unreadable, which set his nerves aflutter. He drew a breath and prayed he would not make a fool of himself in front of everyone.

"I'm ready."

Mari smiled warmly and gestured for him to step forward. Since he'd joined the ranks of the Blue wizards, Tavesin had learned she was a kind soul. Her demeanor eased his anxiety, where the others' did not.

Once he was in position, Virano stepped forward. "This is a day that has been long in coming. The Shining Tower and the Drakkon mages have always shared a friendly alliance, but our friendship was never made formal. Since the onset of the Nameless god's final war, the Drakkon have proven staunch allies to the wizards of this council. It is only proper that our alliance be formally recognized."

Aziarah stepped forward. "My people have long kept to themselves, but the events of the past year have shown us that perhaps our long-held beliefs regarding humans and their magic were misguided. There are more of your kind who could benefit from training in Aethereal magic with the Drakkon, and we will be pleased to accept them as students when they are discovered." She paused to scrutinize Virano. "I will admit, I was at first hesitant to accept your offer, Radiant. Your predecessor hid many things from us—and from your council. A friendly alliance can harbor no secrets between its parties."

"I am in wholehearted agreement," Virano replied. "It is for that reason we are gathered today—to cement our alliance into the foreseeable future." He turned toward Tavesin. "Our youngest Blue, Tavesin Drondes, has been selected to act as liaison between the Council of Auras and the Drakkon."

Tavesin knelt before Aziarah as he'd been instructed to do on the previous afternoon. She chuckled in amusement.

"Rise, Tavesin. You have demonstrated great courage during the past months, and we are not strangers," she said. "In fact, I consider you an equal."

He stumbled to his feet, humbled and overwhelmed by her words. "I… Thank you, Aziarah. I've only acted as I believed was right."

A fond smile touched her scaly lips. "The Drakkon are honored that you have accepted this post, Tavesin." She beckoned to the other Drakkon, and Trozyen stepped forward. To Virano, she said, "On behalf of the Drakkon mages, Trozyen will act as liaison and counterpart to Tavesin."

Trozyen grinned briefly at Tavesin before Virano spoke again.

"The Council of Auras is grateful to be acknowledged by the Drakkon as allies. I shall make a formal announcement to the entire council when we next meet, one week from now." Virano looked between the two liaisons and nodded, satisfied with the arrangement. "I suspect the pair of you have much to discuss. You are dismissed."

There was a shuffle as the audience began to rise and disperse. Tavesin turned from Trozyen as he sought Arra. She remained seated, her eyes locked on him.

"Go to her, Taven," Trozyen said lightly. "Our business can wait."

"Thank you."

He remained fixed in place for a time, uncertain what he ought to say when he approached her. She was clearly waiting to speak with him, which was a sign in his favor, but the words would not coalesce. What did one say to a friend who had suffered greatly, as Arra had? When nothing came to him, he drew an uneasy breath and trudged toward her, apprehensive and unsure. He sat down in the empty chair at her side.

They gazed at one another in silence for several moments before Arra released a sigh. She looked down at her hands where they were folded in her lap and chewed her lower lip pensively.

"I want you to know I'm not angry with you," she said. "I don't blame you for what happened. If you'd been there that night, he would have taken you instead."

He swallowed the lump that was forming in his throat. "I did all I could. I wanted to free you sooner, but everyone told me it wasn't safe. That I'd… That he was using you…"

"Yes," she replied in a firmer tone. "He believed you would follow me. He hoped to lure you to the tower to kill you. It's why I told you it wasn't safe for me to enter the Aethereum, Taven. I was prepared to endure his torture, but I could not risk seeing you captured. Or worse."

"If you truly feel this way, why wouldn't you speak with me before now?" he asked in a strangled tone. The question had plagued him for weeks and demanded resolution.

She sniffled and wiped at her eyes. "I was *ashamed*, Taven. I didn't want you to see me broken and weakened as I was. I couldn't even face myself in the mirror—by the gods, how could I face *you*?"

He blinked, stunned at her revelation. "I thought you hated me," he whispered.

A sob escaped her throat. "Gods, no. You risked everything for me. You're a better friend than I could have imagined."

"I blamed myself for your capture." Tears threatened to spill from his eyes, and he rapidly blinked them away. "They told me it wasn't my fault, but...Garin came for me that night, Arra. He found you instead. How could I not believe myself responsible?"

He was startled when Arra grasped his hand and squeezed it firmly. "Listen to me, Taven. None of what happened with Garin was your fault. *None of it*." She paused to wipe at her eyes again, then said, "We cannot change the past, but we can make the future better. You're a wizard, and one day, I will be as well. I've decided to test for the Greens when the time comes."

Tavesin was unable to stop the hopeful smile that spread across his face. "You're going to stay in the tower?"

"I can't return home," she said in a somber tone. "The Soulless destroyed Bannon's Ford. Your friend with the golden eyes told me it was likely Dranamir's doing. As bad as Garin was, she was much worse." Arra shuddered.

"I'm sorry. I didn't know, and Ravin didn't tell me he'd spoken with you."

She smiled sadly. "He was concerned for you. When I refused to see you, it hurt you deeply, he said. For that, I'm sorry, but I couldn't—"

"I understand now," he interrupted. "I hope... I hope this means we're still friends."

She nodded eagerly as a light blush crept up her cheeks. "You are the greatest friend anyone could ask for, Taven. I promise we'll see each other as often as we can from this moment forward."

He returned her smile, content for the first time in many months. The war was over, he had a new post within the council to occupy his time, and Arra was once more counted amongst his friends. In that moment, there was nothing more he could ask for.

CHAPTER FORTY-NINE

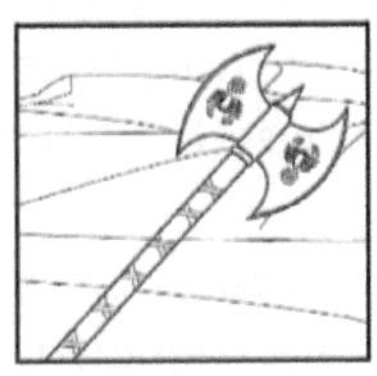

THE CONCLAVE

"*This* is a day I never believed I'd see," Patak stated with a smirk. "My brother, invited to a conclave to determine the next Warleader. And to think you were always the one getting underfoot as a child."

"Patak," Travin growled from Vardak's other side, "if I recall, *you* caused far more trouble for the perimeter guards than either of us combined."

"It's true," Zaria said from behind.

Vardak turned to face their mother with a smile. They embraced, and she held him at arm's length, her dark eyes brimming with pride. "Your father, Aeon rest his soul, would be elated by this event, Vardak. There was a time our people believed he would become Warleader, but when he was killed, that hope was dashed."

"It isn't a certainty," Vardak replied for what seemed the thousandth time since his return to the Stronghold. "There are three others they have been evaluating, and despite my training, my age is not in my favor."

Zaria smiled knowingly. "Ah, but Makta *is*."

Patak snorted and moved side-to-side restlessly. "Has she asked you yet, Vardak?"

He peered at his brother in confusion. "Asked me what?"

Patak rolled his eyes dramatically, opened his mouth for another retort, but was silenced as Emra swatted at his arm. "It's none of your business, Patak," she hissed.

Vardak shook his head. He believed he knew what Patak insinuated, but he wasn't prepared to acknowledge it. Matters between himself and Makta had grown complicated since the end of the war. They'd spent more time together than he'd planned on, and along the way, he'd begun to take note of more than her smithing skills.

"Ignore him," Travin advised. "It's usually the best course of action."

Vardak chuckled and took a moment to look at his family gathered around him. Patak and Emra had decided to remain in the Stronghold once Makta asserted her welcome. Emra claimed she wasn't prepared to return to Balotica and face the king after she'd deviated from his orders, though Vardak suspected it was more to do with Patak's wishes than her own.

His mother beamed at him, overjoyed at the occasion. Behind her stood Maryn, who was only now preparing to leave for his homeland in the jungles. He'd been insistent; he wished to stay in the northern lands to see the outcome of today's ceremony. Vardak was grateful for his presence. Maryn had become his greatest friend and he was loath to see him go, but he understood Maryn's reasons. He missed his people, and though he often denied it, he missed the climate of the jungles.

Travin and Dakna stood to his left, their firstborn clinging to his father's back. Davin was only three weeks old, but strong enough to remain firmly in place as Travin moved about. When Vardak's eyes met his nephew's, the boy blushed and turned his face aside in a bashful display. Dakna chuckled and reached over to ruffle her son's dark hair. Davin already sported a strong resemblance to Travin.

They were gathered in Zaria's sitting room as they awaited the remainder of the guests to arrive. Word would not come from the conclave for several more hours, but in his mother's typical fashion, she'd insisted they arrive early. She'd prepared a feast fit for an army, though she was expecting perhaps a dozen people in her home.

As though reading his thoughts, Zaria said, "I hope the others arrive soon. I'm certain the young wizards are busy, but I don't like the thought of all this food growing cold." She motioned at Patak to move. "You, of all my sons, have never hesitated to eat. Find yourself a plate."

Patak grinned. "You don't have to tell me twice." Emra trailed after him as he made his way to the table, laden with various dishes.

"And, you," she rounded on Travin, "have a young one to feed. Go on."

"Taven and the others can't simply arrive at our doorstep, mother," Vardak reminded her. "They'll have some distance to travel first."

"And I won't have the food grow cold while we wait. Join your brothers. Eat. You as well, Maryn."

He suppressed a sigh and made his way toward the table alongside Maryn. There was no use arguing with her, no matter that his stomach recoiled at the thought of a meal so near to the conclusion of the conclave and the decision of the elders. She would insist that he eat, and if he didn't consume enough, she'd hound him until she was satisfied. Though her sons were grown, some aspects of their relationship had never changed. Ensuring they had enough to eat was one of them.

"For the first time in recorded history, I owe *Patak* two silvers," Maryn muttered. "He told me your mother would insist we begin without the others."

Vardak chuckled. "He won't let you forget it, either."

"No, I suppose he won't. It's just as well—I have parting gifts for both of you. Funded in part by your brother's vast losing streak," Maryn added with a grin.

"A streak I seem to have broken," Patak replied from across the table.

"One moment of Karmada's favor means little," Maryn shot back.

Patak chuckled. "I'll miss this come tomorrow."

Maryn looked down and busied himself with filling his plate. "As will I. The decision to return home wasn't easy, but it's the right thing to do." He cast a longing glance at Davin. "I'm not growing any younger. Perhaps it's time I settled down."

An awkward silence settled over the group. Vardak studied each of them in turn, grateful for the roles they'd each played in his life. Blademon's training may have factored into his present situation, but he believed he'd be nowhere without his family and friends.

A loud rap on the door drew his attention, but Zaria was halfway there before he turned around. She threw the door wide and smiled in welcome. In the corridor beyond, Vardak could make out Owen's tall form, flanked on one side by the two Airess and on the other by Tavesin, Rostin, and Badolo. The trio of young wizards stared at their surroundings with wide eyes; it was the first time they'd visited the Stronghold.

Rostin flashed a grin as his gaze met Vardak's. Vardak smiled; if circumstances had been different when the two were introduced, he suspected he would have grown closer to the boy during his weapons training. As it was, he was pleased Rostin had accepted the invitation. That he'd insisted Badolo accompany him was expected.

Zaria ushered the group into the room with the firm declaration that they should make themselves at home and eat their fill. The trio of wizards greeted Vardak with excited grins and nervous glances before diving into the feast. Coreyaless and Danness came next, while Owen slithered toward the table after signaling he wished to speak with Vardak alone. Vardak suspected he knew what the former knight wished to discuss; it was as though everyone in the room was certain of the conclave's decision regarding the next Warleader with the exception of himself.

"It was good of you to invite us," Danness said. "Vidune Forest is a lonelier place than it was in my time."

"The offer Makta made you still stands," Vardak replied.

Danness chuckled and shook his head, while Coreyaless said, "No, Vardak. Your people have enough new mouths to feed with the Serpentus here. Besides, Vidune Forest is home." She shot a sidelong glance at Danness, who nodded his encouragement. "It won't be terribly lonely for either of us much longer. There is a child in our future."

"Congratulations." Vardak grinned. "If mother learns of this, she'll see to it you eat enough for three."

"It won't be long before she learns," Danness replied. "Once we tell your brother and Maryn, it won't remain a secret." He drew an arm around Coreyaless, and the pair turned away.

Vardak settled himself near one wall and watched the others as they conversed. Patak and Maryn were laughing, while Emra sat between them, a long-suffering look plastered on her face. The three young wizards clustered around one end of the table—the end laden with sweets, Vardak noted with amusement. Travin and Dakna were settled across the room from him, as was his mother; each took a turn feeding young Davin. His large dark eyes scanned the room and the assortment of people within.

Owen sidled up to Vardak once he'd filled a plate. "Vardak, I—"

Vardak held up one hand. "I know what you wish to talk about, but it's premature. The conclave is evaluating four of us."

Owen chuckled dryly. "And of the four, you've already done much for…my people." He looked away, uncomfortable with the admission. "Not all of us are handling the transition as well as we'd hoped. I spent half the night talking Carrelin out of taking her own life."

"I'm sorry." Vardak looked down at his half-empty plate. "*If* I'm elected, I'll do everything I can to ensure the Serpentus thrive. If I'm not, I will continue to support you by any means possible. Your people deserve the chance to make something of themselves."

"Do we?" Owen mused. "Many of us were civilians, captured by the Murkor. I understand their former commander asked to take us prisoners in order to spare our lives. The Soulless wanted us dead, but he had a good heart. It's a shame his attempt to save us ended with us trapped in these gods-damned bodies." He sighed heavily. "I suppose your ancestors felt the same."

"By all accounts, they did." Vardak set the plate aside to focus on Owen. "What was done is nothing short of abhorrent, but you can't give up."

"He's right," Zaria interjected from across the room. "The Scorpion Men struggled for many years in the wake of our own unwanted transformation, yet we persevered. The world must be reminded of the wrongs that were committed against us—and you. If the Serpentus give in to despair and falter, there will be nothing but a written record that will one day be chalked up to little more than legend. Your people deserve better, Owen Greenwaters, if for nothing more than to remind this world that even though Karmada dealt you a sour hand, you overcame it. The Nameless god may be no more, but your people and ours remain as a testament to *why* he needed to die. Without that reminder, people will forget the events of this war in a few generations, and where would we be then?"

Vardak smiled in thanks to his mother. She'd phrased his thoughts far more eloquently than he could have done.

Beside him, Owen nodded, chastised. "Your point is valid. Perhaps I've been thinking of this matter selfishly, but it's difficult to plan for the future when we're not even certain what that may look like."

"No one can foresee the future," Zaria replied, "except perhaps Minora. Make the most of your life, Owen. Tell the others to do the same. Our world is poorer without the Serpentus in it."

It was mid-afternoon when the summons arrived. Travin had been selected to accompany Vardak to the conclave as his witness, while the others would remain behind in his mother's home. The unfamiliar flutter of nerves rippled through him as they followed the messenger, a young woman with reddish hair that reminded Vardak of Janna's.

Absently, he sought the folded note he kept within his shirt pocket, her final words to him. She would have been present today as well, had she not taken it upon herself to acquire the Moon's Eye. A part of him continued to feel responsible for her death, though her decision had been beyond his control.

"Patak's jesting aside, you're far more serious than you ought to be, Vardak." Travin nudged him with an elbow.

He shrugged. "My mind was on other matters. Not this."

Travin raised an eyebrow. "What could possibly be more important than the outcome of the conclave?"

"I was thinking of a friend. One I've lost."

Travin was aware of his story. Zaria had filled him in on Vardak's "adventures," as she referred to them, after Travin's return to the Stronghold. It was just as well; Vardak wasn't in the mood to elaborate further.

Sensing his melancholy, Travin nodded. "I'm certain they would have been pleased to see you today, Vardak—no matter the conclave's outcome."

They walked in silence behind the messenger as she led them through several quiet, residential corridors. They passed few others until they entered the central passage, a broad hall that led between the Stronghold's entrance to the marketplace, training grounds, and the Warleader's spacious quarters. The conclave was meeting there. The interior did not look the same as it had when Sevic occupied it; he and

Makta had spent several days after their return clearing her uncle's possessions from within.

Those they passed nodded to Vardak in greeting. Some slowed to wish him luck. He remained steadfast in his conviction the post of Warleader ought to fall to someone else—someone older, without the burden of an unspoken commitment to both Blademon and Flariel to interrupt their duties. He would keep his vow to Owen, no matter what transpired in the conclave. The Serpentus leader deserved all the support Vardak could muster.

The red-haired messenger paused before the Warleader's door and offered the brothers a tentative smile. "The elders are within. Gods be with you, Vardak."

He took her words as his cue to enter with Travin in his wake. Where Sevic's war table had once stood, a dozen of the eldest Scorpion Men were seated; four men and eight women. The other hopefuls had arrived previously with their witnesses and were arrayed in a half-circle facing the elders. Vardak and Travin took their place at one end of the arc, while Vardak took a moment to study the others. Each was old enough to be their father, and the witnesses were the husband or wife of the candidate. Vardak was not only the youngest, but the only one who was unmarried. It was another mark against him.

One of the female elders rose to her full height. "After much deliberation, we have come to a decision." She gestured to one of the men, whose weathered face was creased and lined to a greater extent than any of the others.

"Essen," he said, "while your qualifications are impressive, we have chosen another."

Essen saluted the elders before he and his witness exited.

"Farric," the elder continued once Essen had departed, "your qualifications were also quite impressive. It was a difficult decision to eliminate you as a candidate."

Farric smiled knowingly as he made his salute. "I understand."

Vardak shifted uncomfortably as the second hopeful departed. He'd assumed he would be the first sent away.

The elder turned to face him. "Vardak, your claim was unusual. Given your unique training and history with the Fireblade's army, your name was selected as a candidate for this position, despite your age.

Makta championed your abilities to great lengths, but I'm afraid your time must wait."

Relief washed over him; he would not be named Warleader. He saluted and turned to leave.

"A moment, Vardak," one of the women commanded. "There is a role I believe you are uniquely qualified to serve, but the decision must rest with our new Warleader. Remain here a moment while we discuss the nature of this post."

Vardak nodded and glanced at Travin uncertainly. His brother shrugged in response.

The male elder turned to face the final candidate, a stern woman Vardak recognized as one of the watch commanders, Ilen. Her dark hair was pulled back into a thick braid. Silver dusted her temples, though few wrinkles creased her brow. Her brown eyes were sharp.

"Ilen, it is with great honor that we name you Warleader of the Scorpion Men. In the weeks to come, you must name your interim heir for succession." He paused, then turned to Vardak once more. "With the addition of the Serpentus to our halls, we elders believe it necessary to name an advocate. One of our people, who will work closely with theirs and see to it their needs are met. It is no secret your words were instrumental in their coming here, Vardak, and you continue to speak with their leader frequently."

Vardak nodded. "That's true."

"With Ilen's blessing, we would like to name you to this post."

Ilen turned to face him, a knowing look in her eyes. "You've demonstrated great leadership in the past months, Vardak. That is not a quality Blademon instilled within you, but one you learned on your own. I can think of no one better for the position." Her lips parted in a mischievous grin. "I would also ask that you lend your abilities to the teaching of new recruits. I've heard you're rather adept at it—even when your pupil isn't one of our own."

He managed a chuckle as he thought of Rostin. "That is also true."

"Then it's settled," she replied. "You will act as instructor in the training halls for our young—and the Serpentus who wish to learn the art of the blade, as well. You will also act as my point of contact when dealing with the Serpentus." She paused to size him up. "I believe we'll work well together, Vardak. You are dismissed."

He saluted once more and made his way outside with Travin. He grinned at his brother, unable to hide his relief any longer.

"It is not the outcome mother was expecting, but it was good, nonetheless," Travin said. "Owen will be pleased."

"Yes. I am, as well."

Travin chuckled. "I see that. I suppose your new role will keep you busy enough, but it will also allow you some freedoms the post of Warleader would not have."

As they turned into the residential corridors, the acrid scent of smoke stung his nostrils. A few steps away, Flariel stood awaiting him, her arms crossed. Vardak's previous good humor evaporated at the sight of the fire goddess.

"I'll tell the others," Travin promised in a low tone before he skittered away from what was likely to become a heated conversation.

Vardak nodded a silent thanks without taking his eyes from Flariel's. "Why have you come?"

The flames that consumed her torso flickered in response. "I come and go as I please, Vardak, and we have unfinished business."

He scowled, but swallowed the litany of curses that swirled through his mind. If he'd learned anything in his dealings with the gods, it was that argument was pointless.

"We are aware of your new post," Flariel continued. "My sister wishes to speak with you on the matter. Come."

She offered her hand, and he eyed it warily. "Will this take long, Flariel? I'd like to say my goodbyes to Maryn before he leaves."

Flariel's lips curved into a faint smile. "You will be gone but a few moments. This is a mere formality."

She gripped his wrist before he could respond, her hand uncomfortably warm. Immediately, he was overcome by a sensation of falling, and in an eye-blink he found himself on the white sands some distance outside of the Stronghold. The noonday sun burned in a cloudless sky above, while heat shimmer rose from the nearby dunes.

Flariel released his wrist with a smirk. "He's here, sister."

A rustle greeted her words, and moments later, another being as tall as Flariel appeared from behind a large dune. Her long, dark hair was bound in a multitude of braids, and her silvery eyes stared at him in silent challenge. Vardak's heart sank; he would have recognized

Karmada's likeness anywhere, but her presence here, on this day, could only mean further complications for himself.

As the rest of her body emerged from behind the sands, Vardak's eyes widened. Below the form-fitting, crimson tunic she wore, her body was serpentine, its gray and emerald scales glittering in the sun. She was Serpentus.

"I have elected to become the patron of the Serpentus people," Karmada stated with an amused grin. "I see Flariel deigned not to tell you of my transformation prior to bringing you here."

He shook his head. He knew he ought to say something in reply, but words failed him. He hadn't been expecting *this* strange turn of events.

"I have yet to reveal myself to the Serpentus leader," Karmada continued. "Given your new role, it was my hope you would arrange a meeting. Misfortune has ultimately led them to you, and luck has placed you in a position to assist them. They have suffered greatly at our dead brother's hands, Vardak. I do not wish to add to their burden, and I believe if the news comes through you first, it will be easier for them to bear."

His previous unease began to melt away. If Karmada sought a meeting with Owen, he would oblige. "Of course."

Karmada smiled. "Flariel believed you would refuse, but it seems you reserve your animosity for her alone."

Vardak clenched his jaw in momentary frustration while the two goddesses shared a laugh.

"I have come to accept what occurred in the Sky Palace," Flariel said after a time. "After the recent events with Solsticia's son, I don't believe it necessary to insist you owe me a debt any longer. Janna chose her fate—*willingly*. Minora at least granted her that."

Though Vardak didn't fully understand her reference to the time goddess, he chose to ignore the statement and focus on her previous words. "Am I free to pursue my life without further interference, Flariel?"

Flariel nodded. "You will not hear from me again, Vardak, unless your skills are required a second time." She offered him a thin smile. "I will return you to the Stronghold and your celebration."

"If the Serpentus are amenable to a meeting, Blademon has offered his temple for the occasion," Karmada said as Flariel grasped his wrist once more.

"I will speak with Owen," he promised.

Another sensation of falling left him outside the door to his mother's abode. Flariel was gone, but he no longer feared she would return without warning. He may not have been named Warleader, but his future held promise. And with Karmada's guidance, he would ensure the Serpentus thrived.

CHAPTER FIFTY

A VISIT TO THE KAL

His once peaceful laboratory was now a source of chronic discomfort, but one Sal'zar was beginning to tolerate. During the first weeks of their return to the caverns, he'd been able to maintain his previously acute focus for little more than an hour before his head began to pound from the strain. Now, nearly two months later, he'd conditioned himself to endure up to six hours of work before the headache became too much to bear.

He understood the source of his condition, and when he'd explained it to the alchemists' caste leader, she'd been understanding. He was an anomaly amongst his people—a Murkor graced with the Ability to wield magic. Their home caverns were shielded as a protective measure against the Soulless who were no more, but it was this same protection that severed him from his power. Before he'd trained to use magic, the shield never affected him. Now, there were nights he wished he could remove the curse of his Ability in order to be more effective in his alchemy.

He'd been at work for almost five hours this night, but could endure no longer. The remainder of his healing salves would have to wait for later. With a resigned sigh, he carefully arranged the glass flasks on his workbench in order to pick up where he'd ended more easily.

He rubbed his throbbing temples as he made his way toward the exit and into the empty tunnel beyond. Jal'den had the night free from watch duty, which meant he'd likely be at the sparring ring with the soldier's caste hopefuls. Sal'zar didn't enjoy visits to the sparring ring—they brought with them painful memories from his childhood—but perhaps he could speak with Jal'den. The other soldiers wouldn't seek to spar with him, in any case; he had no reason to fear a recurrence from his younger years.

The ache in his head diminished slightly as he traversed the familiar tunnels and caverns that would lead him to the sparring ring. His path took him through the bustling marketplace, and he decided on a whim to stop by his father's stall. Sal'daran was a tailor; his skills were always in demand, but became even more so as the nights grew shorter and the summer solstice neared. Caste choosing day was an event that would see him busy for weeks on end, but on this night in early spring, his tidy shop was not overwhelmed with customers.

Sal'zar smiled beneath his hood and waited while his father finished speaking with his current patron. As the blue-garbed woman departed, Sal'daran beckoned Sal'zar forward.

"You are early tonight, Sal'zar. Do you suffer another headache?"

Sal'zar nodded. "They're taking longer to form than they did, but when they take hold, the pain is terrible." He was unable to mask the misery in his tone.

"Perhaps with your alchemy, you will find a cure." Sal'daran patted his shoulder affectionately. "I'm pleased you've stopped by, *ma zan.* I've made something for you—and Jal'den, of course."

Sal'daran turned to rummage through a trunk where he typically stored his fabrics. Sal'zar watched with curiosity as Sal'daran withdrew a folded mass of cloth in shades of green and black.

"Father, what is this?"

Sal'daran chuckled and placed the mound in Sal'zar's arms. "Now that you're both home for good, it's time you mark your dwelling as your own. It's a curtain, Sal'zar. Think of it as a belated gift for your *ujar'havel.*" He paused and seemed to study Sal'zar for a time while his son gazed down at the curtain with a smile. "In truth, I made it some time ago, but it didn't seem right to give it to you with Jal'den away. With the war, I set it aside and forgot about it, but I came across it earlier when Jal'ona was here."

"Thank you, father. This is wonderful. How is Jal'ona?" Sal'zar asked. He was fond of Jal'den's mother and often thought of her as his own.

"Composing music, as always." Sal'daran laughed. "She is well, though she still has not convinced Jal'manan to speak with his son. Sadly, I don't believe that rift will ever be mended."

Sal'zar released a sigh and gazed at the curtain, his father's gift an indication of his support. He was fortunate Sal'daran was accepting of his choice of partners and embraced it. The same could not be said for Jal'den's father. Jal'manan had refused to speak to Jal'den since the night they'd made their intentions known, nearly six years prior.

"We will hang this in our entry, father," Sal'zar promised. "I was on my way to see him, if he has the time tonight. Perhaps we will go aboveground. It seems to alleviate the headaches."

Sal'daran nodded. "Yes, go to the surface if it helps you, *ma zan*. It pains me to watch you suffer."

"Thank you, father," he said again. He turned away, intent on finding Jal'den. He was certain his partner would be thrilled with the gift and the unspoken declaration of support it implied.

By the time he found his way to the sparring ring, his headache had dulled from a roar to a low rumble. He stopped at the ring's perimeter, his eyes on Jal'den's black-clad form. He was practicing stances with one of the gray-clad children, a hopeful to the soldier's caste. The boy wobbled on his feet and struggled to maintain his pose, while Jal'den suggested improvements with an encouraging air.

The boy said something Sal'zar could not hear, and Jal'den laughed. "It simply takes practice," he said. "Given time, you'll rival even me."

"I doubt it," came the response.

It was then that Jal'den looked up and spotted him on the perimeter. "I think that's enough for one night, don't you?" he asked the boy.

The gray-clad youngster scurried away, clearly relieved to be finished. Jal'den chuckled to himself as he strode toward Sal'zar. "He reminds me much of another boy, perhaps twelve years ago," he said quietly once he stood before Sal'zar. He nodded at the bundle in Sal'zar's arms. "What is this?"

"A gift from my father. And no, he was more coordinated than I was, Jal'den."

Jal'den called over his shoulder to the nearest soldier that he was taking his leave for the night. He fell in step beside Sal'zar as they began the return trip to the marketplace. "I don't believe he'll come back, but at least it wasn't a sparring day. He had that in his favor."

"I'd like to go aboveground," Sal'zar stated, desperate to change the subject. His singular visit to the sparring ring years ago was not a memory he wished to recall, though it was the reason behind his initial friendship with Jal'den.

Jal'den tilted his head in a show of concern. "Another headache, *ama*? There must be something we can do."

He shrugged. "I don't know. I'm the first of our people with this…condition."

"Have you spoken to the Kal?"

Sal'zar looked away with a frown. It wasn't a matter he wished to discuss with the Kal, and he doubted the Kal would know of a remedy.

"I will accompany you outside if we speak with the Kal tonight," Jal'den stated. "We need to pay him a visit as it is. Daj'ven returned our book."

Sal'zar's heart stuttered. "Did he…Did he know what it was?"

Jal'den snickered. "You worry too much, *ama.* Yes, but he swore he did not read its contents. I believe him. When he returned it to me, he stated, 'I believe this belongs to you and your lady.' I doubt he would have said the same if he'd opened it, and I didn't correct him."

Sal'zar shook his head in irritation. "I will never be your *lady*, Jal'den."

"I wouldn't change you for the world," Jal'den replied, a grin in his tone. "We'll go to our dwelling, then you can show me this gift from your father. I'll collect the book, and we'll pay a visit to the Kal. *Then* I will escort you outside."

Their visit to the Kal was delayed when Jal'den insisted they hang the new curtain over the entrance to their dwelling immediately. Sal'zar admired his father's artistry; the black bands in the fabric melded seamlessly with the green, creating an undulating pattern across the curtain's width.

They stood in the corridor outside and admired it for some time before Jal'den prodded him into a visit with the Kal. Sal'zar had avoided speaking with him since the afternoon they'd gathered before Ukase in Vardak's command tent, and he wasn't thrilled to be meeting with him now. He remained angry with the Kal's schemes, and weeks later, the wounds remained raw. His headache intensified as they neared the vast central cavern that housed the Matriarch's compound and the Kal's abode.

Red-hooded guards stood sentinel outside the carved, arching doorways. Sal'zar allowed Jal'den to explain the reason for their visit, and they were made to wait upon the broad dais that extended from the front of the compound.

Sal'zar turned away from the guards to scan the cavern. It was largely empty, but he knew in another six weeks it would be filled to bursting with Murkor as the year's choosing ceremony unfolded. Hundreds of delicate yellow crystals were affixed to the walls, providing the area with a soft illumination. As an alchemist, he'd treated countless crystals in his time, infusing them with the means to glow in a variety of pastel tones.

Jal'den nudged him gently as a woman robed and hooded in white appeared in the nearest door. The color marked her as one of the Matriarch's attendants, and by proxy, the Kal's. They followed her into the vast dome beyond the doors without a word. Sal'zar peered up at the crystal situated at the dome's apex, the largest in the vast cavern complex. It shone with a muted white light that caused its numerous spines to shimmer. Jal'den snickered, as Sal'zar had known he would.

He tore his gaze from the crystal and followed the woman into a small side chamber, where she bade them to sit. "The Kal will arrive soon," she promised before she breezed away.

Jal'den withdrew the slim leather-bound book from within a pocket and held it reverently in his blue hands. "The war has taken much from the Kal," he said somberly. "He once told us it was his wish to read this before his death. Do you remember?"

Sal'zar smiled despite himself. "How can I forget? It was during our *ujar'havel.*"

Jal'den wrapped his arm about Sal'zar and drew him close. "It remains my fondest memory, *ama.*"

"Mine, as well." He leaned his head against Jal'den's broad shoulder and closed his eyes. The pain in his temples momentarily subsided, and he breathed a contented sigh.

They enjoyed a comfortable silence for several minutes before the Kal arrived, flanked by a pair of crimson-clad guards. Sal'zar rose to his feet alongside Jal'den, and the pair bowed.

The Kal waved to the guards with a gnarled hand. "Leave us."

Once they were alone, Jal'den presented the book to the Kal. "It's finished."

Kal Aran'jandah ran his fingers over the cover. "I am pleased to receive this. When Sal'zar was taken to the black tower, I feared I never would."

"I completed it while there," Sal'zar replied somberly. "Focusing on our memories allowed me an escape from the Soulless and their followers."

"You are resilient, Sal'zar." He heard a smile in the Kal's tone.

"There is another matter that brought us here," Jal'den cut in. Sal'zar allowed him to explain the headaches that plagued him and his theory behind them.

The Kal was silent for some time. Finally, he said, "It is possible. The Soulless loathed spending time here, but I assumed it was out of disdain for our people. Perhaps it was merely due to their discomfort." His copper hood shifted to look at them each in turn. "I'm aware you have journeyed to the surface often since our return home. Does it ease your pain?"

"Yes," Sal'zar admitted.

"And you can travel as the Drakkon do," the Kal continued. "You have been trained to do so."

Sal'zar glanced at Jal'den uncertainly before making his reply. "Yes."

"Our people are unfamiliar in the ways of magic, but I suspect your condition isn't unusual." The Kal nodded to himself, then went on. "I give you leave to seek a cure, Sal'zar. Perhaps the Drakkon can assist. Perhaps another. You are a talented alchemist, and I know your heart longs to remain home, but this ailment must be addressed. I would not see you suffer."

Sal'zar hung his head. Leaving the caverns was the last thing he wished to do.

"I would not have you go alone," the Kal continued. "Jal'den will accompany you. I will speak to Traj'ani and Dal'janai on your behalf.

The castes can make do without the pair of you for a time. Now, was there anything else you wished to discuss?"

Sal'zar shook his head in disbelief. They were being granted leave from the caverns to seek a cure for his strange malady, a thing nearly unheard of. He had no doubt Traj'ani would be amenable to the Kal's orders; as his caste leader, she was aware of his present condition. Dal'janai, however, would be furious. Jal'den was the commander, Blademon's chosen, her second when it came to caste matters.

"Thank you, sir," Jal'den replied. "We will prepare for departure as soon as Sal'zar is ready."

"Good. Protect one another on your travels, and may the gods be with you." With that, the Kal was gone.

"I can't believe we're leaving so soon," Sal'zar lamented once they were alone.

Jal'den chuckled. "This time, we'll be together, *ama.* Come. I promised we'd go to the surface. Perhaps some time spent gazing at the stars will ease your pain. We can secure provisions tomorrow evening."

Sal'zar smiled beneath his hood as they made their way across the dome and into the central cavern. His headache persisted as they retraced their steps toward the marketplace, then to the exit tunnel beyond. Jal'den spoke to the watchmen on duty as they reached the entrance, as he did each time they made the journey. It was strange to think it would be one of the last such visits they'd make for some time.

It wasn't until they were some distance away from the cavern mouth that Sal'zar felt a sudden burst of energy flow through him as his magic returned. Gone was the constant, muted buzz that plagued him within the invisible shield, and the pain in his head immediately began to lessen. He breathed a sigh of relief, and Jal'den sought his hand, interlacing their fingers.

Sal'zar gazed up at the night sky, untarnished by clouds. The moon was but a sliver as it dipped low toward the Gray Mountains far to the west. Thousands of stars dotted the dark expanse. He'd rarely ventured aboveground before they'd left with the army months ago, but he'd grown fond of watching the stars since that time.

"I look forward to our next adventure, *ama,*" Jal'den said quietly. Rather than look at the sky, his focus was on Sal'zar.

Sal'zar smiled. "As do I, strangely enough."

"We'll find a remedy." Jal'den squeezed his hand. "The Kal did not say it outright, but perhaps we should seek Emra. I suspect she knows more than the Drakkon, and I'm certain she went to the Stronghold after the army disbanded."

"It is a good place to begin," he agreed. "I am glad you will be with me, *ama*."

CHAPTER FIFTY-ONE

A FUTURE OF HIS OWN DESIGN

Ravin examined the exterior of the manor house a final time and nodded in satisfaction. He'd spent the better part of his morning with the smarmy merchant who wished to sell the estate, a man he'd quickly decided he would rather not see again. The manor house was in good condition, the stables and corrals newly built, and the expansive garden behind the house was beautifully laid out and would be well-tended—once Ravin secured a proper gardener.

"It will do," he told the merchant, assuming a false air of nobility. He'd grudgingly dressed the part; he may as well make use of it.

"But, sir, this estate is in prime condition. Surely you can see that."

"It is largely unfurnished," Ravin replied. "The tile work in the kitchen is not to my liking, and the rear door of the stable doesn't latch."

He prayed his excuses would force the man to drop his price. Money wasn't a barrier to his purchase—he'd raided the palace treasury out of spite for the queen upon his return to Delucha—but he would not be taken for a fool, either. He had the means to furnish the manor house easily enough, he didn't care a whit about the tile, and a simple repair would fix the door, but the man was asking too much in the wake of the recent war.

The merchant sighed and tugged at his oily beard. "Very well. Eighteen gold pieces, and the estate is yours."

Ravin narrowed his eyes. "Fourteen, and you fix that damned door."

The man grimaced, then managed a reluctant nod. "We have a deal, sir. Fourteen gold. I have the deed right here." He patted one of his velvet-lined pockets.

Ravin withdrew the required coin while the merchant offered him the deed. He skimmed it silently, noted nothing was amiss, and smiled as he tucked it into a pocket. Adalin would be thrilled. He hoped so, in any case. She wasn't aware of his recent dealings. He planned to surprise her, though she was just as likely to admonish him for the expense. She wasn't aware that he'd pilfered his gold from Her Majesty, either. He could easily have conjured it, but there was no sport in that.

"I'll have my men repair the door immediately," the merchant promised.

"Excellent. I plan to bring the lady here this evening."

"Of course, sir. It will be done before your arrival." The merchant glanced around them uncertainly. "If I may inquire, sir, how did you travel here? I see no horse or carriage."

Ravin flashed a triumphant grin and waved a portal into existence. "Magic."

He blanched. "I see. We will have the door repaired. You have my word."

Ravin chuckled to himself as he entered the Aethereum. Since the war, the mention of magic proved as frightening to most people as references to the Soulless did. Adalin would have scolded him for his antics had she been with him, but the man's reaction had been well worth the effort. He had no intention of harming anyone; he simply wished to have a bit of fun now that his life was truly his own.

He transported himself to the top floor of The Three Roses inn and exited the Aethereum at the end of the hall where Adalin's room was located. He patted his pocket a final time to ensure the puzzle box remained in place and smiled to himself. This evening would prove to be the best of his life—or the worst—depending on her reaction.

As he strode the length of the corridor to her room, a bell began to toll outside. The sound reverberated through the inn's walls. His smile faltered as he pondered the implications; there was a large bell housed within the palace's central tower, to be used to signal the city of important matters regarding the royal family. He immediately considered the young queen's pregnancy and determined she was nearing her due date. Perhaps the bell signified the birth of her heir.

He rapped lightly on Adalin's door. He knew she would hear it despite the clamor from outside, and moments later, she pulled the door open.

"Ravin! You're just in time. The crier is not far," she said in a breathless rush.

He allowed her to pull him inside. He closed the door, then followed her to the open window at the far side of the room.

"Do you believe it's the child?" he asked.

"Shh," she hissed and pointed outside.

He watched as a man clad in gold and ivory livery took up a space in the center of the street below. Townspeople paused in their business to stare in anticipation as the crier prepared to deliver his news. He held up both arms in a plea for silence.

"It is with both joy and sorrow that I bring you news on this otherwise fine spring day," he began. "Our dear queen, Tamarin Serales—"

Ravin snorted indignantly and received a disapproving stare from Adalin in return.

"—has given birth to a son, Morisen. While we are blessed with a future king this day, it is with a heavy heart that I deliver the other portion of my news. The queen did not survive the childbirth. She will be laid in state for a period of ten days as arrangements for her funeral are made. Please keep Lord Jasom in your prayers as he grieves. The late queen's cousin, Lord Daresin Serales, will assume the role of regent until Morisen comes of age."

As the crier fell silent, the crowd below the window erupted. Some shouted questions while others openly wept. Ravin turned away from the scene, his own reaction mixed. He'd witnessed too much death of late, and though the queen had been a murderer, he wasn't certain he wished to see her dead. Merely far away, where she could no longer meddle in his life. For Jasom, his sorrow was genuine. The boy was a victim of the Soulless' schemes, but he'd found love with the queen.

"For the sake of Jasom and the child, this is a tragedy," Adalin whispered, echoing his thoughts.

"Yes. I hope the child will grow up to be a more virtuous ruler than his mother."

Adalin turned away from the window, then groaned. "As nobility, I cannot be seen in public without proper mourning attire. Will you give me a few moments, Ravin? I'll meet you in the corridor once I'm finished—"

"I have a better idea," he interrupted. "You stay here—and perhaps don your riding gear. I'll ask the kitchen downstairs for a portable lunch and return. Then I'll take us away from here."

He'd told the greasy merchant they would return in the evening, but an opportunity had presented itself. He would bring her to the estate, where they'd take their lunch. If she seemed amenable to his purchase, he'd present her with the puzzle box and pray she would not decline his offer.

"I believe it would do us both some good to be away from the city for a time," she replied. "Where will we go?"

He flashed a grin. "It's a surprise, Adalin. I won't spoil it for you."

She raised her eyebrows and gave him a sidelong glance. "A mystery, then. Very well."

Ravin made his way to the inn's common room and placed his request with one of the serving women, who eyed him with a knowing smirk. "You and the lady have plans, I see."

He shrugged in reply, while she laughed and departed for the kitchens. He leaned against the inn's bar, sparsely populated by the locals at this time of day, though he suspected it wouldn't be long before the space began to fill. The queen's passing was an excuse for many to truncate their workday and drown their sorrows—whether real or perceived—in ale. It was yet another reason to take Adalin away from the city; what he wished to do required privacy they would not receive in the bustling common room.

His fingers sought the puzzle box within his pocket. It was a trinket he'd traded one of the Santinians for during the long march between Daesan and the Wasted Land. The puzzle of its exterior was simple due to its small size, but the box itself was exquisitely made. Adalin would have it opened within moments, its contents revealed, as well as his intentions.

An unfamiliar flutter of nerves twisted his stomach into a tight knot. He'd never desired courtship previously, though he now understood it had all been part of Minora's convoluted design. He prayed Adalin would be pleased by his planned proposal. Armistral had advocated for his life, after all, and he hoped the god would bless him anew this day. He dreamed of a life with Adalin at his side, a quiet life without the gods' demands to drive him onward. He wanted a future of his own design.

He was tapping his fingers against the polished bar top, lost in his thoughts, when the serving woman returned with a woven basket. He startled and looked up as she plunked it down in front of him.

"Something on your mind, Ravin?" she asked with a snicker. "I've seen that look on many a man's face over the years. I've no doubt she'll be pleased with…whatever it is you mean to ask her." She winked. "Cook has given you several bacon and cheese sandwiches, a good helping of our first batch of strawberries from the season, and a fresh loaf of bread."

He stared at her, uncomprehending for several moments as he grappled with her initial words. Were his intentions clear to everyone? Would Adalin be surprised, or would she be expecting his actions?

He cleared his throat. "Thank you."

She chuckled again and reached beneath the bar. "Perhaps you'll want refreshments, as well. I hear she likes her mead." She set a bottle down on the bar top with a grin. "I'll add it to your tab."

"I… Thank you," he managed again, uncharacteristically flustered.

"Good luck, Ravin." She grinned and disappeared into the kitchen once more.

He resisted the urge to run his hand through his hair in frustration. If he returned to Adalin's room disheveled, she'd become suspicious—if she wasn't already. Instead, he occupied his hands with the burden of the basket and bottle of mead.

When he reached the top floor landing, he paused to tuck the bottle inside the basket, obscuring it as best he could with the cloth the kitchen staff had placed over their meal. Since the day she'd brought mead with them into the catacombs, the liquor had become a source of amusement between them, a jest with a significant emphasis on events to come. He hoped she wouldn't notice the bottle until he was prepared to reveal it; it was yet another indication of his plans.

As he strode toward her door, he realized he was as giddy with anticipation as he was terrified. Was his experience the same for every would-be suitor? He tightened his grip on the basket and drew a breath as he prepared to knock on her door. He sent another silent prayer to Armistral, then rapped his knuckles against the wood.

Adalin opened the door and ushered him inside with a smile. He noted she wore the same riding outfit she'd donned on that day in the catacombs, months ago. Her dark hair was pulled up into an elaborate twist. She took his free arm and laced her fingers through his.

"I hope your plans make up for the discomfort of the travel," she stated.

"As do I," he replied with a nervous chuckle. "I believe you'll like it."

"Then no doubt I will. Let's be away from this place, if only for a few hours."

With a nod, he created a portal and led her through. Her fingers tightened on his reflexively once they were inside the magical realm.

"Gods, this never grows easier."

He transported them to the garden at the rear of his new estate, then hurriedly led her into the physical realm once more. She breathed a sigh of relief and released his arm to press her fingers into her temples. He frowned with concern as he watched her. With luck, perhaps this would be the last such trip Adalin would be forced to make.

After a moment, she dropped her hands and paused to look at their surroundings. They were in the heart of the garden, near a fountain sculpted in the likeness of the water goddess, Hydralene. Water sparkled in the sunlight as it arced from the statue's hands into a tiled pool. Stone benches formed a circle around the fountain, and behind them were various garden plots, largely barren until Ravin managed to secure a gardener.

"Ravin, what is this place?"

He led her to the nearest bench and set the basket down at his feet. "I've been working on a project, as you know," he said slowly. "I believe I've led you to think it was magical in nature, but it was not. I purchased this estate only this morning."

She studied him, her expression unreadable. "Why, Ravin?"

He drew a breath. "You've mentioned you missed your horses, and I thought—"

"There are horses here?" Her face lit up with anticipation.

He chuckled. "Not yet, but there is a stable and corrals. It's a proper manor house, Adalin. I believe the merchant I bought it from said there was room for six horses, but as you are aware, I know little of the creatures. Perhaps you'd like to take a look?"

"I'd like lunch first, Ravin. Then you can take me on the grand tour of your new abode." She grinned.

He nodded and set the basket between them on the bench. "It, ah, doesn't have to become mine alone."

He felt the heat rising into his cheeks and looked away. He'd faced Soulless on the battlefield and the Nameless god's wrath without hesitation. Yet his confidence was reduced to splinters as he sat before Adalin, his greatest friend and the woman he'd come to love.

She pulled the cloth off the top of the basket, but stilled at his words. Or perhaps it was the sight of the mead that had given her pause. His stomach rolled and turned a flip as he waited for her response.

"Ravin, are you…? Do you…?"

Her voice faltered, and he looked up. Her eyes were locked on his; a hundred emotions seemed to flit through their depths as she attempted to discern his motivation. He swallowed and withdrew the puzzle box from his pocket. The conversation wasn't going as he'd envisioned it, but he'd never anticipated that his nerves would interfere and attain a stranglehold on his tongue. He drew a breath and presented the tiny box to her.

A flicker of a smile graced her lips as she studied it. "A Santinian specialty," she remarked as she ran one finger over its surface. "The mechanism is…ah, here." She flicked her nail against a slightly upraised panel, and the lid sprang open.

Her eyes widened and her lips parted in surprise as she stared at the contents. He wasn't certain if she was pleased or horrified.

He drew a shaky breath. "Adalin, I…I prepared this for you before we faced the Nameless god. Originally, there was a message inside as well. I asked Tavesin to deliver this to you if I didn't survive."

She closed her eyes as tears began to spill down her cheeks. "The estate, this gift, the *mead*… I know what you're going to say next, but let me spare you the trouble. Yes."

He gaped at her. "Yes? You will marry me?"

She wiped at her eyes and smiled through her tears. "Yes. I've wanted nothing more for some time."

He grinned as relief washed through him. His gamble had paid off, Armistral had blessed this moment as he'd hoped, the day was warm, and she'd understood his bumbling attempt at a proposal.

She plucked the ring from within the box and slid it onto her finger. "A sapphire." She held up her hand to examine it in the sunlight. "It's beautiful."

"I think you'll be pleased with the estate as well," he replied. "We'll need to hire a gardener and someone to tend the stables—"

"Let's discuss business later." She leaned toward him to take his hands in her own. "It's perfect, Ravin. I don't know where you found the coin to purchase this place, but none of that matters. It will be nice to have somewhere I can call home again." She paused to study their surroundings once more. "Where *are* we, Ravin?"

"This estate is two miles east of Darvin Mer."

Her smile broadened. "It was owned by the Cantess family, wasn't it? I'd heard the last Cantess was killed during the war."

Ravin nodded, unsurprised that she was familiar with the property's history. "I wasn't certain you'd be pleased with the location. It's not far from your step-son's demesne."

"Darvin Mer was *home*, Ravin. You've given me more than I'd ever hoped for." She looked down at the basket between them and smirked. "When I saw the mead, I *knew*. Although, I believe this was the first time I've ever witnessed you struggle for words."

He felt his face flush. "It was the first time I've attempted a proposal. It went much more smoothly in my head, believe me."

She laughed. "Let's eat, then you can show me the estate. *Our* estate." She beamed. "The future Lady De'vor has never been happier."

Here ends The Relics of War

THANK YOU FOR READING WAR OF THE NAMELESS!

If you enjoyed reading this book, please consider leaving a review.

Information about new books and their release dates will be posted on my website (www.ajcalvin.net), as well as shared via my newsletter. If interested, you can subscribe by visiting my website and clicking on the "Subscribe" tab.

ACKNOWLEDGMENTS

Like its predecessors in the series, War of the Nameless was a long time in the making. More hours than I can count were spent in the writing, revising, reworking, and polishing of this manuscript after it spent nearly two decades untouched.

I would like to thank my husband for his support and patience as I worked to complete this project. I was often scarce, but I believe the end product has been worth the time I sacrificed—and I hope you, the readers, agree.

Another thank you goes to Jamie Noble, the artist who created the cover images for this series, and to Sheena Sampsel, the tireless editor who helped to make this story the best it could be.

And finally, a heartfelt thank you to all of my readers. Without you, writing would not be worthwhile.

NOW AVAILABLE

EXILE: BOOK ONE OF THE CAEIN LEGACY

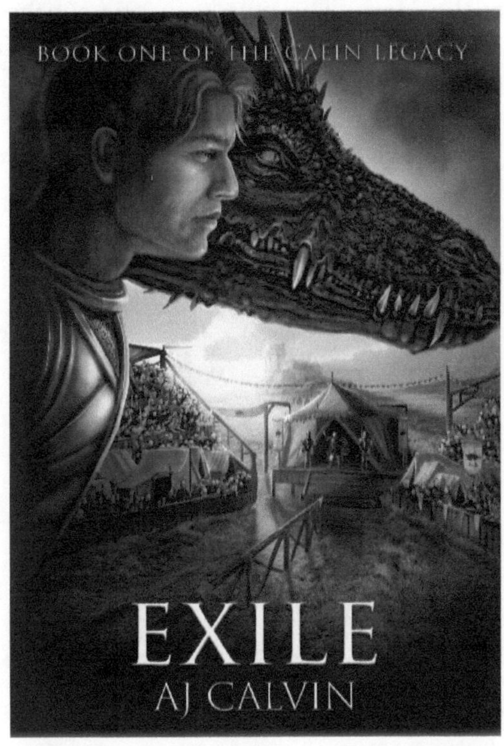

Andrew grew up in the royal palace of Novania, the eldest son of the queen. He went on to achieve fame and glory as a renowned soldier, and was eventually named commander of the king's army. The kingdom believed he would be named heir to the throne, but he has long known he is ineligible. The king is not his father.

The truth of Andrew's lineage is only partially known to the king; the identity of his father is a mystery that even Andrew is unaware of. He knows only that his father was a dragon-mage, and the dragons have fled to another world. Andrew is a skin-changer, able to shift between human and dragon forms, but the laws of Novania forbid his very existence. If the king were to learn the truth of what he is, he would face execution.

The laws are equally hostile to humans born with the Mark of the Magi and the ability to wield magic. Andrew's younger half-brother, Alexander, bears the Mark. The pair keep one another's secrets into adulthood…Until the king dies unexpectedly and Colin ascends the throne. When Alexander's Mark is revealed for all to see, Andrew is faced with a choice: To watch his brother be killed, or reveal his true nature in an effort to save him from the headsman's axe.

ABOUT THE AUTHOR

A.J. Calvin is a science fiction/fantasy novelist hailing from Loveland, Colorado. By day, she works as a microbiologist, but in her free time she writes. She lives with her husband, their cat, Magic, and a fairly large salt water aquarium.

When she is not working or writing, she enjoys scuba diving, hiking, and playing video games.

For more information on the author and news about her writing, please visit her website at www.ajcalvin.net.

www.ingramcontent.com/pod-product-compliance
Lightning Source LLC
Chambersburg PA
CBHW020304030826
48979CB00027B/2090/J

* 9 7 9 8 9 8 8 3 1 9 3 2 0 *